Scarlet Wilson wrote her first story aged eight and has never stopped. She's worked in the health service for twenty years, having trained as a nurse and a health visitor. Scarlet now works in public health and lives on the West Coast of Scotland with her fiancé and their two sons. Writing medical romances and contemporary romances is a dream come true for her.

Fiona McArthur is an Australian midwife who lives in the country and loves to dream. Writing Medical Romance gives Fiona the scope to write about all the wonderful aspects of romance, adventure, medicine and the midwifery she feels so passionate about. When she's not catching babies, Fiona and her husband Ian are off to meet new people, see new places and have wonderful adventures. Drop in and say hi at Fiona's website: Fionamcarthurauthor.com.

Also by Scarlet Wilson

Family for the Children's Doc
His Blind Date Bride
Reawakened by the Italian Surgeon
A Festive Fling in Stockholm

Also by Fiona McArthur

Second Chance in Barcelona

The Midwives of Lighthouse Bay miniseries

A Month to Marry the Midwife
Healed by the Midwife's Kiss
The Midwife's Secret Child

Discover more at millsandboon.co.uk.

MARRIAGE MIRACLE IN EMERGENCY

SCARLET WILSON

TAKING A CHANCE ON THE BEST MAN

FIONA McARTHUR

MILLS & BOON

First Published in Great Britain 2021
by Mills & Boon, an imprint of HarperCollins*Publishers* Ltd,
1 London Bridge Street, London, SE1 9GF

www.harpercollins.co.uk

HarperCollins*Publishers*
1st Floor, Watermarque Building,
Ringsend Road, Dublin 4, Ireland

Marriage Miracle in Emergency © 2021 by Scarlet Wilson

Taking a Chance on the Best Man © 2021 by Fiona McArthur

ISBN: 978-0-263-29784-3

12/21

MIX
Paper from
responsible sources
FSC™ C007454

This book is produced from independently certified FSC™ paper
to ensure responsible forest management.
For more information visit www.harpercollins.co.uk/green.

Printed and Bound in Spain using 100% Renewable Electricity
at CPI Black Print, Barcelona

MARRIAGE MIRACLE IN EMERGENCY

SCARLET WILSON

MILLS & BOON

This story has to be dedicated to my good friend
and Dublin expert Daisy Cummins.

Thank you, Daisy!

Raising a glass to the next time we can get together
with Heidi, Fiona and Iona too. xx

CHAPTER ONE

IRIS CONWAY PUSHED her blonde hair back from her face and yanked at her ponytail band, trying to push it all back into something more reasonable. The stained scrubs were tossed into the nearest laundry basket as she pulled a new set from the trolley in the corner of the changing room. This was the third set she'd worn on this shift so far. Things were not going well.

She shoved her feet into her shoes and elbowed her way back out the door into the noise and bedlam of the A&E department.

St Mary's University Hospital in Dublin was currently in chaos and she hated it. They were four doctors down. Two were on maternity leave, her Spanish colleague had just returned home due to some bad news and a fourth had been involved in an accident on a rugby pitch which had resulted in some emergency surgery. She strode down the corridor and glanced at the board. Every time a space appeared, it was immediately filled. They'd long since breached their four-hour waiting time.

'Rena,' she said sharply, 'I need an update.'

Rena—the charge nurse on duty—appeared at her side, her face pinched. 'X-ray is still backed up, we have six patients waiting for a medical review, three at Surgical, the paediatrician has just appeared—she's got four to review—and there's four patients waiting for casts.' Iris didn't get a chance to talk. 'The two in Resus need your attention again. I have a woman requiring an ultrasound—apparently Obstetrics are just too busy to get here. And Harry's back again. I've just made him a cup of tea and some toast. Oh, and the new doc? She's not coming any more. We're getting some guy—can't even remember his name—instead.'

Iris swallowed down her frustration. Rena looked ready to snap at the next person to say a word to her—not good news for anyone in this department. After a few days of storms, the hospital was full to bursting. There were absolutely no beds left, which was why each speciality was having trouble getting to A&E to review their patients.

Harry was one of their frequent flyers. An elderly man who'd slept in Dublin doorways for years. He never accepted any offer of accommodation, but frequented their department at least twice a week. He would likely be the only individual today that wouldn't hear the sharp end of Rena's tongue. 'Also,' she added, 'one of our new medical students is crying in the staff room, and the other needs to be gagged and handcuffed—thinks he's already qualified and can make decisions.'

Iris sighed. Just what she needed. As a university hospital, St Mary's had more than the average share of student doctors, all at varying stages of their careers. Proper supervision was difficult when she was four doctors down. 'What's she crying about?'

'No idea,' said Rena. 'I haven't had time to find out.'

Iris pressed her lips together. Comforting and investigating why a medical student was in tears would take time she simply didn't have right now—not when the department was like this—and she absolutely hated herself for it. 'Put Joan on our over-ambitious medical student. Tell him he can't do anything without her say-so.'

Joan was one of their fiercest nurse practitioners. Iris didn't usually assign students to her—mainly because they didn't seem to come out of the experience unscathed. But the last thing she needed right now was someone making a mistake. Joan would ensure that wouldn't happen.

Rena raised one eyebrow. 'You'll pay for that,' she said knowingly. Joan was the only other member of staff in here that could give Rena a run for her money.

Iris nodded. 'Oh, I know. And ask Fergus to deal with the other student.' At least he was a safe choice. Fergus, an experienced staff nurse, practically had the word *nice* hanging above his head. He could deal with any upset member of staff in an instant.

That was one of things she loved about this place. She knew the people here like family. In fact, for the last six years they had been her family. Some A&E departments were notorious for their transient staff. It was a high-stress, high-paced environment and people frequently moved on. Many doctors spent a few years in A&E for their CVs, then quickly moved on to other places. Only a few stayed the distance, and Iris was one of them. When she'd been promoted to head of department here, her surrounding colleagues had been quick to congratulate her. She'd fitted in well. Loved the city and loved the people since her arrival six years previously. When she'd adopted her daughter, Holly, on her own, they'd all had her back whenever she'd needed help at short notice. In turn, Holly loved them all, and had tough-nosed Rena and Joan, and soft-hearted Fergus, all dancing to whatever tune she played. These people were worth their weight in gold, and Iris valued every one of them. Her own adoption experience as a child hadn't been good, so she was even more determined to be the best parent she could be to her daughter.

The phone rang next to them and Iris picked it up. Her skin chilled as she listened quietly. She said a few words in acknowledgement, then replaced the phone. Rena knew instantly that something was wrong. Iris pressed the alert on her pager. 'Incoming sea rescue. Four casualties,' she said.

'We need to clear Resus,' said Rena instantly. Iris took a quick glance around the room, hearing the sounding of pagers all around her as staff received the alert.

She strode down the corridor, shouting instructions to faces that appeared from behind curtained cubicles. No one argued. All just giving a nod in agreement and disappearing again.

Part of their earlier conversation struck a chord in her head. 'What happened to our new doc—Claire somebody? Why isn't she coming?'

Rena shrugged. 'She got a better offer apparently. Some hospital in Rio de Janeiro.' She gave Iris a rueful smile. 'Don't think we can put up a fight against their weather, can we?'

Iris shook her head. 'This storm isn't helping anyway. Three days of relentless rain and gale force winds. Why does no one listen to the weather warnings and stay inside? Feels like half of Dublin is currently in our waiting room.'

'Yeah,' agreed Rena, glancing towards the packed room, with steamy windows. Every seat was taken, with plenty of others standing around inside. 'And virtually no doctors to treat them.' The irony dripped from her voice.

It seemed that no doctor on the entire Planet Earth wanted a short-term contract in their A&E department right now. Ridiculous. This was a marvellous place—or at least, it normally was.

She spent the next few minutes stabilising both patients in Resus, and getting them sent on to the A&E combined assessment unit. It was literally only supposed to be used to keep patients overnight while they awaited more tests. Both of these patients should be in beds in the wards upstairs—but Iris didn't have time to wait for that to be sorted. She picked up the nearest phone, paging the doctor on call for the medical wards.

She didn't waste any time when he answered. 'You have six patients in my department—all of whom have breached their waiting time. Get down here, review them and make a clinical decision. I have four fishermen being winched from the Irish Sea and I don't have space for them all.' She put the receiver down before he had a chance to speak.

Iris glanced at the board again and gave a quick look at her watch, making an instant decision. 'Can you get me a foetal monitor?' she asked Rena. 'That poor woman's waited long enough.'

Rena nodded and appeared a few moments later passing over the handheld monitor. Iris sucked in a deep breath and took a quick glance at the chart, then disappeared behind the curtains.

The middle-aged woman was pale-faced, with streaked mascara around her eyes. Her hair was plastered to her head. She'd come in a few hours ago reporting reduced foetal movement. She was on her own, and Iris was immediately concerned about the potential for delivering bad news to someone with no support. She knew immediately that no woman this far on in her pregnancy would have come out in this weather unless she was really worried.

She started washing her hands. 'Hi, Carrie, I'm Iris, one of the A&E consultants. I'm sorry you've had a bit of a wait, but it seems our obstetricians are caught up today. Would you mind if I looked after you instead?'

Carrie gave a quick shake of her head, her hands placed protectively over her stomach. 'I just want someone to tell me if everything is all right.'

Iris nodded and sat down next to the bed. 'I get that. Okay, I see you reported reduced movement. Can you tell me what's been happening?'

Carrie sniffed. 'I feel terrible. I hadn't even realised at first. It was just when I was walking around the supermarket earlier—when the wind dropped for a bit—and I saw someone else with a newborn strapped to their chest, and I realised I hadn't felt any movement today.'

Tears started to flow again. 'I know I felt her last night. Because she woke me up. Kicking like anything when the rain was battering off the windows. But I usually feel her most of the time. And it wasn't until then I realised I hadn't felt anything since then. And I'm an older first-time mum, and I know I'm at higher risk of everything. But all of my tests have been fine; in fact, everything's been fine, up to now.' Her words had just seemed to spill out, and they came to an abrupt halt.

There were lots of things she could say right now. But Iris knew there was only one thing this woman wanted to know.

She held up the Doppler. She spoke slowly and clearly. 'Okay, I'm going to use this to see if we can hear baby's heartbeat. You'll have had this done before?'

Carrie nodded. 'My midwife has used it before. I phoned her today. But she was stuck out on some country road where the storms had made a tree fall. She couldn't get to me and told me to come into hospital and get checked out.'

Which was exactly the advice Iris would have expected her to give her patient. She already knew that the community midwife had phoned in to see how Carrie was, and she made a mental note to try and check up later that the midwife had got back to her base safely. 'This is the one I have immediate access to, so we'll use it first. I want to reassure you, if we don't pick up a heartbeat straight away, not to panic. Sometimes babies lie in an awkward position. Is someone with you?'

Iris knew at this stage she should always be able to pick up a heartbeat, but wanted to hedge her bets for a few more moments.

Carrie shook her head. 'It's just me. Me and Ruthie. That's what I'm going to call her.' She smiled at her belly as she stroked it. 'I never thought I could have children. Tried for years. My husband left me, then I met someone else for a while, and that didn't work out either. Then, out of the blue—' she gave a little smile '—this. But the father didn't want to know. I knew straight away this was my last chance to be a mum and I didn't care about anything else. I don't need a man to do this. I have a good enough job and my own place. My mum and sister-in-law will help out. They were both delighted for me. But I didn't want to tell them about this. I didn't want to scare them.' She blinked, frightened eyes connecting with Iris's. 'I'm forty-four. I thought when I passed all the crucial points I was safe. Twelve weeks. Twenty weeks and the detailed scan. Then, twenty-four weeks. I thought I'd made it past all the bad stuff.' Her voice started to shake. 'I mean, this is supposed to be the final bit. The bit where you just get bigger and bigger and wait for the main event.'

Iris reached out and squeezed Carrie's hand. Empathy was washing all over her. Carrie was forty-four and thirty-five weeks pregnant with a much-wanted baby. She'd already named her little girl and made plans to do this on her own. Some of the things that she'd said struck a chord with Iris—on a personal level that she would never normally reveal to a patient. Her heart gave an unconscious twist in her chest. She really, really didn't want to give bad news to this woman today. She tempered the swelling rage in her chest that the obstetricians hadn't prioritised her. They could well be dealing with some emergencies, but Iris was well aware of the fact that in a few minutes her own attentions would be urgently needed elsewhere.

She lifted the tube of gel and showed it to Carrie. 'I need to squeeze a little of this on your stomach.'

Carrie pulled up her maternity top, revealing her pale skin with some stretch marks and Iris squeezed the gel out. Using the transducer, she spread the gel across Carrie's stomach, holding the monitor in her other hand. She flicked the switch and held her breath.

Almost immediately there was the sound of a rapid heartbeat. Iris couldn't stop the immediate smile that appeared on her face. Carrie gave an audible sigh of relief and her whole body seemed to relax. 'Ruthie,' she breathed.

'Ruthie.' Iris nodded. She moved the transducer a little, watching her black and white screen. The portable ultrasound monitors in the A&E department weren't quite top of the range, but they were certainly good enough for their purpose. She held it steady for a full minute, letting Carrie savour the sound of the heartbeat. 'Everything is in normal ranges,' she said reassuringly. 'Ruthie's heartbeat. Your blood pressure that our nurse took earlier, and the urine sample that you gave just after you arrived.'

'So, I don't need to worry?' Carrie's eyes were wide.

'Everything looks good,' said Iris. 'Do you mind if I get you booked into the maternity hospital for a review tomorrow?' She put her hand back over Carrie's. 'Only because their doctor didn't manage to see you today. I can't find anything to worry about, but we'll give you a chart to complete about foetal movement, and they can have another look at you tomorrow to make sure that they are happy too.'

Carrie looked a little wary. 'You're sure there's nothing wrong?'

Iris nodded. 'I am. I'm a very experienced A&E doctor. All your tests are normal. But I'm not your obstetrician, and if I was, and one of my patients had an A&E visit, I'd want to see them for myself.'

This seemed to make sense to Carrie, and she breathed out slowly. 'Okay, then.' Iris wiped the gel from Carrie's stomach. 'Give me five minutes and one of my staff will come back with the details. But look after yourself, Carrie. And good luck with Ruthie. She'll be in great hands.'

This time it was Carrie who reached out and grabbed Iris's hand. 'Thank you,' she breathed. 'I was so scared when I came in today. You've no idea how relieved I am.'

'I get it.' Iris smiled. 'And I'm glad we were able to help.'

She pulled back the curtain and walked quickly to the desk, giving instructions to one of her colleagues to make the appointment for Carrie and make sure she got home safely.

The thump-thump of the helicopter sounded overhead. Iris could feel the flip inside her stomach—that familiar apprehension over what might lie ahead. All she knew was that a fishing boat had overturned due to the storm and all four crew had been in the sea. She didn't even know yet if all four had been successfully winched to safety. There must have been at least two rescue helicopters out there, and doubtless some of the life craft crew too. All of those personnel would have been exposed to the cruel elements currently battering Dublin.

She could well have more than four critical patients to deal with.

'Everyone ready?' she gave a shout to the staff. It was the oddest thing. Voices quietened in the usually buzzing department. Iris could see that the two patients in Resus had been moved and the trolleys prepared. Two of the other medical patients had disappeared too, leaving two empty bays directly next to Resus.

Emergency trolleys were ready, staff were aproned, gloved and masked. Rena had bags of saline and glucose in the warmers and warming blankets prepared—standard procedures for any unit receiving potentially hypothermic patients.

There was still some background noise, but she could feel the buzz in the air. The hush only emphasised it. She'd spent ten years of her life working in A&E. It had always been her first choice. Always been her home. She'd never felt drawn to any other speciality and this was exactly why.

This was the moment that all department staff drew together. As she looked at the sea of faces—silently wishing there were a few more—she knew she could count on the colleagues around her. It was the same when any major casualties were expected. They were the biggest hospital in Dublin, with over six hundred beds. They always received the majority of casualties. They were always ready. And she was proud to be part of this team.

Iris Conway had done good. From the abandoned baby, to the adopted daughter of two parents who had rapidly became disinterested in her once they'd had a child of their own and then emigrated to Australia as soon as she'd gone to medical school, she only wished there was occasionally someone around to be proud of her and tell her so. That's why she relied on the team around her so much.

The doors burst open behind her, and the air rescue team ran in with their trolley, two of the A&E staff beside them. St Mary's had a helicopter landing pad on the roof, with direct access to a lift that brought them straight down to A&E.

The paramedic spoke quickly as the trolley rolled into Resus. The staff moved automatically, positioning themselves and quickly pulling the patient over. 'Owen Moore, twenty-seven. Part of the crew of the *McGonigal*. We think he was in the sea for approximately thirty minutes. Temperature currently twenty-eight degrees. Bradycardic, hypotensive. On oxygen, saturation ninety-two percent.'

Iris nodded. 'How long has he been out of the water?'

'Eight minutes.'

She held back the wow. These guys were real-life superheroes. 'You have more than one?'

'Second guy is coming in right behind us.' He paused and she knew there was something else.

'What?'

The doors crashed again, and she knew the second patient would be there in moments. He spoke into the radio pinned to his shoulder for a moment, then met her gaze. 'The winds have picked up again. Our second helicopter is having trouble landing.'

She gulped. Hoping her face wasn't showing the immediate thoughts in her head. As soon the first rescue craft had offloaded their patients, she knew it would have taken off again to leave room for its partner to land. These guys were experts.

The second trolley rolled into the room and she listened to the report. Almost identical to the first, only this guy was slightly older.

'Get the clothes off these guys. Both are right on the cusp between moderate and severe hypothermia. Recheck their temps. Cardiac monitoring is essential. Quick check for any other injuries and get me a blood glucose level and I need IV access and a set of bloods on both.'

She moved into position, next to the first patient, expertly sliding a Venflon into his shut-down peripheries. He was young. It was probably the only reason she'd managed to get venous access. She looked up to see Ryan, one of her other doctors, struggling to get access for the other patient. 'Need a hand?'

She could see the frustration on his face and knew he didn't want to give up. Sometimes with a hypothermic patient they had to put in a central line, or even use an infusion into the bone marrow. Taking over wouldn't help Ryan, but she'd do it if she had to. The needs of the patient always came first.

'I'm in,' he said after a few moments.

'Warming blankets,' she instructed, catching sight of the paramedic still at the door. She moved over and lowered her voice. 'Do you need someone to check you over?' Before she could stop herself, she reached over and touched his arm. It was icily cold, and that was through his jacket. 'Fergus?' Her shout echoed down the corridor, and the shaggy-haired nurse stuck his head out from behind a set of curtains. 'Take a look at our colleague for me,' she said, shaking her head as the paramedic tried to object. 'It will be a while before you can get back on duty,' she said quickly. 'I expect you want to hang around to make sure your other colleagues are fine anyway.'

She knew the words gave him the out. She'd been around these rescue guys for too many years. Looking after everyone else was always the priority over looking after themselves. He nodded as Fergus appeared and guided him away. He'd wanted to make sure the other helicopter landed safely and his fellow paramedic had delivered his own patients to the unit.

She moved, still assessing both patients. The second guy, Euan, looked like he may have fractured a rib at some point. The radiographer appeared with the portable machine after a quick call.

The doors at the end of the corridor burst open again, and this time, one of her staff was on top of the trolley doing chest compressions. Relief firstly flooded over her as she realised the second helicopter must have landed safely, then disappeared rapidly at the acknowledgement of how sick the next patient was. 'Let's move these two guys to the bays at the side,' she said instantly, waving to the two patients currently in Resus. They would both still need constant monitoring, but at least they were certainly more stable than the patient on his way towards her.

Sean, one of their experienced anaesthetists, appeared. 'Call me your guardian angel. Just assessed the surgical patients,' he said quietly. 'Want me to hang around?'

'Absolutely,' she said instantly. Her brain wanted to question why he'd assessed the surgical patients instead of one of the actual surgeons, but there was no time for that.

The trolley swished in with the man being resuscitated. He was obviously older. 'Captain of the *McGonigal*,' said the ashen-faced paramedic. 'Was unconscious in the water by the time we winched him out. Had previously been conscious and told us we had to take all his crew first. Rob King. Fifty-seven.'

Her brain was trying hard to keep track of everything. 'Next guy's not quite as bad,' said the paramedic, as if he'd just read her thoughts.

Rena appeared in the doorway. 'New doc's just arrived. The replacement for Claire. He's looking after the two just moved out of Resus and seems to know his stuff. Ryan's breathing a sigh of relief.'

Iris gave a careful nod. Ryan was good, but only a year into the job. He didn't have enough experience yet, and she was glad the new doctor had arrived, because with patients like these, they really needed a doctor each.

She moved next to Sean, who had already expertly intubated Mr King and was attempting to get an IV in place, while the member of staff above kept chest compressions up. Iris wasn't in any way hierarchical. She wasn't going to tell Sean to let her take over, or move her staff member before she should. She seamlessly worked around them, placing the electrodes for the cardiac monitor around her colleagues' hands, taking a core temperature again and then a blood sugar reading. She wordlessly handed the warmed glucose IV line to Sean once he'd finished drawing off the bloods.

The fourth trolley rolled into place and Ryan came in on its heels. 'I'll take this one,' he said.

'What about the other two?'

'New guy's got them,' he said with an easy confidence that let her know they were in capable hands. She didn't even know the new guy's name.

She glanced quickly over at the fourth patient. Younger again, and he looked in a similar condition to the first two. Mr King was definitely the sickest. 'Lori,' she shouted to one of the other staff nurses. 'Come in and work with Ryan.'

Rena was bagging Mr King methodically. 'Wait!' Sean held his hand up to the nurse doing the compressions.

All eyes glanced at the monitor, and after a few moments of stuttering, a blip appeared. The nurse gave a sigh and jumped down from the trolley. 'Well done, Amy,' said Iris, tapping her staff member on the shoulder.

There was a shout from outside and Iris froze at the sound of the male voice.

It was almost like she'd jumped into the Irish Sea herself. Cold flooded through her veins and she was pretty sure her heart stopped.

Another voice joined in. Joan's. She was indignant and obviously giving someone a piece of her mind. Sean looked up. 'All yours,' he said, with a hint of a smile. 'I'll stay with Mr King.'

She was torn. Mr King was the sickest man here, and she was head of the department—she should be looking after him. But something was obviously awry in the next room, and as head of department, she should take control.

She knew exactly why her feet seemed to be sticking to the floor right now. But her brain hadn't really caught up with her body yet.

She could hear the ping, ping of the monitor in the cubicle next door. 'Stand clear,' came the steady male voice again, followed by the familiar sound of a shock being delivered.

'Move!' yelled Joan, and even though the words weren't aimed at Iris, they seemed to have the desired effect on her feet.

She took the few steps out of the resus room and into the bay next door.

A dark, slightly curled head was leaning over one of

the patients from earlier who'd clearly gone into a cardiac arrest. The young medical student was practically pinned against the wall by Joan, an endotracheal tube clutched in one hand. Joan was barely five feet tall, and almost as wide, but she was a formidable force. 'You do not do anything in this department you are not qualified to do,' she hissed as she wordlessly handed a new sealed airway to the doctor beside her.

He glanced up, those familiar dark eyes locking on hers.

For a moment, the world froze. Lachlan Brodie. Her ex-husband. The man who'd stolen her heart years ago, and never given it back.

Lachlan looked just as shocked as she was, but in the blink of an eye, he was sliding the airway effortlessly into the patient's throat, moving to allow Joan to start bagging the patient. It was almost an echo of what was happening in the resus room right now.

She watched, still unable to move, as he turned his head to the monitor, checking the erratic beat of the man's heart. This wasn't uncommon in hypothermic patients. Episodes of ventricular fibrillation could occur in someone as their temperature rose.

'Temperature.' The words came out her mouth automatically, as the rules in these situations came back to her.

'Thirty,' came the curt reply. She grabbed adrenaline from the emergency cart and delivered it into the man's IV. 'Stand clear,' Lachlan repeated as he delivered a second shock.

A few seconds later, the heartbeat appeared again. But Iris didn't have time to breathe a sigh of relief. Because Lachlan straightened up and looked her in the eye. 'Tell me you're not in charge here?'

'Why?' was her stunned reply. Every tiny hair on the back of her neck stood indignantly on end.

'Because this is worst run department I've ever seen,' came the brutal, cutting response.

CHAPTER TWO

IT HAD ALL seemed too good to be true.

Which of course meant it was.

He'd barely registered with the agency when they'd contacted him with a job in Dublin, requiring an immediate start. It had taken two minutes of consideration—one, a quick look at the hospital, two, an even quicker search for the soonest flight.

Apparently one of their senior medics had let them down at the last minute leaving the perfect opportunity for someone with his experience to step in. The hospital manager hadn't cared he'd been out of A&E for the last few years spending time in general practice. His résumé beforehand was so good it practically sparkled and the manager had even offered to set up accommodation for him.

Three months in Ireland. It pretty much sounded like a dream come true. He'd never worked in Ireland before but had visited a few times and always wanted to see more of the place. The university hospital was the biggest in Dublin, with lots of attached specialities. It was set on one side of the city, so that if he chose to stay in either the city centre or the city suburbs, he would still have easy travel.

He'd asked the manager to find him a place in the

suburbs or thereabouts, hoping to see a bit more of the countryside at some point, and the guy had sent him pictures of a gorgeous cottage that had made him instantly interested. A place with character. It's what he'd always wanted in a home.

The first minor hiccup had been when the plane had made three attempts to land at Dublin city airport due to the bad weather. The second hiccup had been when he'd put the cottage postcode into the hire car's navigation system and it had taken him on a tour of Ireland.

After many wrong turns, and asking a few people he passed, he finally made it to the cottage.

From that point, he'd felt as if everything would be plain sailing. The cottage had come stacked with a week's worth of groceries, wood in the wood burner, a local map showing where he could buy further supplies of both and a welcome note from the woman up the lane. She'd also left a tongue in cheek remark saying if he were a 'healthy' type and liked walking, he could take her dog with him. He'd smiled at that one. It had been years since Lachlan had been around dogs and he was more than happy to oblige.

The rain and winds had still been strong, and the sight of three waiting ambulances outside the A&E department let him know what to expect.

He'd had a quick introduction at HR, signed a few forms, shown proof of identity and his doctor registration and been supplied with his staff ID badge. It wasn't until he was walking down the stairs towards the A&E department that he realised he wasn't quite sure who to report to.

Five minutes later, he'd realised that was the last thing to worry about. The place was in pure and utter chaos. Every bay was full. Staff dashed from one place to another. Pagers sounded constantly, along with ringing phones that no one seemed to answer. He'd put his hand on the door of the staff room—heard someone sobbing inside—and realised it might not be the best introduction.

Then, as he'd headed towards the resus room—the most likely place to find the senior doctor on duty—he'd come across a nervous-looking doctor with two very sick patients.

Lachlan did what he would always do. Introduced himself, asked if he could help and assessed the situation. Both fishermen, both hypothermic and both pulled from the sea in the last hour. It didn't matter that it had been more than a few years since he'd looked after a properly hypothermic patient, he still knew all the basics. Raise core body temperature in a controlled manner to prevent any further problems.

The doctor's—Ryan—skills seemed sound. He just needed a bit of reassurance and some low-key instructions. Lachlan hadn't even had time to ask him who was in charge around here.

But there it was. That feeling. The one that he'd missed. The one that he'd craved. In barely a few seconds that frisson of excitement was already flooding his body. The rush of adrenaline, that instant switching on of his brain, acting on instinct, and being back at the heart of things.

The rush he felt working in A&E again was huge. He knew instantly this was the right move. Even if his first impressions were guarded, being put into a situation where he was immediately needed had kicked all his senses back into touch. He'd missed this. He'd missed this so much. And even though only a few milliseconds had passed he knew it had been the right decision to come back. He needed this. More than he'd ever known.

The last few years had been a strain. He'd moved to the English countryside with Lorraine, a fellow GP he'd cared about a lot. Lorraine had fallen ill, but what had seemed like a simple virus had the most horrendous impact on Lorraine. Viral cardiomyopathy, followed by rapid heart failure, and a position on the heart transplant list that had never been fulfilled. Of course, he'd stayed by her side all the way through. They might not have been in love in the traditional sense, but he'd felt genuine respect and affection for her. Lachlan had been the one holding her hand when she'd slipped away. One year on, he'd known the life of a rural GP wasn't for him long-term and he needed to get back to what he loved. This. Emergency medicine.

He could see another two emergencies being rushed in, and immediately realised one was being resuscitated. Whoever was in charge was clearly where they needed to be. When Ryan had disappeared a few moments later, he'd appreciated it was likely a time of all hands on deck.

The curtain between the two cubicles was half pulled, and as soon the monitor started pinging, Lachlan strode around to pull it back properly so he could observe both patients clearly.

All his senses went on alert at the view on the monitor. He reached instantly for the defib, slapping two pads on the patient's chest. 'Stand clear,' he said loudly, checking, before delivering a shock.

He'd barely had time to blink before he witnessed a young man being hauled away from the patient by one of the fiercest nurses he'd ever seen. 'What's going on?'

The nurse glared at him. 'Who are you?'

'Lachlan Brodie, new A&E consultant.' He changed position, focusing his attention on the patient in front of him who'd gone into ventricular fibrillation. His heart

wasn't beating properly and without intervention he
could die.

'Joan,' came the brisk reply. She stopped pinning the
young man to the wall and snatched what he now realised
was an endotracheal tube from his hand. 'Our med student keeps trying to do a procedure he isn't trained for.'

She literally bumped the student out of the way with
her large hips.

Lachlan kept entirely calm, even though he could feel
the rage building inside. Where was all the qualified
staff? Who was looking after all these patients? And
why was a student left unsupervised?

He spoke smoothly as he assessed the young man in
front of him and scanned his chart in a few seconds.
'Well, there are no breath sounds. We need to maintain
an airway here.' He reached his hand out to the nearby
emergency trolley but before he could pull anything, Joan
wordlessly handed him a new sealed airway, tilting the
patient's head back. 'You can watch,' he said to the student at the side. 'We start with a standard airway—not
an endotracheal tube straight away. And we continually
assess our patient.'

He'd barely slid the airway into place before the nurse
had deftly attached the oxygen supply to the bag and
mask and handed it over. Not a word had been said. She
clearly knew what she was doing.

But that was when it all went wrong. That was when
the ground seemed to slide out from under his feet.

It was slow motion. The smell first. That familiar perfume he'd only ever known one person to wear and it sent
prickles across his skin. The sense of someone at the foot
of the trolley. That all-knowing feeling that someone was
watching. For the briefest second he glanced upwards.

No. No. It couldn't be Iris. It was just his mind playing tricks on him.

'Temperature?' came the oh-so-familiar voice.

He answered on automatic pilot. 'Thirty.' He knew exactly why she was asking as he moved again and nodded to Joan to start bagging the patient. He needed to deliver another shock. The person—who he really, really hoped was a figment of his imagination—grabbed some adrenaline from the cart. Patients with a temperature under thirty weren't allowed adrenaline. This guy had made it by the skin of his teeth.

'Clear,' he instructed again, wondering if he was actually still on the plane circling above Dublin and he'd fallen asleep, and this was all just some bizarre kind of nightmare.

He delivered the shock and waited a few seconds, eyes on the monitor. It gave a blip, then a reassuring other blip, followed by something that started to resemble a reasonable heart rate.

Lachlan breathed, and realised his mistake, as he got a complete intake of her perfume again, and all the sensations that triggered in his body. All the memories that related to that smell.

Eight years. That's how long it was since he'd seen Iris Conway, his ex-wife. And right now, eight years didn't seem long enough.

He'd had—what, two minutes of bliss to relish being back in the job? And now, he was tumbling head over heels into some weird parallel universe.

The girl he'd married when they were twenty-three after only knowing her a few, passionate months, vowing never to regret it. Three years later they'd both regretted it and she'd completely and utterly broken his heart.

They'd parted ways, severing any mutual friendships

between them. He didn't need or want to know where she was in the world, or what she was doing. He'd always wanted her to have a good and happy life, but his battered and bruised heart didn't feel the need to see it or hear about it.

Lachlan knew he was unprepared for this reunion. He'd always suspected that Iris would continue in the profession they'd both loved. But the world was a big place and he'd just never expected to run into her again.

He couldn't help all the sensations that bubbled up inside him. He couldn't stop the instant annoyance and blame that spilled over. 'Tell me you're not in charge here?'

He knew his tone spoke a thousand other words. Dripping with sarcasm and holding an edge of contempt. He sensed immediately the staff around him tensing as he continued to work on his patient. Of course it was a mistake—to be the new guy and speak to an existing physician like that. But no one else got it. No one else knew their history. The angry words. The broken hearts. The huge regrets that had bubbled between them. How on earth could they?

'Why?' Iris's response was everything. Indignant. Defensive. And hurt.

And again, he couldn't stop himself. 'Because this is worst run department I've ever seen.'

He could hear the intake of breath all around him. How to win friends and influence people at a brand-new place of work. *First impressions count.*

But somehow, the normally professional, easy-going life that Lachlan usually inhabited had just plummeted off a cliff edge.

For a second he locked eyes with his wife. *Ex-wife*, he reminded himself. Her blonde hair was high in a ponytail and her pale blue eyes raged at his. She was a bit thinner than the last time he'd seen her. It gave her face a pinched edge that didn't suit Iris and gave the overall impression of stress. He'd no idea what had happened in her life since they'd parted company—just like she'd no idea what had happened in his. Maybe it showed in his face too? He'd never really considered it before now.

Her voice had a tiny hint of a tremble, and he wondered if her colleagues noted it the same way that he did. 'Not the time, Dr Brodie. Treat your patients, and we will take this up later. In private.' The words held a special emphasis that almost sounded like a threat. She turned and strode away.

Iris was mad. Lachlan had seen Iris mad in many guises in the past. But today he didn't feel sad about it. Didn't feel like he wanted to run after her and force her into a discussion she didn't want anyway.

Darn it. He should have researched this job better. He should have looked up every doctor that worked here. In his haste to get away from his previous job and memories of Lorraine, he'd taken the first thing available. And if something seemed too good to be true—it generally was. Lachlan had been around the block a few times, he knew this. He couldn't believe he'd allowed himself to be caught out like this.

He blinked and was instantly swamped by the cold feeling around him. He glanced at the patient monitor and barked out a few other instructions. Joan, the nurse, gave him a look that told him exactly where he stood with the rest of the staff. Yep, it seemed whilst he'd thought he was falling off a cliff edge when he glimpsed Iris, the words that he'd spoken to her had dropped him into a sea as icy as the one these fishermen had just been pulled from. Perfect.

Joan followed his instructions as he continued to treat the two young men. The medical student clearly didn't know where to look, so Lachlan just spoke out loud, telling him everything he was doing, and the reasons behind it. He dropped in a few questions, to make sure the student understood and was paying attention.

After around half an hour, Lachlan felt comfortable with the condition of both men. He could still hear murmuring from the resus room next door. His eyes met Joan's steely grey gaze. 'Is assistance needed next door?'

'Dr Conway has everything under control,' she snapped back. She hadn't moved from his side, and unless she possessed telepathic capabilities she couldn't possibly know that.

He stopped himself from pointing out the fact and gave her a half-smile. 'Then perhaps you want to check on your colleague in the staff room. They seemed pretty upset.'

She blinked, clearly surprised that he knew that. But her response was just as quick. 'Fergus is already on that.' She picked up some empty packaging and clinical waste. 'Just like Dr Conway instructed,' she added over her shoulder as she headed to get rid of the waste.

Lachlan took a few moments. He didn't really need to stand over these patients. But he wasn't leaving them unsupervised. The place was still busy. He was sure there were more patients he could be seeing right now, but he'd clearly sealed his popularity around here.

He turned to the medical student. 'Okay, let's start from scratch. Hypothermic patient, brought in like this.' He handed over the chart the paramedic had brought with him. 'Talk me through the complete treatment plan, and the rationale behind it.'

It took a while, and Lachlan knew it was because the

student was nervous. Another doctor appeared and stuck out his hand. 'Ajat,' he said. 'I'm from ITU. I heard these two were coming up to our step-down beds for close observation for a few hours.'

Lachlan gave a nod. It made sense. They weren't ventilated, but could still deteriorate at a moment's notice. He gave a handover for both patients, signed off on the drugs given and stood back as they were both transferred somewhere upstairs. At some point, he would have to take a look around this state-of-the-art hospital.

He'd barely moved out of the cubicles and walked over to the whiteboard to see where else he could be of help before he heard a voice at his shoulder. 'Staff room. Now.'

Iris was standing at his right shoulder. He hadn't even heard her approach.

She didn't wait, just strode off in front of him, knocking the door of the staff room with her hip and leaving it swinging behind her.

Lachlan was almost tempted to smile. It had been a long time since he'd seen an Iris work-related rage.

The staff room was empty, and he realised instantly that she'd known this before bringing him here.

She walked over and flicked the switch on a kettle, before turning around, arms folded across her chest. 'Don't you dare criticise my department. Who do you think you are, walking in here, and talking to me like that in front of my staff?'

The part of his brain that was rational had a momentary explosion. What was it about Iris that made all his functioning parts lose the ability to communicate with one another?

'You're right, I'm sorry. Not the best first impression to make, I admit. But I walked into a department that was clearly in chaos. Every bay full. A doctor who looked out of his depth. A medical student who wanted to tube someone at the first blink of a cardiac arrest. A nurse who had to get him under control. Another staff member weeping. And a department that doesn't have a hope of meeting its target for waiting times—and that's before I've even looked in the waiting room.'

He saw the muscles tense at the bottom of her throat and around her shoulders. 'I'm four doctors down. My most experienced staff aren't here today, and some people have had to step up. You know how that works—it happens in every A&E department. The storm has caused an unexpected surge in cases. The wards are full, we have no beds. St Mary's is currently on a purple alert— as are the other emergency receiving units throughout Dublin. We can't get people discharged home, because ambulance services are struggling.' She licked her lips. He knew she was angry, but the expression on her face was bland, as if she were just reiterating the facts to some nameless enquirer.

'All my bays are full, because the other specialities are struggling to get down and assess their patients. My waiting room is full too, but all patients have been triaged and at least they're safe from the storm whilst they're in my waiting room. I care not a jot about meeting waiting times in a situation like this. I only care about keeping patients safe.'

He broke in before she could continue. 'So, that's why you left a clearly inexperienced doctor and a random un-supervised medical student on the loose?'

She held up her hand as a clear sign he should stop talking *right now*. 'Ryan is not inexperienced. He's perfectly capable. He's been here a year and is still building his confidence. He just hasn't dealt with a half-drowned, hypothermic fisherman before. It's not an everyday occurrence and hardly a crime.'

Okay, Lachlan's insides might have cringed a little. He'd quickly realised that Ryan wasn't incapable and just needed a few prompts.

She kept going. 'Our medical student is brand new. I haven't had time to assess him yet because I've been treating patients. However, Joan—and I know you've met her—is one of my best nurses. She's all over him, and I suspect that's exactly what he needs.'

'What he needs is adequate supervision and a proper teaching environment.'

'Both of which he'll get. Here, under my watch. Heaven help a member of staff take two minutes to wash their hands between patients, Lachlan.'

Lachlan. The way she said his name sparked a million memories. Half of them good. Half of them not so good. But the weirdest thing was, even though his stomach twisted painfully inside, it was the good pictures that flashed into his head. Iris, laughing in her gorgeous wedding gown, holding her yellow flowers next to her face. Iris, leaning forward to kiss his cheek. Iris, sighing happily in the morning, and the glint in her eye as she tried to convince him that it was his turn to make breakfast, knowing full well it was hers. Iris and him, snuggled on their lumpy sofa dreaming about having a family of their own and whether they would have boys that looked like Lachlan, or girls that looked like Iris.

All of those memories rushing out of nowhere and filling his brain in less than a second. It had been a long time since he'd allowed himself time and space to think about Iris.

He straightened his spine and tried to bring himself back to the here and now.

'Criticising your department wasn't a great start. But you still have staff running around like headless chickens and far too many patients waiting to be assessed.' He looked around the empty room. 'And what does it say about a department if you have a member of staff in here, crying?'

Her lips tightened. 'It says we have a place where staff can come and take five minutes out their day when they're feeling overwhelmed and need a little space.'

'It also makes me question if they are getting adequate support from the people around them.' It was a really low blow and he knew that. But the person he usually was seemed to have been left outside in the storm somewhere.

She turned her back to him and took out a mug—two mugs—filling them with a heap of coffee and pouring boiling water into both.

'This won't work,' she said as she handed him a cup.

He didn't answer, not knowing quite how to respond, but completely agreeing.

'It's not a good idea for us to work together. I can't have you disrupting my department like this.'

He let out a wry laugh. '*I'm* disrupting your department?'

For the first time, the rigid expression on her face disappeared and her shoulders seemed to sag a little.

Her eyes focused elsewhere. 'But I've been let down at short notice. So, you can't go until someone fills your place.'

The cottage sprang into his mind. He'd barely even had a chance to see the place and had already signed a three-month lease. He didn't want to walk out on his elderly neighbour and leave her in the lurch.

'I have dog walking responsibilities,' he said with a hint of humour in his voice.

'What?' Iris looked stunned. Whatever she'd expected him to say, it hadn't been that.

He nodded and sipped the coffee. Black, with nothing. Just like how she took hers. Years of working in A&E departments had taught them both that any milk that hadn't been used yet was likely out of date. They'd learned to drink coffee with no embellishments. She'd remembered. She'd remembered how he took his coffee.

Something speared through him. He'd come here to rediscover his love for work. His love for life.

The irony of coming across the love of his life in that process wasn't lost on him. But Iris wasn't his reason for being here.

'If I'd known you were here, I wouldn't have come,' he admitted.

For the briefest second she looked hurt, and then she looked relieved. He didn't even know what that meant.

'Why did you come?' This time the question was in a softer voice. Iris was curious. Curious about him.

More irony. Lachlan had always been certain that as much as he'd never really wanted to know about how Iris was getting on in life, the feeling had been mutual. They'd parted ways, and never expected them to cross again.

He didn't owe her anything. And she didn't owe him anything either.

He ran a hand through his hair. 'I've been out of A&E for a few years. Tried something different, my circumstances changed, and I decided to come back.' He paused for a moment, wishing he hadn't mentioned his circumstances. He didn't want to answer any real questions about his life since they split up—just the most generic things. 'I guess I'm just trying to reignite the fire for my work that I used to have.'

There. It was out in the open. But he couldn't pretend that the tiny flare he'd felt less than an hour ago hadn't happened.

To her credit, Iris let the words sit for a few moments. 'I need someone with experience,' she said slowly. 'And no matter what you've done for the last few years—unless it was time in prison—I know how good an A&E doctor you are.' Her eyes were on his. He saw the briefest hesitation.

He gave a half-smile. 'I can assure you I wasn't in prison.' He didn't offer any more.

She licked her lips and nodded again cautiously. He could see the doubts written all over her face. He knew she was weighing things up in her head.

'This is my department. And I can put the needs of my department before my own feelings.'

'Well, that sounds reassuring.' He shook his head, already knowing where this was going. If he were in Iris's position, would he be saying the same words?

'I need an experienced A&E doctor,' she said steadily. 'One whose work I can trust.'

He leaned back against the worktop in the staff room. 'I'm not too sure I've created the best first impression with your staff. I fear they might want to club me to death in some cubicle.'

The edges of her lips hinted upwards. 'My staff are fiercely loyal. Some of them have been here longer than I have. If you cause trouble, or say anything about me, prepare to be thrown into the Irish Sea.'

He shuddered. 'After the state of those men today? Not likely.'

'I may also ask you to supervise the medical students.'

'It's a punishment, isn't it?'

This time she did smile and shake her head. 'Not at all.

I just know that after our initial encounter, you still spent some time teaching Mr Over-Enthusiastic some of things that I would expect from a mentor working in a university hospital.' But there was a hint of humour on her face. 'And yes, it's your punishment for your initial comment. You are now officially in charge of the students.'

Lachlan stayed silent for a few minutes, trying to sort all this out in his head. He'd landed in a beautiful country, lucked out with accommodation and scored a job in a hospital that would look good on his CV. But could he and his ex-wife really work together?

'What will you tell your staff about me?'

She swallowed. 'The truth. I'll tell them you're my ex-husband. They know I was married before, but I've never given them details.' A tiny flare of hurt crossed her eyes and he looked away. 'It's been eight years. I'll tell them I know you're a good doctor. You came here at short notice to fill a gap that badly needed filling, and neither of us knew about the other.'

She nodded her head as if the idea was cementing in her head. 'Anything else would be complicated. I don't lie to my staff. They'll know that we'll be a bit awkward around each other. They might ask a few questions—but I'd be obliged if our private life could remain private.'

He glanced at her hand. It suddenly occurred to him that yes, it had been eight years. He knew exactly what had happened to him in those eight years, but he'd no idea what had happened to her. She could have happily moved on and be married with three kids right now. His presence might ruffle other feathers in the hospital—what if her husband worked here like she did? He didn't want that. He didn't want his presence to affect anyone else.

'Apart from you and me, will this arrangement cause problems for anyone else?'

It was if she had a moment of fleeting panic. 'What do you mean?'

'I mean, are you married? Do you have a fiancé, or boyfriend, in the hospital or local area that will object to us working together? I don't want to cause any problems. I genuinely had no idea you were here.'

He felt as if he had to say it out loud. Deep down, he had wanted Iris to be happy, and if she was, his being here might impact on that.

'There's no husband,' she said with a nervous laugh. 'No fiancé, no boyfriend. Not right now.' She held out her arms. 'Work keeps me busy, as you can see.'

He gave a slow nod. 'So, we can do this? We can make this work?'

'Honestly, I have no idea. But we're adults. We should at least try.'

Those blue eyes held his gaze for the briefest of seconds before she threw her coffee down the sink and rinsed her mug. 'Now, come on. I have about ten patients I want you to see.'

She was back to business. Back to being head of a department. And that felt easier. Simpler for them both.

So, he followed her lead. Dumped his coffee, washed his mug and followed her back outside into the chaos.

CHAPTER THREE

IT WAS STILL THERE. That instant recognition. That feeling that had shot up her spine at first sight of him. Now, instead of a quick shock, it was remaining a steady tingle, a hum, sending all of her other senses into overdrive.

She'd given her staff the briefest explanation that Lachlan was her ex-husband, and that they'd both been shocked by seeing each other after eight years. Both Joan and Rena had raised their eyebrows. Neither was happy with his initial words about their department and boss, and both had made their feelings known.

But since another doctor had just phoned in sick, Iris had made it clear that he had apologised to her, and the department's priority was to have a doctor with the skills they needed. She'd assured them that Lachlan was a good doctor, good with patients and good with students. It only took a few days for them and the surrounding staff to see that for themselves.

A paediatric emergency, two road traffic accidents and quick recognition of a case of malaria—something they rarely saw in Dublin—seemed to seal Lachlan's abilities in their minds.

But none of it did anything to help Iris's peace of mind.

Things would be much simpler if Lachlan wasn't here. His quiet chat with older patients, his reassurance to anxious parents and his empathetic delivery of bad news to relatives were all sparking memories that sat uncomfortably with her.

He'd always been a good doctor. He'd also been a good husband. Until other issues had driven them apart. They'd both been keen to have a family. Lachlan, as an only child himself with elderly parents, had wanted a large family of his own. Iris had always been honest about being adopted, but she hadn't told him anything of the really tough stuff about her life. She'd been bitterly hurt when her adoptive parents had given birth to their own child and virtually ignored her. She knew she hadn't helped matters by playing up and attention seeking, which had only made their relationship worse. She'd brushed off Lachlan's questions, saying she wasn't that close to her family, and that they'd emigrated to Australia when she started university. Those parts had been entirely true. It was hard to tell the man who had turned her world upside down and captured her heart so quickly that her family had never loved her the way he had. Lachlan was everything to her, and having a family together had seemed like the best idea in the world. Planning their family had started out being fun, and had then turned into a more serious, concerted effort to conceive.

Iris knew that she'd become a little obsessed. Everyone around her seemed to be falling pregnant—everyone but her. After a year she'd wanted to do tests. Lachlan hadn't been so keen, telling her to wait another year and give it some time. She knew that was the normal advice to give in this situation. But this wasn't normal. This was about *them*.

She'd badgered and badgered, and they'd finally both undergone tests. All of which had shown there was nothing wrong—with either of them.

After private consultations, more tests, a few rounds of intrauterine insemination, followed by unsuccessful in vitro fertilisation, their lack of success had left them both ragged and upset. There was no clinical reason for them not to be pregnant. Nothing scientific. Apparently, they just weren't a good 'match.'

It was a useless explanation that left frustration and resentment building in them both. After a while Lachlan had been keen to pursue other options—adoption mainly. But Iris couldn't get there. Every time she looked at the man she loved with her whole heart, she felt as if she'd failed him, and he in turn had failed her.

She'd refused counselling, probably because she'd not been ready to accept that she needed it.

Her mood had dipped lower and lower. When Lachlan had suggested she seek other help, she'd been furious. She knew she hadn't coped well. She knew that she'd fixated on being pregnant, and her whole body had been stressed beyond belief. But none of that helped. And none of that made her want to repair the relationship with her husband that was rapidly deteriorating.

So, they'd split up. Both broken-hearted. Divorced, and walked away to make a fresh start.

She'd never imagined their paths would cross again.

Because she'd never imagined what she'd need to tell him if they did.

Iris had healed—eventually. After a few half-hearted relationships that fizzled out quickly, she'd spent some time on her own, found an amazing counsellor and accepted her life as it was, taking pleasure in her job, her achievements and her friendships.

Her counsellor had spent hours with her, picking apart her own feelings of rejection by her adoptive parents, the fears and resentments she'd had when her husband had suggested they go down the route of adoption and the deep, deep horror that she might ever act towards any child she adopted the same way her parents had.

It had taken her a long time to accept that the whole experience of not being able to conceive and the subsequent breakdown of her marriage had left her with unrecognised, and untreated, depression. Once she'd acknowledged that, her path to acceptance that she was not the same as her parents, had been a less steep hill to climb.

So, when she'd made the decision to look at adoption as a single mother, she'd felt ready to take that step. She'd gone through all the assessment processes and finally been approved. And she'd done all that here, in Dublin, the place she'd come to with her broken heart, to heal and repair herself.

She had close friends outside the hospital who knew her whole story. But she'd always been a little more protective about what she shared with her colleagues at work. They knew she had a daughter. They knew her daughter was adopted. Most of them had met Holly at some point or another. But they didn't know that her husband had once asked her to consider adoption. To think about expanding their family in a way that didn't put her body under constant pressure. To take a break from all the drugs, and the counting days, the incessant calendar watching.

Or to maybe realise that being a family of two was more than enough.

It had been her that had said no. It had been her that had said it wasn't enough for her. It had been her that had refused to take a break, or step away and truly consider adoption as a way forward for them. She just couldn't bring herself to dig deep and tell Lachlan about her own true experience of adoption. She'd spent so much of her life feeling unloved and unwanted that being unable to manage the supposedly simple step of becoming pregnant and giving her husband the big family he'd so freely told her he wanted had made her feel totally useless and unworthy again. All things she just couldn't vocalise to him, too ashamed to admit what she perceived as her failings.

So when adoption had been mentioned, she'd point-blank refused. Wouldn't even properly consider it. And he'd seemed to accept her decision easily, which left her feeling as if it wasn't an option he'd really wanted to pursue anyhow. So, in a way, she'd stolen that option from them both—then stolen it back, entirely for herself.

Now, eight years on, she knew exactly why her stomach turned in knots at the thought of someone revealing to Lachlan that she'd adopted a child.

She couldn't specifically ask her staff not to mention Holly. That was wrong. Holly was the brightest part of her life. But she could ask her staff in a more general way not to mention her personal life to Lachlan. And she did. In the most low-key way possible. 'Lachlan and I used to be married, so you know things might be a little awkward for a while,' were the words she'd used casually. 'He's a great doctor, and a great person, and I want you all to get to know him. So, to keep things simple for us all, it's probably best if you keep things professional and don't talk about us personally around each other.'

She'd noticed the quick exchange of glances. But her staff had nodded as if it were no big deal.

But that hadn't helped the constant churning of her stomach ever since. He was only here on a temporary contract. If he stayed any longer than the three months he'd signed up for, she would tell him. Of course she would—when the time was right. And that was what she kept telling herself.

Dublin was an interesting city. There were a whole load of distillery and whisky tours to be done. Museums were next on the list, with one even at a cemetery. But what Lachlan hadn't counted on was the ever-present coach tours on every country road.

Staying slightly outside the city had seemed like a good idea. He'd spent many a good hour tramping across the countryside with Scout, the fierce terrier belonging to Maeve at the top of the lane. A few quick conversations had made him realise that Maeve's arthritis had slowed her physical fitness, so when Lachlan's phone had rung at nine o'clock one night, he'd assumed that Maeve was checking to see if he could take Scout out the next day.

'Lachlan?' The normally cheery voice sounded distinctly trembly.

'Is something wrong?' He sat up straight away.

'I've had a bit of tumble. I hate to do this, but I can't quite get up. Could you come and help me.'

Lachlan's feet were already in his boots. He kept his phone pressed to his ear as he opened his door and started half running, half striding down the lane. 'Is your door open, Maeve?'

'Of course it's open. Why would I lock it?'

Lachlan shook his head, keeping the whole host of responses he could give a back seat, trying not to think about the fact he'd just done exactly the same thing.

'I'm nearly there. Hold on. Don't try and move. I'll check you over first, before we try and get you up.' He could hear a quiet yap from Scout. 'Is Scout okay?'

Maeve gave a nervous laugh. 'I think he knows something is wrong. He keeps coming over and looking at me.'

Lachlan reached the blue door and gave a few knocks before he entered. Scout almost pounced on him, appearing like a speeding bullet from the back of cottage, giving a few growls, a few barks and then winding between his legs. Lachlan bent down and rubbed his head. 'Don't worry, old guy. I'll sort her out,' he said softly.

'Maeve, I'm here. Let's see you.' Maeve's cottage was similar to his own; it only took a few long strides to go between the rooms. Maeve was lying on the carpet in the main sitting room, in an awkward position between the chair and coffee table.

'What do you mean let's see you?' she said scoldingly. 'What kind of sight is this to see?'

Lachlan knelt down the floor next to her, pushing the heavy coffee table out of the way to get more room. 'Sorry, it's an expression of my gran's.'

Maeve's face was much paler than usual and the smile on her face was clearly forced. 'I'm just a silly old fool. I can't get my legs under me to get back up.'

Alarm bells started going off in his head. 'How did you feel before you fell? Were you light-headed, dizzy?'

She wrinkled her brow. 'I'm not sure.' She winced as she tried to move.

Lachlan moved closer, pulling a cushion from the sofa. 'I'm going to put this under your head, lie back for a moment.'

He gave Maeve a quick check. At this age, it could be anything. A stroke, TIA, hypotension. Bones were so fragile at this age—any fall could cause a multitude of fractures. As he had no pen torch, he pulled out his phone to check her pupils, then gave her a quick pat down, noting she winced as he touched her ribs.

'Has this happened before?' Scout was sniffing around them both, obviously concerned.

Maeve gave a shrug, her breathing a little ragged. 'Once or twice. Only when I get up too quickly.'

'Did you get checked over?'

She waved one hand. 'I was fine.'

'But you're not fine. I'm going to take you to my workplace and give you a check over. I suspect you might have fractured a rib, but I want to check a few other things too.'

'Can't you just help me up? I'll be fine.'

'I wouldn't be a very good doctor if I just helped you up into a chair, and left it to happen again, would I?'

She sighed and rolled her eyes.

'Okay, I'm sure your legs and arms are fine, so let me take your weight and sit you in the chair. Then, I'm going to get my car, and take you for a check at the hospital.'

He could have called an ambulance—and if he'd thought for a second Maeve had broken her hip or any other leg bones, he would have left her on the floor until he had help to assist him. He was also sure she hadn't broken her shoulder and could therefore assist her up without doing any damage.

It only took a few moments to help her up onto the nearest armchair, and make sure she was safe, before he ran back down the lane to pick up his car. He brought it right up to Maeve's front door—much to Scout's indignation—and helped her out into the front passenger seat. His arm was gripped firmly around her waist and he watched with interest when he first helped her upright, saying nothing but clocking her symptoms.

The journey to the hospital was swift—the roads were quieter at this time in Dublin—and he pulled up directly into an empty ambulance bay. Ray, one of the porters, was out straight away, ready to shout at the impromptu parking, but clocked quickly it was Lachlan. 'What do you need?'

'Do you have a wheelchair?'

With a nod, Ray came up alongside and they both helped Maeve into the wheelchair. 'Do you want me to take her inside, or do you want me to move your car?'

It was an easy decision. He handed his car keys over to Ray. 'Much appreciated.'

'No bother, Doc.'

He was grateful. After an initial frosty start, the staff had started to become less wary of him. He'd noticed that none of them mentioned Iris around him—except in relation to patients—and that was fine. The uneasy truce between them still caused mixed emotions. This wasn't the fresh start he'd wanted.

If he walked around the department when Iris was on shift he could smell traces of her perfume. She'd worn it for years, a light floral scent that was more or less her signature. He would hear her laugh when talking to other people, and it seemed to skitter across his skin in a way he didn't want to admit.

His brain was itching to know about the last eight years—but of course he couldn't ask. He deliberately hadn't told anyone about himself. There had been a few casual conversations with physicians from other departments where he'd mentioned working as a GP for the last few years. There had also been a few conversations with the cardiology team around patients that had presented in A&E with partly suspicious symptoms. Fortunately, on two occasions his instincts had been correct, and he'd been complimented on his good catches, leading to earlier treatment for those patients.

He knew he was influenced by his time with Lorraine. It was only natural, and had given him some insights on unusual cardiac symptoms control that could easily be missed.

As he wheeled Maeve straight through to the bays, he picked up a portable tablet to enter her details. Rena appeared at her side. 'You working tonight, Lachlan?'

He smiled and glanced down at his jeans, dirty trainers and navy walking jacket. 'Not really, but looks like it. This is my neighbour, Maeve. She's had a fall and might have fractured a rib. I want to get her checked over and investigate a few things about her fall.'

Rena flashed a smile at Maeve, and from her glance at him he knew she could read between the lines. 'Let me give you a hand.'

He nodded gratefully and they helped Maeve onto a trolley. Rena pulled the curtains, took some quick details and ordered an X-ray whilst Lachlan checked and recorded Maeve's obs. 'Sitting and standing BP?' she asked, and Lachlan nodded.

Lachlan was aware that Rena still gave him the odd cautious glance, but she was a clear winner with the patients and he was grateful for her assistance. Ray appeared again to take Maeve for her X-ray and Rena gave him a few words of instructions for the technicians in the X-ray department.

Lachlan took the opportunity to walk along to the nurses' station to see how the night was going. Everyone on the whiteboard was assigned to a doctor and things seemed remarkably calm. Iris looked up in surprise. She was wearing a pair of black trousers and a short-sleeved yellow shirt. 'You look like a big sunflower.' He smiled as he sagged into the chair next to her.

'What on earth are you doing here?' she said, before glancing down at her shirt. 'And thanks, yellow is my new favourite colour, and pay attention, there are daises printed on this shirt. I did have on a green top, but you know how things are in A&E.'

He pulled a face. 'Vomit or blood?'

She shook her head. 'Coffee, actually.'

'Still clumsy?'

The words came out automatically without much thought. Their gazes connected as a million memories flashed by in his head. Iris dropping their toast, butter side down, on the kitchen floor every other morning. Cups of tea and coffee being knocked or spilled constantly throughout the household. Her occasional trait of walking into half-shut doors or doorframes because she'd been distracted by either her phone or a book—or just too busy talking in general.

Her mouth turned upwards in a private smile and her words were quiet. 'Eternally clumsy,' she replied.

'Are we taking bets on that shirt, then?' He leaned back in his chair and clasped his hands. 'It's too pale for A&E. I give you less than fifteen minutes.'

She sighed and nodded in agreement. 'I should have put on a scrub top. But I'm tired of always wearing scrubs. This was in my locker and just seemed to call to me.'

Lachlan gestured to outside. 'Because it suits the weather?'

Iris groaned and put her head on the desk. 'I can't believe it's still so bad. That's been, what, two weeks?'

He grinned. 'I tell you, none of the travel adverts for Ireland show weather like this—it's all sunshine, cloudless skies and bright green hills.'

She turned her head sideways and narrowed her gaze. 'Hey, maybe it's your fault. Maybe you brought this weather with you?'

This is what it used to be like between them. Easy.

Relaxed. Joking, most of the time. Until it all changed. 'Of course I did,' he said. 'I deliberately brought the bad weather with me. Made my flight circle three times before I landed, overturned those boats in the Irish Sea and continually battered my little cottage with wind and rain so the windows rattle.'

She tilted her head at him. 'You're staying in a cottage?'

'Yep, just on the outskirts of the city, a bit further out.'

She wrinkled her nose. 'Did you want to be outside the city?'

He gave a quiet shrug, wondering how much to reveal. 'I'm in Dalkey.'

Her eyes almost boggled. 'That's the Hollywood hills of Dublin; it must be costing you a fortune. How on earth can you afford that? You do know several celebrities live there, don't you?' He watched as she realised what she had said and put a hand to her mouth. 'Sorry, that didn't come out quite right.'

He gave a slow nod. 'It took me a few days to catch on. Maeve—the lady I've brought in—stays just up the lane. She owns both cottages. They've been in her family for decades and she started renting one out a few years ago to the hospital for visiting nurses or doctors for a small fee. Apparently, she prefers us to the "ridiculous holiday crowd."' He gave a small laugh. 'Wait till you meet her. She does know she could sell both and make a fortune, or renovate and extend them with glass and steel, but she isn't the slightest bit interested.' He gave Iris a knowing smile. In the midst of a generally busy department, it was rare to get some uninterrupted moments. This was really the first time they'd sat and chatted. He'd missed her, he realised. He'd missed her more than he ever wanted to admit. A tiny bit of blonde hair had escaped her ponytail and his fingers itched to tuck it behind her ear.

He'd shut this whole part of his brain off. The Iris part. Because remembering had just been too painful. But now he had no choice but to remember, as Iris was continually in his sights.

'So, what's the cottage like?' She seemed genuinely interested. 'You always wanted something old.'

It appeared that Iris remembered just as much as he did. 'Lots of character. Small but not too small. There's two bedrooms, a main sitting room that the front door opens straight into. A kitchen with the real-life genuine stove, and one bathroom with rattling pipes.' He gave a laugh. 'There's a wood burner installed that gives off a surprising amount of heat, and the place has a new roof, which is just as well.'

'Because?'

'Because a huge amount of heat must stream out the old windows. I'm tempted to find a silicon gun and seal some of the gaps, but I guess there must be some kind of order on the house as a listed building.'

Iris leaned her chin on her hands, her eyes straight on him. 'But think of all the cottages around there that have been renovated and look nothing like the original.'

He shrugged. 'It's not mine, but I'm already starting to love it.'

She made a small clicking sound with her tongue and sat back in her chair folding her arms. 'But you can't *really* love it.'

It was the way she'd said those words. The joke they'd always held between them about their ideal house and what it would have.

He nodded in agreement. 'You're right. There's no room for a library.'

Iris shifted in her seat and pulled a face. 'I hate to tell you this…'

She let her voice trail off.

'You do not?' His voice was indignant.

She gave a not-so-sorry shoulder shrug as her eyes gleamed. 'I do so.'

'You have a library, in your house? Where do you stay?'

He watched something flit across her eyes. She obviously felt the same way he did, reluctant to give too much away. But she'd brought it up. She couldn't back down now. 'I stay in Portobello, in a red brick period terraced house.'

He rolled his eyes. 'Trendy. And as the saying goes, how do you afford that?'

Even though he'd only been there a few weeks, Lachlan had still managed to take a walk around Portobello. The houses were on the pricier side, the area was surrounded with lots of nice cafés, bars and restaurants, and was a short walk into the city centre.

Iris's face fell for a moment. 'Aunt Lucy died.'

His reaction was immediate and he couldn't help himself. He reached out and put his hand over hers. 'I'm so sorry, I had no idea.'

Iris's aunt Lucy had been an elderly spinster, absolutely adorable, with a million stories, sparkling wit and a big heart. She was the only member of Iris's family that he'd met; Lachlan had adored her, and his heart gave a sad lurch to hear she was gone.

But something else came over him immediately. Skin. It was the first time he'd touched Iris's skin in for ever… And although the gesture had been purely for comfort, there was a whole host of sparks shooting up his arm right now. Sparks that were entirely inappropriate, and he was doing his best to ignore.

Iris gave a sharp shake of her head. 'I know you didn't. I did think about trying to find you, but we weren't in touch.' She left the words in the air and Lachlan didn't try and fill the gap with any kind of excuse. They'd both been far too hurt and heartbroken to stay in touch.

'She died around five years ago and left a whole heap of money to her remaining family, which was just my parents, my sister and myself. It seemed she didn't just own her house in Kent, she also owned one in Cornwall and one in France.'

'What?' He was shocked.

Iris laughed. 'That face. That face was exactly mine when I found out. Got to credit Aunt Lucy for playing her cards close to her chest.'

She stared down at where his hand was on hers. She didn't pull away. Just licked her lips and looked back at him. Was she feeling the sparks too—or was she just being adult about the comfort he was offering?

'So that's why I own a beautiful house in Portobello. It needed some minor updating, then I converted one of the rooms into a library.'

'You're killing me,' he groaned. It had been a dream of theirs. They'd often sent random photos from the internet to each other of beautiful libraries around the world, talking about how one day they would build one of their own. Of course, at that point, they'd also been talking about making a mini library for their kids that would take up one half of the room.

'Sorry.' But she was smiling. He could see in her eyes that she obviously loved the room.

'Dark wood or white?' It had been one of their constant debates.

She kept smiling. 'One straight wall, dark wood, specially built library shelves, and the rest of the room is painted cream. I have a pale wood floor and an oriental rug.'

'Do you have a ladder?'

She shook her head regretfully. 'Not yet. I have a stool I climb to reach the top shelves. But a ladder and chaise longue are definitely on the cards.'

There was a ping from the computer next to him, and he leaned forward and pressed the alert to see Maeve's X-ray image. He'd moved his hand automatically and now the palm of his hand felt strangely empty. He leaned forward and Iris did the same. Her shoulder brushed against his and her signature scent drifted around him again. From one comfort, to another.

'Broken rib,' they said in unison.

And it stopped them both dead.

They froze. It was something that had happened frequently, years before. But the repeat event seemed to crash around them.

It was awkward. Even uncomfortable. Because for the first time in eight years they'd actually been chatting easily, teasing each other. Being friends in a way that had existed before but had been snatched from them by their own actions.

All of a sudden Lachlan knew exactly how much had been stolen from his life.

Iris's cheeks flushed pink, as if she were just as uncomfortable as he was. Her hands folded over her chest. 'What else are you going to do for Maeve?'

Work. He was at work. His brain kicked into gear. 'I suspect she's got postural hypotension. There's a marked difference in her blood pressure when she's lying down, and when she's in a chair—that's even without standing her up. I'll go and do a few more checks, review her current medications and take it from there. This has happened more than once.'

Iris seemed to have gathered herself and dropped back into professional mode. 'She was lucky this time with just a broken rib. It could have been her hip, her shoulder or even a head injury.'

'That's what I'm worried about. Don't worry. I'll be thorough.'

'Oh, I know you will.' There was a kind of wistful air to Iris's words as he stood up to go back to Maeve.

'You know, if she wants a female doctor instead, I'm available.' Iris's blue eyes seemed to stand out more in the bright lights of A&E, or maybe it was because of her yellow shirt. Whatever it was, it was hard to look away.

'I'll double-check with her,' he said, looking down at the tablet he'd lifted. Something sparked in his brain. 'The crew of the *McGonigal*, you heard any more about them?'

Iris gave a nod. 'The three younger crew men have all been released. The captain is still ventilated in ICU. Double pneumonia, but still fighting.'

He let out a slow breath. He knew the odds must be against the older man, but he was still here, and still fighting. 'The three young ones are lucky guys.'

She gave him a bold look. 'Must have been the exemplary care they received in *my* A&E department.'

'Must have been,' he agreed as he walked away, laughing to himself. He knew he was going to spend the next three months living down his first statement about the department.

He spent the next hour talking with Maeve, running a few more tests, taking some bloods and making a referral to another consultant. He wouldn't get to the bottom of Maeve's problem tonight. There could be an array of other issues going on—cardiac, endocrine, nervous system disorders. But he could do his best with general advice, and ways to keep her safe in the meantime while other investigations took place.

Rena appeared again. 'Want me to arrange some transportation?'

He shook his head. 'No, it's fine. I'll take her back home and make sure she's good.'

He heard a laugh and looked up. Iris was sitting next to Maeve and they were chatting, as Maeve ate some toast and drunk some tea.

Rena gave a nod. 'The smell of toast always makes Iris appear. When I make some for patients, I always make some for her too.'

Lachlan smiled, struck by the fact the team around here knew parts of Iris like he did—even if they didn't generally say it out loud.

Rena seemed to catch his gaze. 'She's great,' she said quietly.

And before he could help it, he said, 'Just don't try and steal her raspberry ripple ice cream.'

The amused tone in his voice made Rena raise her eyebrows and smile. 'I'll remember that,' she said as she walked away.

He could have kicked himself. They'd made an agreement not to get personal at work and it felt as if he'd just stepped over that line.

Iris disappeared behind another set of curtains as he grabbed a wheelchair and went to collect Maeve.

As he helped her into the car she patted his arm. 'What a nice bunch of people you work with. All of them. And that doctor, Iris? Very pretty.'

He climbed into the driver's seat, knowing that Maeve might know more than she should. 'She's my ex-wife.'

Maeve sighed as she clicked her seat belt. 'What a fool,' she said as Lachlan reversed the car and waited for the punchline.

'What a fool she is for letting you slip through her fingers.'

Lachlan's head turned in surprise as he went to change gear. 'That wasn't what I expected you to say.'

Maeve's eyes widened in pretend surprise. 'Oh, you thought I'd wouldn't be on your side?' She folded her hands in her lap. 'Now why would I do that? I'm Team Lachlan, as they say.'

He threw back his head and laughed. 'Team Lachlan? Where did you get that from?'

Maeve looked out the window as they started down the city streets. 'Just because I'm old doesn't mean I'm not up to date.' She gave him a wink. 'And anyhow, you're the one that walks my dog.'

'Even if he hates me.' Lachlan smiled.

'I think he's warming to you.' Maeve was still watching out the dark windows. 'And just for the record, even though I'm Team Lachlan, I still liked her.'

He glanced sideways, but Maeve's eyes were elsewhere, and somehow he knew she wouldn't let this go.

CHAPTER FOUR

IRIS WAS UNSETTLED. She couldn't help it. Lachlan Brodie was getting under her skin.

Truth was, he'd never really stopped getting under her skin. But having a clean break and being away from him had felt like the right move at the time.

They'd spent a few months still working in close proximity after their initial split, but both had found it too hard. All they did was fight. Pent-up resentment and frustration never did any workplace any good. So, they'd both decided to play at being grown-ups.

Neither had really wanted to leave the huge A&E they worked at in London. But they'd each applied for other jobs. Iris had gone to Melbourne, Australia, for six months, and Lachlan had gone to San Francisco. And after that, she'd lost track of him.

That had been a conscious decision on her part. Iris had been full of regrets, mainly about how she'd coped with things going wrong and the arguments they'd had. It was harder still having to admit to being at fault for some of it. That was a hurdle that had taken a few years to settle in her brain. So many choices made—or refused—and so many what-ifs to come to terms with.

They'd both been far too young to get married, their romance and wedding a whirlwind. They'd barely had time to get to know each other properly before things had started falling apart. Their dreams of a family had led them to start trying for one almost immediately, with all the heartache that had led to. They'd barely celebrated their third wedding anniversary by the time they'd admitted it was over.

Truth was, she'd never in a million years expected Lachlan to turn up in her A&E, and one sight of him had clean taken her breath away.

Sure, he'd insulted her immediately and they'd fought. And even though she'd told him and herself that they'd only reached a mutual agreement for him to stay because she was so desperate for good staff, her own brain kept screaming at her, *That's not true!*

Because whilst seeing Lachlan again was like a punch to the chest, it was also a permanent ache in her soul. Now she was reminded on a daily basis what might have been.

And that made her feel even more guilty. Of course, if she'd stayed with Lachlan, she would never have come to Ireland, made it her home and adopted Holly. She couldn't ever have a single doubt about the best thing that had happened in her life.

But her life, which had felt so put together for the last few years, now seemed to be unravelling again inside her head.

She'd tried to date. But her heart had never been truly in it. She just thought the timing had been off, or she hadn't quite met the right man. But Lachlan constantly being around now was telling her exactly why.

Because none of the men had ever measured up to Lachlan.

The chat they'd had last week when he'd showed up unexpectedly with his neighbour had pulled so many of the familiar strings in her that she hadn't been able to stop playing it over and over in her head.

On the shifts they did together, she could see even more glances between staff. Lachlan and Iris were in sync. They always had been when they'd worked together. It brought out the best in both of them.

Today, he hadn't been working, but something had been niggling away at her.

'Iris?' One of the secretaries tapped her on the shoulder. 'You'd asked me to pull some records from other A&E departments?'

She nodded and took the files. Records in their department were all digital and sometimes it took a little time to get paper records from other parts of the city.

She glanced down and read for a few minutes. 'Does anyone know where Lachlan is today?' The blank looks around her told her everything she needed to know.

He'd flagged something to her a few days ago. An unusual infection in a teenager. Iris had just seen something similar and asked the secretary to make some calls around other A&E departments in the city. Now, she just needed to put the pieces together, and Lachlan would be the best person to help her.

She called up to HR, asking for his mobile phone number. They handed it over but when she called it didn't connect. Sighing, she tried to rack her brains. He was off duty. He'd told her the cottage phone line had gone down in the storms. So, she checked Maeve's record and dialled her listed mobile instead. Maeve answered the phone within a few rings. 'Maeve Corwin speaking.'

'Hi, Mrs Corwin, this is Dr Conway from St Mary's calling—Iris. I hope you don't mind, but I'm trying to get hold of Lachlan. I know the phone line to his cottage is down—would you happen to know where he is?'

If Maeve was surprised at Iris's call, she didn't let on. Instead, she gave a gentle laugh. 'On a day like this? There's only one place that man would be. The Trinity Library, of course.' She paused for a few seconds and then added, 'I thought you might have guessed that one.'

Her insides squirmed. Of course. She should have known. 'I guess I'm a little out of touch,' she admitted, without saying anything more. From Maeve's earlier comment she was guessing Lachlan had mentioned they had history together.

'Nothing wrong with getting back into touch,' said Maeve mischievously, before replacing the phone.

Iris smiled and shook her head, glancing at the clock. She was officially off duty. She turned to Ryan. 'I'm going to see if I can find Lachlan and try and figure out something about a few patients. We might be back in later.'

Ryan looked poised to say something, but then pressed his lips together and gave a nod. 'No problem.'

Iris changed quickly and walked to the car park, snaking her way through the city traffic towards Trinity College.

It was a beautiful day and she knew there would be a queue of visitors waiting to visit the Book of Kells exhibition and great long room of the famous library. So, Iris pulled out her phone and booked her admission online. She was lucky; she could get in soon, and save waiting in the long queue.

She waited for her time, then showed her pass and walked straight in, passing quickly through the front entrance.

She entered through the dark wood doors and immediately looked upwards at the barrel-vaulted ceiling, inhaling deeply the scent of the ancient leather-bound books. She would never get tired of that. There were benches at either end of the middle of the long room, with green ropes keeping the two hundred thousand previous books safely out of reach. Marble busts lined the length of the long room's two-storey main chamber, as if keeping guard of the rows of books at their entrance points. Aristotle, Homer, Shakespeare and Socrates were all on duty, with high oak shelves behind them, varying in number, books crammed together and a long metal ladder to assist those important enough to touch the previous volumes.

The room was busy, with several older citizens just sitting on the benches that resembled old church pews and gazing up at the ceiling and second floor.

Iris gave herself a moment. It had been a few years since she'd been here. With work, and Holly, there just hadn't been the time. She smiled as she started to walk slowly along the rows. At any point she could lean forward a little and try to make out the faded text on some of the ancient books, wondering at the titles and what information lay beneath the covers. This place really was a wonder.

Voices were hushed as this was every book lover's dream. She wished she could actually sit down in here for a whole day and study. Instead, there were other parts of the library for that, as this long room and the exhibition was one of Dublin's top tourist attractions.

Iris wove her way through the crowds, scanning for Lachlan's dark hair. Eventually she glimpsed his broad shoulders, dressed in a pale blue shirt, his short dark curls bringing a smile to her face as she made her way towards him. He was next to the bust of Sir Isaac Newton, doing much as she'd done a few moments earlier, and squinting at some of the book titles. She could see his phone in one hand where he'd taken a few notes of titles, and he had a book of his own tucked under one arm.

She gave him a gentle nudge. 'Guess your phone doesn't get a signal in a place like this?'

He started and turned towards her, surprise written all over his face. But it only took a few seconds for the edges of his mouth to turn upwards. 'Switched the ringer off anyway,' he admitted. 'This is hallowed ground.' He turned the phone towards her, so she could see there was absolutely no signal in here at all. His brow creased. 'Is something wrong?'

She waggled her hand. 'I'm not sure. I wanted to talk to you about the case you mentioned to me a few days ago. There's been a few more. Can we grab a coffee?'

'Sure,' he said quickly, and gestured for her to head to the exit.

'Sorry to ruin your day,' she said over her shoulder as they headed to the exit.

He waved his hand. 'No worries. I was only going to sit outside somewhere with my book for a bit. Then, of course, go back and walk Scout, who maybe only hates me about eighty-five percent right now.'

She laughed. 'Maeve's dog hates you?'

'Of course. By the time I wear him down, either me or him will be heading for the Pearly Gates.'

'Don't tell me you created the same bad impression with him that you did at the hospital?'

Lachlan put his hand to his chest and had the cheek to look offended. 'Me? Create a bad impression? No.' He shook his head. 'That was just timing, and shock.'

'Shock at seeing me?'

They weaved their way out of the exit and across the grass towards the nearest street lined with coffee shops. 'It's not every day your ex turns up.'

She shook her finger at him. 'Oh, no, it wasn't me who turned up. It was you. Invading my little space with your big hair.'

He caught a glimpse of himself in a shop window. 'What's wrong with the hair? Too long already?'

It had been a constant joke when they were married. Cut short, his hair had just a hint of the dark curls. Left any longer the curls seemed to multiply in space and volume overnight, making Lachlan's hair the butt of many jokes.

She'd always dreamed of having a little girl with dark curls like Lachlan's, and a pang of sorrow twisted inside her. It had been a long time since she'd thought like that.

'Your hair is fine,' she said a bit more sharply than she meant to. He gave her a curious stare and directed her towards a coffee shop with tables and chairs outside in the sun.

They waited a few moments for a young waitress to take their order. Iris went to the nearby display cabinet to pick a cake, but Lachlan did what he always did. 'A coffee and a doughnut, whatever you've got.'

She smiled again. 'Still with the doughnuts?'

'Why not? They're good in any shape or form—jam, custard, apple, plain, iced.' He smiled. 'I could go on for ever.'

'I thought your cake selection might have improved over time.'

'Why fix what's not broken?' There was an awkward silence between them. It was clear their minds had just gone back to their own, very broken previous relationship. But this was about doughnuts. Not about them.

'I got a bacon doughnut once.' Lachlan was obviously trying to fill the silence.

She wrinkled her nose. 'Where on earth did you get that?'

'America. I was working in an ER, and a bakery around the corner started doing bacon doughnuts. It became the standard breakfast food.'

'I'm surprised you didn't stay.' She couldn't help it. She was curious about where he'd been, even though she didn't want to be.

He paused as the coffee and cakes were sat down by the waitress. 'I thought about it. The career opportunities were good, but after a while, I wanted to go back to England.'

'Where did you go?'

This time when he looked at her, she saw something in those brown eyes. Something that he clearly didn't want to share. She glanced down at the strawberry tart she'd ordered and wondered how on earth she could eat it without getting sauce everywhere. It seemed easier to concentrate on that than anything else.

He didn't answer the question, just moved smoothly onto something else. 'So, what is it you wanted to talk about?'

She pulled out her phone and showed him the notes she'd taken. 'You remember that kid you saw a few days ago—the one with nothing you really could put your finger on?'

His forehead creased. 'Yeah, the seventeen-year-old with the minor temperature and muscle aches. He definitely wasn't telling me everything, and I couldn't really treat him with so little to go on.' He groaned and leaned back. 'Don't tell me, he's back and I missed something.'

She shook her head. 'No, but we've had a few other teenagers all reporting similar symptoms across the city in the last two days.'

'What have they been up to?'

She leaned her head on her hand as she tried to break

up her strawberry tart with a fork. 'And why didn't they just to go to their GP?'

'So, what are you thinking?' he asked.

'I'm thinking that there could be more to this than meets the eye.'

Lachlan took a bite of his doughnut. 'The most obvious thing for teenagers is glandular fever, but it doesn't fit.'

'No, it doesn't.'

Lachlan pointed to a newspaper headline at the shop next door. 'What about that?'

Iris turned her head. '"*Spate of break-ins at designer properties.*"' She raised her eyebrows. 'That's close to your new neck of the woods. How can they be connected?'

'Because the radio this morning said the police suspect teenagers. There's been some minor damage, but at most of the break-ins it's been consumption of alcohol and use of the property that seems to have been the main motivation.'

Iris gave a slow nod. 'It could be. But does that mean there's something toxic at one of those houses?' She pulled a face. 'Or illegal? Are we going down the entirely wrong route?'

Her phone rang and she answered quickly, her eyes gleaming as she looked at Lachlan. 'Fergus, I think I love you. I'm with Dr Brodie now. We were just discussing the cases. We'll be in soon.'

Lachlan was already grabbing for his wallet to pay the bill when Iris stopped abruptly. 'What's wrong?' he asked.

She took a moment, then gave him a serious glance. 'I'm sorry, it's your day off, and you clearly had plans.' Her eyes went to the book grasped in his other hand. 'I shouldn't have assumed you would be happy to work without checking first.'

He gave her an amused smile. 'As long as I'm back later to walk Scout, my day is yours.' He settled the bill and turned to her. 'Besides, you've already worked today, shouldn't you be worrying about yourself?'

She looked at the clock on her phone screen and grimaced. Holly was due out of school soon. She'd be picked up by the childminder, but this could take longer than the childminder usually stayed. 'Give me two minutes to make a call, then we can head to the hospital in my car. Or—' she glanced around at the streets that were full of parked cars '—did you bring your own?'

He shook his head. 'I took the DART today. Decided to be a cross between a local and a tourist.' He took a few steps away. 'You make your call and I'll wait for you.'

She was grateful he gave her a little space, conscious that at some point she should really mention Holly. It was beginning to feel a bit awkward—all on her side, of course. But she just didn't want to start arguing again with Lachlan. Telling him she'd adopted a child on her own would bring up a whole conversation, a whole pile of feelings that she just wasn't comfortable discussing with him. He'd likely be hurt—maybe even angry—and it felt as if she and Lachlan were just reaching a place she'd never imagined they could get to: friends. Plus, he was only here for three months, and a few of those weeks had passed already. Was it really worth telling him something that might cause a huge amount of tension between them for the rest of his stay?

She'd been well aware she wasn't the only one with a broken heart when they'd split. She was treading carefully, but it seemed as if Lachlan had reached some equilibrium in his life. Would admitting she'd moved on from

their marriage, and created a family of her own without
him, be like rubbing salt in an old wound? She certainly
didn't want to do that to him.

Once she finished her call they walked quickly to her
small red car. She laughed as he folded his long legs into
it. 'You realise you've set the hares running already,' he
said.

'What do you mean?' She pulled out into the city traffic.

'You told Fergus you were with me. People will wonder why you're spending time with me when we're not
working.' There was a hint of amusement in his voice.

She raised an eyebrow at his teasing. 'I already told
Ryan I was coming to find you, and if anyone else asks,
I'll be just as honest. The case that annoyed you, started
to annoy me too. I dug a little deeper and thought it was
worth trying to join the dots.'

'So, what does Fergus have for us? I take it another
case has come in?'

'A case that was seen yesterday at Dublin Memorial
has presented at St Mary's. Fergus gave me a call, because I'd told anyone to let me know if we got any further
cases. According to him, this kid has taken a downhill
turn.'

'Let's try and get a better history. I think the young
guy that I saw wasn't entirely truthful about where he'd
been. It might give us a clue to whether this is actually some kind of disease, infection or an environmental thing.'

They chatted easily as they reached the hospital, pulling into the staff car park. Part of her insides were glowing. For a few moments she'd cursed herself for making
assumptions about Lachlan wanting to come back into
work—she had no right to do that any more. But when

she'd stopped, and corrected herself, he'd been only too happy to help—just like he'd always been. Over their eight years apart, there had been major changes in her life; she suspected there might have been major changes in his too. But it was still good to know that, at heart, Lachlan seemed the same man.

Fergus looked up as they entered A&E. He gave the two of them a half-knowing smile. 'Good, you're here.' He looked at them both, 'Want to get changed, or just want to see the patient?'

Iris glanced down at her white trousers and pink shirt, knowing just how much she should get changed, but Lachlan laughed and gave her a nudge. 'Go on, take a chance. Risk it.'

She sighed. 'Who needs white trousers anyhow?' she asked as they both washed up at one of the nearby sinks.

Fergus took them into one of the cubicles. 'This is Tyler Brooks. He's seventeen and presented an hour ago, with a temp of thirty-nine, a dry cough, headache, muscle pains and shortness of breath. I've taken some bloods and he's had a chest X-ray...just waiting for the results. He was sent home last night from Dublin Memorial with no treatment, but his symptoms weren't as bad last night. He also reports a few episodes of D&V at home. I gave him some paracetamol for his temperature.'

The young man looked completely worn out. He was attached to a standard monitor and had a probe on his finger and an oxygen mask on his face.

Lachlan stood at the edge of the trolley. 'Hi, Tyler,' he said quietly. 'I'm Dr Brodie and this is Dr Conway. We've seen a few sick teenagers in the last couple of days, and we're trying to find out why.'

Tyler's eyes flew open and he instantly looked scared.

Lachlan put his hands up. 'I'm not here to get you into trouble. I just want to find out what's wrong with you.'

Iris moved around the other side of the trolley. 'Do you mind if I have a listen to your chest?'

Tyler shook his head and Iris listened to the front and then the back, shooting a look at Lachlan. This young man's lungs sounded far from good. She'd guess at the least he had pneumonia, which was unusual for someone this age.

She lifted his chart. 'Can I just double-check? No history of asthma, or any chest complaints?'

Tyler shook his head, then started to cough. She saw something flare in Lachlan's eyes at the sound of the cough.

He waited until the coughing stopped, then spoke quietly to Tyler again. 'Have you been somewhere different in the last few days?'

Tyler shot him a glance, and Lachlan didn't need the answer out loud.

'Okay, so is there a chance you touched something you shouldn't have? Chemicals, gardening supplies?'

Tyler closed his eyes again, clearly exhausted. 'We didn't touch anything like that. Just had a few drinks, and went in the hot tub,' he sighed.

Hot tub. Lachlan's vision connected with hers. 'Is it a hot tub you'd been in before?' he asked.

Tyler shook his head again. Lachlan patted his arm. 'I think we might know what's wrong with you. Let us check your blood results and chest X-ray and we'll be back in a minute.'

They walked to the nurses' station and pulled up the chest X-ray. Tyler's lungs showed signs of pneumonia, with consolidation at the bottom of both lungs.

'Want to take a guess at his bloods?' asked Lachlan.

Iris pulled them up and nodded as she looked at them. 'All abnormal, low sodium levels overall.'

'He has legionnaire's disease.' They both nodded at each other.

Lachlan started pulling up another record. 'Do you think the other kids might have had Pontiac fever? It's the same disease, just milder.'

She looked at the notes on her phone. 'It could be.' She glanced anxiously back to the cubicle. 'But there could be more that have legionnaire's—likely from that hot tub. We might not have seen them yet.'

Lachlan looked thoughtful. 'The police should know which of the houses that were broken into had hot tubs. If they'd been sealed up while the owners aren't there, and the kids just fired it on without knowing any of the treatments to use, it's likely that's where they've picked up the disease.' He gave her a smile. 'How about I deal with Tyler, and you talk to environmental health and the police?' He gave a small shrug. 'I figure you know more people around here than I do.'

She picked up a phone. 'And I figure you want the easy bit, instead of all the paperwork.' They were teasing each other again.

He picked up Tyler's chart and walked back towards the bay. 'Some people might think that you know me,' he quipped over his shoulder, and threw her a wink.

The easy remark let a whole warmness spread over her body. Reaching parts that she'd forgotten she possessed for quite a while. She looked down and her hand started to tremble. Once it started, it didn't stop.

Iris quickly checked to see no one was watching her and hurried along to the changing room, closing the door behind her and leaning against it.

Her heart was clamouring in her chest.

Tears brimmed in her eyes. This was ridiculous. Ludicrous. They'd had a fairly normal couple of weeks working together. Her heart told her they were on their way to being friends. They were even beginning to joke around each other.

She sucked in a breath and started coughing. All the stuff that she'd kept deep down inside her for years was trying to push its way to the surface. And all it had taken was an off-the-cuff remark from her ex, about what people might say about them.

No one else in the world would get this. She couldn't explain this rush of emotions if she tried. But that cheeky glance, those casual words and that blooming wink had sparked more memories than anything else had.

Because that's how life had used to be between them. And she'd never, ever met anyone else who had made her feel the way that Lachlan had.

It had taken her right back. Way, way back to the start of their relationship when they were so in sync. When every time she glanced at Lachlan Brodie her heart skipped a couple of beats. When even a brush of a hand could make them want to head to the nearest room with a locking door. When she felt totally loved, adored and safe around him. When the whole of their lives stretched out for them like a beautiful winding path they would walk together.

Of course, there were a few things she hadn't told him. Everything had seemed so instantly good between them that she hadn't wanted to tell him anything that might make him think less of her. So, although he knew she was adopted, she didn't tell him the true relationship between herself and her adopted parents. She didn't tell him how abandoned she'd felt when their newly conceived baby had been born, how useless and unworthy—or how much she'd played up for attention, making everything worse. He hadn't asked too many questions. Particularly about how her parents hadn't come to their wedding. She'd made a few half-hearted excuses about Australia being too far away, and how they'd married at such short notice, that there hadn't really been time to make arrangements.

Guilt threatened to swamp her. Guilt that she'd kept secrets. Guilt that her driven obsession of starting their own family had ultimately driven them apart. Guilt that she'd ruined their relationship and their future.

No. No. Iris took some deep breaths and started to think rationally. She pressed her hand against her heart, which was still beating too fast.

Life had taken them in different directions. Yes, she'd missed his company, his love and the life they'd had together. But she couldn't go back. *They* couldn't go back.

And the most ridiculous thing was she didn't even know if he would want to. She was being pathetic. One wink, and a smart remark, and she was in the changing rooms, crying like a baby.

But the attraction was still there for her. Those knowing brown eyes had seen too much of Iris. They'd seen her at her worst, and at her best, and she couldn't pretend that a tingle hadn't shot up her arm when he'd touched her when they were talking about Aunt Lucy. The feel of his skin against hers...

She shook herself. She couldn't allow herself to go back to that place. It was torture to her. Torture to remember what she'd lost, and to see it walking around in front of her again. She was trying so, so hard to be a grown-up about this.

She wiped her eyes, starting to get angry with herself. She had a job to do. She had a child to get home to.

A daughter who loved her, was definitely the boss and regularly told her off.

Maybe Lachlan working here wasn't such a good idea after all. Yes, they'd got to the bottom of something today, in a way that was so familiar to her. That's all this was. She was having a weird, momentary flashback, because they'd relived how well their working relationship used to be. But in the scale of life, it was nothing.

She wiped her eyes and washed her hands, checking her appearance in the mirror and putting on some lipstick. She still had those calls to make. There could be other kids in this city who'd been exposed to legionella.

She wasn't worried about Tyler. Lachlan would have started him on the right treatment and taken care of him. She had no doubts about his abilities as a doctor. But she needed to find out if he'd got a better history of where those kids had been.

She took a deep breath and walked out to find him. 'Any idea where the house with the hot tub is yet?'

He was typing up some notes as he started speaking. 'I think it might be the one close to where that rock star lives.' He looked up. 'Iris? What's wrong?'

Darn it. She pressed her lips together. 'Nothing's wrong.' Her tone was dismissive because she couldn't handle this conversation now.

He looked at her strangely, then turned over a chart and scribbled something on the back. 'Here, Tyler roughly told me where they drove to. I don't know that part of the area too well. You might have a better idea.'

She stared down at the pencilled map and nodded. 'This will do.'

She went to walk away but Lachlan grabbed her arm. Concern was written all over his face. 'You would tell me if something was wrong, wouldn't you?'

She held her breath, looking at those dark brown eyes again. The ones she used to love and trust with her whole heart.

She blinked and straightened. 'No,' she answered truthfully, not reacting to the surprise on his face. 'We're long past that part of our lives.'

Then she turned on her heel and walked away, ignoring the fact that she knew he was watching every step she took.

CHAPTER FIVE

LACHLAN BRODIE HAD no idea what was going on in his life.

He'd found a perfectly nice cottage to stay in. He was loving the ability to tramp over the fields with Scout and keep an eye on Maeve while her medications were reviewed and she was undergoing a few other tests.

In theory, work was going well. The fire in his belly had been well and truly lit again working in Dublin's A&E. He'd talked to the four other A&E departments around the city, and they'd developed better ways to flag children who presented frequently across all five hospitals after working alongside their IT colleagues.

It was a system used in other cities he'd worked in, and had been one of the first things he'd thought about since being back. In a world dominated by IT now, all A&E departments should talk easily to each other, but it didn't always happen. Lachlan hated to think of a kid with bruises being taken to one hospital, then presenting at another with a broken bone, and no one connecting the dots. The staff around him had been enthusiastic; all he'd had to do was present the system, and gain some permissions to use it. After that, it had been adopted easily, and he was proud.

He was fast becoming enamoured by this beautiful city and its people. He loved being so close to the sea.

The area around the harbourside was becoming a favourite. A few of the other doctors had invited him out for drinks at the local pubs and to join their football team.

In lots of ways, he was enjoying his time here. Except for one thing. The giant, beautiful thorn in his side that was Iris Conway.

He had absolutely no idea what was going in inside her head.

One minute, he'd thought they were on their way to being friends. The sparks were still there. Although she was eight years older, and—just like him—had a few little lines around her face, she was every bit as attractive as she'd always been. At times when they chatted things felt so natural. So...before.

Before all the issues that had driven them apart. He wished he could turn back the clock. He wished he'd been more direct with her. He would have done anything to keep her happy back then, so he'd agreed with all the avenues she wanted to pursue and those she hadn't. They'd both had dreams of a family, and she'd been determined to never put those aside.

But, with time and retrospective thinking, Lachlan wished he hadn't been so obliging. He wished he'd sat his wife down and told her to stop. Told her over and over that *she* would always be enough for him. That, just them, growing old together, was his happy-ever-after. Children would have been a welcome addition, but not an essential part of their future together.

And he had tried to say those words to her. But they had been lost in amongst the tears and fights. Now, when he looked at Iris, he saw eight years that he had lost with the woman that had once owned his whole heart.

He had never really verbalised to Iris how much of the blame he'd felt for their break-up. He realised now he'd spent way too much time talking about how much he wanted a big family: a couple of boys who might look like him, a couple of girls who would look like Iris. They'd also, in their youth and inexperience, dreamed of names for those children, with imaginary personality traits. All of that was wonderful, until the harsh wake-up call that their dreams wouldn't become reality. He'd known she was adopted, and hadn't pushed when she'd rejected the suggestion to try that route themselves.

Hindsight was a wonderful thing, and he knew now that there were lots of conversations they hadn't managed to have that they should have had. And that still bothered him. He should have encouraged her to talk to him about adoption. But every word had seemed to hurt her without him trying, and he would always regret letting her walk away when she wanted to. Maybe if they'd been older, married longer—maybe if they'd had a bit more life experience—they would have had more resilience to weather the storm of infertility. But it was far too late now.

Even though he knew Iris would always hold a part of his heart.

As all his regrets played out in his head, he wondered if they might ever have these conversations out loud, as older, wiser individuals. But where on earth would they have them? In the staff room? On the stairs between floors?

Part of him wondered if it was stupid to think like that. Rehashing the past wouldn't help anyone.

Yet at times when their gazes meshed, it felt like whole other conversations were going on.

It all seemed so random. Him, turning up here, and seeing Iris again after all this time. Realising the connection that had once been between them still seemed as if it were there.

But for the last few weeks, Iris had been colder towards him. She'd tried to distance herself from him. There was no laughing, no casual conversations, and every time he watched her walk in another direction, deliberately avoiding him, a little part inside him died.

His house phone rang and he answered quickly. 'Hi, it's Rena. Don't suppose you can cover at short notice?'

'Sure, what's wrong?'

'Ryan's wife has gone into labour. Only a week early, but he needs to leave.'

Lachlan felt a little pang inside him. 'Aww, of course. Wish him well from me. I'll leave in the next five minutes.'

He grabbed a few things and made a quick call to Maeve to check she didn't need anything before he left. It was a Tuesday night. He could literally toss a coin to see if it would be busy tonight or not. Generally, Thursday to Sunday night shifts were always busy, but Monday to Wednesday could be a hit or a miss. Quiet shifts were a killer. Lachlan wasn't good at sitting still.

By the time he reached the department he was reassured that there were only a few people in the waiting room. As he walked through the department he blinked in surprise as he noticed Iris in the plaster cast room, winding a fibreglass cast around a woman's wrist.

'Hey,' he said.

'Oh, you're here.' She didn't sound exactly happy to see him. He hadn't expected her to be the other doctor on duty—there were always at least two, but somehow he guessed she might have tried everyone else before him.

'No problem,' he said. 'Where do you want me?'

'Now there's a question,' the female patient responded quickly with laughter in her voice.

Iris's cheeks flamed and she shook her head without meeting his gaze. 'Can you just deal with the cases on the board?'

'No problem.' It was a less than stellar handover. But Lachlan was more than capable of filling in where required.

He quickly checked over a kid with a football injury, an older man with a swollen ankle and a very angry baby with colic. The mother was tearful and upset, mainly at the thought of being powerless to control her child's symptoms and blaming herself for wasting A&E staff's time.

Lachlan recognised instantly she needed some time out. He spoke to Rena, who was still on duty, and got her to show the mum to the canteen to get something to eat, while he paced the corridor with the screaming baby on his shoulder.

He watched as Iris dispatched the woman with the purple cast before she strode down the corridor towards him.

'What's going on?' She looked mildly irritated.

Lachlan swapped the little boy onto his other shoulder. 'I'm taking a turn holding little angry Aiden here, so his mum can get some peace. He's been like this for over an hour.' He rubbed the baby's back. 'I imagine he'll do much better in a month's time when he's old enough to start weaning, but until then…'

Iris put her own hand onto the baby's back and looked up and down the corridor. 'Go on, then. I'll take a turn too.'

'Are you sure?'

'Don't look so shocked.' She looked at Aiden again with a hesitant smile. 'Boy, can this little fellow scream.'

'Oh, yes,' laughed Lachlan, 'which is why I thought mum needed a break.'

She lifted the baby from his arms and adjusted him onto her shoulder. Aiden continued to scream. 'Okay, you make the coffee. There's doughnuts in the staff room.'

He gave her a sideways glance. 'Anyone would think you knew I'd be working.'

She rolled her eyes. 'Ryan brought them in tonight. He wasn't expecting to get called away.' Then she grinned wickedly. 'I am going to torment him all night by sending him pictures every time a doughnut leaves the box, all whilst his wife is in labour. It will send him quietly mad.'

'Now that's just mean.'

'Just the A&E way of life,' she said as she started down the corridor, rubbing Aiden's back and whispering quietly in his ear.

By the time Lachlan had made the coffee, Iris had managed to quieten Aiden. She walked back into the room tugging a wheeled crib behind her and looking critically around the room. 'Mind if I put the lights down a bit?'

He shook his head. 'You must have the magic touch.' The words came out easily, and then he cringed a little, realising how that could feel for a woman who'd wanted a family.

But Iris didn't seem to notice. 'No magic touch,' she said as she laid him down in the crib and lowered the lights. 'I strongly suspect he's just exhausted himself.'

She sat down next to Lachlan and reached for her coffee, letting out a sigh.

He could almost hear the silence echoing around them. He took a sideways glance. Iris had her hair in her usual ponytail and was wearing pale blue scrubs. She had some light make-up on her face and looked a little tired.

He took a deep breath, wondering where to start. 'I like Dublin.'

'You do?' She seemed surprised by that statement.

He nodded. 'It's a beautiful city. Lots of character. The people too, they're very welcoming.'

She took a sip of her coffee. 'Sounds like you want to stay.'

'I might.'

Iris froze. He knew that he'd taken her by surprise. But she also knew he only had a three-month contract right now.

He moved, turning to face her on the central chairs. 'But it feels like yours.'

It was best just to say it out loud.

She frowned. 'What do you mean—it's mine?'

He shrugged his shoulders. 'It is. It's your city. You've been here a while. You're head of this department. You bought a house and built a library.' He gave a gentle laugh. 'For anyone that knows you, that's pretty much a sign you plan on staying here long-term.'

She bit her bottom lip, watching him carefully. 'I do,' she agreed. 'I like it here. But I can't put my name on a city and call it my own.'

He felt his heart break a little at the way she said those words, reading everything she wasn't saying out loud. This was her place. And he was likely outstaying his welcome. Just as well he'd already agreed to a new contract somewhere else.

'We both know that if I'd known you were here, I wouldn't have taken this job.' It didn't sound nice saying it out loud. But he was only being honest for them both. 'It was never my intention to appear unannounced.' He lowered his gaze. 'I honestly didn't think we'd run into each other again.'

'Nor did I,' she agreed quietly.

His arm was on the back of the chair between them. 'So, what now?'

He looked back up and held her gaze. Lachlan could almost swear there was a giant ticking clock somewhere in the room, counting out the seconds of silence in the loudest possible way.

'I don't know,' she finally whispered.

'Do you hate me being around?'

'No' was her immediate reaction, but then he saw her take another breath. 'And yes,' she added.

It was painful. Just the way he thought it would be. She was slowly cutting thin wafers of his heart and tossing them away. But the way she was looking at him told him something else. Even though the lights were dim, he was sure his eyes weren't playing tricks. She was looking at him as if…

Her voice was husky. 'It's confusing,' she murmured. '*You're* confusing.'

He shifted a little, subconsciously getting a little closer. Her blue eyes were on his.

'How do I confuse you?'

She gave a soft smile. 'Because sometimes I just hear your voice, sense your presence or listen to your laugh, and it takes me back to a whole other world.'

'I know the feeling,' he replied in a low voice. 'I never expected…' His words tailed off, unsure if he should actually say what he was thinking out loud.

'To see me again?'

He gave a little laugh but shook his head. 'Well, there was obviously *that*.'

'But?' There was a hopeful edge to her voice that he just couldn't ignore. Not when it was just them. Not when they were here like this.

He held his palms upwards. 'I just never expected this again.' He kept his eyes fixed on hers. He had no idea how she felt about all this. He knew it confused every part of him. He couldn't be sure that he was reading things right. He knew that he found Iris every bit as attractive as he ever had. He knew that any time he was around her, he itched to get closer. Just to be nearer, just to be in her presence. Was he crazy? Because it was starting to feel like he was.

But Iris's pale blue eyes held his gaze. He watched her nervously swallow. 'What is this?' she whispered.

He dropped his gaze and shook his head as the low laughter bubbled again. 'I'm darned if I know.'

She shifted next to him. He hadn't meant to make her feel uncomfortable. 'I can go,' he said quickly. 'And I will go. I've agreed to a three-month contract in Glasgow after this.'

'You have?' There was a small hint of panic in that response. And before she knew it, Iris had reached out to him. The warm palm of her hand pressed down on his bare arm. He was almost scared to look at their skin-on-skin contact. Scared of how easily it made his heartbeat quicken and his pulse feel as if it echoed in his ears. His heart was contracting so hard he knew he had to speak. He had to say some of the words out loud. He could sense an air of desperation about her, and he understood it, because he felt it too.

'I only ever wanted you to be happy, Iris.'

Her fingers tightened on his arm and he looked up to see a single tear fall down her cheek. 'I know that...' Her voice shook and he pulled her into his arms.

His reactions were automatic. Iris's tears had always broken him. The sense of heat against him was intense.

Her head nuzzled into his neck, and her arms wove around his waist, clinging on tight.

For a few moments, they stayed like that. That closeness, those curves against the lines of his body, reminded him of how much they'd always felt like a perfect match. No one had ever invoked the same kind of sensations in him that Iris did. They had seemed to connect in a way he'd just never managed with anyone else.

As he breathed in, he inhaled her scent. Not just her perfume, but the shampoo in her hair and the soap on her skin. Tingles shot across the surface of his skin. He gave a little groan. 'Iris,' was all he managed to say.

It was as if the sound of her name set her alight. She lifted her head with a gleam of determination in her eyes. She shifted position so quickly he didn't even have time to think, kneeling astride him and moving her lips to his.

If Lachlan had been trying to keep things subdued and controlled, that was all out of the window now. He matched her kiss for kiss, hungrier for her by the second, his hand sliding up the inside of her scrub top and up the length of her back.

Iris couldn't get any closer, but she tried. Sliding her fingers through his hair, laughing as he let out another groan, then clasping the back of his neck as she ran kisses down the side of his face.

'I had to know,' she said breathlessly as she kept kissing him.

'Had to know what?' He wasn't really paying attention to the words, as he was far too distracted by what her hands were doing now.

She nibbled at his ear. 'Had to know if it was still there. Still us.'

He couldn't help his deep throaty laugh. 'Oh, it's still there. You can't deny that chemistry.' Relief and heat were igniting every cell in his body. He wasn't crazy, and he hadn't imagined it. This was every bit as real as he thought it was. *Too* real, in fact.

But Iris pulled back and closed her eyes. She looked every bit as overwhelmed as he felt right now. It was almost like she was trying to catch her breath and collect her thoughts. Lachlan pulled her towards him again.

A little murmur sounded behind them.

They both froze. Lachlan was sure he could hear their hearts beating above any other noise.

After a few frozen moments he let out a strangled whisper. 'Scared to move.'

Her head was right next to his ear. 'You should be.' Her voice was barely audible. 'Little guy is looking me straight in the eye.'

Lachlan started to laugh too, his chest reverberating against hers. 'I guess you can say we were caught red-handed.'

She gave a half-hearted smile and swung her leg back over and slid on to the chair next to him. 'I'm innocent. I was just trying to get closer to the jam doughnuts.'

There was a pang deep down inside him. He wanted to *talk* to her. And he could sense Iris retreating again. Their chemistry was electric, but it was clear there was still so much of herself she wanted to keep hidden from him.

He'd been burned before. They both had. And the truth was, Lachlan wasn't sure he could go through that again. It had been too hard, too painful, to get over. He'd spent the last eight years trying to replace what he'd lost, without success.

Reigniting the fire again could cause even more damage. He wasn't sure how much he could hold together if things between him and Iris backfired as spectacularly as they had before. The vibe he was getting right now was that Iris was still the same person. Still someone who didn't want to dig too deep, and be really, really honest about things. He couldn't let his heart get tangled up with her again. Not unless she could be more open with him.

'What is this, Iris?'

The humour left her eyes. She knew exactly what he was getting at. He didn't need to spell it out for her.

Iris paused and the wait seemed to be killing parts of him.

She looked down at her hands. 'I don't know. So much has happened. There's a lot about me you don't know.'

His stomach muscles clenched. He had to resist the urge to offer platitudes or say anything that made him sound the way he really felt like now. No. He was long since done being that person around Iris. He took a deep breath. 'I'm only here for another—what? Seven weeks? There's chemistry between us. That's never changed. So, why don't we just take the opportunity to enjoy it?'

Short term. With no long-term damage. He could do that. But that was about all he could do.

Iris stood up. He could tell she was considering saying no. So, he reached out his hand and took hers gently. 'It's fine,' he said gently. He couldn't pretend that every cell in his body wasn't currently been driven crazy by the hormones racing around his system. That kiss with Iris had reignited something in him.

She shook her head. 'No... I don't think I can do this.'

But while she said it, her blue eyes met his gaze, and she stopped holding his hand and instead threaded her fingers through his, giving him a little tug towards her.

'Okay,' he said slowly, 'I'm getting mixed messages here. Because I can't read you any more, Iris,' he admitted. 'I sometimes wonder if I ever could. You need to tell me what you want.' He couldn't keep the sadness out of his words. Because it was there. And he didn't feel the need to hide it from her.

'You could always read me, Lachlan.' Her voice was hoarse. 'Often better than I could myself.' She was staring straight into his eyes, and he wondered if this was it. A repeat of past history. Another chance to walk away.

'Kiss me,' she said suddenly.

He blinked. He'd thought she was going to move. He'd thought she was going to step away. But her hand reached up, oh so slowly, and she trailed her fingers through the hair above his ear. 'Remind me of that chemistry.' Her voice was low and husky.

He dipped his head to hers. Kissing her slowly, gently. Conscious they may well have a small pair of eyes on them. Pulling her body next to his, and feeling the tight tension relax as they melded together.

This time, it was him that pulled back. She was breathing hard. 'Seven weeks.'

He nodded. 'Seven weeks.'

'I'm not sure if I'm ready for this,' she admitted. She looked up at him. 'I won't deny the chemistry is still there. But how about we start out as friends? I think that's about all I can promise right now.'

He swallowed hard and nodded.

'I missed you,' she admitted. 'More than you will ever know, and more than I could ever cope with. I just don't know what I can realistically deal with again. Because it's not just you, Lachlan, it's us, and everything that happened between us. Every fight, every damaged moment, every little bit of heartache. I can't just get back the good memories, the bad ones will come too.'

It was clearest thing she'd ever said to him, and it took Lachlan a moment to process. She was right. Their history would always be part of them. For him, it meant they should have fought harder for each other, but he wasn't entirely sure that was what she meant.

Aiden grizzled and Lachlan nudged the crib back and forward. 'But history—no matter how much we hate it—has made us who we are. We've moved on. We've grown. We can't wipe it away.' He gave a nod of his head. 'Seven weeks, as friends. I think I can manage that.'

His stomach squeezed as he saw Iris give a sigh of relief. She reached into the crib and picked up Aiden, nuzzling him into her neck and rubbing his back.

Iris would have been a great mother. But that was completely the wrong thing to say here, even if watching her actions made him ache inside.

She put her hand on her chest. 'But I still need a bit of space. *We* still need a bit of space.'

'I can live with that.' It was the easiest thing in the world to agree with. Because he wasn't quite sure how he was going to handle this. He still felt as if Iris was keeping her cards close to her chest.

She stood for a few moments, watching him carefully. He could see her start to relax, her shoulders ease and muscles stop clenching. It was almost as if all the anxiety was draining from her body. 'I better get this guy back to his mother,' she said, heading for the door.

Lachlan walked alongside and opened the door for her. 'Friends,' he said in a low voice. 'For seven weeks.'

She nodded, glancing outside to see if anyone was watching them. 'Friends,' she agreed. The corridor was empty.

As she stepped out into the corridor, his arm brushed against hers. 'Friends—' he smiled, then gave her a wink '—with chemistry.'

Then he strode down the corridor before she had a chance to reply.

CHAPTER SIX

IRIS HAD CHANGED three times, much to the amusement of Holly, who sat on her bed, legs crossed, eating chocolate and watching something on her iPad. 'Where are you going, Mum?'

'Out. Not sure where.'

'Then how are you supposed to decide what to wear if you don't know where you're going?' Holly made it sound all so simple. Her long dark hair fell over her face and she was engrossed in the latest episode of a kids' TV series.

Every time she glanced at her daughter Iris's heart swelled. Part of it was circumstances. Background information was limited, but Holly had been given up because neither of her parents had wanted her. Iris didn't know what their circumstances had been, but from the moment she'd met this little girl she'd felt such an affinity to her. Iris knew that Holly had experienced the misfortune of being given up by her parents, then being in a number of foster homes before her placement with Iris when she was four, and Iris still occasionally caught a haunted look on her daughter's face. One that she recognised well. That glimpse of some kind of memory that might not be welcome.

Iris had done her absolute best to ground Holly and fill her life with love and attention. Letting her know she was always safe and secure with her, and that they were family. Holly was, without a doubt, the most important person in the world to her, and her heart ached with the thought that Lachlan still didn't know she existed.

Iris looked around at the black dress, red trousers and white top, and black trousers with a whole host of coloured tops that she was still undecided on.

'Looks like a tornado has swept around this room,' said Holly casually. She was giggling now, because this was an expression that Iris frequently used to describe Holly's room. She laughed too and started hanging things up again. No black dress. No red trousers.

She pulled the black trousers on, along with some flats, and stood staring in the mirror trying to decide what top would be best. Smart? Casual? Or sexy?

No. Definitely not sexy. It was too soon for that. She and Lachlan were treading carefully around each other, almost like a pair of lions stalking prey. She'd had coffee with him a few times. They'd gone back to the library together. All daytime activities. And now, he'd finally suggested they go for dinner. Which was making her nervous—a) because it was a definite night-time activity, and b) because she'd had to arrange a babysitter for Holly and make some excuse for him not to pick her up at home.

The babysitter part had been very easy. Holly was going to stay with her school friend overnight. It was an arrangement that happened frequently between the two families, usually due to the work commitments of both working mums. But this was the first time Iris had asked due to a personal reason. A social reason. And it felt almost like she was taking advantage.

Holly's bag was packed in the corner, waiting for Iris to drop her off on her way into the city centre. She was as excited about the stay, and full of giggles, but was clearly picking up on her mum's nerves.

'That one.' Holly pointed, with a huge grin. 'It's pretty.'

'You're right.' Iris picked up the burgundy top, with a few sparkling sequins scattered across the neckline, and pulled it straight over her head.

Her make-up was done and she shook her hair out, slipped in a pair of earrings and grabbed her leather jacket and bag. She gathered Holly into a huge hug. 'Thank you so much for helping me choose. Now, are you ready?'

Holly was still smiling. She knew her mum was going out with a friend from work, but Iris hadn't mentioned a name. Holly blinked and looked at her mum. 'Is this a girl work friend, or a boy work friend?'

Iris smiled, as she inwardly cringed. She liked that fact that Holly knew no matter where Iris was going, or with whom, she was always completely indecisive about what to wear. She could avoid the truth here, but she didn't want to do that with her daughter.

'It's a boy work friend. He's new to Dublin. But I've worked with him before.' It was clearly a very abbreviated version of life, but it was as much as an seven-year-old should need to know.

Holly stuffed another last-minute toy into her bag. 'What do you think we'll have for breakfast at Katie's tomorrow?'

There it was. Her daughter's favourite subject. It seemed that Iris was sadly lacking in the breakfast department. Katie's mother seemed to dream up things out of nowhere for the girls. Shaped pancakes, flavoured porridge, French toast, home-made waffles. Iris's usual toast and box of cornflakes were never going to make the grade.

The two climbed into Iris's red Mini and five minutes later—after a long conversation about the latest kids' TV show—Holly wrapped her arms around Iris's neck and smothered her in kisses. 'Love you, Mum.'

'Love you, honey. Have a good time and remember you can phone me anytime if you want to.' Holly grinned and then skipped up the stairs in Katie's house with her friend.

Iris's heart gave a little pang as she thanked Katie's mum and said goodbye. Adopting Holly was, without a doubt, the best thing she'd ever done. That settled like a weight around her shoulders. She still hadn't told Lachlan about her daughter. They were treading so carefully around each other right now she was afraid to rock the boat.

The answer was simple, really; she just had to gather her courage and tell him. But she wasn't quite sure how he would react to the news. When he'd mentioned adoption to her in the past, and she'd no, he'd dropped it, so easily. He hadn't pried. He hadn't pushed, and it made her wonder if he'd really only ever been fixed on having children of his own. Would he even be interested in Holly? And if he wasn't, how would that make her, Iris, feel? No, she really needed to get a better sense of things first.

Timing was everything, she told herself. But each day that passed seemed like another opportunity lost. As friends, they were getting closer. Every time they were together she could feel the barriers that had been built between them gradually breaking down, little by little. The kiss had certainly helped. At least, it had certainly given her a few sleepless nights.

She shivered, remembering it in delight as she pulled into a car park in the city. She'd made an excuse for meeting like this, and quickly checked her make-up before climbing out of the car.

Lachlan was leaning against his own car, smiling at her. She walked over to meet him. 'Well, are you going to tell me where we're going?'

It was a beautiful mild evening. The streets were busy with people casually walking around. 'I'm going to surprise you,' he said as he held out his hand to her.

She hesitated for the briefest of seconds, then reached and slid her hand into his. Was this a step too far for friends? But the feel of his hand encompassing hers made her smile all over again. They'd always held hands. Never while they were working. But all the time in their previous daily lives. This felt natural. It felt good. And she wanted to capture some of those moments again.

They started walking through the streets, stopping to look in the window of a bookshop, and then again at an antique shop. He gave her a sideways glance.

'What?' she asked, checking her appearance in a nearby window—had she smudged something?

'You've got your hair down. It's lovely. You always have it up at work.'

She'd forgotten she'd left her hair down and gave it an unconscious shake. Her blonde hair had always fallen in natural waves. Products and styling were not required.

Lachlan had always loved it.

Her free hand came up and twisted a lock around her finger. 'Yeah, I don't wear it down much these days. Too busy. Too much time spent at work.'

'You need to get out more. Enjoy yourself.' There was a hint of something in his eyes. She liked it. It sparked something down deep inside her, like a slow burning flame.

'Hungry?' he asked.

'Absolutely. If you don't tell me where we're going soon, I'm going to raid the nearest bar, and order twenty-five bags of crisps.'

He laughed. 'Oh, we can't have that.' He gave a nod to the other end of the street. 'It's just along here.'

She tilted her head, trying to see any of the approaching signs, but her vision wasn't quite that good. It took her a few moments to realise where they were going. 'Here?' she asked, her eyebrows rising.

Lachlan nodded and gestured for her to enter the well-known hotel. Iris couldn't help but smile as they walked through the foyer and took the lift to the top floor. The restaurant in this hotel was extremely popular. It had floor-to-ceiling windows all the way around, a large circular bar in the middle and breathtaking views of Dublin city and the mountains.

The wooden décor was cool and funky, and there were booths at the windows, offering a little privacy, along with the spectacular scenery. Iris couldn't stop smiling as they were shown to their seats. 'I've always wanted to come here.'

'You haven't been before?'

She shook her head. 'I was supposed to come here once, for a colleague's leaving do, but I ended up having to cover that night and couldn't come. I was livid,' she admitted as the waiter handed over their menus. 'I'd already picked what I wanted on the menu that night.'

He shook his head. 'Well, I'm glad I've brought you somewhere that you haven't experienced yet.'

They ordered drinks and Iris leaned back into her comfortable seat and looked out over the city and mountains. 'It really is a great view,' she sighed. 'People tell you about it, and you can see it from the gallery photos on the website.' She sucked in a breath. 'But actually *being* here, and seeing it for yourself, is entirely different.'

She looked across the table at him. Lachlan always managed to look good no matter what he wore. His black polo shirt was casual, but smart, his hair was at the perfect stage where it was still short, but had just enough hint of his natural curl. There were a few tiny strands of grey around his temples, but it was always the deep brown eyes that got her.

There was so much behind them, so much depth. Sometimes she thought she could read his whole mind by just looking into those eyes. As she glanced at the menu his hand crept across the table and his fingers intertwined with hers.

She gave a deep sigh and looked back him, struck by the fact that Lachlan hadn't even realised that he'd done it. Eight years on, and they could still fit back into their old loving habits. And instead of making her panic about moving too fast, it gave her the greatest sensation of comfort. Love. Eternal love, that she'd always thought she would never find again.

No one had ever made her feel the way Lachlan had done. No one had ever set her on fire like he did, engaged her mind and her body. Understood her in ways she didn't understand herself. In the end, none of it had helped keep them together—and she pushed that last thought out of her head because this night she just wanted to remember the good.

The waiter appeared to deliver their drinks and take their order and Iris didn't hesitate. 'Can I have the roast pepper, paprika and sweet potato soup, followed by the pan-fried salmon, please?'

Lachlan gave her a nod of approval. 'I'll have the same,' he said, handing back his menu.

'Don't you want the steak?' she asked in surprise as she took a long drink of chilled rosé wine.

He shook his head. 'After eating it for around five years straight I realised I had to change my eating habits.'

She lifted her glass to him. 'You're learning to widen your eating habits?' It was something she'd gently chided him about regularly.

'Oh, there's lots I've learned,' he teased.

She glanced around. 'So, how did you know about this place?'

He smiled widely. 'I asked my local expert where the best place for a first date would be.'

First date. The words sent a shiver down her spine. 'This is a first date?'

'I think so.' He looked at her curiously. 'Why? What would you call it?'

She wrinkled her brow. 'I'm not sure, a reunion?' She shook her head. 'No, that doesn't seem right. A blast from the past?' She shook her head again. 'No, a drink between friends?' None of the terms seemed to fit them.

Lachlan took a drink of his beer. 'No, this is *definitely* a first date. And that's how we will treat this. Two new people, out for dinner—' he gave her a wink '—dressed to impress, in a beautiful setting, with a lot of promise in the air.'

She couldn't help the mischievous words. 'You think there's promise in the air? Well, that means you'll have to impress.' She raised her eyebrows. 'Think you've got the skills?'

He raised his bottle of beer to her. 'I guess we'll find out.'

Tingles darted down her spine. This is what she'd wanted. This is what she'd missed. That chat. That banter. The playful promise of what might come next. It had been so long. Sure, she'd dated. Sometimes for a few months at a time.

But nothing had replicated the relationship she'd had with Lachlan. And now, in this beautiful restaurant, with the three-hundred-and-sixty-degree views around them, she was drinking in the view of the man she'd loved so long ago.

His hint of curls, thoughtful brown eyes, the tiny wrinkles around the edges of both his eyes and his lips. The broad shoulders, and wide chest. The way when he was next to her, his large stance made her feel protected, shielded from the world. She could have done with that over the last eight years.

'I'm so sorry,' she blurted out.

He blinked and froze. 'For what?'

The waiter appeared and sat down their soup. Iris stared at it for a few moments as she tried to find the words. 'For…just…everything.'

She didn't look back up. It was all so overwhelming. Being here with Lachlan was something she'd wanted to be fun. But she had to say something out loud—about their past, their history and their break-up. They'd never really had that final conversation. They'd just packed up as agreed and gone their separate ways. It had all been so civilised, even though they'd both been tremendously sad.

Iris had been utterly heartbroken. But she'd never wanted to admit it to herself when she'd been the one to push for them to part.

Lachlan's hand reached back across the table and touched hers. 'I know,' he said quietly. The buzz up her arm was instant. 'And so am I.'

That was just like him. He didn't take the opportunity to apportion blame and lay it at her door. Another reason he'd always had her heart.

'Eat your dinner,' he said in a joking tone, clearly trying to lighten the mood. 'Don't get bogged down by the past tonight. Let's just enjoy ourselves in the here and now. There's plenty of time for the other stuff later. Deal?'

She looked up and he raised his bottle of beer. It was as though the wave of guilt and regret that had flooded over her just ebbed away again. He'd given her permission not to linger on past regrets. And for tonight? She could do that.

She clinked her wine glass against his. 'Done.' She picked up the spoon and tasted her soup. Her taste buds exploded. It was delicious. His leg brushed against hers under the table and she smiled as another kind of zing shot through her. This night had started with hand-holding and she had a deep suspicion she knew where it might go.

Three hours passed in a flash. The wine, beer and food flowed. The lights outside grew dimmer and by the time the waiter had cleared their plates away the sky was a mixed range of oranges, purples and dark blues.

'Coffee?'

'Irish,' she said promptly.

'Hmm…' said Lachlan as he watched her, nodding to the waiter. 'Two Irish coffees, please.'

'I'll need to get a taxi,' she sighed, leaning back against the padded booth.

'*We'll* need to get a taxi,' Lachlan corrected.

'A late-night walk through the city might be nice. Especially at sunset.'

Lachlan looked out at the spectacular evening colours. 'Next time we should take a drive out to the mountains. Watch the sunset from there.'

'Next time?' She knew that her voice sounded hopeful, but she wasn't ashamed to admit it.

'Why wouldn't there be a next time,' said Lachlan, his voice casual. Part of that annoyed her, and part of her was amused by it. Was he really so relaxed about what was happening between them again? Every time his leg brushed against hers, or he touched her hand, she felt the sparks in the air between them.

She let herself drink in the warmth those words spread through her body, pushing aside the little voice in her head that warned her there were still some things she needed to be honest about with Lachlan.

She was sure there was just as much she didn't know about him. He'd been distinctly sketchy about the last eight years—and, for now, that was fine. She wasn't ready to hear about anyone else he might have loved in her place. She knew no one had featured in his place in her life, but *he* didn't know that, just like he didn't know about the decision she'd taken around parenthood. And she would tell him. Soon.

It wasn't like there hadn't been dates before. Holly had only ever met two men that Iris had dated, and she'd cut both relationships short when she'd realised she'd never consider anything long term with either of them.

But now?

She'd thought for ever would be Lachlan Brodie. And it hadn't been. The voice in the back of her head kept reminding her he was here on a temporary basis and he already had another job waiting for him. If this amounted to anything, it would be short, and maybe a little bittersweet.

Yet a fire burned deep inside her. The chemistry between them still seemed so strong. Part of her longed to push forward, to see if they still connected in the bedroom the way that they previously had.

The coffee laced with whisky warmed her even more. And when the bill had been settled and they started walking the darker streets, it was easy to let Lachlan slip his arm around her shoulders and for her to lean her head against him and slip one hand against his flat stomach.

Their pace was slower, both sedated by the good food and alcohol. Iris guided them to the nearest taxi rank. She turned to face him and he said the magic words. 'Would you like to come and see my cottage?'

She knew the taxi ride to her house would be quicker. But her house showed signs everywhere of the fact she had a daughter. Even though Holly was staying with a friend tonight, she couldn't take him to her house without being honest with him—whether Holly was there or not.

She slid her arms around his waist. 'I'd love to see your cottage.' And the truth was, she did want to see it. He clearly loved his temporary accommodation, as he mentioned it frequently. She was curious about how much of himself he had imprinted on the place.

A taxi drew forward and Lachlan opened the door for her, giving the driver the address as he climbed in.

Around twenty minutes later he signalled the driver to drop them at the bottom of a well-lit lane and paid the fare.

Iris was already smiling as he took her hand and led her towards the grey brick cottage with a slightly wonky-looking roof. The lane was wide enough for cars and had several lights along it. Lachlan's cottage was around halfway along and had a dark blue door.

He drew out his keys and opened the door. She was instantly hit by the rush of warmth against the cooler night air.

She stepped inside and looked around. The door led straight into the main room that had two double squishy sofas, a central coffee table, a side table and large fireplace. One window looked out onto the lane, and the other looked back over the countryside.

She walked over to the back window immediately, then took a few moments to finger the dark red checked curtains. They just looked so right. The inside stone window ledge was wide enough to sit on and she turned back around and looked at the rest of the room. The sofas were dark green, and had red cushions to match the curtains, and there was a thick red rectangular rug under the coffee table stretching out across the room.

'Wow,' she said, realising the deep scent she was smelling came from the bowl of old-fashioned potpourri on the wooden sideboard.

She held out her hands. 'This place is just so…cottagey!' she finished because there was just no other word that fitted.

Lachlan let out a deep throaty laugh as he locked the front door. His head was only a few inches underneath the ceiling height of the room. But he was obviously used to it, because he didn't duck or stoop. 'Of course it is. Why do you think I love it so much?'

Iris kicked off her shoes, sat down on one of the sofas and tucked her legs under her. This place was instantly comfortable.

'Oh, no, you don't,' said Lachlan. 'You've not had the full tour.'

'I'm getting a tour?' she asked.

'Of course. It's your first visit. Isn't that an unwritten tradition?'

Iris sighed and pushed herself off the sofa, moving over to his side and nudging him with her hip. 'Go on, then, give me the tour.'

They stepped into the kitchen and she was impressed

by the large traditional cast-iron stove, and the pale green kitchen around them. Anywhere else it might have looked quite twee, but here, it was just perfect.

'Do you want something to drink? Tea? Coffee? Wine?'

'You have wine?'

He nodded and pulled a bottle of white from the fridge and two glasses from one of the kitchen cupboards. Her foot caught something on the floor. Two dog bowls. 'I thought the dog was Maeve's?'

Lachlan gave a guilty smile. 'Yes, he is. But he spends quite a bit of time around here. I thought it made sense to get him some things.'

'You realise he's playing you, don't you? Should we call him two-dinners Scout?'

Lachlan handed her a glass of wine. 'Oh, one hundred per cent he plays me, but I've not told Maeve about the dog bowls. I figure, what happens between us boys, stays between us boys.'

She shook her head as he led her back out to the main room and showed her the obviously repurposed bathroom, alongside a smaller room that Lachlan was using as a study, and finally, he pushed open a large oak door to reveal his bedroom.

Iris wasn't shy. She stepped inside and sat on the edge of the white uncovered duvet. 'This is bigger than I expected.'

Lachlan nodded. 'This room and the room at the side were a later extension of the cottage. The bathroom was doubled in size then too.'

'So, if all this was taken off, that was the original size?'

'Apparently. Maeve said she's got old papers that stated a family of eight used to live in here.'

Iris immediately drew her arms in as if she were being squished. 'Eight? That must have been a tight squeeze.' Her hand brushed over the duvet cover and she looked around again. There was a large armchair next to the back window in the room. She could see one of Lachlan's jackets, a few pairs of shoes and a couple of books perched on the deep windowsill. At the other side of the room was a dark wood wardrobe, and she could see what she'd once called his 'doctor's bag.' It was brown leather, old and battered. Not like the modern lightweight waterproof bags that were available now.

'I see you've still got your old friend,' she murmured, taking a sip of her wine.

He gave a nod of acknowledgement, and she watched as the memories flitted across his eyes. 'Stethoscope, stitches, scalpel, aspirin, blood pressure monitor, pocket airway mask, finger oximeter and glucometer. A few other bandages and drugs.'

'You still take it with you?' Her voice echoed with nostalgia for Lachlan and the fact he'd used to throw the bag in the boot of whatever car he was travelling in, no matter what the purpose of his journey.

'Of course I do. Never know what you might need in an emergency situation.'

'I bet it could tell a few tales.'

'Oh, it absolutely could.' He was leaning against the door jamb. He'd only taken a few sips of his wine.

Iris looked at him. The guy that even after all these years, one glimpse of, set her heart racing. It seemed ridiculous that one person could still do that to another, with absolutely no contact, after all this time.

But she couldn't ignore the fact, and she absolutely didn't want to.

'What?' He gave her a soft grin. Darn it, still sexy.

She gave up any pretence of resistance. 'I'm just wondering, how it is possible, that after eight years apart, you still make my heart beat just as quickly as ever.'

His lips turned upwards even further. It was almost like a licence for him to move. He took a few steps towards her, stopping midway between the door and the bed. 'Pheromones,' he said in a low, deep voice. 'Compatibility. History. And who knows what else?'

She stood up and took a step towards him. Her skin tingled to reach out and touch him. But she wanted to know it wasn't just her. She wanted to know that he felt exactly the same way she did.

'Is it the same for you?' she whispered.

He gave her a blazing look. 'It is.'

It was all she needed to hear right now.

His voice was husky. 'Are you going to stay the night?'

Of course. Holly was safe with someone else. The night was hers to do what she wanted with.

And she knew exactly what she wanted to do with it.

She stepped forward and put her hand to his face. 'I think I could be persuaded.' She smiled.

He dipped his mouth towards hers. And persuaded her.

Iris woke as the early morning sun hit her face. Pure and utter comfort. That was her first thought. The second was a bit more alarming. She was in that hazy spot, where the brain takes a few moments to orientate to time and place. The heat from the bed wasn't coming from the covers, it was coming from the warm body tucked in behind hers. A large arm was wrapped around her body and rested on her stomach. Her bare stomach.

Every part of her tensed. It was an automatic reflex as her brain finally reminded her where she was. The clothes lying scattered at the bottom of the bed told the story of their evening. She couldn't even see her bra and had no idea where it had ended up.

Last night had been scary, but also very, very natural. Two people who had known each other intimately before, coming together with no hesitation. The familiarity had given them both confidence. The memories of each other remained, but being a few years older had made Iris appreciate just how great their mutual chemistry was. She'd never experienced pleasure in bed with anyone like she had with Lachlan.

She'd actually begun to tell herself that she'd imagined it. It couldn't quite have been as good as she'd remembered, and that she might have been overplaying it in her memories.

But no. Last night had heightened and reinforced every memory she'd ever had. Her skin still tingled at the mere thought. It was simple. Lachlan had ruined her for any other man.

'Hey,' the soft voice murmured in her ear. 'What are you doing awake so early?'

She blinked and smiled, turning around to face him. 'What time is it?' she asked sleepily.

'Five o'clock. Guess I forgot to close the curtains.'

She kept smiling. 'I think you were distracted.'

He dropped a kiss on her lips. 'I think I was.'

He laughed. 'Did that really happen, or was something in the wine last night and I just hallucinated the most spectacular dream of my life?'

She reached up and touched the edge of his cheek. 'It happened,' she agreed, her stomach turning over. After the passionately intimate night they'd just spent together, she knew she had to be honest with him. She had to take the bulk of the blame for their split, and she had to let him know exactly how she'd moved on. She had to tell him about Holly.

'Lachlan,' she said quietly.

His eyes opened. He'd heard the wary tone in her voice. 'What's wrong?' His hand was stroking gently up and down her back.

'I have to tell you something.'

'You can tell me anything, Iris,' he said, with a quiet reassurance that made her more nervous than ever.

She kept her hand on his cheek. It anchored her. But as she spoke she closed her eyes, because it made her more comfortable. 'You know you mentioned adoption to me in the past. And I told you no.'

She felt his body stiffen a little next to hers. Even though she wasn't watching, she knew he would be looking at her right now. 'I know you were adopted yourself. I respected your decision to say no.'

She swallowed awkwardly, wishing he'd said a bit more back then.

'Being adopted wasn't a fairy-tale experience for me,' she said quickly.

His hand continued to stroke up and down her back, as if he were doing it now to offer comfort. 'Tell me about it.'

'I don't have a lot of early memories. I have to assume I was happy initially. My memories really start with my mum telling me she was having a baby of her own.'

'Okay.' It was a statement, but he made it sound more like a question.

'I remember her stomach getting bigger. I must have been around six then. I learned later that they'd desperately wanted a baby of their own, it hadn't happened, and then after they'd had me for a few years, it just happened naturally.' She opened her eyes now. 'The way that everyone tells us that story.'

Lachlan gave a slow nod. They'd had multiple friends offer similar stories when they'd been on their own fertility journey. 'Stop trying' had been a favourite recommendation. But friends often didn't realise how much their own words and stories could hurt.

'So, what happened?' he coaxed.

Iris pressed her lips together for a second, trying to stop the tears forming. But they were there. Telling the story made it all so real and painful again.

'My mum was completely distracted during her pregnancy, totally focused on what was happening to her. Suddenly, I was too loud. Too demanding. I had too many activities. I wanted too much of her time. In the end, my parents stopped my dance lessons and my swimming lessons, telling me they would be too busy to take me when the baby came along. It was like as soon as they knew they were having a baby of their own, I became nothing more than an unwelcome inconvenience to them.'

'Iris, that's terrible.' A deep furrow creased his brow.

She shrugged. 'It is. But that was my life from then on. My sister was born, and it seemed like I couldn't have a second of their time. They didn't celebrate my successes. When I did well at school, it was like they didn't even care. My sister was always the centre of attention. And because there were six years between us, as the years passed, I did what most kids would probably do. I acted out. I misbehaved. I got into trouble. Anything really to get some kind of attention from them, but it just made everything worse.' Tears were falling now. 'It took a teacher, who recognised what was going on and helped me realise the opportunities I could let slip away, to focus on myself and my studies again. Mrs Kelly helped me with my application for medical school; she made it possible for me to attend the after-school lessons by dropping me home afterwards. Both of my parents had said they couldn't possibly pick me up, and the school bus service had always finished by that time. It felt as if she were the only adult that ever noticed me.'

Lachlan brushed a tear away from her cheek. 'That's awful. I want to kill them. How dare they treat you like that? What kind of adults do that? I always wondered why they didn't come to our wedding. You said it was because they were in Australia, but I still thought it was strange they didn't even phone or send a message.'

Iris shook her head. 'I don't think they would have come even if they had been in this country.' She moved her hand from his cheek and pressed it against her chest. 'They never made me feel loved. I never felt wanted. I always felt as if I just shouldn't be there. And when you suggested adoption to me as a possible way forward for us...'

She let the words tail off.

She didn't want to have to spell it out for him. She wanted to move on. She wanted to tell him that she'd finally healed. She wanted to tell him about Holly now.

But Lachlan never gave her the chance.

He sat up quickly, unwrapping himself from around Iris so he could look at her clearly, without mounds of pillows and blankets in the way. His brain was trying to piece together everything she'd just revealed about herself.

Had he ever actually known Iris at all?

'Why didn't you tell me all this before?' was all that he could start with.

Iris looked hurt he'd pulled away, and she pushed herself up too and sat back against the pillows. 'Because I was young. I was in love. My husband wanted a family. *I* wanted a family. And when it didn't happen—' she held up her hands '—it seemed that everything just fell apart.'

Lachlan couldn't help what he was sure was a look of disbelief on his face. He still couldn't find the right place to start. 'This was important information, Iris. I was your husband. This was the kind of stuff you should have told me. Don't you think I could see how much you were falling apart? Why didn't you trust me enough to tell me about your childhood? You knew that I loved you. I would have done anything for you, Iris. But you didn't tell me any of this, which would have helped me understand you better, and you just kept pushing me further and further away.'

Iris looked hurt but she nodded. Her pale blue eyes met his and her voice trembled. 'But how do you tell the first person who actually loves you in the universe that no one else thought you worthy of love before? What if I tell you something like that, and you decide I'm not worthy of love either?'

It felt like a slap in the face. He'd noticed her change in tense. She'd changed from the past tense, to the present. Her words cut him to the bone—the fact this his wife had actually *felt* like that and hadn't told him. Clearly still felt like it. Just how much damage had her parents done—and did they even know, or care?

Now he realised what drove her so hard to wanting children of her own, and what had inevitably led to her falling apart after she'd failed to conceive.

He kept his voice low. His own emotions had to be contained, because he could see how much those words had cost her.

'These were things you should have told me—or I feel as if I should have just known or realised. I thought we knew all about each other, Iris. I spilled my guts to you about everything. Our connection felt so real, so in tune.' He swallowed. 'But I obviously didn't give you the security that you needed. And I'm sorry, because I thought I had. I thought our marriage started out somewhere close to perfect—' he gave a sorry excuse for a laugh '—but I was clearly blind. Our marriage was nowhere near as healthy as I thought. If it had been, you would have felt safe opening up to me. We might have had a chance to work through all this if you'd been able to talk to me.'

Her fingers reached over and stroked the back of his hand. 'If only we could turn back time.' She shook her head. 'I wish I could have had the knowledge and experience I have now, back then. I was desperate to have a perfect life. But it wasn't just us that was affected, Lachlan, it was everything in my life. I struggled to open up to people because of the constant fear of rejection. I understand that now.' She gave a half-hearted smile. 'A good few years in therapy helped me unpick all that.' She sighed. 'If I could turn back time for us, I would wait.'

He frowned. 'Wait? You mean, not get married?' He was surprised how much that hurt.

But Iris shook her head. 'No,' she said sadly. 'I would always have married you.' And those words gave him a little comfort, as she continued. 'But I wouldn't have been in such a rush to start a family. To go through everything that we did. If we'd taken a bit more time together, before we got swept away with the idea of creating a perfect family, then I think we might have discovered each other a bit more. Had a little more resilience for what lay ahead of us.'

Lachlan's heart squeezed. It struck him that he still knew barely more about Iris now than he did back then. What other things might he not know about her? They'd clearly moved too fast yet again, carried away by the incredible chemistry that still existed between them.

His alarm sounded loudly, making them both jump. Iris glanced at the clock. 'Darn it. I need to get home and get a change of clothes before heading to work.'

She swung her legs out of the bed and started grabbing last night's clothes. 'The cars,' he groaned. 'They're both back in the city centre. I'll call us a cab.'

He made the call first, then quickly washed and dressed for work. He would be able to drive straight to work once he picked up his car. Iris, however, would need to make a journey home first. He wrinkled his nose. 'Do you want me to go and ask Maeve if she has anything she can lend you?' He looked down at her dress trousers and sequined top.

The air was weighted with sadness. Something had changed. The conversation had dragged up parts of the past they'd both pushed aside for a while. And it was clear they were both aware of it.

Iris shook her head. 'Then she would tease you mercilessly. Some secrets should be kept.'

Their eyes met and he saw Iris flinch. She'd only been talking about their night together, but the words just seemed ill-timed in light of their previous conversation. The taxi beeped outside the door and she seemed only too relieved to open it.

'Let's go,' she said, and Lachlan nodded, locking the door behind them slowly, his brain still whirring—not entirely sure what might come next.

CHAPTER SEVEN

IRIS WAS FEELING kind of melancholy. She was even more confused than ever. Lachlan had been distant for the last week. She kept going over in her head how hurt and disappointed he'd been after she'd told him about her past, that she'd not confided in him before. How on earth would he take the news about Holly, because now, more than ever, she felt as if she had to tell him.

He needed to know. He deserved to know. And maybe she was panicking about nothing. It could be that Lachlan would have no reaction to the fact she'd adopted a child on her own. It was her right, of course.

But part of her was fearful. Their night together had been wonderful, and she couldn't get that chemistry and connection out of her head. She'd already thought he might have ruined her for any other man, and now she was sure. What they had between them was special. It seemed that there was more at stake than ever.

So, she really, really needed to have the conversation about Holly. He needed to know all her truths. It no longer mattered to her that he only had a few weeks left of a three-month contract. No matter where he was going in this world, she wanted him to know that Holly existed. She had no idea what that might mean for them. But if she was only ever going to have this kind of connection with one man, then she needed to be honest with him. Could there ever be a future for her and Lachlan? She didn't know. She might spend the rest of her life as a single mum with Holly. If that happened, she would be happy. She would. But she also had to be true to herself and her feelings for Lachlan.

Iris walked through the unit. It was busy today. A typical Saturday afternoon, building up to likely a busy Saturday night.

She scanned the board. Fergus was working, alongside Ryan, Joan and Lachlan. With those senior staff, she expected everything to be under control.

Joan was triaging, rapidly assessing all patients. Ryan was looking after someone in Resus, and Fergus seemed to be co-ordinating the floor.

'Have you seen Lachlan?'

Fergus nodded. 'He's in bay four with a sick kid. Running a few tests. It looked just like some regular virus, but Lachlan's worried.'

Iris nodded and walked over to the nurses' station, picking up a tablet and having a quick scan of what was recorded.

She made her way to the bay and pulled back the curtains. 'Good afternoon,' she said to the man at the side. 'I'm Dr Conway. Just in to see how your little boy is doing.'

Lachlan looked up and lifted his stethoscope from the child's chest. He scribbled a few notes and handed them to her.

Temperature for last few days. Rash. Swollen lymph nodes. It could literally be any sick child in the world.

Children often came in, with parents in near tears with worry, only for them to perk up a few hours later as if they hadn't been sick at all. She'd witnessed it herself with Holly. The resilience of children was never to be underestimated—alongside the ability for the parent to feel like a panicking fool. Even though she was a doctor, Iris had worn that badge herself, more than once.

But this little guy looked exhausted. His chest was bare, and he was curled up on his side.

Lachlan was talking quietly to the little boy. 'Here, Fletch, I'm just going to take a look in your throat. Can you open your mouth for me?'

The little boy obliged, and Iris wondered if he had some kind of tonsilitis. But Lachlan then sat down in a chair next to a man who she presumed was the dad, and took one of Fletch's hands. He took a few moments, and then stood and lifted the hospital blanket and glanced down at Fletch's feet. Something inside her brain switched on. Lachlan gave her a nod, as if he'd realised she would catch on to what he was thinking.

He turned to the dad. 'Alan, you were absolutely right to bring Fletch in. I think there's something a little more wrong with him than just a virus, but the first thing I'm going to say to you is that this will be entirely treatable.'

Iris moved closer. Now, she could see the cracks at the sides of Fletch's lips, his puffy eyes and how swollen his fingers were, just like his toes. Classic signs, that could on occasion be missed by a less skilled physician.

'I'm almost sure that Fletch has something called Kawasaki disease. It generally affects kids under five, and Fletch has all the signs. A temperature for more than a few days, a rash, the cracks around his lips and his swollen fingers and toes. He might also develop some peeling skin from the palms of his hands and feet.' He put his hand on the sleeping little boy. 'It's important this disease is picked up quickly and treated. So, we'll admit him to Paediatrics and start him on some immunoglobulin. The best way to get the medicine into him is through a drip, so I'll have to put something in his arm. We also have to give him a medicine we don't normally give kids. You'll have heard of it—aspirin.'

Alan wrinkled his brow. 'The health visitor said we're not allowed to give him that until he's twelve. He's only three.'

Lachlan nodded. Iris couldn't help but admire how good he was being with this dad and this little boy. He had a gentle manner, but was also very clear when explaining things. She would expect any doctor to be like this. But watching Lachlan was making her heart squeeze.

'He is. And this is one of the only occasions we'd use this medicine. It's likely he'll need to take it for a few weeks.' Lachlan stood up and held his hand out to Alan, shaking it in a reassuring manner. 'Let me go and talk to my colleagues in Paediatrics, they'll come down and see you straight away. I'm going to go and get some cream to numb Fletch's skin so he won't feel the needle when we put it in.'

Iris followed him as they walked back to the nursing station. 'Checking up on me?' he asked. She knew he was joking but his expression was serious. It was clear he was worried about the little boy.

'Good catch,' she said. 'Someone else might have missed it.'

He shrugged. 'Let's just say I have a vested interest in these things. The paediatrician had been notified to come down, but we had a baby with suspected meningitis earlier, so I suspect they are still dealing with that case. I'll give them a phone.'

Iris was stuck on the first part of the sentence. 'What do you mean you've got a vested interest?'

He paused as he picked up the phone. 'I'll explain later.'

She held her tongue and let him do his job. Kawasaki syndrome could lead to heart conditions in children. Fletch would need to be monitored for the next few years. She'd never seen a case herself, but knew that not all children had the specific symptoms, and sometimes things were missed. The fact that Lachlan had caught this on first examination was impressive.

She treated a few patients herself while waiting for him to finish, then joined him in the coffee lounge.

He had a strange look on his face when she sat down next to him. 'Are you okay?'

He gave a tight-lipped nod, then shook his head and leaned forward, resting his arms on his legs. 'Just brought back some difficult memories for me.'

She was careful now, conscious there was a whole eight years she knew very little about, and even more aware that she still had important things to share with him too. 'Okay, tell me.'

He sighed. 'We haven't told each other much about the last few years. But I'm sure you'll have lived your life, just like I have.'

She gave a nod, her chest tight. She had a horrible feeling she wouldn't like what came next.

'I met someone. Her name was Lorraine and we were good friends, comfortable around each other. We decided to get out of the city and bought a house in the countryside to make a few changes to our lives.'

'You didn't work in A&E any more?'

He gave a short laugh. 'You'll hate this, but I did my GP training. Looking back, it wasn't really for me. But it suited me at the time. It suited us.'

She was astonished. Lachlan had always liked being

in the thick of the action, much like she did. He had mentioned doing something else, but he hadn't given much away. But it was the other words he'd said that she was fixating on. Lorraine. Every part of her had an instant irrational dislike to whoever this person was. You didn't buy a house and change your whole life for someone who was just a good friend.

'So, what happened?' Her voice felt a bit wobbly.

He took a deep breath. 'Lorraine was a doctor, just like us. She picked up a virus—like we all have, a million times over. But this virus became viral cardiomyopathy. She became sick very, very quickly. She ended up on the heart transplant list but never managed to get one.' He ran his hand through his hair. 'The truth was, she probably would never have survived the surgery. Her consultant was astonished at the rate of her disease progression. It was all just so quick.'

Iris was shocked. She didn't know quite what she'd expected to hear, but it certainly wasn't that.

'So, your partner died?'

He nodded and gave her a sad smile.

'I'm sorry, Lachlan. That must have been so hard on you.'

'It was,' he acknowledged. 'And today might have been a different disease, but we know what can happen if Kawasaki syndrome goes undetected and the damage it can do to hearts.'

'How long has it been since she passed away?'

She was feeling utterly selfish. She'd been so wrapped up in her own secrets, she hadn't really considered Lachlan's. He hadn't used the word *love* when talking about Lorraine. But she had to assume it had been there.

'Over a year since she died.' He sighed. 'And it was only a few months ago that I realised I wasn't really living any more. I didn't enjoy my job. I didn't enjoy my life. I needed a new place, and a chance...' His voice tailed off and he didn't finish.

Iris wanted to fill in the space. There were so many ways she could finish that sentence: a chance to start again, to look for love, to rekindle a romance?

Or maybe she was being too hopeful. It could be: a chance to get away from everything, to forget about the past—which would put a whole other slant on things.

So many things were racing through her brain as she thought about the words he'd just used to describe Lorraine. Good friends. Comfortable around each other. But had he loved the calm, sensible-sounding Lorraine more than he was revealing after the turmoil and trauma of their marriage? All of sudden she felt on even more shaky ground.

'A chance to what?' She couldn't let her mind keep filling in the blanks.

He held both hands upwards. 'A chance to do this again. A chance to get a fire in my belly for my working life again.'

He reached out and took her hand with a sigh. 'It's also given me the chance to see you again.' His deep brown eyes looked at her. 'I wanted to apologise. I've spent the last week thinking about it, and I know how hard it was for you to tell me about your childhood. I'm sorry I didn't react the way I should have. It should never have been about me. It should always just have been about you. I felt as if I'd let you down because you didn't feel you could trust me with this before.' He squeezed her hand. 'And I know you probably needed space and time away from me to do that. I just wish things could have been different for us.'

For the first time in a week she felt bold enough to

ask a question out loud. 'So, what about now? Are you glad that you came to Dublin? Are you glad that we've met again?'

Maybe it wasn't appropriate to ask that question now. But Iris felt as if Lachlan had just pulled the carpet out from beneath her feet. She'd no idea he'd lost a partner relatively recently. And all of a sudden she wondered if the connection she'd relived during their night together had just been pure fantasy.

Lachlan gave a small laugh and squeezed her hand. 'You were a surprise. A blessing almost. Although I'll never get over the shock of looking up and seeing you standing there.'

'I'll never get over the horror of hearing you tell me my department was a mess.'

He shook his head. 'Not my finest moment. In my defence, I was pretty stunned.'

His thumb started making little circles on the inside of her palm. It gave her confidence to ask another question.

'So... Lorraine?'

Lachlan looked at her. She could see the softness around his eyes.

'What about her?'

'Were you married? Engaged?'

He shook his head. 'No. Nothing like that.'

'But you bought a house together. Moved to the country together. You must have loved her.'

'I did,' he said without hesitation, and Iris found her breath catching in the back of her throat. 'Lorraine was a good person. She'd had a previous relationship that hadn't worked out. She'd been hurt—like I was.'

The hairs pricked on the back of Iris's neck. He was talking about *them*. She shifted uncomfortably on the chair.

Lachlan kept talking. It was so matter-of-fact. 'Lorraine was easy. She was comfortable to be around. We didn't fight or argue. If I had a bad day at work, we could come home and talk about it. If I came home and wanted to tramp about the hills for a few hours, she never minded.' He lowered his eyes. 'I cared about her a lot. I loved her in the way that you love a good friend. We were companions more than anything. Sure, at times, things were physical between us, but we didn't have huge plans for the future. We never talked about marriage or a family. I think she very much felt the same way I did. Happy to have someone to share things with and be comfortable around.'

Iris was struggling to get her head around this. She understood the words, but not the emotions. She'd never had that kind of relationship before.

But Lachlan wasn't finished. 'But when she was diagnosed and became sick, it all got too real. Lorraine was terrified. It was as if, right from the beginning, she understood how ill she was, and how things would go. She was calm but scared. I spent most nights just holding her. She cried for all the things she wasn't going to get to do, and she used to get really upset when I tried to placate her and say that things would be fine.'

'But that's understandable. I get it. She must have felt as though her life was being stolen from her. The unfairness of the disease is horrible.'

'But I was overwhelmed by how much it made me realise what Lorraine meant to me.' Iris's insides twisted. She wasn't sure she liked this, but now she'd asked the question, Lachlan couldn't seem to stop talking.

'At that point, she was my best friend. I hated she was sick. I hated that she hadn't got what she wanted out of this life. I did everything for her. Helped her into the shower. Sometimes helped her get changed. Washed her hair. Made the dinners. And she hated being help-less as much as I hated seeing my friend suffer. It was so unfair. In the meantime, I was still working as a GP, and supporting other families that were in similar posi-tions to me—nursing a family member with a terminal condition. I always thought I understood and got it, but I realised then that I hadn't. It had all been assumptions and sympathy on my part. Then I understood not being able to sleep at night and not really being able to work out why. I understood why I could reach the end of the day, realise I hadn't eaten a thing all day and wonder why I hadn't been hungry. It all made sense to me. And I started looking at those people differently, talking to them more. Calling them into the surgery to ask them how they were doing, instead of waiting for them to ap-pear with symptoms.'

The words made sense in Iris's head, and she realised herself that since Lorraine had been gone, Lachlan prob-ably hadn't talked to anyone about this. All the fears and petty jealousy that had flitted through her mind vanished. She put her other hand over the one Lachlan had inter-twined with hers. 'It sounds as if you were a very good friend to Lorraine. She must have appreciated every-thing that you did for her. It must have given her relief, knowing that she was living with someone who would do anything for her and follow her wishes.'

He nodded and let out a long, slow breath. 'I would have done anything for her. I just wanted her to be com-fortable. When she finally died, I followed her wishes for her memorial and then...there was just nothing left for me.'

He looked almost embarrassed. 'I hated the house that we'd bought. I hated the view from the windows. I felt trapped there. All of my patients had known Lorraine.

But they talked about her as if she'd been the great love of my life. To say anything else would have felt like a betrayal. We'd never really explained our relationship to anyone. It wasn't anyone else's business. I started to resent my job, and my patients, and knew I just had to get out of there.'

He turned to face her. 'So, coming here, to this place—finding that cottage, and getting this job—just seemed like all my dreams coming true.' He ran a hand through his hair. 'And then, there was you.'

'Me?' Her voice was shaking.

'You,' he said, and the way he looked at her made her heart soar.

'I'm glad you came here,' she said softly.

He smiled at her as she reached up and touched his cheek. 'And now we've talked,' he said. 'And got things out into the open.' He paused for a second, before looking at her with hopeful eyes. 'Do you think we could see where things take us from here?'

Her chest tightened as she nodded. She wanted to take this chance with Lachlan again. She wanted the chance to be with the person who made her feel whole. But the fact she had kept something else from him was eating away at her. He'd just told her a big part of his history. He'd lost someone he'd cared deeply about. And she believed every word. Lorraine might not have been the big love of his life, but he'd clearly had a lot of affection for her and looked after her. It all seemed right to Iris—and so like Lachlan. She no longer had that tiny pang of hurt or jealousy. She was simply sorry that Lachlan had lost someone. It sounded as if he'd pretty much done it all on his own, and that made her want to hug him even more.

'I've missed you more than I could ever tell you. I have so many regrets,' she admitted.

'No.' He shook his head. 'Let's just take it from here. This could be good for us.'

Her heart was flipping over and over. She wanted to tell him about Holly but was conscious that at any moment another member of staff could walk into the room. When she told him about Holly, she wanted it to be just them, uninterrupted, so they really had a chance to talk things through.

'I have an idea,' he said suddenly. 'Let's go for a walk after work.'

'You're on until eight,' she said, trying not to look panicked as she thought frantically what to do with Holly.

'Eight will be perfect. Come back and we can leave from here. It will just be starting to get dark. There's some place I want to go. And something I want to do with you.'

He was looking at her with such warmth that she couldn't possibly say no. 'Okay, I'll come back. I'll be back here for eight.'

He dropped a kiss on her lips. 'Perfect. Now, let's see some more patients before the rest of them come hunting for us.'

Lachlan felt lighter. He'd shared with Iris about Lorraine and what he'd gone through in the last few years. And she'd been fine about it. She seemed to understand that he'd held Lorraine in a lot of affection, rather than being heartachingly in love with her.

No one could ever hold his heart the way that Iris could.

After spending the night with her last week, processing things and having their heart-to-heart tonight, he was keen to move things along. He didn't want to pretend with Iris. He wanted to wear his heart on his sleeve. He knew there was still so much underneath they would have to talk about again, and still come to terms with. Children would likely never happen naturally for them, and Lachlan had long since accepted that children may never be part of his life. But he didn't want to be afraid to bring up the subject with Iris; he wanted the opportunity for them to reach some common ground. She would always be enough for him—it was time for him to reiterate that, and it seemed like now she might finally be ready to hear it and accept it as the truth. Eight years was a long time. If she'd had a change of heart and wanted to consider other options for a family going forward he'd be willing to talk about it. Whatever they were going to do, he was sure he wanted to do it together. And tonight, he wanted to make it a sign of their fresh start.

Dead on eight o'clock he threw his scrubs into the locker room laundry and pulled back on his jeans and navy polo shirt. Iris was waiting outside.

He walked out into the pleasant evening and didn't bother to check who might be behind him as he held out his hand to her. He was glad when she didn't hesitate and let him lead her along one of the streets away from the hospital. The dim evening light was pleasant, the street lights just starting to turn on. 'Where are we going?' she asked.

She'd let her hair down again and was wearing jeans, trainers, a navy-blue jacket, and he could see a hint of bright pink jumper at her neckline.

'I hope you're not hungry, because this is strictly a no food date. This is something else.'

Her nose wrinkled. 'I grabbed some food when I got home. You said a walk, so I dressed appropriately.' She raised her eyebrows. 'But you better not try and hike me into the mountains.'

He shook his head and stopped at a coffee shop that was clearly open late. 'Let's grab something to drink in case we get a little cold.'

She waited while he bought them both coffees, but still took her free hand as they headed down the street. This was her city. He was sure she would guess where they were going soon. But it didn't stop the wave of excitement that fizzed in his stomach.

It was strange. He'd been married to this woman for three years. He'd proposed to her in bed of all places. But tonight, he was even more nervous than he'd been all those years ago.

They started down towards the River Liffey and he suspected she thought he might be taking her over towards the main streets lined with bars. But as they walked along the side of the river, he realised he couldn't have hit a more perfect time.

The evening sky was dimming all the time and lights on the white bridge in front of them were glowing. There was green underneath at either side, with yellow and white towards the middle and reflecting off the dark river.

He stopped walking and turned to face her. She tilted her head to one side and looked at him quizzically. 'What?'

He nodded his head slowly. 'Okay, to some people this is just the pedestrian bridge from one part of Dublin to another. To others, this is the Ha'penny Bridge.'

She laughed. 'I've been over this bridge hundreds of times. Why have you brought me here?' She lifted one hand. 'You do know we're not allowed to put any of those lock things on it, don't you?'

He nodded. 'I know. I was thinking about something else. Something for us.'

He took her hand again and led her to the bridge. It

was well used, and several other people were crossing at the same time. They walked into the middle of the bridge and he stopped, turning to face her again. He was certain the time to do this was now. It had come to him out of nowhere after what had happened today, and he'd wanted to mark something between them. He wanted to let her know how serious he was, and that he wanted an entirely clean slate for them to work from. Iris was the most important person in the world to him.

She swallowed nervously, wondering what Lachlan was about to do. She'd made an excuse to her neighbour that she had to run back to work and would likely be a couple of hours. But at some point, she needed to get back home to Holly.

He held up one hand to the scene around them. 'So, we're in Dublin. I know you've lived here for a while, but for us, we have no history here.'

Iris gave a slow, thoughtful nod. That made sense. 'Okay.'

With her nod, enthusiasm seemed to grip him. 'So, we're over the River Liffey. It's a beautiful evening. We couldn't find a more perfect spot.'

Her heart skipped a few beats and she looked around. Surely he wasn't going to suggest something unexpected? They'd only just agreed to give things a chance. For a second, her mouth went dry. She still had to sit him down and spill out her whole heart to him—to tell him all about Holly and how her life had changed becoming a mother at last. It only took her a moment to realise they were entirely alone. The rest of the pedestrians had disappeared into the night. The sky was filled with deep mauves and the river seemed to twinkle with the reflected green, yellow and white lights. A few coloured buildings lined the side of the river. If she didn't know she was in Ireland right now, she might think she was on a movie set, or at a popular American theme park.

Lachlan pulled something from his pocket and this time her heart almost stopped. But it only took a second to realise what it was. An old-fashioned halfpenny. 'Where did you get that?'

Iris leaned forward. These hadn't been in circulation in her lifetime. She'd only ever seen them online before.

'I've had it for a while. My old auntie gave it to me as a good luck charm years ago. I found it when I was at the cottage the other night and thought it might mean something.'

'What do you mean?'

He pulled a sorry kind of face. 'My original thought was that we could come here and make a wish together and throw it into the river. Something to signify a new start for us.'

She smiled at him; honestly, this guy could touch her in places she didn't even know existed. Her fingers reached out to touch the shiny coin. She already knew there was a but coming.

'But?'

'But I thought that a ha'penny might not be too good for the river. So, I thought of something else instead.' He dug into his pocket and pulled out a small but perfectly formed flower.

Iris let out a gasp. 'Where on earth did you get that?'

He tapped the side of his nose. 'Never you mind. Just know, it was last minute, and I had to have some help.'

She leaned forward and looked closer. He had a small perfectly formed peach-coloured rose. It looked as if it might have come from some kind of bouquet. 'What are we going to do with this?'

Lachlan pulled one small petal from the rose. He held it in his hand, then let it go over the water, mouthing a few silent words. He turned back and smiled. 'There,' he said in a deep voice, 'I've gone first. A wish and a promise for what might happen next.'

'But you didn't say it out loud.' She felt a bit cheated. 'I want to hear what you're wishing for.'

He gave her a smile. 'Okay.' He pulled another petal. 'This one is for a new promise between us. A chance to start anew.'

Hope filled her heart as he sent the little petal down onto the river. She leaned over and saw it carried on the current away from them.

She leaned over and plucked a petal herself. 'For a new beginning.' She copied his actions and let it fall from her hand.

'For no regrets,' said Lachlan, and did it again.

Her heart panged as she copied him. She meant it, she wanted to have no regrets between them.

'For love,' he said as he pulled her closer. 'I love you, Iris. I always have.' The heat from his body flowed to hers. She wrapped her arms around his neck and pressed her lips to his. She was secretly stunned. She hadn't been prepared for this. But as much as she loved this moment, it was never clearer to her that now was the time to tell him her whole truth. He knew part of her story about her upbringing and how it had impacted on her initial thoughts about adoption. Her fears, and the fact she had worked through them. But now he needed to know about Holly.

She let her lips move away from his and pulled another petal from the rose. 'For love,' she said as she held it in her fingers. 'Now and always.'

He grinned at her, picking her up and spinning her around. When he set her feet back on the ground, she wound her fingers through his hair. 'I can't remember the last time I was this happy,' he whispered in her ear.

'Me either,' she agreed. She took a deep breath and put her hands on his chest. 'But there's something else I want to talk about. Something that's really important. And I hope you'll understand.' Her stomach was currently doing backflips.

It must have been the expression on her face, either that or he could sense how nervous she was. He pulled back. 'You can tell me anything, Iris. No secrets between us.'

'No secrets.' She nodded in agreement and took a deep breath.

'Help!'

The scream made them jump apart instantly. Both of them turned. There was a man lying crumpled on the path by the river. Another man was by his side, grabbing at his friend and clearly trying to revive them.

Lachlan started running, and it took Iris a second to join him. She'd just been about to tell him—tell him about the most important aspect of her life. And now this. She pulled her phone from her pocket and dialled the number she needed. Lachlan was already on his knees performing CPR. The man who'd collapsed looked in his fifties and had the classic pallor of someone who'd had a myocardial infarction. She spoke to the emergency services, giving the situation and their exact location before kneeling down to assist.

For two emergency doctors the process of resuscitation was second nature. But frustration simmered just beneath the surface for both. They had no equipment, no drugs and no means to shock his heart back into rhythm. The odds of survival for cardiac arrest in the street were slim, but Iris was determined that this man would at least stand a chance.

The ambulance appeared quickly, with the two personnel jumping out. There was a nod of acknowledgement when it was clear they recognised both Iris and Lachlan. The man's condition didn't immediately improve, and when it was clear he would need to continue to be resuscitated, Lachlan looked at her with sorry eyes. She knew exactly what he wanted to do.

'Go.' She nodded. 'You need to help.'

'But what about you?'

She shook her head. This ambulance would be heading to another hospital that was slightly closer, not their own. And she knew she had to get home soon to Holly. She couldn't allow herself to get caught up in something else. Lachlan and the paramedic were more than capable of getting this guy to hospital.

'I'll see you later.' She was full of frustration and regret. But it wasn't the time and it wasn't the place. It just seemed like the last few chances when she'd wanted to tell him about Holly, something else always got in the way.

Lachlan climbed into the back of the ambulance with the man's friend, giving a swift wave of his hand. 'Talk later,' he said as the door closed.

She watched as the ambulance took off with the lights flashing and gave a deep sigh. She'd promised Lachlan a fresh start. And she wanted that for them both. But the truth was, until she sat him down—without other distractions—and told him about her daughter, neither of them could ever have a fresh start.

And that made her heart hurt in a way it hadn't for years.

CHAPTER EIGHT

LACHLAN FINISHED THE EMAIL, asking the estate agent to put his house on the market back in England once the lease was up. There was no point keeping it. He would never go back there. Not now. He hadn't even managed to have that conversation with Iris yet. But he was sure she would be happy to hear he was staying in Dublin.

His hand brushed the inside rough brick of the cottage. He loved this place. Scout was currently rooting around his legs, apparently impatient to get back outside. Starting a new life with Iris again would undoubtedly mean leaving the cottage. Although he hadn't seen it, she clearly loved the red brick terraced house she'd bought in Portobello. Maybe he could persuade her to look at dog adoption? He'd quickly grown used to having Scout around and he enjoyed the fact of having a constant companion. He smiled as he took Scout for a final walk before heading to work. Ireland was bringing him a whole new life again. Part of him wondered what might have happened if he'd waited a few more weeks before making the decision back home that he'd had enough. This job would likely have been taken. He would have ended up somewhere else and never met Iris again. That made his stomach twist in a way he didn't like. Did he really believe in fate, or was this all just dumb luck?

An hour later he returned Scout to Maeve, giving her a quick, unobtrusive check over. Her meds had been changed after they'd discovered she had adrenal insufficiency. She had no other big symptoms of Addison's disease, but Lachlan, and her consultant at St Mary's, were keeping a careful eye on her.

'How's things with the beautiful Iris?' she asked. He'd quickly learned that Maeve would always be known for her persistence. She didn't let things go.

He gave a warm smile. 'Good. Better than good. Let's just see how things go.'

He moved over to her table where he glanced some paperwork. 'What's this?'

His eyes scanned the drawings.

But Maeve was still lost in romantic thoughts. 'Love reunited. I like that, it's like some old-fashioned love story.'

'I'm thirty-four,' he laughed. 'I'm not completely out of the game yet.'

Maeve looked up. 'Oh, those.' She waved a hand. 'Before you moved in, I had big ideas. I fancied myself doing all those renovations that other people have done and leasing the place for a fortune.'

He blinked at the wall on one side of the large, extended cottage plans, made mainly of glass. A bit like the house up on the hill where the kids had got sick from the hot tub. It made him shiver.

'Maeve, far be it from me to comment, but the best part of the cottage is the natural features. The old-fashioned brick. The rough stonework.'

'What about the gaps around the windows and the irregular plumbing? I know you're there on your own, but what if you had more guests? There isn't much room.'

He nodded, his thoughts going to earlier. He didn't

imagine he could persuade Iris to move to the cottage, but even if he did, it would be a tight fit for two. There was very little storage space, and he could almost hear her voice echoing in his ears: 'Where would I put the vacuum cleaner, or the ironing board?' Both things that he'd never had a requirement for in the last few weeks.

'You're right. There isn't much room. But is there any way you can extend but keep everything in the style it is now, with just a few subtle updates—' he smiled '—like the windows and the plumbing?'

She gave a nod. 'I suppose I could. But don't all the youngsters and trendy people want glass everywhere?'

Lachlan shook his head. 'I guess everyone is different. But I guess if I was picking a place to stay for a holiday, I would think your cottage was perfect. If I wanted to come with friends, I'd just want some more space. A few more bedrooms, a bigger sitting room and maybe another bathroom, and maybe another entrance where all the muddy boots could go after walking in the hills. Hey, can you hire Scout with the place?' he joked, bending down and scratching Scout behind the ears.

Maeve looked thoughtful for a few minutes. 'I might talk to the architect again. I'll see what he can come up with.' She looked back at Lachlan and grinned again. 'I made you a cake.'

'What?'

'For you, and your colleagues. Take it to work with you. It's on the counter in the kitchen in a metal tub for you. Irish apple cake.'

Lachlan's stomach immediately growled at the thought of it. 'You're supposed to be taking things easy right now. But I'll just say thank you and take it anyway. I'm hungry already.'

He smiled as he left and drove to the hospital. He deposited the cake in the staff lounge with a note on it and quickly changed and headed to the nurses' station. He'd been trying to think of some place local that he and Iris could go to in the next few days. There was still so much of Dublin he hadn't seen yet, and having his own personal guide would be a perfect bonus.

Iris was on duty, and he could hear her talking behind the curtains as she reviewed a patient. He grabbed the details of the next patient on the list—a woman with acute abdominal pain—and went to see her.

By the time he'd finished, Iris appeared looking a little flustered. 'Okay?' he asked.

She pressed her lips together. 'Can we get a chance to sit down together, maybe later on?'

'Do you want grab lunch together?'

She shook her head. 'No, not here. It's not something I want to talk about at work.'

Lachlan stopped for a second. 'Something wrong?'

The way she hesitated before answering was like a punch to the guts. 'Yes, no, maybe.' Iris looked distinctly nervous. It wasn't something he was used to seeing on her.

He reached out and took her hand, not caring who around here saw him. 'What's wrong?'

She sucked in her cheeks, then forced a smile on her face. 'Nothing. Let's just leave things until later. It's just really, really important that we have a chance to sit down together and talk, Lachlan. I've tried to talk to you a few times but something else always comes up.'

His guts churned. This wasn't like her. At least, not in any way he could remember. Perhaps she was going to tell him she didn't want to try again. He'd just reached the desk when the red phone began to ring. Lachlan had enough experience in A&E to know exactly what that meant. Someone was calling a major incident alert. It was midday, and it was during the week. This was unusual. Most major incidents happened at weekends or in the evening. All around him, other phones started to ring.

He kept calm. 'St Mary's.'

'Major incident alert. There's been a mudslide causing a train derailment. Ambulances just on-site. Casualty numbers will be available soon. St Mary's is listed as twenty major casualties. Can you confirm those numbers for me?'

Officially, Lachlan should check at this point with the head of the department in case there was anything else going on in the hospital that meant they wouldn't have room for the potential patients. But he didn't need to. He knew A&E was relatively quiet this morning. They could clear the patients they had in the next twenty minutes. 'Confirming St Mary's for twenty casualties.'

People had already gathered around him. He replaced the receiver and raised his voice. 'Train derailment. More details to follow. Confirmation of potential casualty numbers for St Mary's. We'll get a call back to let us know how many will actually be coming. Ambulances are on-site. So, it'll likely be soon. Can we clear our patients, and alert all other services? Speak to the surgeons, tell them they need to delay routine surgeries. We should know soon.'

Noise erupted around him. Joan appeared at his side with a checklist. She shouted orders to people like a military sergeant. He smiled and put a hand on her shoulder. 'Thank you.'

He saw a flash of yellow and Iris pushed her way through the people, her face pale. 'Was it a train? Was that what you said?'

He nodded. 'Mudslide, derailment.'

'What train? Where?'

He shook his head. 'They didn't say. But they'll get back to us shortly.'

Iris leaned against the wall and pulled her phone from her pocket. Her hands were shaking. Several people were asking him questions all at once, and Lachlan answered them as best as he could. 'Did they ask for an emergency team to attend the scene?'

He shook his head. It wasn't unusual in a major incident for ambulance services to ask for additional support. A&E teams were trained to attend if required.

He pushed his way over to Iris, putting his hand around her shoulders and taking her away from everyone else. The nearest place was the laundry store and he closed the door behind them. 'What's wrong?'

It wasn't just her hand that was shaking, it was her whole body. She tried to push past him. 'I need to find out. I need to find out about the train.'

He shook his head. 'Did you have a friend travelling by train today? Is that's what wrong?'

Her hand was still clutching her phone. The screen was lit and he could see she was on one of the well-known social media sites that gave a constant stream of news.

The words didn't seem to form on her lips. From the cupboard, Lachlan could hear the shrill ring of the red phone again. 'Let me get that,' he said, regretful that he'd have to leave her alone.

He strode quickly back to the desk and picked up the phone just as Joan was about to. 'St Mary's.'

'We have seven casualties coming your way. Two major—both adults, one head injury, one multiple fractures. The five other casualties are schoolchildren aged between seven and ten. It seems there were three different primaries on a co-ordinated school trip.'

His hand gripped the receiver even tighter. His skin prickled. There was always something horrible about knowing children were involved in a major incident. 'Can you give me details of what train this was, in case we have enquiries?'

He listened carefully. When he'd finished, he replaced the receiver and repeated the news to the staff. 'Prepare for two adult majors, one with head trauma, one with multiple fractures. Five children all minor. See if we can get a paediatric team down here.'

Joan tugged his elbow. 'Five children?' She was frowning.

'Apparently some school trip.'

'What school?'

He shook his head. 'They didn't say. But there were three different primary schools on that train.'

'What train?'

He repeated what he'd been told and heard a strangled sound somewhere. Of course. He wasn't sure what school it was, or where it was situated in the city, but some of the staff in the hospital might have family members affected.

He moved his way through the people, watching faces, catching the flash of yellow in the distance heading into the treatment room. It was his favourite of her shirts. She looked good in it. Now it was calling him like a beacon.

All the staff around were moving dutifully to their places, preparing for their patients. Seven was actually quite a small amount following a major incident, and with only two with serious injuries, the department would be able to cope without problems. But what on earth was going on with Iris?

It might have been a few years, but he'd worked with her before when there had been major incidents. She was always calm and organised. He didn't recognise her right now.

He got stopped numerous times on the way to the treatment room, answering queries easily. Unusually, the door was closed. As she pushed it open he watched. Iris was leaning across the sink retching. Her words were coming out in between. 'She is on that train. She is on that train.' Joan was holding her hair back for her and rubbing her back. 'It will be fine,' she was murmuring in a low voice. 'She's probably lost her phone in the panic. That's why she's not answering. I'll see if I can get patched through to the commander. Find out if anyone has her name.'

Joan's eyes lifted and she started when she saw Lachlan standing there. She leaned forward and whispered something to Iris, who snapped her head back up and stood back from the sink. He couldn't ever remember seeing her look so distraught.

'I'll give you a minute,' said Joan. 'See what I can find out.'

Lachlan didn't quite get what was going on. Clearly the news hadn't gone down well with Iris, but she hadn't mentioned friends or relatives with kids, or anyone who worked on the trains, so he couldn't quite understand what was going on. Iris had never been the kind of person to panic or overreact to these kinds of situations.

He let the door close behind him, stopping himself from immediately holding her close. Something was telling him to wait. She looked terrible. He could see a snapped ponytail band on the floor and her blonde hair was in complete disarray all around her face.

He watched Iris carefully. Her breathing was ragged beneath her yellow shirt. 'Tell me,' he said. 'Tell me who you are worried about on that train. Who is on that train that has you in this state?'

He couldn't stop himself. He moved the few steps and put his arm around her. Iris's wide blue eyes looked at him. She looked as if her heart was in pieces. 'Holly,' she breathed. 'She's on that train. She's on a school trip. She's not answering her phone.'

Something lanced through his heart. He knew the answer before he asked the question. 'Who is Holly?'

There was only the briefest pause before Iris answered in a sob. 'My daughter.'

His brain went everywhere. The kids on the train were between seven and ten. He and Iris had split eight years ago. But no. Iris wasn't pregnant then. That was the reason they'd split up. So, if she'd had a child since then, she'd moved on from him pretty quickly.

Last night, they'd agreed to move forward and yet Iris hadn't told him she had a daughter. It was a pretty big non-disclosure. But he could get over it. He could. Even though he couldn't for the life of him understand why she wouldn't have mentioned her daughter before now. A child wasn't something to hide.

There wasn't time for this now.

'Okay,' he said calmly. 'Holly. Is her second name the same as yours—Conway? Can we ask ambulance control if they have her? Let's do that.' He was trying to be logical. Putting things in order in the way that Iris clearly couldn't right now. But she was a parent. She wasn't a doctor right now. And she was doing what any parent would—panicking while they waited to know if their child was okay.

He pushed everything else aside. This was too important.

'I meant to tell you. I was going to tell you. I was going

to tell you tonight,' Iris sobbed, her whole body heaving. 'That's why I haven't invited you back to my place. I had to tell you about Holly.'

There was a definite wave of panic flooding through Lachlan. It was filling in any possible reason for Iris not telling him she had a daughter.

The age pinged again in his brain. Was Holly his daughter? Again, the possibility of Iris being pregnant with his baby when she left filled his irrational thoughts. The IVF had been over. But they'd still been sleeping together. Almost right up until the end. They'd never managed to get pregnant when they'd tried before, but could some quirk of fate have allowed her to become pregnant just before she left and they now had a seven-year-old daughter?

His head just couldn't compute that. Iris would never have had their child and not told him. That was an unimaginable betrayal.

He couldn't ask the question. He couldn't ask it out loud. He touched her shoulder. 'You stay here. Let me find out what I can.'

He walked back out into the claustrophobic atmosphere of the department, his gut clenched solid. He moved over to Joan. 'Any news?'

She knew exactly what he was talking about, and didn't make any pretence about it. Something struck him. All these people must have known Iris had a child and none of them had mentioned it. Why not? Had she asked them to keep it a secret? He tried to dampen his anger down. He was starting to feel numb with shock.

Joan passed him a number. 'There's ambulances at the scene from all across Dublin and the surrounding areas. I'm on the phone to one depot. You try this one.'

He picked up the phone automatically and dialled. 'Hi,

it's Lachlan Brodie, consultant at St Mary's. I'm trying to trace a child. Do you have a note of who is in all of your rigs following the train derailment? Yes, I'll wait.'

Joan glanced at him. 'You on hold?' He nodded. 'Me too. I hate this.'

He was finding it hard to look this woman in the eye. She was talking so easily to him. How could she, if she'd deliberately been hiding a child from him?

It gave him a bit of reassurance. His mind was just racing away and making up stories. There was only one person that could tell him the truth, and she wouldn't be in any fit state to do that until she knew her daughter was safe.

Another phone rang; a nurse answered and gave a quick shout to her colleagues. 'Our two major trauma cases are arriving.'

Lachlan was torn. He'd told Iris to stay where she was, and she wasn't in a fit state to see patients right now. He put a hand on Joan's shoulder and handed her his receiver too. 'You do the phones, then check on Iris. I'll triage these first two patients and take care of them.'

Joan gave a nod of her head, and as he walked to the resus room he saw Rena already running through some drip lines.

Fergus came into the other side of the room and both he and Rena exchanged glances. They were expecting another doctor in here. They were expecting the head of their department. 'I'll run both cases,' said Lachlan without hesitation. 'I suspect both will end up in radiology since one has multiple fractures and one has a head injury. But full assessment first.'

It was only a few moments before both patients were rolled in. As he worked steadily alongside Rena and Fergus, he was confident that everything was being done for both patients. The older lady had been going on a day trip. She was conscious, with low blood pressure, probably due to her injuries. She'd broken her shoulder, her right arm and her right leg with the way the carriage had rolled. He suspected there might also be a few ribs involved. Thankfully, two of the orthopaedic surgeons were on hand quickly, to join in the assessment process and take her off to surgery. The second patient was a middle-aged man; he was dressed in a suit and had a large gash to his head and had been unconscious since he was found. His investigations showed a subdural haematoma, and a specialist surgeon was available to take him to Theatre to release the pressure on his skull.

As Lachlan was treating these patients, he was pleased to see a number of his colleagues from Paediatrics file past the door. Two doctors and an equal number of nurses from the ward had come down to help with the schoolchildren. He wanted to go out and ask if Holly was among them, but he knew his priority had to be to treat these patients, so Iris was free to try and find her daughter.

Joan appeared at the door. 'We've several more patients coming in. No majors. Equal numbers of adults and kids.'

'How many?' He was staring at her intently and she gave the tiniest shake of her head as she replied, 'Three of each. We'll cope. We have plenty of staff.' The message was there. Iris still didn't have news of Holly.

Lachlan waited until the man was wheeled out of Resus and snapped off his gloves. He took a brisk walk around the department, checking on every patient and all the staff working on them, making sure there were no problems and he was not needed.

Bays had been cleared for the new patients expected, and staff were ready. He moved into one of the bays where a young girl in a school uniform was getting her elbow stitched. 'You're every brave,' he said, giving a nod to the paediatrician stitching her. 'What's your name?'

'Ruby,' she answered. 'Is my mammy coming soon?'

The doctor stitching looked up and smiled. 'She'll be here soon. I've spoken to her. I told you that.'

He really wanted to ask Ruby if she knew Holly, but he also knew just how inappropriate that was. He glanced at Ruby's school jumper sitting on the nearby chair. The school name and badge were easy to see: St Regent's.

'Are my friends okay?' asked Ruby. He wanted to send a silent signal of thanks upwards. It was just the opening he needed.

'Give me the names of some of your friends and I'll see if I can find out how they are.'

Ruby rattled off a whole host of names. Even if he'd had a notebook and pen in his hand he couldn't have kept up. But one of those many names was Holly.

He held up his hand. 'Holly Conway?'

Ruby nodded.

'Were you all sitting together?'

Ruby shook her head. 'Mrs McLellan made us go in pairs. She did it by names. We didn't get to sit together. I wasn't next to any of my friends.' There was a distinct amount of pouting.

'Okay.' Lachlan nodded. 'I'll try and find out which of your friends are here.'

He gave a nod to the other doc and went back to the treatment room, but it was empty and the door was lying wide. He scanned the department and couldn't see any sign of the yellow shirt. Where was she?

It only took a few more tries to find her. She was in one of the rarely used offices, on the phone to one of the other emergency departments.

He could see the list in front of her with the names scored off in turn. As she replaced the receiver her shoulders sagged. 'I can't find her. No one knows where she is. She isn't in any of the other hospitals, and no ambulance has her.' It was clear the frustration was driving her crazy.

'Will they let us go to the site?'

She shook her head. 'I've tried that. The police say no way. They're still pulling people out. What if she's trapped there, scared and alone? Why can't I get to my baby?'

It didn't matter how many questions of his own Lachlan had right now. He wrapped his arms around her and let her sob on his shoulder.

He couldn't think what else to offer to do. Part of him burned. If this was his child, what would he do? The thoughts played on his mind. He took a deep breath. 'Let me call ambulance control again. Maybe we're asking the wrong questions.'

He still remembered the number from earlier and dialled again. 'Lachlan Brodie from St Mary's. The children on the train who weren't injured. Where have they been taken? And what arrangements have been put in place to contact the families?' He listened carefully. 'So, they've all been checked over by your staff. Do you want to bring them all to St Mary's for a second opinion, or at least a central waiting place? We have room here.' He actually didn't know that. And he didn't care. He didn't baulk when the commander at the ambulance station told him he didn't need a second opinion. However, the offer to take the children away and co-ordinate the return to their parents was a different story. It wasn't just St Regent's children that had been on the train. There had been two other schools, all on a co-ordinated trip. Even though the police were helping too, they had children in a variety of places. Getting them all in one place would help. Apparently, that would free up some of their staff that were needed for other duties. Lachlan replaced the receiver. He stuck his head out of the door. 'Anyone seen Rose?'

Two minutes later, Rose Reid, the hospital general manager, appeared. He held out his hand and took hers, shaking it, and not letting go. 'Don't kill me.'

Her brow narrowed. 'What have you done?'

'I've offered to take the uninjured children off ambulance control so they can keep dealing with casualties. Apparently, there are a number of kids that they need to contact the parents for. I told them we had space and staff to assist.'

Rose raised her eyebrows. He'd seen her dashing about for the last few hours, helping wherever she could. He hoped he hadn't played this wrong. She waved a hand. 'Is that all? No problem at all. I'll take them all along to the paediatric outpatient clinic. Plenty of things to keep them amused. I'll get some food from the kitchen and some admin staff to get in touch with the schools to see how best to assist.' He saw her gaze go to Iris behind him. She lowered her voice. 'Anything else I can do to help?'

He shook his head. 'The controller said the children will come with a police escort.'

Rose nodded. 'Give me five minutes and I'll be ready. I'll send some staff round to help take the children along to outpatients.'

Rose disappeared out the door and Lachlan turned to look at Iris again. Last night, they'd stood on a bridge and tossed rose petals onto the river, along with all their promises and wishes for the future. How could he create a future with someone who kept secrets from him—possibly the biggest secret of all?

Right now, he walked over and put his hand on Iris's

shoulder. 'Why don't we go and wait for those schoolkids to arrive?'

Iris swallowed nervously. It was clear she was still trying her best to keep calm. She nodded and followed Lachlan to the entrance to the department. There was so much he wanted to ask her. So much he wanted to say. But he still understood that now wasn't the time. For all he knew, Holly might not be among these children. She could—as Iris dreaded—still be trapped on the train.

A police car pulled up, with a few police vans behind. Lachlan moved over to greet the lead officer, just as an admin staff member hurried to join him. They exchanged a few words and he was conscious of Iris, her eyes fixated on the faces in the vans. The doors opened and the children started to climb out. A few were nonchalant, others looked bedraggled, a few others slightly stunned; all were dressed in some form of uniform, with or without jackets, and one young boy had only one shoe.

Lachlan moved over next to them, ushering them all to follow him. At just the right moment, Rose Reid appeared and clapped her hands, telling them all she'd look after them until their parents could come for them. One of the Guardai moved over to join her and between them they started to filter the children along. The admin staff took names as the children got to the entrance. But Lachlan knew that Iris wasn't waiting for a name. She'd started to pace, staring into the various vans, frantically searching for her daughter. After a few seconds she let out a yelp and hugged a little girl who stepped down from a van. His heart leapt in his chest until he heard the words. 'Esther, I'm so glad to see you.' She clasped both of the little girl's cheeks before giving her another giant hug. 'Let me look at you again, are you okay?' The little girl nodded.

'Is Holly with you?'

Esther shook her head. 'She's in another van. Can you call my mammy?'

The spark of light that flared in Iris's eyes was obvious from even a few steps away. He could see her breathe a huge sigh of relief. Someone had seen her daughter alive and well. This little girl had told her she was in another van, which likely meant she was uninjured, and on her way. He watched Iris blink back tears as she pulled her phone from her pocket and started talking rapidly to someone. 'Frank. Esther's here. She's fine. She's just been brought to St Mary's to co-ordinate collection for the parents.' She let out a nervous laugh. 'No, I've not seen Holly yet, but Esther tells me she's in another van.' Iris handed the little girl over to the member of admin staff. 'Esther Reilly, St Regent's Primary. Don't worry, I'm talking to her *daidi* now.'

She reluctantly let Esther go, then spun back around to watch the other vans appear. It was a slow process. Since the vans were coming from a few different venues, they all arrived at different times.

Lachlan was nervous. He couldn't pretend that he wasn't.

As one van after another pulled up, he helped the children down, casting a careful eye over them, and giving a nod to the staff for the ones that seemed upset. At last a van pulled in and he sensed Iris's emotions straight away. 'Holly,' she breathed, clearly spotting her daughter's face at one of the windows.

She started waving frantically as large tears poured down her cheeks.

He wasn't quite sure what to do with himself, or what to think about the way his heart currently felt like a clenched fist.

The admin assistant was being methodical with the

kids. Every time a child set foot from a bus, she took a
name, a school and a date of birth if they knew it. He
wondered if she would bypass all this when Holly was
obviously Iris's.

Iris couldn't wait; as soon as the doors opened on the
bus she ran straight up the steps and disappeared from
view. Lachlan pretended his throat wasn't bone dry, and
his heart rate wasn't pounding in his ears.

She had a right to reunite with her child in private.

He kept telling himself that, as the minutes seemed
to stretch on for ever. A few other kids came off the bus,
and he moved beside the admin assistant, casting a quick
eye over them all.

Finally, a tear-streaked Iris appeared, her eyes bright
with relief, with a little girl tucked under her arm.

Lachlan breathed deeply, not sure what he could say.
But Iris stepped down and rattled off details to the admin
assistant: Holly's name, school and date of birth.

The date of birth registered in his brain instantly.
Holly was seven, so the dates didn't quite fit. He couldn't
rationalise the wave of emotions that rolled over him.
There was no way she was his daughter, and he didn't
know if he was sad, or relieved.

His heart sunk like a stone, and his brain couldn't
compute. If Holly had been his daughter and Iris had
hidden her for years, then he would have been unimag-
inably angry. Now he knew that wasn't a possibility, so
why did he still feel a knot of cold fury deep inside him?

This whole thing was making him crazy.

'Do you want me to check her over?' he asked Iris
through tight lips.

For a moment, she paused. He could see a million
emotions flitting across her eyes. But being a parent came
above everything else. 'Yes,' she breathed.

* * *

He knelt down. 'Hi, Holly, I'm Lachlan, one of the doctors that works with your mum. Bring her with you and we'll make a quick check to make sure you're okay.'

Holly pulled her head out from where it was carefully tucked into Iris's side. She was a frail, pretty little thing with light brown long hair, brown eyes and freckles on her face.

He gave her a reassuring smile and Holly gave him an unsure glance.

He held out his hand to let them go inside in front of him. There was a squeal and he watched as Joan appeared out of nowhere and wrapped Holly in a hug. She started talking rapidly to Iris, and dropped a kiss on the top of Holly's head, before glancing back at Lachlan. Her eyes flitted between Iris and Lachlan as if she didn't really understand what was going on.

'I'm going to give Holly a quick check. Why don't you help me?' He could see Joan's professional status slide back into place.

'Of course,' she agreed, then picked the seven-year-old up in her strong arms and carried her over to the nearest cubicle, perching her on the edge of one of the examination trolleys.

Lachlan let his years of experience take over. This wasn't a time for unwelcome emotions. Iris was a colleague, whose child had been involved in a major incident. Although he was sure the ambulance personnel had checked all these kids properly—for a colleague, he would always check again.

Joan spoke quietly in his ear. 'One of the paediatric doctors is around at outpatients, just keeping an eye on all the children before their parents come.'

He nodded. She'd read his mind. Someone from this

hospital was checking all these kids. Kids were a resilient bunch. But sometimes symptoms, particularly emotional and psychological impacts, weren't immediate. Right now, he had no idea what any of these children had seen or been exposed to. They knew there were some serious injuries, but he still didn't know if there had been any fatalities at the scene.

He took out his pen torch and showed it to Holly. 'Do you know what this is?'

Joan was helping her out of her school cardigan. 'My mum is a doctor,' Holly said in a quiet voice.

'Okay, then. You know what it is. I'm going to take a quick look in your eyes, if that's okay.'

Holly gave a nod as Joan slipped a pulse oximeter on to her finger.

Iris was standing silently, but he could see her breathing easing. Her eyes never left her daughter for a second.

Lachlan kept things methodical, checking Holly for any unidentified injuries. Her observations were all entirely normal, and apart from a few marks on her arms and legs, where it was likely bruises were starting to form, there seemed to be nothing out of the ordinary.

When he'd finished, Joan gave Holly another hug. 'Do you want some chocolate?'

Holly glanced quickly at her mum, and then nodded. 'I lost my bag,' she said in a tiny shaky voice. 'It had my phone in it. And I don't know where my blazer is.'

It was almost like she'd just remembered these things. Delayed reactions could be common in children involved in accidents. Iris knelt down in front of Holly. 'Your bag, phone and blazer can be replaced. I'm just glad that you're safe, honey. I was so worried about you.'

Holly hugged her mother tight. Lachlan immediately felt like he was intruding on the family reunion. 'Everything looks good,' he said, picking up the chart with Holly's details. 'How about you two go home?'

Iris gave a grateful nod.

Lachlan wasn't sure how to feel about anything. The woman that he'd realised he loved on the bridge and had wanted to plan a future with only last night had lied to him. It might have been by omission. But it was still a lie.

As if she were reading his mind, Iris shot a glance in his direction. 'We'll talk tomorrow,' she said as she helped Holly back into her cardigan.

He watched as Iris walked out the department, hand in hand with her daughter, and he couldn't understand why his heart ached so badly.

She'd wanted this for so long. And he'd wanted it for her too.

So why did it hurt so much?

CHAPTER NINE

AT MIDNIGHT IRIS received a text.

I'm glad your daughter is safe. But we definitely need to talk. Tomorrow.

There was no question mark. It wasn't a question. It was a statement and she understood entirely why.

Iris couldn't sleep anyway. This had been the worst day of her life. The feeling of being powerless—to get information, or to help Holly in any way—had almost destroyed her.

Part of her felt a bit pathetic. But her stomach had ruled her at the beginning, and the tears of frustration had spilled over when it felt as if no one could really help her find her daughter. Rena had talked sharply to her when she'd wanted to jump in the car and drive on down to the scene of the accident, holding her by the shoulders, and telling her not to get in the way of the emergency services doing their jobs. What if her actions affected the welfare of someone else's child? It had been a blunt reminder of the types of conversations she'd had to have with patients' relatives over the years, and she'd hated every second of being at the receiving end for once.

She also hated that Lachlan had found out this way.

She'd wanted the chance to sit down and tell him calmly about Holly. About how she'd come to be a mother, and how fabulous Holly was. They hadn't even formed the conversation about family again after their previous history.

It had probably seemed too soon to Lachlan to have those conversations. But Iris had known better. And she should have done something about it.

She'd seen the look of confusion in his eyes today. She'd seen the hurt. It was as clear as day. But he didn't even know the real story yet, and although she hated it, there was a good chance it might hurt him even more.

As she watched her daughter sleep, Iris was sure of one thing. She and Holly were a package deal. No matter how he felt at the news, Lachlan needed to understand that any relationship with Iris would be a relationship with Holly too, and her stomach twisted at what the outcome of that conversation might be.

School was off tomorrow for obvious reasons. And she just wasn't prepared to leave Holly on her own. Her little girl hadn't spoken much about the accident since she'd got home. Just pushed her scrambled egg about her plate, eaten only a few mouthfuls, then asked if she could go to bed. She was clearly physically and emotionally drained. And Iris's priority was to be her mum. She couldn't invite Lachlan here. Not when she was unsure how he might react to the news she still had to tell him. So, whether he liked it or not, Lachlan Brodie was going to have to wait. In another day, she could meet him at one of the local cafés. Somewhere neutral they could talk, with no one else around. It might not be what he wanted. But it would have to do.

Lachlan hadn't really slept in the last two days. Yesterday, he'd done an extra shift at A&E to cover—and to keep his mind from other things. Even Scout couldn't cheer him up on the two long walks they'd taken across the country fields. His mind was working overtime and he fully acknowledged that wasn't doing him a bit of good.

As he approached the café in Portobello, he could see Iris already sitting there. Her hair was around her shoulders and she was wearing a green jumper. He hated that his heart always skipped a few beats at every sight of her. What he really needed right now, and what he deserved, was answers.

She looked up anxiously as the door clang signalled his arrival. He slid into the seat opposite her at the window table in the café, far enough away from other tables that their conversation wouldn't be overheard.

When the waitress approached, he only ordered coffee, not even sure if his stomach would take that.

Iris was clearly nervous.

'How's Holly?'

'She's good, thanks. Her bruises have come out now, and she's a bit stiff and sore. Most of her friends who were in the accident are all okay. One was knocked out, but has recovered, one broke a wrist, another their tibia. The teacher's assistant seemed to get the worse of things. She was trapped for a while and had to be cut out. I'm not sure exactly what her injuries are.'

'Did Holly see anything she shouldn't have?'

Iris shook her head. 'I don't think so. Most of them were just in shock, really. They were disorientated after the carriage rolled and didn't know which way to get out. Thankfully there were a few businessmen on board, all standing near the doors. So, they stopped the kids getting off until they knew things were safe.'

The waitress appeared with the coffee and left it on the table, leaving them both in an awkward silence.

Iris looked up, her pale blue eyes on his. 'I guess I should tell you about Holly now.'

'I guess you should.' His words came out tight and he couldn't help it. He sat back in the chair. 'You should know that when I first heard about her, I wondered if she was mine.'

Iris's eyes widened in shock. 'What? Why would you ever think that? I would never have done that to you.'

He shrugged his shoulders. 'The kids were aged between seven and ten. We parted ways eight years ago. It did occur to me that you might have been pregnant when we split, and just not told me. It wasn't until I saw her date of birth and saw when she turned seven, that I realised we were out by several months.'

It was clear that the possibility of him thinking this had never even entered Iris's mind. She tried to reach out her hands towards him but flinched as he pulled them back.

'No, Lachlan. Absolutely not. I would never do that. Never.' Her expression was sincere, but even though the words should have helped, they didn't.

'But you didn't tell me about the daughter you did have. Even though we were dating again. Even though we'd slept together.'

He said it as a statement, although it was actually so laden with reined-in emotion that Iris winced. 'I know, I'm sorry. You're absolutely right. You have to know I had every intention of telling you. But I just couldn't find the right time.'

'Before we fell into bed might have worked. Or before we made those promises on the bridge. I didn't think I was making a whole host of promises to a woman who was keeping such a huge secret from me.'

Iris put her head in her hands. He knew he was being

hard on her, but he was also being honest. Until they'd talked things through truthfully, he couldn't possibly know if there could be any hope for them going forward.

'I'm sorry,' she said, shaking her head. 'I intended to tell you after we slept together, but things got snarled up once I explained about my childhood to you, and then suddenly we had to get to work. Then, I was absolutely going to tell you on the bridge, but that man became unwell and I just didn't get the chance.'

He paused for a second, then spoke again. 'I assume you met Holly's father not long after we split up?'

Her face was blank for a few moments, then she shook her head frantically. 'No, not at all.' He couldn't understand why her face looked even more pained. 'Holly isn't my biological child,' she said carefully.

Now Lachlan's brain jumped all over the place—all in a few seconds. He'd already had pictures in his head of Iris being pregnant. He had no reason to think anything else. He just assumed that the reason he and Iris couldn't get pregnant together was because they weren't a good biological match. It had always been in his head that there was a chance she could get pregnant with someone else, and he, in turn, could have had a family with someone else.

The idea that she hadn't been pregnant at all just didn't make sense. His brain searched for other family members. Iris didn't have brothers or sisters with children that she could have been left to care for. He couldn't even remember any cousins. Had a good friend maybe passed away? It was the only thing that made sense.

'What do you mean Holly isn't your biological child?' he asked.

She licked her lips nervously. The coffee in front of him had already gone cold and he hadn't even taken a sip. Iris rested her head on one hand. Now, she bit her bottom lip. He knew she was stalling.

'I mean… I adopted Holly.'

He froze. 'What?' It was the last thing he'd expected to hear. Every hair on his arms stood on end.

'I know you tried to talk to me about adoption. I know I was dead against it, for reasons I hope you understand now. But after we split, and I spent some time on my own, I started to re-evaluate things. It took a long time, with the help of a good counsellor, but after a number of years, I finally felt ready. I applied for adoption and spent over a year being assessed. Holly was placed with me when she was four. I adopted her three years ago.'

He could swear there was roaring in his ears right now. So many thoughts whirling for space in his brain. It was like he couldn't quite process what he'd heard. The words just seemed to have tumbled out of her in quick succession—as if she couldn't say them rapidly enough.

He leaned across the table towards her. 'But you were always so against it. The reason I didn't push for adoption was because I suspected you had issues you weren't ready to share. I let it go because you meant more to me. Even though it was a route I wanted to explore. When you said no, so completely, so absolutely, I knew I could live the rest of my life happily with just you.' He was shaking his head the whole time he was talking. It just seemed so incredible to him. 'So, I put the idea to bed. Because it was what you wanted. It was always about what you wanted, Iris. But it turns out you were keeping a whole host of secrets from me.' He sat back. All he could feel was disbelief and disappointment. 'If only you'd told me the truth. If only you'd confided in me—told me about your childhood experiences and your fears about adoption. We could have worked through them together, with a counsellor. We could have done all this together. Eight years. Eight years of our lives together lost, because you wouldn't talk to me, trust me.'

She looked stunned. But she couldn't be. What on earth had she expected him to say? This wasn't a punch to the guts—this was being dumped on by steel block. After refusing to listen to him, after not even considering the possibility of adoption, she'd gone off, and taken that option on her own. Without him. He was a fool. An absolute fool.

Tears sprung into her eyes, but he was done with Iris crying. She'd ripped his heart clean out of his chest. He hadn't thought that was even possible any more. Oh, how little he had learned.

'Please, Lachlan, let me explain. I just wasn't ready to accept that path when I was with you. I couldn't think straight, I couldn't sleep, I couldn't do anything because I was an emotional mess. The whole IVF thing just finished me off. Finding out we couldn't conceive without any real reason absolutely ruined me. I needed the science. I needed the facts. It would have been a million times better if it had been my fault, if I had blocked tubes, or no eggs. Or your fault, with sperm that couldn't swim. But telling us that everything was fine, just not when we were together, made me feel like such a failure. Useless. Worthless. I hated myself so much that I saw no other way out than for us to split up; I wanted you to be free to have what you always wanted—a child of your own. The one thing I couldn't give you. I couldn't even begin to think about adoption, especially after my upbringing. I wasn't ready. It took me three full years to sort myself out, Lachlan, before I started the process of becoming an adoptive parent. That's when I finally accepted myself for who I was and focused on making things work for me. We'd lost touch by then. I had no idea where you were in the world.'

He didn't speak. He didn't say a single word. Because he couldn't find any.

The woman he was looking at had been the person he'd loved most in this world. The person he'd hoped to build a life with again, here, in Ireland. Coming here and finding her again had been like being gifted a whole new start. How much of a fool he had been.

Iris was panicking. Even though he was right across the table from her, she could see Lachlan retreating further and further away from her.

Nothing she said was right.

She was grasping at straws, struggling to put their history and the last eight years into some kind of perspective for him. But the explanation she was giving him seemed poor, even to her. What she wanted to do was to reach out and grab hold of Lachlan. Tell him that she loved him with her whole heart. That meeting him again had lit her up in a way she never thought possible.

The worst part was the hurt she could see all over his face. And she was the cause of that. She should have told him straight away about Holly.

'I'm sorry, Lachlan. I just wasn't ready to hear you back then. But you were right. You were absolutely right all along. I should have considered adoption. It was a real option for us, although I couldn't see that at the time. Believe me, I will always regret that. Just like I'll always regret not fighting harder for us. I just didn't have the energy or the belief in myself any more. My counsellor eventually made me see I'd been suffering badly from depression and not realised it at the time. I just thought the low mood, the lack of concentration and energy, the lack of appetite was all due to the effects of the IVF, and the subsequent failures. I thought being miserable was an entirely normal state of mind. I couldn't focus on anything else.'

Lachlan's face remained blank, almost frozen. It was like he'd stopped listening to her. And she should understand that, because eight years ago that had been her, shutting down and not listening to him.

But then he focused his gaze on her. 'I asked you speak to someone about it. I begged you to talk things through with a professional counsellor.'

She closed her eyes for a second. 'I know that. I know you did. But, Lachlan, what can I say? I wasn't myself. I didn't feel like myself. Now, I feel like I did when we were first together. Obviously I'm older, and hopefully wiser. And now I'm a mum.'

She pressed her lips together, realising how hard this had to be for him.

'You looked me in the eye the other night on the bridge and made a whole host of promises to me, based on a life you hadn't told me about. It was all a lie, Iris. How can I ever trust someone who keeps secrets like that? Your daughter. She should never be a secret to keep— you should be shouting about her from the rooftops.'

He just looked entirely disgusted by her and it made her even more uncomfortable. She pressed her hand to her heart. 'Of course I should. And I do.'

'Did you ask all your colleagues to lie on your behalf?'

She cringed and sucked in a deep breath. 'Not exactly.'

'Not exactly?' Icy sarcasm dripped from his voice.

'I simply asked them not to discuss my personal life when you first arrived.'

'So, the first thing you thought about doing when

we met again was lying to me about where you were in life. Nice.'

'Don't make it sound like that. I just thought this would be a difficult conversation. I remember how good you were about everything. I remember how you wanted to look at adoption, and I didn't know how to tell you that I'd gone ahead and done it myself.' She lowered her head. 'Because even to me, that seemed awkward and we had to work together for three months.'

Iris shook her head. She had to try and get back some control of this conversation. She had to make sure Lachlan knew exactly how she felt about everything.

'Adopting Holly has truly been the best thing I've ever done. I might have made a mess of this with you, but I won't make a mess of anything to do with Holly. We're a package deal. If you can find it in your heart to understand why I kept this from you, I'd need you to be happy to be a part of both of our lives, not just a part of mine.'

He blinked and looked at her.

'Holly isn't the problem.' His voice was deathly low and the look in his eyes froze her. 'You knew exactly how I'd feel about this. You didn't want to be together eight years ago. I've had to live with that. We couldn't have children together naturally. I lived with that too, and accepted it. You've had every right to live your life however you've wanted for the last eight years—just like I have too. But at least I was honest with you about what happened in my life. I told you about Lorraine, my career change and my reason for ending up back here. I felt as if I owed you that—' he put his hand on his heart '—because *I* wanted this to work. I wanted to take this second chance for you and me and find a way to make it work.'

'And I do too.' She reached for him again, but Lachlan snatched his hands from the table, as if he couldn't bear her touch. 'I love you, Lachlan. I love you with my whole heart. Tell me how to make this work. Tell me how to make this right with you.'

'I can't get the past the fact you looked me in the eye, spent time with me, made promises to me, *made love with me*, and didn't tell me about one of the most essential parts of your life. That you adopted a child makes my head explode—probably because you shut down that option cold for us. But more than that, I can't think how on earth you thought I'd be so shallow as to only want my own biological children. Didn't you know me at all, Iris? Where on earth did those thoughts come from? The one thing you should always, always have known is that I am *not* like your parents.'

She looked a bit stunned, but he continued, fury driving him on. 'I absolutely know you have every right to make your own choices, time has moved on, and things changed for you. But in here?' He put his finger up to his head, then put his fist to his chest. 'And in here? I just see the woman I thought I loved again who couldn't be honest with me about the most important thing in her life. Who supposedly couldn't find one moment to tell me about her daughter's existence. Haven't you learned anything about keeping secrets? You've already torn my heart out once, Iris. I have no intention of hanging around for you to do it again.'

Before Iris could get a chance to say another word, Lachlan stood up and walked from the café.

She was shell-shocked. She knew she'd brought this all on herself. But somehow, she'd thought she might be able to make him understand. She'd no idea that he might have considered that Holly could be his daughter. It hadn't even occurred to her. Now she felt worse than ever. She should have spoken to Lachlan sooner about all this. But until that moment on the bridge, she hadn't really realised that he was going to tell her he loved her and wanted to start all over again.

Lachlan had truly pictured a life for him—for them—in Ireland, and she'd just snatched it all away from him.

Iris sagged her head down into her hands. She couldn't have made a bigger mess of this if she'd tried. How could she repair the damage that she'd done?

CHAPTER TEN

IRIS WAS GOING through the motions. Turning up at work, treating her patients and going home again. The atmosphere at work was terrible. Everyone knew that she and Lachlan weren't speaking. The staff were tiptoeing around them all. She'd heard Rose talking to someone else, saying that Lachlan had enquired about ending his contract early. Rose had told him if he left before they found a replacement it would put stress on the department. But knowing that he was trying to get away from a place he could easily have settled in—and it was all her fault—made her feel a thousand times worse. She'd tried to speak to him a few times, but Lachlan had made it clear their relationship was strictly professional.

Most of all, she missed him. Spending all her time with Holly would always be wonderful, but even Holly had noticed something was wrong.

'Why are you so sad, Mum?'

'I fell out with a friend even though I didn't mean to.'

'Can't you just say sorry?'

'I did, honey. But he's not happy with me. I'm not sure I can fix it.'

Holly forehead creased and she looked up from her schoolwork. 'Well, that's really sad. Maybe you just need to give him some time to think about it.'

Iris looked at her in surprise. 'Where did you hear that?'

'Mrs McLellan. When there are fights at school, she makes everyone say sorry. But we aren't always friends again until the next day. She says sometimes people need a little time to think things through.'

Iris smiled and rubbed her daughter's back. 'Well, I think Mrs McLellan is very wise. I guess I'll just need to wait and see how things go.'

Holly leaned her head on her hand. 'Which person at work is it? Is it Fergus? Or is it the new one?'

Iris smiled. There wasn't much she could get past her daughter. 'It's the new one, honey. His name is Lachlan.'

'The girls at my school said he was cute.'

'What?'

'He helped some of them at the hospital. Then he went along and talked to some of them when they were waiting for their mums and dads.'

'That's because he's a very nice man.' Iris smiled again sadly. 'And I wish I hadn't upset him. But you're right. I just need to give him some time.'

Holly wrinkled her nose. 'That bad smell is coming in our house again.'

'What bad smell?' Iris stood up and put her hands on her hips, sniffing deeply. Holly was right. There was a bad smell—one she didn't like.

'The one from earlier. We smelled it walking home from school today and out in the back garden. It's yucky.'

Iris's skin prickled—her senses suddenly alight. She turned to Holly. 'Honey, maybe we should…'

But she never got to finish the sentence before a huge boom echoed somewhere and she was blown from her feet.

Lachlan put the fifth apple cake that Maeve had baked for his colleagues into the staff lounge. It didn't matter how often he told her to rest, the woman seemed incapable of listening.

It didn't help matters that she was as astute as they come. She'd been badgering away at him the last two weeks. Asking him what was wrong, if he wanted to talk about things, what had happened between him and Iris. The expression 'being like a dog with a bone' didn't come close. Maeve should have probably been a private investigator.

In the end, she stopped asking questions, and started nagging him. It was the only word he could use to describe it.

'You're clearly miserable. Whatever has happened between you and Iris, you need to get over it and make things right.'

When that didn't work, she tried a different approach.

'The first time around didn't work with Iris—are you going to let the second time slip through your fingers too?'

It was clear she was getting exasperated by his closed lips.

'You're torturing yourself seeing her every day. There needs to be an end to this—a line in the sand. Make up your mind, Lachlan, are you in, or are you out?'

This time he'd snapped.

'I'm out, and I wish you'd stop going on about it. Since when did you become Team Iris?'

A smile had hinted at Maeve's lips and he realised she'd got what she wanted—she'd tricked him into talking about it. She straightened in her chair. 'I'm not Team Iris. I am, and always will be, Team Lachlan. But it seems like my team doesn't know what's good for it. So, as an older friend, I feel obliged to point out the glaringly obvious—that you need to talk to her.'

His shoulders had sagged. 'I've done that. She disappointed me. She let me down. She wasn't honest with me when she should have been. Talking gets me nowhere.'

Maeve had nodded her head. 'You talked, but did you listen?'

He'd looked at her. 'What do you mean?'

Maeve had folded her hands in her lap. 'You know exactly what I mean. Now, pick up the cake from the kitchen.'

And just like that the conversation had been over and it had bothered him ever since.

Fergus appeared at his shoulder. 'More of Maeve's Irish apple cake?'

Lachlan nodded and pushed the tin in his direction. 'Help yourself. How are things out there?'

Fergus pulled a face. 'It's one of those days where you know not to say anything.'

Lachlan groaned. It was a well-known fact, in A&E departments across the world, that if you ever made the mistake of saying 'things were quiet,' it was like a licence for chaos.

He walked through to the front of the department, quickly checking the boards. He already knew Iris wasn't on duty today, and it was a relief to know there would be no awkward exchanges.

He was considering his position here. He had to. He'd thought Ireland was the perfect place for him, the perfect place for a new start. He loved his job again, liked the people he worked with, and finding Iris had made it feel as if all the jigsaw pieces that had been jumbled for the last eight years had finally settled into place.

Until the mudslide and train derailment and he'd found out she'd been keeping secrets.

Some of his self-reflection in the last few days had

made him uncomfortable. He'd been thinking a lot about how Iris had spent the last three years bringing up Holly as a single mother, and the journey she'd taken to get to that stage. A tiny part of him wondered if he was actually a little bit jealous—and that didn't make him like himself much at all. He would have loved to have kids. Whilst others might run at the thought, he'd always wanted a family. His heart was big, he had a lot of love to give, and he couldn't help but envy the life that Iris had been able to give to Holly.

He heard running footsteps and turned around to see Fergus again with a phone in his hand. 'Anyone seeing these?' he shouted, his voice carrying across the department.

One of the admin staff stood up. She was talking on her mobile. She also reached for the remote for the TV that played in the patient waiting room.

The news wasn't playing, but a ticker tape message was running along the bottom of the screen.

Report of unidentified explosion in Dublin

There was a collective hush as people appeared from everywhere, pulling phones from pockets. The admin worker lowered her phone. 'My husband says it's in Portobello.'

Lachlan's skin went cold. They must have waited a few seconds before the department phones started to ring.

He snatched receiver up. 'St Mary's.'

'St Mary's, explosion of unknown origin confirmed in the Portobello area of Dublin. Residential area. No known casualty numbers as yet. Please confirm your ITU status.'

'Four beds available.' He signalled to a staff member to make the call to the ITU department.

'Two mobile teams required. Can you confirm?'

He knew every eye in the place was on him. 'Confirming two mobile teams from St Mary's.'

'Pick up in five minutes. Stay safe.'

The phone was replaced and Fergus was already in the cupboard pulling the emergency kits. It wasn't often that A&E staff had to attend incidents in other places, but all staff were trained for the contingency.

Lachlan's head was spinning. Portobello. Where Iris and Holly lived. He felt sick. 'Fergus, you're with me. Ryan, get kitted up, and, Rena, you're with him.'

The news was apparently already filtering throughout the hospital as a few other doctors from other departments appeared. Lachlan slipped the large jacket on with fluorescent writing saying 'Doctor' across the back of it. He opened the emergency pack and double-checked all the equipment he might need. He grabbed some extra gloves and stuffed them in his pockets.

Fergus appeared beside him with his emergency pack on his shoulder. 'Ready,' he said. He'd changed his normal lower scrubs and was now wearing waterproof trousers and a pair of trainers.

'Done this before?' asked Lachlan.

'Last time was a couple of years ago in a multicar pile-up in a thunderstorm. Was out there for six hours.'

Lachlan nodded. They walked to entrance and, when the ambulances pulled up, climbed in. 'Any more information?' asked Lachlan as he strapped himself in.

'Could be a gas explosion. Unconfirmed report that people in the area had reported a smell of gas a few hours earlier.'

'Any word about the damage?'

'Fire services are on-site. They say that a whole block of terraced houses is affected. One almost obliterated, two are half-collapsed and a number of others have significant damage.'

'What's the street name?'

The paramedic repeated it and Lachlan sagged back in his seat. He glanced around at Fergus. 'That's Iris's street.'

The two of them sat in silence while the blue-lighted ambulance raced through the dark streets. There was radio chatter. Confirming it was a gas explosion and services were on-site. There was some debate about whether it was safe for staff to assist.

Lachlan wasn't even there and he could feel his blood boil. But the paramedic alongside him rolled his eyes. 'We'll be going in, and so will the fire crews. I'll get you a hard hat and visor, Doc. We won't be leaving patients behind.'

The ambulance turned the corner and pulled to a halt. Fergus and Lachlan jumped out of the rig, and took a moment to survey the damage, as Ryan and Rena jumped out of the other ambulance behind them. The damage was significant. One house looked like barely a shell—the roof was gone, and the side walls had collapsed. The houses on either side seemed to have lost half of themselves, collapsing precariously.

Other houses had damaged roofs. Windows were blown out, and curtains were fluttering in the wind. He could see a few people who had clearly been evacuated from their homes. Some in a state of undress. All shell-shocked.

The Guardai had taken command of the situation. One commander pointed Ryan and Rena towards some people who looked as if they had been hit by flying debris.

'Do we know how many people are in each household?' asked Lachlan.

The commander looked up. 'We're having to go on what the neighbours are telling us right now. Someone from the city will join us shortly with more details.' He pointed to the partially destroyed street. 'Number sixteen, a mother and three kids. Father works away. No one's sure if he's home or not, but his car's not there. Number twelve, a mother and one kid. Number fourteen, elderly couple, adult son and teenage grandson. That's where the focus is right now.'

Twelve. Was number twelve Iris's house? He didn't know for sure. He walked swiftly over to where he could see some of the neighbours gathered together. 'Excuse me, can I check? One of my colleagues stays in this street. Iris Conway, do any of you know her?'

The first couple shook their head. But another woman frowned. 'Is that Holly's mum?'

'Yes, yes, it is.'

The woman's eyes were filled with tears. 'Yes, that's their house over there.'

She pointed to one of the half-collapsed houses and Lachlan felt his stomach heave. 'Thank you,' he said, before making his way over the fire and rescue crews and grabbing a hard hat and visor for himself and Fergus. 'Do you have anyone you need me to treat right now?' he asked.

He could see a variety of rescue crew in bright clothing dotted amongst the debris. Some attempts had been made to try and make these buildings safe, with walls propped, but all the staff working here would know there were risks involved.

Lachlan had a job to do. He was happy to take those risks.

'We need a doc here?' A hand waved and Lachlan and Fergus ran over.

'I've got someone trapped under some rubble. Need to check it's safe to move them.'

Fergus glanced around. 'Want me to take this one?'

Lachlan hesitated. What he really wanted to do was wade into the rubble that was Iris's house and start heaving bricks out of the way, and try to find either her or Holly. But he knew that was crazy. He knew he had to let the other services do their part of the job first.

'We'll do it together,' he said to Fergus, and they made their way over. It was the older man, and he was pinned partly beneath a piece of furniture that a wall had subsequently collapsed on. Lachlan and Fergus took some time to stabilise him, check for any other issues, then gently eased him out as the fire crew relieved the weight by just a few inches. He was transferred quickly onto a stretcher and back to the main hub where Ryan and Rena would take care of him.

'Doc.' Another shout. This time it was Iris's house. 'I've got a kid trapped. Not sure if she's injured. She won't talk to me.'

Lachlan sprinted over, his heart leaping in all sorts of ways, making his way over unstable rubble and family items. Toys, kitchenware, a set of yellow curtains. His insides were roiling over and over. These were Iris's things, Holly's things. Things belonging to living, breathing people that he knew.

He put his hand on the shoulder of the rescue worker. The guy looked up. 'I've got a kid down here. Through the gap. I think she's under a kitchen table. Right now, the only way out is through this gap. But I can't persuade her. Can you try?'

Lachlan dropped to his knees. 'This little girl was caught up in the train accident just a couple of weeks ago. She might be having flashbacks. Let me see what I can do.'

'Sure, Doc. I'll be right behind you. Let me know what I can do. Poor kid.'

Lachlan pressed his face toward the thinnish gap. It took his eyes a few seconds to adjust to the dimness. He turned to the guy. 'Do you have something I could use to pass something down to her?'

The guy nodded. 'Give me a sec.'

Lachlan took a deep breath. 'Holly, this is Lachlan. I'm one of the doctors that works with your mum. Can you hear me?'

There was sniffing, but no real answer.

'Holly, I'm here to help you. I'm here to help your mum. Can you let me know if you're hurt at all? Or if you're stuck?'

There was a tap on his shoulder, and the rescue worker handed him a long rod with a pincer at the end. Perfect.

Lachlan wrestled his phone out of his pocket. He could only begin to imagine how scared Holly was. He flicked on the torch on his phone and disabled his fingerprint status, then he put it in the pincer. 'Holly, I'm going to send down my phone to you, so you will be able to see a bit better. The torch is already switched on, so it might dazzle you for a second as it comes down. Okay?'

There was a murmur that sounded like *okay*.

He, ever so slowly, sent the rod down the thin gap with the phone going first. When he was sure it had reached her, he shouted some instructions. 'Holly, grab the phone. Can you reach it?'

He felt the movement before he heard anything. 'Got it,' was the small reply.

Lachlan breathed a sigh of relief. 'Okay, honey. Give

yourself a minute. I think you might be trapped under the kitchen table. Can you tell me if that's right?'

'Ye…es,' came the wobbly answer.

'Okay, are you there yourself, or is anyone there with you?' His chest felt tight as he asked the question.

'Just me…'

His heart sank, but he focused on what he needed to do. 'Okay. Are you hurt anywhere, Holly?'

'No…'

'Good. Can you move about okay?'

'Yes, but there's not much room. And it's creaky.'

Lachlan quelled his panic, thinking the table was likely creaking under the strain of the weight on top of it. 'Great. Do you think you could get through this space and come out to me?'

There was silence, before finally, 'I don't know you.'

Lachlan did his best to put himself into Holly's point of view. 'Okay, do you remember meeting me at the hospital with your mum after the accident?'

'Maybe.'

'Well, your mum would want me to make sure you're safe. Only way I can do that is if you can get through this space to me. Can you do that?'

The silence lasted for ever. She was scared. 'Is my mum there?'

Lachlan bit his bottom lip and wondered if he should lie. Truth was, he had no idea where Iris was, or if she was still alive. Every part of him wanted to throw this building apart to find her, but he knew he had to prioritise Holly. That was what Iris would want him to do. He could do that for her.

Something came into his head. 'Holly, do you know how to work those phones?'

'Yes.'

'Okay. Find the app for the photos. If you can do it, look right back at the beginning.'

He held his breath. Would she notice he hadn't answered the question about her mum?

'Have you done it?'

There was a little gasp. 'Is that my mum?'

He sighed. 'Yes, it is. We knew each other years ago. There's just a couple of photos. But I want you to know that your mum and I have been friends for a long time. You're safe with me.'

'She's laughing,' said Holly. 'You're laughing.'

'We used to do that a lot.'

There was a signal from behind him. Fergus. He bent forward and spoke in a low voice. 'It's Iris. They've found her.'

'Is she alive?' Lachlan mouthed the words so Holly would have no chance of hearing them. Every muscle in his body was tense right now. All he wanted to know was that she was alive. If she was injured, he could help. No matter what had happened to her. If she needed care— he would do it. All he wanted to do was help the woman that he loved. He'd been a fool. He'd seen the fact that Iris had moved on with her life in a real, positive way yet he hadn't listened properly to everything she'd been telling him. He'd been so wrapped up in what he thought was her deceit that he couldn't see the bigger picture.

Fergus gave a nod, and Lachlan's heart soared. 'Give me five,' he mouthed, and turned his full concentration on getting Holly out.

It took some coaching and reassurance. But Holly finally squeezed her way through the hole that had been made. As soon as she was within arm's reach, Lachlan gently lifted her the rest of the way, talking the whole time. He gave her a quick check over. She turned the phone towards him and he looked at the picture she'd kept on the screen.

It was ancient. Iris and Lachlan were sitting on the grass together in Kensington Gardens in London with the swan pond in the distance. They were laughing at something a friend had said and the moment had been captured perfectly on camera. It was an old photo that Lachlan had scanned digitally years ago. It had been in amongst his digital storage and he hadn't looked at it, or the other few that he had, in years.

Seeing them back then tore at his heart. 'You look so happy,' Holly said with a wistful tone in her voice.

'We were.'

'But you're not happy now.'

Lachlan stiffened. 'What do you mean?'

'Mum told me she upset you and she was sad.' Holly swivelled her head from side to side. 'Where is she?'

She'd been sheltered from this. She likely hadn't understood that the gas blast had almost destroyed her family home. She started to shake, and he wrapped his arms around her and carried her away from the area. 'I'm just going to see your mum now, Holly. As soon as I've checked her, I'll make sure you can see each other. But I'm taking to you Rena now, and she will look after you while I'm getting your mum.'

Holly looked at him again. 'You're not upset now?'

It was an odd question for a child whose house had just disintegrated around her to ask. But children had many different coping mechanisms, and Lachlan figured that, right now, thinking about this instead of anything else was Holly's. He gave her the most reassuring smile that he could. 'I'm not upset with your mum now, Holly. I promise. This is nothing that can't be fixed.'

He walked over to the temporary aid station that had

been set up, and Rena gave a shout of glee when she saw Holly, rushing over to get her. Lachlan gladly handed her over and made his way back to the partially collapsed building to find Fergus.

'Here, Doc!' He saw the wave of Fergus's hand as he picked his way through the debris. Iris was pinned underneath rubble, her hair covered in dust and only one arm visible. Three rescue crew were working around her, trying to find the best way to extricate her safely.

Fergus had already put an oximeter on her finger, and an oxygen mask on her face. He'd used scissors to cut the sleeve on Iris's top, to reveal her arm properly. 'Was just going to get some IV access. Want to take over?'

'Gladly,' said Lachlan, sliding into the space that Fergus vacated.

He could see at a glance that Iris's oxygen levels were slightly lower than normal. He slid a needle into her arm quickly, inserting the cannula and securing it, before checking her blood pressure. Low. She could have other injuries. By the time he looked up, Fergus had already run some IV fluids through a line and was holding it out to him.

He fastened it quickly and put his head down next to Iris's. He reached out and touched her face. 'Iris, Iris, it's Lachlan. There's been a gas explosion. I'm here to help.'

There was a faint groan as he stroked the side of her face. Her eyelids flickered. She automatically tried to move her body and let out a sharp yelp of pain. 'Holly,' she breathed. 'Holly.'

'I've got her, Iris. She's safe. We're just going to find a way to get you out too.'

She started to become more alert. 'Lachlan?' She looked confused, as if she didn't really believe what she was seeing.

'Yes,' he said. 'I'm here. So is some of the team.'

'What happened?' she blinked again.

'There was a gas explosion. Took out some of the houses in the street.'

'That smell,' she groaned, turning her head to the side. It was as if she realised she was trapped. She tried to sit up but couldn't. 'Lachlan?' There was panic in her voice.

He took her hand. 'It'll be okay, Iris. The rescue crew are going to find a way to get you out. Till they do, I'll be here. And Holly is safe with Rena.'

Iris took a few stuttered breaths. 'Can't move, can't breathe,' she gasped. She tried to pull the mask from her face.

'No, leave it, you need it right now,' he ordered.

'Move, Doc,' came the order from behind him. He turned to see the fire and rescue crew with equipment that looked as if it might take some of the weight to allow Iris to be pulled out.

Another crew member appeared with an orange flexible sliding board. It was clear they were going to try and get it under Iris, to try and get her out quickly as soon as the weight was lifted.

Fergus didn't even need an instruction. He picked his away around the rubble to assist at the other side.

'Iris, we're getting you out. Fergus is at your other side. The crew are going to try and slide something under you. Can you lift your back at all?'

She gave a cough. 'Yes, a little. I can lift my shoulders.'

Fergus gave a thumbs-up. 'Perfect, just a little more shuffling and we'll be ready.'

Lachlan glanced around, watching everyone prepare. *Please let this work.* All he wanted was to get her out safely.

Lachlan couldn't help himself. He took Iris's hand and squeezed it.

A few moments later there was a commanding shout. 'Ready? We're doing one, two, three and pull.'

There were shouts of assent all round and the lead fire and rescue officer shouted clearly. 'One, two, three, *pull*!'

There was some loud creaking, a waft of dust, and Iris was pulled out. She was pale and looked shell-shocked. Lachlan let go of her hand and grabbed one of the handholds in the sliding board. The rescue crew all picked their way across the rubble and over to the emergency tent.

Iris was moved onto a nearby trolley and Lachlan grabbed his stethoscope, leaning over her and touching her face. 'Let's see what we can do to make you feel better.'

'Let me sit up,' she said. She pulled the mask from her face and took some deep breaths, choking a bit.

He was scanning her whole body, assessing everything. There didn't appear to be any obvious injuries.

'Mum!' Holly came running in, and Iris gave a little cry of relief. They hugged and kissed, as Lachlan stood to one side. Fergus stood smiling at the entranceway.

'You're safe,' Iris kept repeating as she hugged her daughter.

Holly's eyes flickered to Lachlan. 'Your friend helped me,' she said.

Iris looked over at Lachlan and gave him a nod. After she'd examined her daughter from head to foot, Fergus took a step inside, clearly sensing the vibe. 'All right if I go and find Holly something to eat and drink?' He held his hand out to Holly.

Iris glanced at Lachlan, then gave Fergus a grateful smile, dropping another kiss on Holly's head. 'Thanks,

Fergus. I'll come and get you in a few minutes,' she said to her daughter, who left quite happily with Fergus.

Silence fell between them. All Lachlan could feel right now was an overwhelming sense of relief that both Iris and Holly were safe.

After a few moments, Iris gave a weak cough, then looked him clean in the eye. 'Why you, Lachlan? Why are you here?' There was a hint of confusion in her voice.

He didn't hesitate. 'Because I knew it was your area. I wanted to make sure you and Holly were safe.'

Her eyes blinked again and she kept staring straight at him. 'But why?'

'Because I love you, Iris. I always have. And I'm going to stay right by your side.'

She took a deep breath and her eyes widened. 'You hate me,' she said simply.

He put his hand on her shoulder and shook his head. 'I love you. It's always been you, Iris. No one else has ever come close. I just reacted badly when you told me everything, and I'm sorry. But you have no idea the wave of fear that came over me when I thought something might have happened to you just now. I couldn't bear that. Not for you, and not for Holly.'

'You helped my daughter,' she sighed.

'And I'd do it again in a heartbeat.'

He took both her hands in his. 'Iris, I know that what happened in our marriage was also my fault. Deep down, I knew there were issues we needed to grapple with, and I didn't try hard enough to work with you on them. I should have made you sit down and talk to me about it. But I didn't. At twenty-three, maybe we were too young to be married. We certainly made a mistake rushing into try-ing for a family—' he put his hand on his chest '—and I take equal responsibility for that. What I want—' he took a deep breath '—and what I hope you also want, is for us to sit down together and find a way to make things work. I'm not letting you slip through my fingers once again. We're going to fight for this, Iris. We're going to fight for this together.'

He could see she was blinking back tears. 'But what if we argue? What if we still struggle?'

'Then we'll work it out together,' he said firmly. 'I love you, Iris. Nothing is going to change that. This is it. We're older, and I hope we're much wiser. I don't want to lose this chance. Fate put us back together again for a reason, Iris.' He smiled at her. 'We can do this. I have faith.'

She closed her eyes for a second. 'What about Holly?'

'Holly is your daughter. Holly comes first. We'll take things at a pace that suits her.'

He pulled her close to him and dropped a kiss on her forehead. 'We can do this,' he vowed again.

Her face crumpled and she raised her dust-covered face to his. 'Promise me,' she whispered fiercely. 'Promise me we will get through this together. Because I love you too.'

He didn't hesitate for a second. 'Now, and always.'

EPILOGUE

Two years later

'READY?' LACHLAN ASKED. He was standing behind Iris as she checked herself in the full-length mirror one more time.

She spun around, her hair in long curls and her knee-length wedding dress flowing out as she turned. She lifted her hands, one clutching her orange-flowered wedding bouquet, and wrapped them around his neck.

'You look quite handsome today.' She smiled. 'Going somewhere special?'

She'd never looked so beautiful. 'I'm going to get married to a mysterious woman who has stolen my heart not just once, but twice,' he said as bent down to kiss her.

'Taxis are here!' shouted Maeve.

She was standing at the doorway of the extended and newly refurbished cottage that Lachlan, Iris and Holly were now calling their home. Although Iris's home had been rebuilt, they'd both decided that the cottage would be a new start for them all, so they'd sold it.

Holly was dressed in a bridesmaid dress of her own choice, with matching flowers in her hair. She had something in her hand. 'Mail,' she said.

Iris and Lachlan froze. They'd been waiting for something and had been anxiously checking the mail for the last week. The envelope was official, white with a blue insignia.

'Let's leave it until after the wedding,' said Iris nervously. 'Just in case it's bad news.'

Lachlan hesitated, then gave his wife-to-be a smile. 'Have confidence,' he said as he took the envelope from Holly's hand and pulled it open.

As he slid the letter from the envelope, he knew everyone else in the household was holding their breath. There was only one word he needed to say. 'Approved!'

'Yes!' shouted Holly. 'I get a brother or a sister.' She was jumping up and down.

Iris had taken the crumpled paper out of Lachlan's hand, and kept scanning it for a second. 'How about both?' she said, beaming from ear to ear. 'We've been matched with twins!'

'Twins?' Lachlan's mouth fell open, and then he started laughing. He picked up Iris with one arm and Holly with the other and swung them both around.

The taxi tooted loudly outside. 'Dublin City Hall is calling!' said Maeve. Scout gave a bark, turning his head to try and gnaw on the bow that had been tied around his neck. 'Let's go, people. Honestly, you two will be late for your own wedding!'

Maeve, Scout and Holly climbed into the black taxi with a bright orange ribbon that matched Holly's dress, and Lachlan and Iris climbed into the other adorned with a cream ribbon.

She snuggled into his side as the taxi started down the lane. 'I'm going to get make-up all over your handsome suit,' she sighed.

'And hopefully lipstick all over my face,' he replied, smiling.

She sat more upright and turned to face him with a

broad smile on her face and her eyes gleaming mischievously. 'I don't think we should wait until the ceremony. I think I still need some convincing.'

Lachlan moved too, and settled his hands around her waist. 'That sounds like a good idea to me.' He grinned. 'I think we should definitely get some practice in.'

And so, the bride and groom, both slightly dishevelled, arrived at Dublin City Hall to the cheers of their friends and walked hand in hand up the steps to start their new life together.

* * * * *

TAKING A CHANCE ON THE BEST MAN

FIONA McARTHUR

MILLS & BOON

Dedicated to my dear friend Carolyn,
who was there for my first book
and tragically gone for this one.

I will always feel a smile when I think of you,
and I bet you're causing mayhem in heaven. Fi xx

CHAPTER ONE

JUST A WEEK since Domenico Salvanelli had first locked stares with her across the room and Isabel Fetherstone had been made inconveniently aware of a man seven years her junior. To make it even more awkward, there could be no doubt he was aware of her too.

Now, at her niece Faith's wedding rehearsal in Lighthouse Bay, Isabel tried to ignore the tingle in her fingers where they rested on the powerful forearm of the groom's twin.

Dom didn't smile, causing much concern to all, Isabel thought wryly, yet despite the angst emanating from him she thought of him as Dashing Dom. Couldn't help it. Though as the spinster aunt, fifteen years older than the bride, she'd never said Dom's pet name out loud. She'd sworn to be sensible, the one in control, and there was nothing controlled about such a delightful buzzing from a young man's steely arm.

Dashing Dom was a widower buried in grief but before too long, like a male version of Sleeping Beauty, he would be in need of a new love.

He'd also be in need of a new Salvanelli heir. That ruled her out.

An heir sounded so old-fashioned—but there was the aristocratic old-world Italian culture of passing on gilded Florentine estates. Both brothers were ridiculously wealthy, and she had no doubt that they'd each want as many spares as possible.

As they walked together back up the aisle, best man and matron of honour, she tried not to inhale the particularly divine aftershave drifting next to her, or glance across at the impressive masculine chest stretched so delightfully close.

He made her feel a little wicked—almost as if they meant to brush against each other, invading mutual space—but they weren't. Or she wasn't. No, she couldn't accuse him of crowding, but his fierce concentration rippled her deep pond of serenity and made her aware of their proximity.

She wasn't one for flirting with toy boys, though the darkness behind his coal-black eyes belied naivety.

Secrets. Guilt. Baggage.

Dom had mountains of tormented baggage and the man would be high maintenance. But darn, he was pretty and made her blush.

Seriously, she wished she didn't find his gaze on her every time she turned around, not saying anything, not helping her awareness. Watching her. As if he was trying to understand a divine puzzle.

As if she attracted him.

Again, ridiculous. Too young.

She didn't need a fling to divert her from this absolute highlight in her tiny family's life, if that was what he was trying to instigate. This was all about her niece Faith, who deserved the happiness she'd finally found with this man's brother. And Isabel was the sensible aunt. Always sensible. Always.

It was two days before the wedding breakfast in Lighthouse Bay and they stood in the church like puppets. And you know what? Weddings made her itch. Or they did with Dom beside her.

She thought about the last wedding she'd stood in as bridesmaid—her late sister's disaster—and promptly pushed away the memory of the desertion that husband had visited on his wife and daughter. And her own fiancé's desertion. Pushed them both far away.

Isabel had to believe Faith's marriage would be perfect because Faith and Rai were so much in love.

The groom and his brother—they were such uber males these Salvanellis—certainly knew how to convey dark and inscrutable, but now there was nothing mysterious about Rai. All she could see was blazing joy shining from that dear man's eyes. Isabel smiled warmly at him.

Beside her, Domenico leant in, his scent swirling like fine aromatic spice in a souk's dark alley. 'Why—?' he started, before another instruction from the jolly Catholic priest cut him off.

'We will start again,' the priest interjected. The Father had driven in from a nearby town to preside over the non-denominational chapel for the real event. And he wanted everything right.

Obediently, Dom closed his beautiful mouth, spun on his heel and returned to the altar to stand beside his brother. They restarted the rehearsal.

Isabel compressed her lips to hide her smile. Ah, Dom. Like a good Catholic boy, she thought, amused that he'd been thwarted, and trying not to flashback to the way his toned backside was cupped by his dark trousers as he stalked back.

'I think he likes you,' Faith's voice teased as Isabel took her arm to wait for their signal to begin another stately bridal walk.

'Who? Father Paul?' Teasing back. With a tinge of

pride Isabel noted how calm and unfazed her niece had remained as her wedding day galloped towards them. A month wasn't long to arrange a wedding. Especially just before Christmas.

Isabel, acting also as the one to give away the bride, had no doubt Faith would be happy in marriage because these star-crossed lovers had waited a long time to rediscover each other. Five years of misunderstandings and interference from others. Enough time had been wasted. Now their future beckoned with wide open arms.

Faith pulled a non-bridal face. 'No, silly, not the priest. Dom fancies you.'

'Ah, that's what you mean.' As she smiled she hoped the twitch didn't look as false as it felt. Isabel tried not to think about that one time she too had thought she'd found true love. Or the man who'd left her when it was discovered how unlikely it would be for her to bear his child.

Or even, since then, on how she'd missed out on love completely by being the one in control, pulling back as soon as any man looked like being attracted to her.

This was Faith's wedding and she loved Faith, and her daughter Chloe, very much. She would do nothing to jeopardise that love. Certainly not come on to the groom's brother in a fit of ill-suited attraction.

'Dom is too young for me,' Isabel said, sounding calm as she and Faith waited together in the arched entrance for their next instruction. 'And we all know he has issues.'

Faith tossed her hand in the direction of her soon-to-be brother-in-law. 'You know how to deal with issues. You're the most level-headed person I know.' A waggle of eyebrows. 'And he's gorgeous.'

Yes, he was. 'You think he's hot because he looks like your husband-to-be.' But she couldn't stop the heat creeping up her cheeks. Just as her gaze crept up the long lines of Dom's body as he stood straight, tall and well-muscled beside his brother.

'True. But...' the bride's eyes strayed to her man '...Rai is hotter.' Faith's gaze came back to rest on Isabel's face. She studied her, unexpected glee in her eyes. 'I've never seen you blush before.' Her brows creased.

Suddenly thoughtful, her eyes became piercing. More serious. 'When that hunky locum doctor asked you out last week you weren't flustered,' she mused.

That man had been Isabel's age. Good-looking. Well-adjusted. Eminently suitable. And he hadn't interested her enough to accept a free dinner. She wondered if she would have said yes to Dom. Which was ridiculous. Disastrous. And a little scary.

For Isabel, the next few minutes were blessedly question-free, until she floated back down the aisle with Domenico's hot, corded muscles taut beneath her fingers. *Sigh.*

This time they strolled more companionably towards the exit, with the rehearsal ceremony finally concluded and only the practice waltzes to complete.

'Isabel,' he began again, his strong accent stretching the word out as if stroking her name with his long, strong fingers. 'Why are you not married?'

Why the heck did men say that to her? As if the world revolved around women lucky enough to find a man. Oh, she could find one. Just didn't trust them. Look at her sister's marriage. And her own broken engagement.

His comment made her impatient. 'I choose not to be.' She arched her brows at him. 'You've been a widower for six years. Why haven't you remarried?' She knew as soon as she'd said it she shouldn't have. It was an indication of how much this man unsettled her, and so unlike her to respond less than kindly. And he had so much angst.

She'd guarded her heart so well, been so independent, and now this young stranger addled her brain! Scattered her wits. Where was her level head now?

Dom's face darkened. 'I doubt I will ever remarry.'

The words were accompanied by such a look of despair she wanted to shake him. For goodness' sake! She got that he was heartbroken, and to lose a child would be the worst thing in the world—the absolute worst—but six years was a long time to grieve, feel guilt and grow old. She knew that. She'd done it for more than twice that and for the first time in all that time she wondered if she'd been a fool.

Dom should not be a fool. Especially if he had the ability to father another child. 'You're a young man.'

'I have been blessed once. And I failed to protect them.'

Guilt. Isabel knew about guilt. Especially unfounded guilt. Faith had told her his wife and child had been killed in a horrific balloon ride accident and that Dom had not gone with them on the day because of work. But too much guilt was harming this man. It harmed everyone. They all knew that.

The priest had followed them out and he smiled as he came towards them. Isabel dropped Dom's arm. 'Yet you have a dynasty to pass on.' She looked at the cleric.

'Father Paul, I always thought that God's plans could not be understood by mere mortals.' She felt Dom stiffen beside her.

The priest smiled benignly at them. 'So true. Repentance brings peace and new beginnings. Guilt and shame and blame have no place in God's world.' He waved his hand up at the heavens and floated away to speak to the bridal couple like a whimsical white-frocked cloud. Leaving an anvil of emotion in storm cloud Dom.

He rose to his full height, towering over her. His face a mask, transitioned to a hardness she hadn't seen before. Impressive. She'd obviously struck a nerve and the priest had been a little more on the knocker than she'd bargained for.

'I lost my wife. And my son.' His face came closer. Very softly he continued, 'You, a spinster who eschews marriage, you have not had a child. You do not understand.'

At Dom's words her breath caught somewhere under her ribs, sharp and stabbing, as a wave of long-checked agony burst through her like a knife. Lacerating. Lancing her. Licking with pain.

'That's true.' Almost. She'd never married and she'd lost a baby, not a child. Only Faith knew. This was a secret she didn't share, not even with her closest friends.

Dom's stab in the dark had drawn blood. Touché. Hers had too.

Few knew of the stillbirth, nor of its aftermath, when she'd been told her uterus was misshapen and an inhospitable place for pregnancy. She'd tucked that away in her deep, dark, sorrow-filled soul, desperate for a child of her own.

She'd been stupid to comment. Stupid to ask the priest to comment. Now, forcing calm, she lifted her eyes to the man by her side. She looked right into his tortured eyes and said, 'I'm sorry for your loss.'

She walked away.

Two days later, at the front of the church, Dom's face felt hard like the painted granite around him as he stared inscrutably ahead in his matching black suit. It was difficult, in this time of joy for his brother, not to think of his own tragic marriage and the loss of his family. And when he did think of new beginnings, as his twin had suggested so often, then guilt chewed at him like a carnivorous beast.

'Brother?' Dom turned to look at Rai as he spoke, and some of the strain eased away. 'Today is for rejoicing, yes?'

'Indeed.' His twin was in love. *Amore*. Domenico felt his mouth kink upwards. 'I rejoice. You managed to wait a whole month before you married your Faith.'

Rai laughed quietly. 'It was not possible for more speed or it certainly would have been sooner. Thank you for being here.'

He had only just made it. It had been difficult to extricate himself from the many technicalities of an incinerated business, and a lethargy steeped in despair had slowed him even more, but he had known he would have to come if Rai married in Australia.

He had to sympathise with his brother on the irresistible attraction of the Fetherstone women. Sadly, his brother had noted how Faith's aunt, Isabel, had caught his eye as well.

At the wedding rehearsal Isabel had brushed off Domenico's attention as if she were the older, wiser woman fussed over by a boy. It had been amusing to Rai, Dom knew, when Isabel was only seven years the elder and yet he had been markedly ruffled by her dismissal.

His reluctance to leave Florence when matters were urgent meant he'd had every intention of hurrying home as soon as the nuptials were completed. Though, to Rai's delight, it had taken just a few days in the company of Isabel Fetherstone for Domenico to mention to his brother that he might stay 'perhaps a little longer'.

After the briefest of honeymoons, Rai and Faith would return here to live. Lighthouse Bay, where the sea breeze blew through the open windows of the houses along with the noisy crashing of waves.

This bay, this place, held magic the like of which Dom had never felt before.

He glanced over his shoulder to see Faith's friends and colleagues in the congregation. They had already become Rai's associates. Though his brother might fly home many times, he doubted he would leave his new family behind or stay away from this place for long.

A car pulled up outside. Doors opened and his brother drew a deep breath beside him, impatient for his bride.

Dom too leaned forward.

The music started and a rustling at the door and a shift of light drew all eyes to the entrance.

Ah. The little flower girls. His niece Chloe like a daffodil in her sunshine-yellow dress, the lilac sash so pretty, her dark hair plaited around her sweet, serious face as she solemnly sprinkled yellow rose petals down the aisle for the bride. A little girl followed her, her own basket of dewy softness on her arm as she copied her friend. They looked like fairies as their glowing faces spread joy like the petals among the congregation.

Isabel stepped into view, head up, large eyes excited, yet her face was serene, her mouth curved in the happiness of the moment, and Dom tensed beside his brother. *Sì*, she was a vision.

Faith's aunt waited, stepped sideways, the maid of honour who refused to be bridesmaid. The pale lilac dress highlighted the dark auburn of her hair, the silk that slid and slithered over the slim body was modest but with that hint of allure his twin had found in Faith. And Dom had found in Isabel.

Isabel's face rose as the music lifted to a climax and

the bride stepped alone into the doorway. Then she reached out and rested her hand lightly on Isabel's arm.

Isabel would give the bride away for safe keeping, into the arms of the man she loved, as he had been told she would.

What was Isabel's story? Dom needed to know.

The reception was held at the surf club and after the photographs the bride and groom entered to the fun strains of a modern love song while the guests clapped and cheered. Isabel followed with Dom and the children, and she smiled at the happiness as Faith and Rai waltzed their way around the room smiling at each other. It was so beautiful to keep the momentum and excitement going.

Except now Isabel would have to dance with Dom when they joined the newlyweds in the centre of the room.

She could do this.

Isabel waited, her feet shifting on the wooden boards of the surf club with her fingers lost in Dom's large, firm hand as the first song ended and the slower waltz began.

Faith beckoned them to join.

Dom's other hand eased against the skin of her back, just above her buttocks, burning through the thin fabric of her dress as he pressed her into a closed stance. Standing there, so close, the scent of him was like rolling wine around in a glass and tasting. Delicious, flavoursome, intriguing. Darn him.

She felt tiny in Dom's arms. Feminine. Fluttery. It was certainly foolish to feel such things, but today was for celebration. For joy. For a little abandon.

The music began—*oom-pah-pah, oom-pah-pah, oom-pah-pah*—as Dom stepped sideways, leading her with a firmness and grace that, of course—cruel universe—

she'd always searched for in a dance partner and never found. Typical.

Her lilac dress slithered against her skin; his arms were solid steel bands and perfectly positioned to allow her to flow with the music, an invitation to immerse herself, and she couldn't help the tiny smile. Letting herself go should have been harder with Dom. But she loved to dance and her hand on his shoulder unconsciously softened into trust.

He glanced down, his gaze intent on her expression, and though nobody could call it a twinkle in his eyes there was some kindlier emotion than some they had shared.

His mouth bent close. 'You dance well in my arms, Isabel.' The warmth of his breath stole a fragment of her composure and she would have stumbled if he hadn't had such control over them both. Perhaps his gaze held a touch of complacency that he knew she wasn't immune to his nearness. Yes, he could sense that her body responded to the feel of being held in his steady embrace. She could give him that. But his words implied that he had control. Not so.

She might be aware of his heat, his big body and his masculine scent but she wouldn't lose herself, throw good sense to the wind and let him dance her off to wherever he wanted. She wouldn't. Even if the idea had delightful merit.

A sensible woman wouldn't be feeling these things. But she couldn't help the softening of her body. The loss of herself to the step and sway in time to Dom's direction, clever, masterful dancer that he was.

The *oom-pah-pah* of the dance thrummed through her senses and his arms were so easy to glide in. She turned her face so he couldn't see her expression.

'Good,' he said. 'I will not let you fall.'

No. He wouldn't. Intrinsically she knew that. But she might. Fall. Fall for him. She understood the danger with a fear that was unlike anything she'd felt before. What was it about this man that called to the impulsiveness she'd denied for so long?

It was closing her throat. Speeding her heart until sense talked her down again. *It's just a dance.*

And it should be fun. This was a joyous occasion.

Why not let her hair down and enjoy these moments in an excellent dancer's arms?

'Can you be impulsive, Isabel?' His question startled her, the train of conversation so close to her own thoughts.

No. Yes. Could she?

Isabel tilted her chin at him. 'Of course.'

'Then do it.' He bent his face sideways. 'Let us enjoy the moment.'

He was right, darn him. Consciously she eased the remaining tension in her shoulders, loosened her grip and allowed him to lead more fully. Allowed herself to be whirled away. The guy could dance and she rarely had the chance. She lifted her face and smiled into his eyes. Impulsive behaviour had been absent from her life for so long.

Other couples joined them. Isabel immersed herself in the moment and swayed and spun again and let herself be held in this man's arms and savour it. To be rash.

Her mouth curved wider as she smiled up at him. The music soaked into her. His arms held her firmly, strongly leading them, his feet perfectly in time with hers. She could do this, have fun with this serious, seriously handsome young man. Her nephew by marriage.

The music stopped, yet for a moment they moved on—

until Dom slowed and then stepped away, his hand sliding from her back.

She blinked and pulled her fingers down from his shoulder to clasp her other hand in front of herself. Her smile faded as she returned to the real world.

'Thank you for the dance,' she said quietly.

'We will do this again.'

His words made her nervous, but she pretended they didn't. It was just a dance. Fun. Nothing deep and meaningful. And he'd be going soon.

Isabel tucked her oddly trembling fingers against the sides of her pretty dress and looked around. Saw tables of happy people. The wedding breakfast served. Saw something that made her brows crease with concern.

She crossed to the older woman, Mrs Cross—a stalwart of the Ladies Auxiliary at the hospital—who normally enjoyed non-stop conversation, yet clutched her throat with shaky fingers. Her shorter, rounder husband hovered and waved at Isabel.

Isabel avoided a dancer as she neared their table in a few fast strides. 'Is everything okay?'

'Cynthia doesn't want to spoil the wedding.' Mr Cross's whisper was oddly strident. 'Won't let me tell anyone.'

His wife hushed him.

'What's wrong?' Isabel could tell something wasn't right. Mrs Cross's face seemed ringed with red and her neck had welts rising as Isabel watched. Allergy? 'Did you eat something that doesn't agree with you?' Isabel had had a friend with severe allergies; she knew about the dangers.

The older lady nodded forlornly at her plate. 'I think the salmon.' Her voice sounded hoarse and cracked. 'I love salmon. I'm not allergic to the salmon, just prawns.

But now I'm not sure. My lips feel funny and numb.' She coughed. 'And I'm having trouble breathing.'

'She has a needle for prawns.' Mr Cross patted his pockets and pulled out a silver case which opened to reveal the plastic barrel of an EpiPen. 'But she's never been allergic to salmon before.'

Epinephrin? Isabel felt her heart thump. Serious allergy. She looked around for help without causing a scene, but everyone was watching the dancers. She caught Dom's eye; he was watching her.

She waved him over and took the pen from Mr Cross as his wife coughed. She knew about pens. This wasn't a good time to wait for the airway to close. She unwrapped the plastic from the barrel, flipped off the top cap, pushed the orange base against Mrs Cross's upper leg and pressed the pen into the side of her thick thigh until it clicked.

Dom arrived and took Mrs Cross's wrist in his hand. 'EpiPen,' she said. Their eyes met and he nodded.

'Waiting, one, two, three,' Isabel said to Mrs Cross then removed the needle. 'It's done. Nobody noticed. Let's slip you down to the hospital to get checked. Dr Salvanelli will come with us in your car; that will be faster than an ambulance.'

She knew the dose of epinephrine would boost Mrs Cross's falling blood pressure and reduce the swelling, but the older lady needed observation away from the wedding reception. Isabel suspected Faith's guest would have quickly progressed to full anaphylaxis if treatment hadn't been at hand, bless her husband.

Said husband had shakily pulled car keys from his other pocket and Dom and Isabel ushered the woman out of the door unobtrusively, taking her tottering weight between them until they could carefully help her into the car.

It was all over in moments. The drive down the hill. The stop at the hospital doors. Their charge handed over to the emergency staff.

A relieved Mr Cross refused to let them walk back up the hill and drove them back to the reception before turning his car again. They didn't talk on the drive, but Isabel mulled over the event.

Dom had been great. It was nice to have discreet medical backup, she thought. Someone who was quietly efficient. Calm. As she had been herself. And barely anyone had noticed the emergency, certainly not the bride and groom, much to Mrs Cross's relief. Isabel smiled at that.

They did have things in common.

And things that kept them apart.

And still that attraction.

Back at the reception, Faith and Rai came over to them with puzzled looks on their faces. 'What happened? Where did you go? It's time for the speeches.'

Isabel and Dom silently agreed to play it down. She let him talk. 'All is well, brother. I will tell you later. Let us have speeches.'

Domenico Salvanelli watched his twin brother's car disappear down the hill, his new wife at his side. He saw them drive past the inflated, red-suited St Nicholas who stood on, of all things not holy, a surfboard at the end of the street. Past the sign to the beach and the lighthouse.

Nine days since he had arrived in this sun-drenched bay of white sand and strange, yet compelling people on the coast of eastern Australia. And only five days until the day he dreaded the most every year. Christmas— without his family. Which was why he was flying out of this joyful place the day before the best and worst memories of his life.

Yet since his arrival in Australia he was realising he needed to change. The catalyst of the factory burning down had left him at his lowest but now, with his brother's wedding today, this place had seemed to halt the deadly slide.

He'd been existing not living since Teresa and Tomas had been lost, and suddenly there was this place. A vibrant place of sun and smiles.

And this amazing woman, Isabel, who had made him consider himself in a different light.

But still he held back.

For a moment the strangeness of standing here, half a world away from his home in Florence, overwhelmed him. In his home city frosty air would be rustling the huge decorated tree and nativity scene in Piazza del Duomo.

Here in Australia it burned hot and strange and Santa had replaced Saint Nicholas. He couldn't see a single manger, though Chloe, his brother's newly discovered five-year-old daughter, had told him there were such to be found. He couldn't see even a Wise Man in a garden.

But women? Perhaps he had found a wise woman. He looked towards Isabel, so prudent and practical when he looked into her calm face. Yet, despite her composed neutrality towards him, in only these few days he'd realised she intrigued him more than any woman in years.

Isabel's understated beauty called to him. She rippled his previously frozen world like the warm sea wind tossed the dark riot of her hair around her face in soft strands. Her hair was like the woman, with hidden depths—a ruby in the depths, glowing like the heart of her. He wished to stroke the texture of both and discover if she were as soft as she looked.

He'd been in mourning for so long, the fact that suddenly this woman attracted him was shocking for him. How had he let her overtake his thoughts in this way? Was his brother right? Could he come to Australia with the idea of making a new start, perhaps? Was he in the perfect place and time to be attracted to someone new, even as this thought terrified him?

He'd tried to work out Isabel's attraction for him.

To see the charm of Isabel.

But it was no one thing.

She danced like an angel. Cared for all with her goodness. Yet spoke her thoughts without fear.

Her mind shone with flashes of brilliance and subtle strength—mostly disguised but never fully contained and deeply intriguing. The impenetrable wall she had erected between them made her unobtainable and even more desirable. He had not experienced such barriers before or after his loss of Teresa. And when had he been able to think of his wife without searing pain? He could not remember.

The recognition of a kindred soul had jolted him at his first sight of Isabel. So much so he'd started in surprise. She'd shown no such discomfort. She rarely did. That fascinated and annoyed him, used as he was to his volatile and flamboyant countrymen and women in Italy.

Then he'd begun to notice other things. Her care and consistent compassion towards her niece Faith and greatniece Chloe, and her obvious approval and delight in his brother's love for Faith.

Rai had said this sensible woman had been a rock for his Faith and Chloe, and that Isabel held few prejudices.

Yet?

Towards him, he felt a strong prejudice. An annoying wall that made him want to ripple her serenity in retaliation for the confusion she left him feeling.

Between them some barrier stayed, contained and controlled and repelling even his most subtle advances. Yet he'd sensed from the beginning that there was a passionate woman underneath the façade, and he was drawn to that in her. Had sensed it from the dancing. Holding her in his arms had been a revelation. A joy. Almost an addiction.

But he couldn't understand why he thought so. Or why she was the one. It was as if an unexpected fairy tale had opened before him.

He thought of that conversation outside the church on the rehearsal day. She seemed to have forgotten, yet he regretted it every night in his bed. The memory had robbed him of sleep. He could still see her stricken eyes after he'd cruelly called her a spinster who would not understand.

He'd seen that quick flash of pained emotion, and yet she had sounded so calm. He remembered her response. 'That's true,' she'd said. 'I'm sorry for your loss.'

But he sensed a deep well of pain in this woman and knew he'd caused it. He wanted to know how and why.

He had apologised the next day. Yet she had waved off his apology as unnecessary. As if it hadn't mattered to her at all. But he wondered. Suspected. Doubted.

And earlier today, the moments when she'd taken control of the situation with the anaphylactic woman at the wedding as if it was not worthy of comment, which for a layperson it surely was. Yet when he'd asked she'd brushed that away too, mentioned a friend. He didn't understand Isabel. But he wanted to.

Today, watching her niece drive away with his brother, their child's fingers clinging to hers, the intriguing angles of Isabel's face drew him again. That and her quietude. She was like an island haven in a sea of tempests. While he was a raging sea of conflicting emotions.

Turning her lithe body towards Chloe, he saw Isabel gently squeeze the little girl's hand. When her gaze lifted to his it was as if she sensed his melancholy. He forced a smile, avoided her all-seeing green eyes and looked at Chloe.

Chloe's lips quivered, her face pinched, and her free hand reached to dash away the glint of tears from her cheek as the car bearing her parents disappeared from sight.

For Dom, a surge of renewed pain of loss for his own wife and child pierced him with familiar despair. Six years. And yet in the last year he'd seemed to be grieving more deeply as time went on, not less. It was an illness that needed treatment, or a great change in his life, his brother kept saying.

He turned from the child. He needed to go home to Florence. This place unsettled him.

'Let's have pizza tonight for dinner, Chloe.' Isabel's calm, pleasing voice carried to him as he began to walk away.

'Do you like pizza, Uncle Domenico?' a piping, uncertain voice spoke to his back. The forlornness in the words froze his movement. It called to him, penetrated his own misery.

He had felt like that. Bereft.

He turned and saw the worried frown of his little niece, so unexpectedly like his own dear mamma's face and yet not, and dragged himself from the past.

His son Tomas, barely two years older than this child when he had died, had loved pizza. But Tomas was gone, as was his Teresa, and his brother had dragged him here to his new family across the sea for the next few days. He needed to lift himself and pretend he didn't want to join his own family in death, forget that he'd been spiralling this past year into a darkness he felt he could not escape.

'Sì.' He straightened his shoulders and forced another smile. 'But your papa has a new special oven in his house. I could make us all pizzas when the last of the workmen go home. Would you like that?'

The constant clatter of tradesmen from the tall dwelling across the street ceased at five in the afternoon until seven the next morning. The whole renovation would be completed soon, when his brother and his new wife returned from their brief honeymoon.

Then finally, just before Christmas, Dom would fly home.

'Can I help make them?' Chloe's eyes were imploring and only a sterner man than he would have been able to deny her.

He looked at his new relation by marriage for permission. Isabel nodded, though he couldn't tell if she was pleased that they would now join him for the evening meal. Her composure was a pleasant mask he wished to remove with a growing desire, but the key eluded him. She was like the lighthouse across the bay. Eye-catching, standing tall and watchful. But locked.

'Your aunt says yes. So sì.' He nodded. 'First I must go down to the shops and buy a few items. But I will call for you when I am ready to begin the preparations.' It would give him something to do. He hadn't cooked for years. The child made him smile. Something else he hadn't done for years.

And Isabel would be there. Perhaps he would learn something about her. The idea excited him in unfamiliar ways. He might discover something more than the few scant details she had shared so far and, if he was careful, perhaps he could penetrate the shield she held between them. And, in doing so, was there hope for restoration of their rapport and even, down the road, more than friendship?

Isabel drew Chloe towards their gate—her gate, now she had taken over the freehold ownership, with all of Chloe and Faith's belongings tucked into the new built-in wardrobes and drawers across the road in the Captain's house. She still smiled when she thought about Rai's impulsive purchase of the imposing turreted building the day he'd discovered his daughter. And the relentless renovations that had ensued since then.

The Captain's house stared haughtily over the roof of her own small dwelling. But her windows gazed across the blue waves of the inlet to the tall white tower on the oceanside cliff face that gave the town its name. Lighthouse Bay.

She could not imagine Dashing Dom being as impulsive as his brother. But damaged men were rarely impulsive, unless in the worst way possible.

Of which Rai had warned her.

Dom's endless despair, guilt. And pain.

The thought made her cold.

She understood why mental illness drew people to remove unbearable suffering for ever. Yet during this morning's wedding there had been moments when she had seen the man Rai had assured her was inside his brother. He had so much to be proud of.

The dapper best man. So tall and handsome.

The delightful dancer who'd smiled into her eyes and held her during the bridal waltz.

The doctor, there when she'd needed him earlier today.

Despite herself she'd wished he were a decade or two older, past the age of wanting children, so that she could act on the spine-tingling attraction she still fought. And do something for him that proved life was for living. Her cheeks warmed and she looked down at her hands. *Tsk, Isabel, when did you last think about seduction?* The thought sent a low, tickling warmth through her belly and she squashed the excitement it brought. Darn shame indeed.

No! Stop.

The last thing this man needed was to become fond of her until she stepped away. Heaven knew he needed a young, fertile wife to give him many children. Men were capable of fathering well into middle age, while she wasn't capable of childbearing at all.

Isabel had never been one to allow herself torment over what she couldn't have. Or, when it arose, the fact that others could, so easily. Like when her niece hadn't intended to fall pregnant over five years ago with Rai. Because the result was Chloe, a gift for all of them.

Certainly she didn't anguish over young men, out of bounds not only because of the age difference but because they had empires to pass on. And they were related by marriage. Isabel considered herself blessed to have shared the upbringing of her dear older sister's daughter and later Chloe. Her own loss had been eased by that sharing.

She was happy being the favourite aunt—so happy with that. She had a job she loved—not the midwifery she'd once practised but hadn't been able to face after her own fertility issues were discovered, but as part-time receptionist at the hospital—and was involved in many of the small town's social clubs and charity works. Life was good. Men asked her out—some young, some not so—but she rarely went twice. That way she had no need to explain her dysfunction as a woman if someone began to care.

Her rules. Though now she had passed forty she could look at older men with no wish for children in a more permanent way. Strangely, the ones she seemed to meet just didn't feel right.

Thankfully, this next year she would return to her travel and try to resurrect her contacts she'd made in the travel writing industry before Chloe had been born.

Freedom again. She wasn't needed now, superfluous.

Faith's needs had changed: she was married with a husband, and Chloe had found her lost father.

Isabel's travel writing and photographs had been sought after in the past and would be again.

With the changes in Faith's life came changes in Isabel's. New opportunities, including the chance to return to her great love: travel. Life was good and soon, she decided, it would be even better.

CHAPTER TWO

DOM BEGAN THE preparations for the evening meal and shook his head in wonder. Who would imagine a device to slice vegetables could give so much pleasure, both to the user and the observers? Dom thought, still surprised at his own enjoyment.

He'd found the gadget in the tiny supermarket and had hoped it would protect his young niece's fingers from the need to use a knife.

His gaze met Isabel's over the top of the small head that bent so industriously over the chopping board. He smiled at her and she smiled back, one of the most delightful acknowledgements he'd had. Except for the dancing.

She looked away. He did too. Back at Chloe.

One small hand gripped the protective cover of the chopper, fiercely anchoring it to the wooden board, while the other stiffly spread palm beat violently down on the spring-loaded top in a deafening rata-tat-tat. In rapid slices the blades within the clear dome dissected the vegetables holding the shards captured.

When the green pieces were almost too small he said, 'Bravo, Chloe. Your capsicum is perfect.'

'Heh-heh-heh.' The short, satisfied chortle from the child—very much like the wicked witch's cackle in some fantasy film, he thought—made him laugh out loud. The sound from his throat was unfamiliar and he glanced up to see the amused raised brows of the woman opposite.

He gestured with his hand. 'Her laugh…'

'I know. Classic.' Isabel's amusement crinkled her face and more warmth flooded him. Dom passed the little girl the thick ham on a new board. Normally he would have torn it, but watching her chop made all of them smile.

'I don't know why I haven't bought one of those before,' Isabel murmured, shaking her head at her niece. 'Perhaps for your next birthday?'

He was pleased with himself that he could tell the lovely Isabel was joking. His new need to impress and begin to know her excited him, though Dom pretended this was not so, and only inclined his head sagely. He held her gaze when she swung it his way. 'There is much pleasure to be had.' To his delight Isabel blushed and he wondered if she too felt the pull between them, the double meaning in his words.

'What else can I chop?' Chloe's eyes, sparkling emerald-green like a precious gem, showed all of her pleasure at their industry. She had her mother's eyes. And her aunt's. And why did his thoughts always end back at the aunt?

'Will you eat mushrooms?' Dom asked. He knew the fungi were often disliked by children.

Chloe wrinkled her nose and he suppressed his smile. She looked up, her eyes imploring for more to cut. 'I could chop mushrooms. Perhaps we could put them on one side only of the pizza if I share with Aunty Izzy?'

'We can do that,' Isabel said. She scooped away the capsicum onto a saucer and replaced it with a mushroom.

'My son Tomas did not like mushrooms either.' Dom stopped. He never ever spoke of Tomas. This was huge.

Memories had been suppressed because of the pain. But just this once he spoke of him to his new niece Chloe, a flame of hope for the future, as all children were. And with Isabel, because of her kindness and understanding, it did not seem too bad; it seemed almost natural. In sharing a memory he experienced such a feeling of relief to let the words out.

Chloe paused her cutting and small arched brows drew together as her eyes met his. The child's regard seemed wise beyond her five years. 'Mummy said Tomas and his mamma died before I was born.' Before he could say anything she went on. 'My nana died too. And sometimes Mummy or Aunty Izzy say I'm like her. Was Tomas like you?'

He swung his face to Isabel, expecting her to stop the child speaking of loss. She didn't. She smiled. Perhaps ruefully or perhaps with some expectation that he would answer.

Dom found himself closing his eyes at the remembered inquisitiveness of a child. The sudden sweetness of faith that the adult would know all the answers.

'*Sì.* He was like me. And like his Uncle Raimondo.'

'My papà.' She nodded sagely. The silence lengthened. Her lips parted in a smile. 'Can I chop cheese now, please?'

He pulled his emotions back under control. Moistening dry lips with his tongue, he spread his hands. 'Sadly, I have cheese already grated.' Ridiculously, he was sorry he had not chosen a block that Chloe could dissect. 'But you could have tomatoes to attack. And then basil.'

An hour later, Isabel sat well-sated with pizza, hers with lots of mushrooms, on the upstairs veranda.

The view lay before them on the outdoor first-floor

space. Across the street her own house perched below through the wrought-iron railing and then across the bay, past the lighthouse and out to sea, the view swept on. Chloe's new father had purchased a telescope with a wheeled base and steps for the one cupolaed turret so she could watch ships on the ocean and imagine adventurous quests. Faith had said already the turret was a frequent hideaway for Chloe. They'd all looked through the telescope and Isabel had been surprised how clear the view had been.

For Isabel, this time with Dom and Chloe had been an evening of pleasant surprises. The man had been different, almost social at times.

Small pleasures. And not just the delicious food.

'Does it snow in Florence at Christmas? Like the North Pole?' Chloe rested her chin on one small hand as she watched her big uncle sip his tea.

Surreptitiously, Isabel watched him too. Dark brows. Espresso eyes. Sensuous lips. She watched as he sipped and felt her skin warm. Pulled her eyes away. It seemed he'd acquired the taste for their favourite green ginger tea, judging by the satisfied way he put his cup down. That surprised her, this big man enjoying caffeine-free tea. But then he'd surprised her a lot this evening.

The sea breeze stirred a swirl of dark hair across his high forehead, the shadows of the evening making the sharp lines and angles of his aristocratic face smoother. Less grim and forbidding than the normal frown which seemed habitual.

'It does not snow often in Firenze.' He looked at Chloe to explain. 'That is the Italian word for Florence.'

The little girl nodded. Rai had been teaching her some Italian words so she understood the concept.

They'd decided not to turn the lights on as night crept

in on them, but she could see enough to know his face had softened for real at Chloe's question.

'Turin, in the north, is a place people go to see reliable snow and to ski on the mountains. In December, Turin has its annual Luci d'Artista, where the city and its people light up buildings and artworks in wonderful ways. Your papà would no doubt take you there to show you if you asked him.'

'That sounds nice.' Chloe wasn't interested in Turin or the festival, Isabel could tell, but Isabel most certainly was. She would love to visit again…had revelled in the cobbles of the streets, the red of the flowers and the history of villages tucked away on the hills. Yes. She could go back.

'I've never seen snow,' Chloe said thoughtfully. Her head swung towards her aunt, dark plaits swishing in the air. 'Have you seen snow, Aunty Izzy?'

'Yes. And I have even been to Turin in December. It is very beautiful. I will show you my photographs tomorrow if you like.'

Chloe nodded before continuing on her quest for more personal knowledge. 'Have you been to Florence? Where Papà and Uncle Domenico lived?'

Isabel smiled. She had the feeling that Chloe had beaten Dom to the question.

Dom sat forward as if interested.

'Where your uncle lives now? Yes. Another beautiful city.'

'Firenze is *the* most beautiful city,' Dom corrected, his voice a deep rumble in the night, almost teasing, his dark-as-night eyes intense on her face. Deep in her belly she could feel that smoulder of forgotten rolling, pulsing heat flicker into flame. For goodness' sake, had it really been more than a decade since she'd fancied a man? It might be time to go home, away from the warmth in his gaze. Back to safety.

As if totally unmoved, Isabel recalled herself to Dom's statement and agreed. 'I admit to a special charm in Florence, yes.'

'Pah!' he murmured in pretended disgust. 'Firenze is not charming; she is a gilded, glorious goddess of a city, with great beauty and wondrous art.'

That made her laugh. All he needed to do was to stand and throw out his arms. He was like a small boy who had been disagreed with. 'She is.'

His gaze shifted and caught hers. 'You should come to Florence. When Rai brings his bride.'

Good grief. She tried to break the link. 'And why would I do that?'

He shrugged those massive shoulders.

She arched her brows as if not understanding. 'I'm minding Chloe for their three-day honeymoon in Queensland. The rest they will do as a family.'

'But if we left when they returned? The whole family, including you, could have Christmas in Florence instead of the newlyweds waiting here for the festive season to pass. They could take their time, stay longer in Italy with just the two travelling at first, knowing Chloe was in the same country with you.'

Domenico's voice rumbled, low and persuasive, beside her. Were they to have Christmas in an aircraft flying over the ocean? She imagined Chloe's disgust, let alone Chloe seeing her parents disappear to have fun. Isabel glanced sideways with mild amusement at him. 'And what would Chloe and I do while waiting in Florence during their initial grand tour?'

'There is much to see.' He lowered his head until his eyes met hers and, though he didn't truly smile, his choc-

olate eyes darkened and the corner of his mouth rose minutely with a sensual slant. It was quite shocking after all
the serious faces and grim expressions she'd seen from
him until now.

Mentally Isabel stepped back. He was too darn attractive for someone she wasn't encouraging, but those sexy
insights this gorgeous man threw her way left her belly
warm and her toes wanting to curl. It was most inconvenient to say the least.

'Funny you think that.' Now she sipped her own tea
and continued sipping, pause, sip, until she had herself
under control. 'I'm sure Rai is happy to spend time with
his newly discovered daughter. And Faith has never been
without her.'

'Of course. He is besotted with the child.' He waved
his hand again, a more open smile tugging at his lips as
he glanced at the young girl in question, who had stood to
look at a ship from another viewpoint. 'I too find the child
delightful. I would show you both around, of course.'

He wiggled a big hand as if saying could she not see
the idea of the parents wanting to be alone for some time?

Isabel laughed. She hadn't thought he had it in him.
Nice to know he wasn't all doom and gloom and tortured
looks. 'Thank you for the invitation. But I am happy to
agree with what Faith has decided on.'

'Do you not follow the impulse? Do what *you* wish?'
His dark brows drew together solemnly, as if sad for her.
There was emphasis on the *you*.

In return, she smiled sweetly and turned away to look
at the view. 'I can be impulsive. And I always do what
I wish. When I decide. I'm determined. Right now, it's
time for Chloe to go to bed.'

Chloe piped up, 'I was in hospital.'

'And that was not too long ago.' She turned to Dom.

'I'm sure your brother mentioned Chloe had a secondary immune response and low blood counts that left her very ill. Time for bed.' Isabel stood and of course, as she'd expected, Dom stood immediately in response. 'We shall say goodnight to your uncle and thank him for the pizza.'

'Thank you for the pizza, Uncle Domenico.' Chloe stretched out his name again, to ensure she had it correct.

He smiled at her. 'Perhaps it would be easier to say Uncle Dom.'

'Yes.' Chloe breathed out a sigh of relief. 'Uncle Dom,' she repeated and stepped forward to throw her arms exuberantly around him.

Isabel saw Dom close his eyes for a moment as if in pain and then his big hands came down to the young girl's shoulders and he hugged her to him. 'Goodnight, little one.' He released her and looked across at Isabel. 'Thank you for the company.'

'And you for your hospitality,' she said and, despite her intention to remain cool, she couldn't help the flash of amusement that spread through her as she remembered Chloe's endeavours in the kitchen. 'I must buy a vegetable dicer.'

'Yes.' He inclined his head, his eyes twinkling, and she was glad his mood had lightened with Chloe's company.

'Goodnight.'

'Goodnight, Isabel. Perhaps you too could shorten my name?'

'Perhaps.' But she didn't say Dom. Because that would be the first admission that his name left her feeling flustered and feminine and fluttering like a moth under his bright gaze.

Not that she was afraid to use his name out loud. Was she? No.

'I will walk you across the street.' He held the veranda door open for them to enter the house and go down the stairs.

Chloe skipped through and Isabel murmured as she passed, 'You could watch from here.'

'But I will come nevertheless.' His words were low and determined and not quite close enough to brush her neck as he stepped in after them. Her skin tingled as if he had and she remembered the dances they'd shared. His breath in her ear. His arms hot and hard. His thigh against hers.

'I've travelled the world on my own.' *Darn sexy man,* Isabel thought. *I can manage to get across a street in my own town.* But, because she was supposed to be the sensible, composed woman everyone thought her, she didn't say that. Coolly, she hoped it looked that way as she walked ahead of him to follow her niece out of the door.

True to his word, he followed them across the road and to their gate.

'Goodnight,' she said again. But she still didn't say his name. Although she rolled it silently around in her mind.

She could have said his name, Dom thought with unexpected irritation. Or turned around to look at him as she closed the door quietly. Not as if he wasn't standing outside watching them walk away.

He turned and strode under the streetlights downhill towards the beach, his footsteps sounding a little too forcibly on the footpath. The salty breeze lifted the hair around his face and blew back the collar of his shirt to cool his neck in the ridiculous heat of December.

Christmas. Weddings. Small children. All things he dreaded. And yet his heart felt lighter than it had in a long time, a frisson of excitement piercing the darkness of his soul—though admittedly with some exasperation for the nonchalance of the woman he had just left. The woman who unsettled him.

He swivelled his head and looked at the unfamiliar festive lights. It was the place that unsettled him. So different from home. Not Isabel causing him to be disconcerted.

The beach came into sight with the moon climbing from the waves to the sky. Yes, his brother's new hometown was a beautiful place. And it had beautiful women residing in it. Or at least one beautiful woman.

He laughed grimly. He should have gone home straight after the wedding, but Rai had asked him to stay so that the bride might feel even more at ease leaving her daughter for the three nights.

As Isabel had said, Chloe had been ill recently and he was a doctor, if not practising often. The demands of the pharmaceutical company had been all-consuming, but his credentials were still there. Used rarely, at his brother's urging.

But watching over his daughter had not been Rai's only reason for asking him to stay. He knew Rai had been worried about him.

About the darkness Dom held inside. His state of mind. His intentions for the future.

Dom stood on the edge of the sand, looking out over the ocean where waves collided and smashed, and was suddenly glad the swirling water held no attraction to walk towards the horizon until the water closed over his head.

His brother was right. He did need to make a life change. Find joy in small things that had eluded him for too long.

His grandfather's factory, the millstone that had once saved his sanity in his hour of need, was gone, recently lost in flames and destruction, with reams of red tape all that was left if he wished to rebuild someone else's dream. It was the reason he had to leave Lighthouse Bay very soon and fly home or the family would lose the opportunity to rebuild.

It had never been his dream, more a deathbed promise he'd gladly been buried under after Teresa and Tomas had died. With the recent fire and destruction, the excuse to block out the world with his grandfather's legacy had also been left in ruins.

He had no focus. No goal to strive for. No desire or duty to drive him to rebuild something he had never felt passionate about. But there were many legal and financial responsibilities he needed to complete speedily when he returned, before the end of the month or the permits would expire. He'd let things come to such a pass with his lowered mood.

This morning Rai had suggested he return here once his business was completed, that they open a general medical practice together in Lighthouse Bay. A trial of one year. It had been the first mention of the subject, to be discussed later.

He'd been astounded. Had denied the possibility of a return to medicine. He was a pharmacist now. Had been in charge of his grandfather's pharmaceutical company for years.

Though perhaps it was not so astounding.

Of course, such a venture would involve further refreshment of his knowledge. He'd need more medical expertise than the work in Third World countries he had occasionally been drawn into when his brother had needed him.

Such a venture would also require that he gained registration in another country, though in Italy his volunteer work had kept him legally registered.

But to move across the world? To this strange town on the edge of the ocean?

He would need to find a place of residence because he would not live with newlyweds.

His mouth lifted in a small smile. He doubted that Isabel would allow him to sleep with her in her house.

Madonna. His breath sucked in, held low and hot in his chest as he stared dumbfounded at the moon. Imagined himself in Isabel's bed. Had his attraction to Isabel gone so far? Had he forgotten his wife? His loss? His loyalty?

Six years.

His breath hissed out. Perhaps his fun-loving, tempestuous Teresa would not have expected life-long mourning from him; he wondered why for so long he had.

CHAPTER THREE

'AUNTY IZZY, AUNTY IZZY, there's a rainbow.'

The next morning Isabel woke to a cloudy sky with sunbeams piercing her windows.

A small child flew through the air to land on her bed. She pulled her feet to the side quickly to prevent toe squashing and made a space for Chloe to wriggle and bounce.

'A rainbow?' Her face stretched into a yawn and her hand came up to cover her mouth. 'Did it rain this morning?' She must have been more deeply asleep than she remembered. It had taken her so very long to sink into slumber, thanks to the irritating Italian next door. Libidinous thoughts were not the norm for her. Or conducive to rest. Good grief, she'd actually felt sexually frustrated last night in her bed.

Isabel turned her head to look from her niece to the window and, sure enough, prismed colour gleamed in a semi-circle to the left of the pane.

'Can we take a photo for Mummy?' A particularly energetic bounce on the bed made a pillow hit the floor. 'And for my papà.' Chloe's addition made Isabel smile. Chloe still wasn't used to having that extra person in the family but loved inserting 'my papà' into most conversations now.

Isabel sat up and pushed her hair from her eyes. 'Of course.' She'd tried showing Chloe ways to compose photographs and her niece had been a precociously apt pupil. 'Though we may have to find a good vantage spot to work the whole rainbow in.' She slid from the bed and absently grabbed the nearest pair of shorts, bra and top and headed for the bathroom. 'You'd best get dressed if we're going up the hill. We'll have to be quick to catch the light.'

Chloe catapulted off the bed in a leap and disappeared.

Five minutes later they slipped out of the front door just as the tall, dark, brooding neighbour across the road did the same. Isabel suppressed a sigh. Darn it. She knew what would happen now.

'Uncle Dom, Uncle Dom, there's a rainbow. We're taking a photo for Mummy and my papà. Will you come and find it with us?'

Yup. She'd known. And here she was, dressed in her shortest gym shorts and a skimpy singlet top. Not what she would have worn if she'd thought ahead sensibly; running into their neighbour was always a possibility in their quiet street.

Lack of sleep to blame. Nothing else.

Isabel lifted her chin. Closing the gate after the little girl, she looked up to smile calmly into the dark gaze of the man who had invaded her dreams most inconveniently. He was studying her in the thorough way of Italian men regardless of their age. He'd better keep his hands to himself or he'd lose them.

'Your timing is impeccable.' Her voice might have sounded a tad dry, so she softened it with another smile.

'Sì.' There might even have been an amused twinkle

in the dark eyes. 'And there is a rainbow, I am told. May I join you?'

Isabel felt like saying '*Sì*, I have no choice.' But she didn't. 'Of course,' she said instead and smiled tranquilly.

The two adults followed the skipping, hopping, trotting girl up the hill, past the row of crofts on the right that clung to the edge of the cliff. As they walked past they could glimpse the magnificent views over the bay between the houses.

'Who lives there?' Dom's interest seemed significant and she felt a tiny disquiet at his question. Could he be looking for a property? She thought it unlikely he would imitate his brother, but she still didn't trust these Salvanelli men not to buy real estate on a whim.

Isabel pointed them out. 'My friend Myra and her husband Reg, and next door is Sam and Ellie, and next to them Finn and Trina. Midwives and their doctor husbands—all friends of Faith and Rai who you met at the wedding.'

'And friends of yours, of course?'

Funny. She always thought of them as Faith's friends. Like a younger sibling's friends. 'Yes, my friends too, but they're a younger crowd. I have more in common with Myra as an older woman past childbearing age.'

Now why the heck had she said that?

She wanted to turn around and walk back down the hill. She never ever talked like that. Maybe she could knock her head against the wall once she was safely inside her house in private. Why was she so insecure about her age, especially in relation to him? Why was she so convinced that he needed to produce an heir that it made their relationship impossible? He'd never actually said that to her. Indeed, it seemed her age didn't matter to him. What was holding her back?

Being comfortable alone? Lack of confidence that she could hold the attention of so young and virile a man? Fear that she would fall in love and he too would walk away?

She couldn't pinpoint it. But fear was there. No doubt about it.

This man unsettled her—made her blurt out the weirdest things—and she wasn't happy with herself.

But she couldn't abandon Chloe by scuttling off home. Instead, she increased her pace and tilted her head to stare pointedly at the rainbow. They passed the last house and the path widened to a seating area overlooking the bay.

'Here's a lovely spot to take the photo, Chloe. I think it's starting to fade so you'd better be quick.'

Isabel pulled her phone from the small bag she'd stowed it in, found the camera app and handed it to Chloe. 'Watch your horizons are level.'

Chloe took the phone carefully and began to take various angles, not just standing feet planted and front on. Isabel nodded in approval. 'Good girl. Nice composition.'

'She knows of photography?' He'd come up beside her while she'd been watching her niece and she inhaled that spicy scent he wore. Straight from the shower, she guessed, but she chose not to feel unwashed and underdressed. Not at all.

She needed a diversion. 'I'll buy her a camera soon. I believe children can learn camera basics very early. It seems a shame not to make the best of an opportunity to share knowledge. Rainbows are always fun to shoot.'

Dom tried not to stare at the long, strong and shapely legs and arms displayed in the micro shorts and thin-strapped top. It was difficult. *Dio*. Most difficult. There had been no instance in the last few days that Isabel had not been covered and demure. And this morning so much wonderful woman was on display that for the first time in many years he felt the hot surge of desire.

He guessed she'd left the house hurriedly for the child and the thought amused him. She would dislike that, though he didn't know how he could be so sure of it. But he was.

Sure and delighted.

Yet still she showed no outward sign of awareness of her attire. She was an unusual woman and Dom suspected that she sold herself short if the few years between her niece's friends and her own age seemed such a huge gap. Perhaps this Myra was of the same age.

He then considered if this mindset could be the reason she had displayed such detachment.

Hmm. Did she consider him in her niece's younger age group and therefore too young for her? The thought piqued him. Did she not know she was a desirable woman, attractive to all men with eyes? That he was a man worthy of her?

He watched as woman and child studied Chloe's results of the rainbow chasing expedition, heads together. Chloe's hair was tied back in a rough ponytail and Isabel's features softened by glints of red amongst the free strands waving about her face like Aphrodite's.

His belly clenched with want, with the need to move on and open his heart to other women, to Isabel, and his brows drew together. There was no doubt he felt physical attraction to her. But was there any chance of reciprocation or just the spectre of more pain when she refused? She'd made no secret of the fact she wasn't interested in a dalliance.

Chloe skipped across and displayed her favourite

frame to him and he dipped his head to study the screen. Indeed, the horizon sat straight and the composition did not look childish. It was a shot any amateur photographer could be proud of.

'A wonderful photograph of clouds and the rainbow.'

'Aunty Izzy taught me how to take pictures.'

He looked at Isabel. 'Your aunt is an excellent teacher.' Then back at the child. 'And you an excellent pupil. Your mother and papà will certainly enjoy this.' He listened to himself, stilted and awkward with the child. How had he fallen out of the way of talking to children? With people really.

This was good for him, this interaction. Rai would be pleased that he was, at least, trying.

'Can we send it now?' Chloe had spun to hold out the phone to her aunt.

'Now that we have the photo you want, let's go back to the house and have breakfast and dress properly for the day. We can send your surprise after breakfast, when Mummy has had a chance to wake up as well.'

'She won't be sleeping now.' Chloe looked askance at her aunt and Dom suppressed a smile. He doubted his brother would be sleeping either with his new wife in his bed.

Calmly, as she seemed to do everything, Isabel inclined her head. 'Just in case. Mummy has had a couple of very big days. It would be a shame to wake her if she were sleeping in.'

The child screwed her face until it cleared. 'After breakfast then. Can we ask Uncle Dom to breakfast?'

If he wasn't mistaken Isabel's face twitched before it returned to being expressionless. Dom felt the sudden unexpected mirth slip out from him in a small laugh. He put Isabel out of her misery. 'Thank you, little one, but I have already broken my fast.'

Isabel's expression did not change but he thought her shoulders loosened. Tiny nuances were there if he watched carefully. It seemed he liked watching carefully.

The child appeared determined to spend time with him. It gave him an unexpected warmth. But also forced his company on Isabel. He could see that wasn't her wish.

And why was that?

A devil inside him stirred. Yet he spoke to the child. 'We could meet for lunch, down at the beach kiosk.' Another twitch from her aunt and he suppressed his smile. 'I have not yet eaten there and would like to try it before I return to Italy.'

'Can we, Aunty Izzy? Lunch at the beach with Uncle Dom?'

'That's sounds delightful.' She smiled blandly and he inclined his head, a spurt of masculine pleasure shooting through him. He would give her delightful. Oh, yes.

A few hours later Dom read the email that confirmed with his secretary in Firenze that his flight would leave Australia on Christmas Eve. All the while he watched out of the window for Isabel.

The door of the house across the road opened and two females, one tall and one tiny, stepped along the path and out through the gate. Isabel did not glance his way but he noticed Chloe avidly searched for him, her gaze scanning the house from window to window. He huffed out a small laugh. His niece appreciated his company anyway.

He watched them turn to walk down the hill to the beach. Isabel was fifteen minutes early so he allowed them privacy to go ahead instead of rushing to join them for the walk, but still he closed his email and followed as soon as he could. He could see them ahead of him and took pleasure in watching Isabel sway sedately while his niece scampered ahead on the path.

His gaze returned to rest on Isabel, her dark auburn, sun-kissed hair tied back at her long, slender neck, head angled high, straight spine, this morning's long legs hidden by the swirl of a colourful ankle-length skirt. Isabel covered the ground gracefully like a dancer and he remembered again what it had been like to hold her in his arms at the wedding.

And the rehearsal before that.

She had been yielding and compliant, her breasts soft against his chest, her lovely body inherently balanced and responsive to his direction as the music slid over them both during the waltz. Yet it had not been enough. It had been in the dancing that his first moments of intrigue had turned to strong attraction, surprising him with unfamiliar longing after so long an abstinence.

When he'd come back into his brother's house this morning after the rainbow hunt, his anticipation for sharing lunch with Isabel and Chloe had also surprised him. He was eager. Though it was not a *date* as the Australians said. He doubted the self-sufficient woman would allow him to pay for her meal, even though it was his idea to go out, but that was a small battle he could win another time.

His chest felt lighter than it had for years as he closed the distance between them, noting in the periphery of his vision the rainbow of pastel cottages, colourful but paler than those in Cinque Terre or Burano yet still pretty.

The gardens were neat and colourful, and decorations abounded. The town seemed to smile and there was something healing about the sound of the sea as a constant gentle drumbeat in the distance.

The quiet path was a joy to travel on foot. Or was the joy in watching the child and woman ahead? His gaze lingered on Isabel and his heart lifted further.

The intrusive sound of motorbikes grew louder in the distance and he decided this place felt too somnolent for young bloods, hotheads and speed. The engines of the bikes screamed closer, which didn't fit with the narrow streets and curving paths of the village, and he hoped the riders were as skilled at manoeuvring as they were at destroying the quiet.

The bikes and riders appeared like two red blurs, travelling far too fast, and he saw the moment Isabel reached the corner at the bottom and took the child's hand to pull Chloe to her.

The first bike braked, slowed and slewed to a stop at the unexpected T-intersection. Far too fast, the second bike tried, failed, slid out of control, tipped and spun sideways, the engine roar dropping as the rider tumbled off to bounce across the bitumen. The horizontal bike kept moving, shooting sparks in a roaring, grinding slide, the pings of flying gravel and the scream of metal scoring the road as it veered at alarming speed sideways towards Isabel and Chloe with unstoppable momentum.

Time slowed. Dom's vision sharpened and sounds rushed in. His breathing quickened, his mouth dried and his heart pounded with a sudden surge of energy. Dom began to run.

Isabel knew the bike would hit her but instinctively she swung her niece backwards towards the soft grass behind them where the little girl gasped at the unexpected shove, landed and rolled. Isabel felt the blow, the impact low and solid, taking her feet out from under her at the ankle, the rush of air as she was tossed through the air, but not by the bike.

By a man.

She'd been knocked aside from the machine by Dom, who landed on top of her, his big body covering hers as if to take the impact himself.

Her forehead hit the grass with a thwack and her body followed with a bone-jarring puff of breath exploding from her as weight crushed. The screech of metal and the crash of glass reverberated as the machine whooshed by with millimetres to spare and smashed into the telephone pole with a crumpling *whoomph*. The machine settled, tinkling a confetti of headlight glass and crumpling metal. Gradually the sounds died until only the sound of the sea and the *tink-tink* of a hot engine rose in the air. And the gallop of her heart.

The broken machine lay mere centimetres away, circling the pole like the palm of a tightening fist.

Chloe's frightened sob cleared Isabel's head of the shock from the impact and she tried to move.

'Chloe,' she gasped, struggling to pull air into her squashed lungs while her ears rang from the bump to her head. 'Get off me.'

Dom shifted swiftly and with only a little stiffness, thankfully, she could breathe again.

Her heart pounded like a manic piston in her chest as he reached down to offer his hand and she took it, grateful for something solid to hang onto as everything else swam in her vision.

But thankful also, when she had time to think about it, for the fact he'd saved her from being mashed by the huge motorbike and hot metal against the unforgiving pole.

But Chloe first.

Isabel's ankle throbbed where she'd twisted to throw

Chloe and then been hit by Dom. When she put her weight on her left foot, her lower leg screamed in protest and gave way. She would have fallen if he hadn't held her.

'Are you all right?' he asked.

'I think I've twisted something. And my head and shoulder hurt.'

He made a fast assessment of her face and body and lowered her again. 'I will bring Chloe to you. Then we will look closer.'

Seconds later he placed Chloe gently on the ground beside Isabel. Chloe's eyes were wide and confused and she reached for her aunt, who slid an arm around her.

Chloe stared into her face accusingly. 'You pushed me.'

Isabel dredged a smile from somewhere—goodness knew where it had been rummaged from—her heart still jolted and she couldn't stop thinking about how close to being hit she and Chloe had been. 'A good thing. I pushed you and Uncle Dom pushed me.' She pointed at the pole and wrecked vehicle. 'We didn't get squashed by the bike.'

And that was the gist of it.

Across the road the local policeman, still carrying the daily newspaper he'd just collected from the tiny newsagents, was gesticulating to the stationary motorcyclist and gesturing to Faith and Chloe on the footpath. Along with the hapless motorcyclist, who limped awkwardly, they all began to cross towards them.

Dom moved in front of Isabel and Chloe. To the men he said, *'Lo stupido.'* To the officer, in a cold rigid voice that, despite the lack of emotion, froze like dry ice, 'My family are both shaken. It is best we do not speak to these reckless people at this time.' He handed the policeman a card. 'My lawyers will be in contact with them.'

Isabel blinked. Lawyers? His card?

She said from the ground, tiredly, 'Nobody was hurt.'

Dom spun on her. 'You *are* hurt. Chloe is bruised, I am sure. You both could have been dead.'

Yes, Chloe could have been killed. She shivered as cold slid over her skin in slivers of sick horror.

Then she saw the absolute terror in Domenico's eyes and with sudden insight wondered if he'd had a flashback to when he'd lost his own family. Not a lot of give in those eyes glaring back at her. He needed time-out more than she did. 'Take us home, please.'

He replied shortly. 'To the emergency department first, and then home.'

Dom said something else to the policeman, something low and gruff that she didn't hear, and the other men moved away towards the little police station across the street.

CHAPTER FOUR

WITHIN MINUTES OF Dom speaking to the policeman, a constable arrived in a police car to drive them across to the little hospital a few hundred metres away.

Dom carried her in, his strong arms holding her as if she were a precious porcelain doll, not a full-blooded woman capable of limping in herself, though if her head hadn't been swimming and her ankle aching so, she probably would have enjoyed the sensation of flying in Dom's arms.

Chloe followed with Isabel's handbag and a pinched worried frown on her little face. Poor Chloe.

What a mess this all was, Isabel thought, and wished they'd stayed home for lunch.

The emergency nurse ushered them to a stretcher in a cubicle and Dom made sure the staff knew he was a doctor and he wanted Isabel thoroughly examined. He asked for X-rays and an emergency doctor in a most demanding way.

'Sorry, Ro,' Isabel said quietly. As if they wouldn't get the best care. Despite her headache, she murmured, 'Domenico, let her do her job. Roseanne is very efficient.'

His attention shifted to her. 'You are hurt. I am partly responsible.'

Despite her awkwardness at his insistence to the nurse

Isabel knew very well, there was a crazy, if illogical, delight in the fact he was so concerned about her. 'Thank you. But I'm good.'

Roseanne smiled at Isabel. 'He's fine. I can see he's worried.' She proceeded to assess Isabel's blood pressure and pulse. 'Normal.' And then checked her pupils. 'Both equal in size and briskly reacting to the light from my pencil torch,' she said as much for Dom as for Isabel. 'You've knocked your head. And we'll check your leg. Dr Southwell is coming.'

Isabel touched Dom's arm. 'Dr Southwell, Reg, is my friend Myra's husband.' *So be nice to him.* She didn't say it out loud, but his raised brows and slight smile said he got it.

'Ah,' he said, and glanced at his watch as if to say he should be here already.

The nurse smiled at Isabel. 'Lucky Reg is in the hospital.'

Isabel closed her eyes. 'So it seems.'

Reg arrived, rubbing the cleanser into his thin, age-spotted hands, his wrinkled face calm and kind. 'Isabel.' He looked at Dom.

Isabel said, 'You met Rai's brother, Dr Domenico Salvanelli, at the wedding. Dom, do you remember Dr Reg Southwell?'

The men nodded at each other and Reg turned back to her.

'Now, my dear. What have you been doing?' He took the chart from Roseanne and checked the observations then pulled on fresh gloves and crossed to her. Resting his fingers briefly on her wrist to feel her pulse, he said, 'I hear we had some less than intelligent motorcyclists causing problems.'

'Not for long,' Dom muttered.

There was a slight smile on Reg's face as he reached out and tilted her face so he could see the bumps and abrasions. He gently touched the place on her brow which was the worst of it and she winced. Dom stood at his shoulder watching and narrowed his eyes at her obvious discomfort. She wished he'd go outside and wait but she doubted anyone would be able to get him to leave. Again, a silly delight rose at the thought.

'Her ankle also is twisted. I hope not broken,' Dom said.

'We'll check that,' Reg said patiently. He moved down to examine her leg. Glanced at Dom. 'What do you think?'

'I think badly sprained but not broken, but would prefer confirmation with an X-ray.'

Reg smiled. 'I agree.' He looked at Isabel. 'Are you happy for us to send you through to X-Ray? Perhaps Chloe's uncle could stay with her here, while you go through?'

By the time she returned, reassured by Reg, who'd come back when the X-rays had been processed and both he and Dom had discussed her leg bones ad nauseam, Isabel was allowed to go home in Dom's care.

The constable had waited and then driven them back up the hill to Isabel's house.

Once back at the top of the hill, Isabel tried to climb out of the vehicle under her own steam, despite the pain and the spinning in her head.

'Do not attempt to stand on that ankle.' Dom's growl came from behind her head and stopped her as she opened the front door of the patrol car. He was out of the back and at her side, his face grim and eyes flashing at her attempt at independence. Seemed she'd lost that one too.

'Why do you persist in foolishness?' he muttered and scooped her out and up as if she were lighter than Chloe. He stood, holding her, his arms securely pulling her against his big chest. 'Thank you,' he said to the policeman, dismissing him.

'Come, Chloe, perhaps you could find the keys to the door to your aunt's house in her handbag.' Chloe was still clutching it like a talisman through all the upheaval and drama of the morning.

Isabel shifted in his arms. 'I'm Chloe's great-aunt. Not her aunt.' As if reminding gave her some control. 'And the door is unlocked.'

He glared at her. 'Your foolish great-aunt.' And carried her into her house. He muttered a pithy comment about the fact the door was unlocked but Isabel ignored that particular point because it wasn't worth worrying over.

But his arms. They were a worry. Strong, so strong, yet tender, warm and very, very safe.

She couldn't remember the last time a man had carried her. Long back in childhood before her parents had passed. Never against such a broad, steel-banded chest, and seriously, that aftershave was to die for.

He placed her cautiously on her long sofa. As if she would break if he wasn't careful. 'We will pack and both you and Chloe will sleep across the road with me tonight.'

'No.'

He returned with two pillows from her room. 'Yes.' He placed them behind her then stood back and crossed his arms over that massive chest.

She raised her brows at him. Seriously? 'I'm not moving into Rai and Faith's house for the night.'

She needed an aspirin, or a paracetamol. Or a thimble of brandy. No. She couldn't have a brandy. Child-minding.

Memory sliced back to the accident.

She shivered. She and Chloe could have died. She'd pushed Chloe and Dom had saved her.

Still no reason to move in with him for twenty-four hours. Not happening. She wasn't losing this battle of wills.

Dom loomed over her as she sat with her legs up on the sofa.

'You need care. You must elevate the leg and should not walk. Walking on a sprained ankle is not advised.'

'I am aware of that. But it is only a sprain.'

He spoke impassively. 'Then you are aware that your ankle needs time to heal before weight-bearing. Twenty-four to forty-eight hours minimum. Weight-bearing too soon may slow healing or cause further damage. Then it could be a week of immobility.'

No, she didn't want that. 'I'm aware.'

'You are also possibly concussed and need cold compresses for your ankle.' Dom's face remained expressionless and hard, as if chiselled from the rock cliff-face down on the point of the bay. The one the waves beat against and never seemed to imprint.

He spread his fingers in that Mediterranean gesture so many Italian men seemed to love. 'How is your five-year-old niece going to look after you?'

She'd manage. In private. No big dark Italian to watch her struggle. 'We'll be fine.'

His lips compressed in a firm tight line, but his expression said he doubted that very much. She wondered if eyebrows could be arrogant as she watched his rise with exasperation up into his dark hairline.

She closed her eyes, feeling light-headed and silly with shock, and said in a small voice, 'If you'd like to do something I can't ask of Chloe…' She flicked open her lashes and reassured herself Chloe was still fine. Her niece looked none the worse for the morning's excitement, playing with her dolls as she explained about motorbikes and being careful on roads to her plastic friends. 'I would very much like a cup of black tea with some sugar or honey, please.'

Dom made an odd snorting, infuriated noise, but turned away for the kitchen. She'd missed the opportunity to see what the noise had meant. She closed her eyelids again and rested back on the heaped pillows he had scooped from her bed.

Scooped from her bed.

He'd seen her bedroom.

That left her with an odd, tingling feeling she was so not going to examine.

It seemed like seconds later but must have been minutes because the kitchen electric jug had been cold and her tea steamed beside her with wafts of sweet honey scent. Dom knelt beside her leg to examine her ankle without touching. Waiting for her to open her eyes.

'You slept.'

'I did not.' Had she?

Dom didn't bother arguing. In his hand lay two round white pills. Paracetamol, she recognised. She took them and sipped from the glass of water beside the tea.

'We will hold off on the ibuprofen until your headache is gone, in case of concussion. Later you may start them for the swelling of your leg. But I have ice for your ankle.'

He crouched down beside her and that wondrous, masculine Dom scent wafted over her. Clean and spicy and too darn yummy. 'May I check again that it is not showing signs of more than a simple sprain?'

He'd already had her checked, he'd checked her, along with Chloe, and everyone had been satisfied that there were no broken bones.

It did hurt like the blazes, though. 'Fine. And thank you for the ice.' Manners. She needed to watch those manners, which seemed to go haywire in his presence. 'And the tea. And tablets. It was very kind of you.'

There. She sounded more like herself again.

He glanced up at her. Smiled. As if he'd heard her thoughts.

'It must be very tender.' His long fingers slid along the red swelling on the outside of her calf, carefully probing. The slight pressure made her wince. And his touch made her warm. All over. He'd removed her shoes as soon as he'd put her down, so the polish on her toes winked like little red eyes when she shifted her feet. For some weird reason she found that embarrassing.

Her ankle would be fine. There was no odd shaping despite the raised bump, but the whole lower leg had turned red and swollen.

He straightened and stood. 'Ankle tendons are strong, but sudden overstretching and strain—' here a brief shrug '—such as caused by a large man knocking you sideways can cause damage.' He dipped his head. 'My apologies.'

Her cheeks felt hot. Too much large man too close. 'I forgive you for saving my life,' she said lightly, but she was feeling anything but light with Dom's hands so recently on her ankle. It was as if the heat was still there. And creeping higher.

He smiled and the warmth of that curve of his lips did something inside her she couldn't control. An unfurling and wanting she couldn't think about. Unfair. Too beautiful and caring for a man she barely knew and had banned herself from giving false hope to. Banned from giving herself false hope.

He turned his big body sideways and took the bag of ice he must have made up from her freezer trays and wrapped in one of her tea towels. He lowered the pack slowly and gently on top of her lower leg and sat back.

Then he handed her the cup of tea and made sure she could reach the table to put it down again.

'You should come to Raimondo's house for the night,' he tried again.

'No.'

Dom sighed, perhaps with some long-suffering edge to it, and glanced instead around the room. His gaze settled on the large soft white leather reclining armchair she'd bought last week, a little luxury she planned to curl up in and read her book now that she was the single occupant of the house. The seat swivelled all ways and towards the windows looking out to the small ocean-facing veranda. 'Then I will stay here. I will use that chair.'

'What do you mean, stay?' She'd turned Faith's room into an office. There was only Chloe's single bed. And hers.

'Once I have returned with my laptop and phone charger I will visit with you and Chloe today. I will come and go. Tonight, I will sleep—' he pointed one long finger imperiously '—there.'

'No, you won't.'

He didn't argue that either, but she knew darn well that didn't mean he'd agreed to sleep in his own bed across the road. The worst of it was, she probably needed him. And that only made her more uncomfortable. She didn't want to need anyone because when she had trusted a man to be there for her before he'd abandoned her.

Her head ached and her leg throbbed. She would deal with this other—larger—irritation later.

'You need to rest. Avoid activities that cause pain, swelling or discomfort. That means walking. We will use the ice pack for fifteen to twenty minutes and repeat every two to three hours while you are awake. But I will check every hour if I am not already here.'

All sensible advice. She didn't argue.

He frowned down at her. 'I will set my phone alarm and ensure that we follow this timing. But first, compression. I wish to reinforce the flimsy bandage they have applied, to help stop the swelling.' He held up a wide bandage she suspected he'd found in her first aid box.

Hourly checks, alarms? The man was pedantic.

And how had he discovered her emergency medical supplies?

As if hearing her aunt's thoughts, Chloe appeared at her side. 'I showed Uncle Dom where to find the bandages.'

Oh. 'Thank you, Chloe. That was very helpful.'

Chloe's worried little face relaxed, as if she'd been unsure if she'd done the right thing. She handed Isabel a small packet of hand freshener wipes. 'You have dirt on your face.'

Poor little mite. Such drama and strangeness to face when her mummy had just gone away. 'What a clever girl you are.' She took the wipes and cleaned her hands and face. 'Does that look better?'

Chloe nodded and smiled. 'And my dolls and I showed Uncle Dom where the bags are to put the ice in. And the tea towels for wrapping.' Now she looked mighty pleased with herself.

'You and your dolls are such wonderful people to have around when I have a sore ankle. And you are playing so well.'

Chloe would be fine with just the two of them. She was an independent little girl with a sunny nature and biddable disposition. Which Isabel believed came from the absolute knowledge that everyone loved her and that she was a big help to her mother and aunt. Discipline had always been loving and gentle and the rewards were in front of her.

'Do you know how to use your aunt's phone, Chloe?' Dom's voice startled Isabel out of her rambling thoughts. Her phone, she saw now, had appeared on the table beside her. When had that happened? Another thing he'd asked Chloe for?

'Yes,' Chloe said, instantly bright-eyed and eager.

Dom picked it up. Swiped and looked satisfied it wasn't automatically locked. Proceeded to add a number to the contacts.

He could have asked first. 'Lucky I haven't a photo of myself in a bikini as a screenshot.'

'Or bad luck,' Dom said with a straight face.

Just like a man. She deserved that. She held back a smile at the thought.

'You can press this number—' he showed Chloe the screen '—and I will answer, if you or your aunt need my help when I am not here.'

In between those hourly visits? Isabel felt her cheeks heat. Did he think she couldn't survive between his welfare checks? Good grief. 'She won't have to do that,' she said.

'Perhaps not. But if she does need me... Would you prefer she cross the road to my brother's house without a chaperone?' He tilted his head as if speaking to someone whose sense had deserted them. 'This is better.'

Isabel's hands tightened in her lap. No Mediterranean gestures for her, but she wanted to throw them out in a 'Good grief' gesture like he had. And, worse, she knew the darn man was right. She had fallen asleep just minutes ago.

Discreetly she blew an easing sigh and let the tension

go. 'Of course. Thank you.' Her voice sounded sweet. Maybe a bit too sweet but that was the best she could manage. Her usual common sense and desire for independence felt torn and shredded, as if it had deserted her where this man was involved. And her head ached. She needed to go to the bathroom and wondered if she could hop across while Dom was gone. But she suspected it would be fraught with the weakness she still felt.

'Rest your eyes, *cara*. I will return soon.'

CHAPTER FIVE

DOM SHUT HIS MOUTH. Felt his face harden in shock. *Cara?* His Teresa had been *cara*, not this woman he'd met just over a week ago.

He put down Isabel's phone and turned to the door. 'I will be back in twenty minutes to remove the ice.' He ignored Isabel's 'Chloe can do that,' called after him and strode out.

His mind whirled. His chest thumped. His skin itched. It had been an unconscious use of the endearment. Just a slip of the tongue. Concern for a woman in distress and an unintended softening.

It meant nothing.

Or did it mean he was changing? Opening his heart to Chloe's Aunty Izzy, calling her *cara*, the first time the word had passed his lips since that dark day of his loss? Or was it only delayed shock from the events of the morning and not his heart at all?

Cara Isabel?

Faith's rock when Rai had failed her.

Dom's damsel in distress whom he'd injured in saving.

Isabel's presence had shoved him by the shoulder that first day until his senses opened and he saw her. Saw her calm, her empathy and her ability to manage the unexpected. Saw her humour directed at him, understated but skimming the surface in the glances he caught from her. She would make someone a good wife. The thought furrowed his brow at the thought of another man with Isabel. Or she could make him a good wife.

Why was he thinking this? He did not love her like he'd loved his Teresa, but…

The way she managed Chloe—managed everything and everyone—made him consider the thought with more calm. Less emotion.

Suddenly it seemed he did miss not having a partner in life. A wife to lie down with at night. To wake up to with the sun. To share his thoughts and his body and his soul. In fact, in the awareness between him and Isabel, something powerful could grow if only she would help him nurture it.

This new wanting of her was making him a little crazy.

Isabel Fetherstone had been hurt but could she really be cast as a woman in distress when she was so capable, so steady, so sensible? Isabel's distress came from having to rely on him, not from the fact that he had wrenched her ankle and forced her head to the ground.

She'd saved his niece. She had thought very quickly to ensure Chloe's safety and not her own. She could have been crushed against the pole by the metal monster. But she hadn't been. He'd saved her. He'd saved Isabel.

At that thought his mind cleared and the tension in his shoulders eased somewhat. He needed to apprise his brother of what had happened, but he'd wait for Isabel and Chloe to be present before making the call.

Their planned time for lunch had passed and no doubt Chloe would also be hungry. So much for his booking a table at the café. Perhaps the establishment would do takeaway in the circumstances and deliver.

He pulled out his phone as he crossed the street to his brother's house and pressed the café's number.

Twenty minutes later Dom knocked and pushed open the door to Isabel's cottage. He carried a small overnight satchel with toiletries, his computer and chargers. Soon a large box of food would be delivered here.

Strange how the idea that he was compelled to attend to an invalid, and to a night's sleep on a chair, did not bother him.

'You're back.' Isabel's demeanour appeared less shaken, the tea and water had been consumed, and a light blush of colour had returned to her cheeks. She looked rested. Unruffled. Breathtaking.

He cleared his throat and stamped down his sudden urge to cross the room and sit by her. 'I have ordered for lunch to be delivered.'

She smiled, her face alight with a touch of mischief, an appreciation of his actions and a cordiality that was growing between them. His chest warmed. Such a smile was worthy of more than a box of food. She gestured towards the back of the cottage. 'Chloe is playing with her dolls in her room.'

Good. This meant the child was over the shock of the accident. And gave him a chance to be alone with Isabel?

'I have come to remove the ice.' He put his overnight bag down beside the chair and moved across to lift the soggy towel of ice from her ankle. He carried it across to the sink, then returned to crouch beside her.

'Let me look.' The skin above and below the bandage where the ice had lain was pale with cold but not swollen. He slid his finger carefully on the uninjured side to feel the tightness between her skin and the bandage. 'Firm but not too tight.'

He glanced up at her face. Her eyes twinkled at him though her expression remained composed.

'Everything is good. You have an excellent bedside manner,' she added.

Was she teasing him? But she seemed serene and sincere. So he answered honestly. 'A bedside manner is not something I practice often.'

'You are a doctor, yes?'

He was not a doctor. Not any more. Though lately he had thought... 'Apart from some crisis relief with my brother in Third World countries, and occasional relief in one of the poorer villages for a friend of mine, I have mostly been a pharmacist for many years.' One of the brothers had had to promise their grandfather they would carry on the company. With his wife and son dead, Dom hadn't cared about anything. It hadn't mattered. Nothing had mattered. No. He had not been a doctor for years.

'You still have medical skills. Look at your care for my ankle. It feels better already.' She cast him a quick hopeful look. 'In fact, it feels so much better you really don't need to stay.'

Ha. He understood her tactic. 'But I do. I shall plan to stay tonight.' He shrugged. 'Tomorrow we will see how independent you are.'

He thought her lips might have compressed and wasn't sure why that amused him. Her eyes did not meet his. Deliberately? To hide her expression?

They both stared down at her leg. It was a very nice leg.

He asked softly, 'And your headache?'

Unconsciously she lifted her hand to her forehead, where a small bruise blossomed beneath the graze that marked her brow. 'Better.'

He wondered how 'better' it really was and would have

liked to smooth it. But her defences were up, he could tell. 'May I check the reactions of your pupils again?'

'Of course.' Her head lifted and he saw how such a request gave tension to her shoulders. Was this because it brought him closer? He hoped so. Because when he was close he could breathe her floral scent and admire the sheen of her skin. And he liked the way she blushed.

He took her chin in his hand and shone the torch. Once he was satisfied that both pupils were equal in size and reacting to the light from his small torch, he stood.

Before awkwardness could descend on their silence, a knock sounded at the front door.

He felt movement at his side as he crossed the room and when he opened it Chloe was peering out with him. It was the food.

He'd ordered for ease of consumption. Chicken and salad wraps for everyone, Pizza Margherita to share and a bowl of finger-sized whiting fillets with chips. For dessert, small pots of ice-cream and berries. A takeaway cappuccino for Isabel, cola for him and a milkshake for Chloe.

Anything that wasn't eaten he could leave in Isabel's refrigerator for her convenience later.

Her gaze was on him as he crossed the room and she said, 'I've been waiting to call Faith and Rai.'

He put the box on the round table she used for meals. 'I thought also but waited for you. You look well enough to do this now. And that we both agree they should be told and reassured.'

Isabel nodded. 'I thought Chloe could phone them. That way, Faith will know she's fine right from the beginning and then we can both reassure them.'

So they did. On speaker phone—not something he was fond of.

Chloe's explanation startled him. 'Mummy, it's Chloe.
I'm on Aunty Izzy's phone and a motorbike crashed.
Aunty Izzy tossed me onto the grass, so I'm fine. Uncle
Dom's not so good at tossing Aunty Izzy. Now she has a
sore leg and a headache.'

Dom froze, horrified, and then he bit his lip to stop
his smile, turning his head to Isabel, who held her hand
over her mouth. Her eyes danced like green gems in the
light and their gazes met and connected. He had forgotten the joy of a child's viewpoint and sharing it with Isabel was even more delightful.

A sizzle of awareness zinged between them, pausing
his breath. It seemed he had also forgotten the strength
of a visual connection across a room from a woman he
desired.

On the phone speaker, Faith's exclamations of horror
came with an instant offer to return home.

'May I talk to Mummy, please, Chloe?' Isabel accepted the phone from her niece. 'You're not coming
home because of this. You'll be back the day after tomorrow and I'm feeling much better already.'

Dom held back impatience but as words continued
between them—a back-and-forth negotiation that was
going nowhere—he held up his hand. This could be long
and drawn out in the way of women. 'I wish to speak to
Raimondo, please.'

Isabel narrowed her eyes at him. Dom blinked as she
frowned. Such an expression! She was holding his gaze
with what looked like censure.

What? he wondered and closed his mouth. He thought
about her frown as he waited and replayed his request
in his mind. Or had it been an order? In six years had
he grown out of practice in dealing with those who did
not work for him?

'Domenico wishes to speak to Rai,' she was telling Faith. Her voice held a trace of astringency. 'Chloe and I are both fine. We just felt we needed to make you aware of our adventure.'

He should have called his brother on his own phone. That would have been a simple solution without machinations. He held up his hand.

She paused again, still annoyed. The slight frown was unaccustomed censure from this woman. She said, 'Just a minute,' to Faith.

'I will phone Raimondo myself. You are not to be rushed in talking to Faith.' He inclined his head, acknowledging that he had been abrupt. 'My apologies.'

Isabel lifted her gaze and her face softened. She nodded. 'Dom said he would call Rai himself. Yes, I will tell you what happened in more detail now the men are sorted but everything is fine. Honestly.'

Dom heard the shortening of his name and hid his pleased smile. She had referred to him as Dom. The first of many barriers he wanted gone. Perhaps the start of her letting him in. They had been through fraught circumstances of course, but still…a good sign. He opened the front door and pressed the number for his brother.

Isabel watched Dom leave the open-plan house to step back into the front courtyard. Two mobile phone conversations would have been annoying, so it was good he was gone. That didn't stop her from wishing she could hear his side of the conversation with Rai.

'Tell me again?' Faith's voice recalled her to the phone in her hand.

She explained again in more detail and after five more minutes, and another quick conversation with Chloe, Faith sounded satisfied that all was well and the call ended. Isabel had played down her sore ankle which, although feeling better after the ice and the pain medication, she knew would be a nuisance.

Dom had still not returned and Chloe drifted to the box of wrapped food and aromas filling the room with a woebegone look on her face. 'Can we have lunch now?'

'As soon as Uncle Dom is back. He's talking to your papà.'

'What if he takes hours?'

'That would be a problem.' She looked at the little girl. Chloe needed her lunch and was still tired from her recent illness. She needed a sleep after such an exciting morning. 'I'll text him.'

She found the number and did it quickly, before she chickened out.

Chloe is starving. Would you mind if we start without you?

Twenty seconds later Dom returned, smiling. He looked ten years younger when he did so and the smile was so rare to see it took her breath away. Though the seven years younger thing was a worry. She was feeling particularly old just at this moment.

'Thank you for reminding me of the lunch,' he said as he closed the door behind him. 'Of course Chloe must eat. The food will grow cold.'

He moved to the table but Chloe tugged on his trouser leg. 'Uncle Dom. We have to wash our hands before we touch food.'

Isabel sucked in her breath and winced. She'd need to prompt Chloe gently not to boss adults.

Dom's head lifted and, to her relief, she saw the effort he made not to laugh. 'Thank you, Chloe.' He crouched and looked at his niece. 'That is true. Thank you. It has been such a busy morning I am forgetting things.'

Chloe nodded approval and showed the way to the sink and proceeded to wash her own hands. 'That's okay. Aunty Izzy always says I am a good girl when I remember.'

They shared the soap and the water and Chloe offered her hand towel to dry. 'This is my special towel. Aunty Izzy sewed a lighthouse on it for me. You can use it.'

Dom looked across at her and she shrugged. Yes, she could sew. He looked back at the child. 'Thank you, Chloe.' His big hands were too large for the small scrap of material.

Then they attacked the box of goodies. Isabel wiped her fingers again with one of Chloe's little wipes and tried not to laugh as Chloe directed Dom on which things to serve her.

They ate off plastic plates because that was the cupboard Chloe could reach and Dom filled Isabel's plate with small portions of everything. The coffee when sipped had stayed hot enough and Isabel closed her eyes as she drank. Bliss. Perhaps her headache hadn't been helped by missing her coffee. She'd somehow omitted this morning's caffeine. The time for their planned lunch was well past now and she needed it.

Dom sat across from her, consuming his food economically with little attention, but paying attention to Isabel's needs, while she encouraged Chloe to finish so she could have a rest. When Chloe had finally eaten what she wanted she drooped as she sat, and Isabel shifted to rise.

'No.' Dom gestured. 'Stay.'

No? Stay? She was tempted to reply with a 'Woof'. Funny how she was lying down for these orders she'd normally rail against. Her head must be woozy.

'May I tuck you in, Chloe? That way, Aunty Izzy can keep her leg up.'

Minutes later Dom came back from Chloe's room smiling the new amused smile that Chloe seemed to drag out of him. It looked good on him. 'She is a quaint child with a kind heart.'

Isabel reran those words through her mind. Quaint? Kind? Such old-fashioned words. But true, yes. Chloe was both of those things and it pleased her that Dom could see these admirable qualities in his niece. 'She likes you.'

His eyes rolled at that. As if it wasn't true. Of course she liked her big handsome uncle. The man had issues.

'Through no effort of mine, I believe. I look like her new papà, that is all.' He shrugged those massive shoulders and, despite her attempt not to, her gaze followed the stretch of the fabric as he shifted. Such an impressive build and yet not too heavy. She marvelled that she hadn't heard the creak of tortured fabric. Remembered she was staring and pulled her eyes away.

Funny how she noticed Dom's broadness. While many men were built with strength and size, she wasn't drawn to smooth their skin or want to bury her face in their chests. Just his. Dom's. Every angle she had of Dom— and at the moment he soared above her—looked delightfully attractive to her.

Isabel murmured, 'You don't look exactly the same as your brother.'

He repeated the shrug and again she enjoyed the show. Straight-faced, he said, 'I am the more handsome, of course.'

Isabel blinked and returned her gaze to his face. He did not just say that, did he? Then she got it. 'You made a joke?'

His brows went up. 'Have I been such a sorry soul this shocks you?'

'Shock?' she murmured. Then shut her mouth. It might have been shock. Certainly surprise. 'No. Of course not,' she continued calmly. Settled herself after all the silly emotions that seemed to be floating and spinning in her addled brain. 'I'm pleasantly relieved, Domenico.' Her own joke.

He smiled. 'Come. You have called me Dom once. You can do so again. From now on, I hope.'

It shouldn't have been so hard to say his name out loud. 'Dom.' She said it a little too forcefully and darned if her cheeks didn't grow warm with heat.

He smiled. Getting a lot of those, she thought. Seemed a girl needed to be almost killed to start him smiling.

'How is your headache?' he asked, his expression growing serious with concern again.

She couldn't have that and smiled airily. 'Almost gone. The coffee helped, so thank you for bringing me that much-needed caffeine.'

'You are most welcome.'

The conversation had run its course and silence fell between them. This time the emptiness filled with tension and awareness. Their eyes met and held. Enough. She needed space. Air to breathe because he was stealing it from her lungs. She had to try again to make him leave. To get some space to regain her senses, which were now topsy-turvy from more than the effects of the accident.

'As I said, there really is no need for you to stay with us here when you have things to do. You've barely seen anything of the bay and you're leaving soon. We both know how to contact you if we're desperate.'

'And yet I will stay.' An expressionless man, no longer smiling. 'Would you be more comfortable on your bed for a rest while Chloe is asleep? I will sit out here in case she wakes. You could give the last of your headache the chance to disappear if you slept.'

It was a good idea. But she suspected Dom would feel the need to carry her into her room and the idea made her squirm with tension, and heat and want. She wasn't supposed to want those things. Not if she wasn't going to encourage him.

She remembered the last time his arms had held her. Safety and strength and scent.

Could imagine it again. Far too easily. But the bathroom would be good.

'You think too much,' he said quietly and stood, all man and all ready to take command. 'We both know it is a good idea. Are you stubborn, Isabel?'

She suspected she was acting that way. Sighed in defeat. 'If you give me your arm I would like to go to the bathroom.'

He leaned forward. 'I will give you both of my arms.' He said it simply and just as simply he picked her up and carried her through to the bathroom, stood her on one leg beside the sink and ensured she had a firm grip. 'Are you steady and balanced?'

'Yes. Thank you.' Primly.

She was relieved he left without looking back. No man had ever taken her to the ladies. Good grief.

Isabel stared in the mirror as the door shut. She had a graze on her cheek, but even the one not grazed looked pink from embarrassment. Blushing, at her age. The bump on her forehead looked purple. She grimaced.

Grow up, Aunt Isabel. Think of him as a male nurse. That made her chew her lip with amusement.

Then urgency reminded her she was here for a reason.

* * *

Once she'd finished in the bathroom, washed her hands and cleaned her teeth, Isabel knew she couldn't stand much longer without falling over. Her ankle had developed a throbbing pulse of pain with every heartbeat and the ache grew more insistent the longer she hung it down. She hopped to the door of the bathroom and opened it, looking for her nurse.

Dom rose from the white chair and crossed to her. He studied her face, which she'd noticed in the mirror had paled, and bent towards her. 'Your bed, I think.'

His arms and hands and fingers came around her again. Big, warm, safe. BWS. Like the initials of an Australian liquor store chain and just as addictive as its wares.

He reminded her of one of those dark, silky chocolate whisky liquors. A heady mix. Intoxicating and smooth as it burned and warmed and slid all the way down her throat. Like heat down her body. Like hot fingers on her skin.

Whoa there. No fingers were sliding anywhere. She was going down on the bed to rest.

He'd slowed. Stopped walking. Stood before her door and looked down into her face, untroubled by her tall frame in his arms, as relaxed as if she weighed no more than Chloe.

'What?' Caught by something he saw in her face. 'Are you daring me to kiss you, Isabel?'

Good grief. Had he read her thoughts? She hoped not. 'I've always thought dares were silly.'

'And what if I dare you to kiss me?'

'I am not so foolish.' But Isabel's body had melted to soft and languorous with her thoughts.

'Scared?' His dark eyes crinkled wickedly. His face drew closer.

'No. Not scared.' Her gaze dropped from those all-seeing eyes to his mouth. Full, curved lips. Sexy lips. Sinful lips. The impulsive Isabel of old would have tilted her face and pulled his head down to hers. She wanted to.

His voice caressed as his lips parted. 'Prove it.'

A dare the old Isabel would have taken.

And the new Isabel?

Isabel leaned up and he leaned down. Their lips brushed. Tingled. Supped in sliding, seductive sideways nibbles. A tide of longing surged between them, tossing her intentions of a fast peck aside and forcing her mouth more firmly against his. Her fingers tangled with the silky strands of his hair and her lips parted. She opened to his hot and honeyed mouth and heat blasted. Scorching and terrifying.

She froze, wiped the expression from her face and eased away.

'Do not stop,' he whispered. 'Come back.'

'I choose not to.' She battled not to flush with her thoughts.

She tried not to hurry into speech but the words came out too fast. 'Put me down, Dom.'

She needed to be out of his arms. Before she threw her own around him. 'We're grateful you were here when all this happened. Thank you for pushing me out of the way, Domenico.'

'Dom. And we know I added a little to your injuries.' Words tumbling as if to hide the kiss.

She mumbled, 'It could have been so much worse if the bike had picked me up in passing and squashed me against the pole.'

And that was true. She had been lucky. The thought

of that—and getting that worst-case scenario out of her mind and into words—strangely settled her. As if there were worse things than enjoying being in the arms of a handsome man. Kissing Dom.

His fingers tightened their hold until they gripped her a little too firmly, as if affected by her words. 'I do not like to think of that possibility.' He looked into her face, his strong features so close to her own. 'The thought of you being hurt pains me.'

Don't kiss me again. She hid her thoughts beneath her eyelids.

'Would have pained me too. Thank you.' Trying to lighten the mood, she attempted a smile but it wobbled around the edges. His hold eased as if he realised he was clutching her too tight.

'You are most welcome.' He tilted his head as if struck, and his eyes widened as if he'd just noticed her agitation. 'Now you are nervous in my arms. From one kiss?' A slow, teasing smile tilted his lips that were again too close to hers. He began to walk again. 'No need for that. We will play more dares another day.'

Oh, my. Another day. Isabel tried to disperse some of the response from her body but tension pulled her tight. Heating her belly. Tickling her skin with awareness. She wanted to say she wasn't nervous. Of now or the future. Liar. After that kiss, something was going on with her responses that she couldn't shut down.

'Not nervous,' she blurted but her cheeks burned and she tried to look away to hide her lying eyes. Dom held her captured in the depth of his scrutiny. Delving into her thoughts, as if seeing something he'd missed before.

His brows drew together. Then his eyes widened. 'And not the truth.' He laughed. 'Isabel, dissembling is not your forte. A woman who cannot lie. There is fun to be had with you in this.'

Oh, great, she thought, and was pretty sure her ears were burning too with embarrassment.

'But not while you are injured,' he clarified thoughtfully while his mouth tilted more. 'For now, it is time for you to rest.'

And what the heck did that mean? Did he have plans to carry her around and tease her another day? Play truth and dare with her? Did Italians even know that game? She turned her face away so he couldn't see her expression, but she felt flushed and embarrassed and after that possibly too stimulated for sleep.

As he lowered her she saw that while she'd been in the bathroom he'd brought the pillows back from the sofa. Plumped up and soft, he'd put two pillows at the head of the bed, and one positioned lengthways for her leg.

Inside, her chest tightened. She had always been the one to pick up after others. Be the support in crisis, yet always in the background. The one who put other's needs before her own. Even in her very few relationships, no man had done little comfort things for her like this.

Dom had even found the soft blanket on the chair that she kept for cool evenings. The space he'd created on her bedcovers looked inviting and he leaned over and placed her gently in the centre of the quilt like a fragile flower.

Then in one movement and with experienced hands he floated the fluffy throw over her until warmth settled feather-light around her. As if she were a child. Or precious. The softness against her skin settled some of the emptiness she felt at his release.

'Thank you.' Still feeling oddly small in the middle of the mattress with him looming over her.

He stepped back, as if he read her reaction. 'Rest.'

He left her staring at the ceiling.

He needed an heir. He wasn't for her. But, for the moment, it felt secretly special to be the recipient of such care. And despite the thoughts chasing and the sensations still thrilling in her ribcage she was able to close her eyes. Another amazing thought was that she could trust him to keep Chloe safe if she fell asleep, and that was good.

Three hours later Dom woke Isabel with tea. It was time to add ice to her leg anyway. He'd placed his own cup beside the window chair in her room and gone back for hers, hoping she would wake with the coming and going, but she hadn't.

It concerned him that she should sleep so heavily after a knock on the head. And a kiss that had shaken them both.

He'd been anxious for an hour now and had slipped in to count her heartrate twice to check she was medically stable. Her delicate wrist had pulsed slow and steady and she'd murmured once in sleep, turning her face to him with a soft smile. Definitely not awake, because she did not look at him with that gentle pleasure when conscious.

He wanted her to feel pleasure when she looked at him. The way he did when he looked at her. He remembered her mouth on his and wanted it again. But kissing in a dare did not really count. He wanted her to see him as a man with desire for her. Possibly—some time in the future—even *her* man, not just a young male relative by marriage she'd had to rely on.

At this moment she looked so peaceful and he resisted the urge to stroke her cheek with his finger. Concerned he would startle her, now he placed the cup on her bedside table with a small clunk and she stirred and opened her eyes.

'*Buonasera*, Isabel,' he said, and leant forward to offer his hand to help her sit up. 'Chloe is awake and colouring in her book quite happily.'

'I slept,' she said, and he smiled.

'Indeed. It is four p.m. and I thought you would not sleep tonight if I let you sleep much longer.'

Her eyes widened at the passage of time. 'Good grief.'

It was her favourite saying, he decided, pleased to have this one personal insight. 'How is your headache?' he asked.

She closed her eyes and opened them again. He saw the pupils contract and nodded. Then he was so distracted by the emerald pools he couldn't help staring into them until she looked away.

'Headache is fading,' she murmured.

The bruise was not. The mark on her forehead seemed a deeper purple than before.

He retreated to the chair beside the bed and sat down. Yes, he was being unfair, standing over her in her room. 'I hope you don't mind. I brought my own tea to share while you have yours.'

'Of course.' She looked through the door to where he knew she could see Chloe. 'Thank you. I could get used to you bringing me tea in bed. Though I'm a coffee girl in the mornings.' She put her hand up. 'I'm joking, of course.'

She blushed for some reason and it was so delightful he'd have liked to discuss the concept of him being here in the mornings. Tease her. Watch her blush more. But she was hurrying on. 'It seems I did need your welfare check if I slept through Chloe waking. I know what a little chatterbox she is after a nap.'

'Sleep is a good healer.' Though he had never found it so. He touched his own head to explain. 'You need ice on your bruise as well. After you finish your tea, we will see to that.'

The rest of the day was more of the same, Dom trying to anticipate Isabel's needs, Chloe ridiculously happy to have them both close and attentive. Isabel, it seemed, was too sore to care that she had lost her independence for the moment. The doctor in him watched her carefully for complications. The man fell more under her spell each hour that he spent with her. She was like the princess in the fairy tale he had never believed in. He still wasn't sure that he did believe.

CHAPTER SIX

ISABEL WAS WOKEN the next morning by a phone call from Faith to say they were coming home a day early.

'I'm disappointed,' Isabel said out loud when she'd completed the call.

Dom stood at the door of her room with a cup in his hand, an enquiring look on his aristocratic face. The man looked like a Renaissance hero; she could imagine him reaching down to pull her onto his horse, hard thighs against hers, his chest a wall behind her, one arm around her to ride away...

Good grief. Thankfully the aroma of coffee swirled into the room on a drift of air and dispelled the dream.

She wanted coffee. And him. But she could only have the first one.

'You are disappointed in my *caffè*?'

What? Oh. She'd said 'disappointed'. She had to laugh. 'No. Coffee smells wonderful, thank you. I'm disappointed in Faith and Rai coming home early.'

He stepped closer and placed the aromatic cup beside her on the night table then leaned and took the pillow from the quilt, tucking it behind her head and helping her to sit up. As if she were a weightless leaf from a tree rather than a full-grown woman.

Morning assistance from her magnificent nurse.

Then she remembered Faith. 'They're coming home today. Have already left.' She huffed. 'Their brief honeymoon was already too short!'

'They have a life together now.' Dom didn't seem fazed but then he would be free of responsibility once Chloe returned to her parents. 'And if you had been in your niece's place? Would you have stayed away?'

Darn it. No. She would have been back last night.

That realisation made her cross and she never got cross. Well, not often before Dom swashbuckled into her life.

She looked at the tall man watching her face with amusement. Amusement was good on him and she squashed the spurt of irritation in herself. He'd brought her coffee. Had slept in a chair between his self-imposed three-hourly attentions. She owed him thanks and serenity and a modicum of good humour.

What was it about this man who made it so hard to stay settled in her quiet life, content with her few friends, ecstatic with her privacy and the solitude of her new home? Dom's arrival and intrusion into her life had affected her ability to remain even-tempered and she didn't know how to stop that snowball of emotion rolling down the hill all the way to the beach below.

But she'd have to stop it. Build a wall again. Think normal thoughts.

She sipped her coffee slowly—it was so good, just right. She rarely managed to make it so delicious even though she'd owned the machine for years.

Dom sat opposite and drank his own small cup in the chair by the window.

Apparently he'd claimed that chair for himself.

She suspected it wouldn't look right now without him in it.

Once she'd drained her cup she slid back the covers and lifted her damaged leg across and out. Pain pulled, better but still there, and she hissed her attempt to hold it in.

'Do you need the bathroom?'

'No.' Her eyes narrowed at him. 'I need my independence.'

He shrugged, refusing to respond to her ill humour. 'Which you cannot have until your ankle has recovered.' He tilted his head at her. 'I did not think you would be a difficult patient, Isabel, but I see I was mistaken.'

She huffed out a laugh. 'I'm trying, and you're right, not always successfully. And if you were in my place,' she muttered, referencing his previous comment about Faith coming home.

He laughed. It was short and awkward, as if he were out of practice and he'd surprised himself. He'd sure as heck surprised her.

'Of course, yes, I would be the same. So perhaps I do sympathise with your frustration. I will send in your niece, who has been waiting for you to wake up, and she will be delighted to find your clothes for you. Then I will help you to the bathroom.'

By the look in his eyes she could tell he'd decided to carry her.

She could fight it—should fight it—she was being weak, turning herself into a wimp wanting to be coddled. But you know what? He'd be gone soon. Why the heck would any sane woman refuse Dom in all his glory?

Because it was bad for her.

Like eating a whole box of chocolates at once.

Sweet Dom. Strangely, she found her good humour restored.

'It is almost time for the ice again,' Dom said with a check of his watch.

Isabel sought her usual Zen state of calm and sense. When the twenty-four hours had passed, they could stop the ice. Three hourly cold compresses for twenty minutes each through the night, attended to by Dom, and one trip to the bathroom being carried. The man had arms of steel, shoulders to die for, and being held against that ripped manly chest meant she could breathe in his incredible scent up close. And relive the kiss.

This all should have kept her in a state of agitation totally opposed to sleep. And yet…

Every time Dom had left her tucked in, her toes had curled with delight and she'd sighed happily off again into a deep restful sleep.

This morning she was embarrassed at just how much caring he'd had to do for her and how easy it was for her to let him. Totally not what she would have thought she'd feel.

Several hours later the phone call came that the newlyweds were almost home. Isabel had hoped her ankle would have improved enough so she could meet them when they arrived. To try out her weight-bearing, she swung her leg off the sofa and limped to the sink to fill her water glass. Not so successful. Once across the room, she dreaded the trip she would need to get back again.

Dom rose from his chair, where he'd been engrossed in his computer screen. 'I wish you would sit down. I could have filled that for you. You had only to ask.' He gestured to the child, who was peering out of the front window watching for the car. 'Or Chloe would have liked to help.'

He offered his arm and, wrapping her fingers around the steel of his muscled forearm, she was left with no doubt he'd manage most of her weight easily. Yet still she wobbled. Her breath sucked in as he picked her up so easily, becoming so fabulously familiar, and nestled her weight gently on the sofa with a 'tsk'.

When she had her breath back she chided, 'You'll hurt your back.'

His haughty brows rose. 'I am not so poor a specimen.'

No, he wasn't a poor specimen, she repeated to herself as she sank back into the cushions and hoped the pain would ease with the height of her limb. Her ankle throbbed now and he put the ice pack back into place.

'Please leave it there for an extra five minutes.' A command she had to agree with as the relief was almost instant as the cold penetrated.

And yep. She knew. Dumb idea to get up.

Dom frowned down at the stubborn woman. 'I will take Chloe outside to wait. Will you stay there until I return?' When she didn't answer, Dom nodded, cautiously satisfied. 'She is too excited to stand still in the house. I will hold her hand until the car is stopped.'

Isabel's mutinous mouth made him want to smile but he didn't. Watching carefully, he saw the moment she reached for her usual serenity. Drew it around her like a trusty cloak. Pretending that she wasn't affected by his touch. Or his orders. He wasn't fooled.

Such a mistaken trap one could fall into. The woman wasn't placid at all.

Outside, they could see the Lexus coming.

Chloe held Dom's hand as she jumped up and down on one spot until the car pulled up outside his brother's house. Dom looked down at her. The child's cheeks were flushed, green eyes shining with excitement, but obediently she waited until the car stopped and the road was safe. As soon as Dom let go of the child's hand she flew out of the gate and crossed to her mother, who had leapt from the car and wrapped her arms around her as if they had been away for a year, not two nights.

The way Teresa had wrapped her arms around Tomas. The memory was bittersweet but precious. He was changing.

Chloe's sweet voice carried back to Dom. 'I missed you. We had an exciting time,' she added. 'Uncle Dom carried Aunty Izzy and put her in the police car.' Then, as if remembering her manners, 'Did you have a nice time?'

Rai met his gaze and his brows lifted, as did his mouth in a smile. It did sound quite spectacular put like that. Dom acknowledged the truth with a nod and thought wistfully that his brother had found a wonderful family.

Faith hugged her daughter. 'Yes, darling, but we're sorry to hear that Aunty Izzy was hurt.'

Dom walked across to Rai and they shook hands in greeting. 'She is much better this morning.'

Chloe prattled on. 'Uncle Dom has been looking after us. I've been showing him where everything is in the house.'

'What a clever girl.' Faith smiled and cuddled her daughter to her again. She looked up at him. 'How have you managed her, Dom? Has she been this excited the whole time?'

'Chloe is a credit to you, Faith. A lovely child and very helpful.'

Rai said, 'And Isabel?'

He looked at his brother. 'Isabel does not like being an invalid, but the ice and compression has repaired some of her ankle strain. If she would stay off it. This morning she said her headache has gone.'

Behind him he felt—hadn't heard, yet sensed—the approach of Isabel.

He turned and there she was, the crutches supporting her body weight off her injured ankle somewhat precariously. 'You could not wait until Faith came to you?'

She assumed her tranquil guise. 'I appreciate your suggestion, Dom, but I'm fine. Hello, dear Faith.' She leaned over and kissed her niece's cheek, offered that smile Dom looked for. 'You look happy.'

'As she should,' Rai said as he too leaned down to cheek Isabel's cheek. 'She has been cossetted and spoiled by her new husband.'

'Lucky woman,' Isabel teased but her face had pulled into the expression Dom had come to realise was Isabel masking pain. 'Chloe and I have also been well cared for.'

'Are you sure your ankle feels fine?' Dom couldn't help himself.

'I wanted to come out and join the welcoming party.' He noted she didn't answer the question.

'Then perhaps I should have brought out a chair,' he almost growled. Foolishness. Stubborn woman.

'What a lovely idea,' she agreed equably. 'But not necessary. Now that I've seen the arrival, I'll leave you all. Faith can visit me when she's settled.'

She waved at Chloe's head, bent against her mother's middle. 'Chloe has packed her bag ready to come home. You can pick it up later. I'll go back and pop my leg up.'

Dom raised his hand at his brother. 'Welcome home.' But his eyes were for Isabel. 'I will help you up the steps.'

She took his arm and he felt the weight she tried to keep off her ankle. She limped badly. He huffed out his disgust, took the crutches from her and handed them to his brother, then picked her up.

Isabel hissed, 'Put me down.'

'No.'

Neither looked back as she was carried back inside.

Dom could hear his brother laughing behind him and Faith admonishing him to silence. He was pleased they didn't bring the crutches in just then.

He thought when he had her resting on the sofa that she would berate him.

Instead, she turned to face away. 'You were right. Walking down the steps outside hurt too much to be worth it.'

And his ire fled. It appeared she was more annoyed with herself than with him. He'd held back the frustration he wanted to direct at her for causing herself such pain but instead he blew the breath out. 'You know it will heal quickly if you let it. Would you like to lie on your bed for half an hour and I will put ice on your leg?'

'Thank you.'

He realised it must be extremely painful for her to agree so easily. 'Perhaps you require some medication for the discomfort?'

She turned towards him and smiled, though the smile was crooked and showed strain. 'I don't know that I deserve something after that foolishness.'

He bent, slid his arms around the now familiar curves of Isabel and lifted her from the sofa where he'd just placed her. She felt good in his arms. Wonderful. Not only because it needed to be done. He felt the tension inside his chest loosen. They had formed a rapport between them then.

'Perhaps if I was in your place I would do the same.'

She rolled her eyes. 'Right.'

Isabel lay on the bed where Dom had propped her, let the gentle relief of the mild analgesia he'd given her seep into her bloodstream and thought about the morning. She could hear him clattering around in the kitchen and she suspected he was making her a cup of ginger tea. Perhaps one for both of them, judging by the clunk of mugs on the bench top.

He really should go back to medicine because he was a caring person.

And a lovely man.

But not *her* far too young lovely man.

The sooner he was out of her house the sooner she could reinforce those thoughts. Wanting closeness with someone as damaged as Dom could be dangerous— though hopefully only for her and not for him. But it was hard to resist when he cossetted her so delightfully and in her miserable useless ankle state she could use some fun.

Though it had been embarrassing when he had picked her up in front of Faith and Rai. There would be some explaining to do and she doubted her niece would wait long to have a comfortable 'chat'. Probably less than an hour to wait. Isabel huffed a small laugh.

Living with Faith, and her single mother for Faith's teenage years as well, had given them a very close understanding of each other. Faith was the daughter she'd almost had. But now never would.

Dom reappeared with the tea and she turned her thoughts from that wistful subject. She inhaled the waft of aroma. Yep, refreshing ginger. 'Thank you. Just what I feel like.'

'I'm pleased. May I sit with you while we share tea?'

'Of course.' Didn't he always? He'd been in this room so many times tending to her she couldn't understand why he'd asked. But now? The idea made her smile. They didn't have Chloe chaperoning, perhaps?

Dom was such a delight to admire but she wasn't going

to pounce on him. Or he on her. Sadly. No, *not* sadly. She was not in any way, even a little, disappointed with that.

He offered her favourite cup, the one sprinkled with tiny violets she'd bought in the Côte d'Azur, and sat on the chair under the window with his own. She tried to distract herself from studying Dom too much and noticed the one he'd chosen. The cup with the red fox, with a picture of the animal instead of the word. A gift from someone at work who'd been amused. She wondered if Dom understood the meaning. It was appropriate for her mixed and violent feelings about this man.

For fox sake.

Dom crinkled his brows at her unexpected smile. He was aware he'd missed something that amused her.

She didn't enlighten him so he added, 'Chloe will be happy to have her mother home.'

'Yes.' Isabel leaned back at the thought of Chloe across the road, chatting nineteen to the dozen to Faith. 'She's a charming child but she's a mummy's girl. Most definitely.'

'And yet her aunt is also charming.'

Was she? Instead of responding to this she corrected him gently. 'I'm her great-aunt, not her aunt.' Saying it out loud, often, reinforced their considerable age difference and made her feel more secure that she wouldn't be foolish over this man. 'You forget my relationship to Chloe and my age.'

His brows lifted. 'Age does not obsess me.' He paused. 'As it seems to obsess you.'

Dom continued, 'My brother tells me you have lived with Faith's mother, and then Faith since Chloe's birth?'

'True both times. They needed help to work and raise a child, although both would have managed if they'd had to. It seems the women in our family don't have much luck with relationships.'

He frowned, and maybe that had sounded too general so she continued, 'My sister's husband left when Faith was small. But I can see that Rai is going to change that luck now,' she hastened to add.

'Indeed. My brother is very happy.' He inclined his head. Looked at her with intent eyes. 'I wonder if you include yourself in that generalisation of ill-fated love?'

And she'd manoeuvred herself into this conversational minefield with her own stupidity. She sipped her tea to give herself time to think.

She supposed she could share a little of her background. In the broadest of brushstrokes.

'My one attempt at true love—more than fifteen years ago, mind you—left me abandoned by the man I thought would be there in my time of need. I'm not willing to feel like that again. My life has been happy as a single woman. I've travelled, loved it and made a living wage from writing and photography, and yet was able to be with my family when needed. I have friends. My family. Few regrets.'

She didn't mention the midwifery career that she'd dropped after the loss of her baby. She regretted that. She'd loved the wonder of being with a woman giving birth.

There was regret for the loss of faith in the man who had left her when they'd found out she was unlikely to ever be a mother. Perhaps even her loss of faith in all men was a regret.

Her inability to carry her own baby to term was too big a loss to call it a regret. That would take much finer brushwork than she was prepared for.

Time to change the subject. 'Faith tells me you and Rai were orphaned and lived with your grandfather as children.'

'*Si.*' A sigh. 'That is correct.'

'Rai and Faith have that in common then. Being raised by another family member other than their parents.'

His face twitched. 'Not so similar. Faith had you.' He made an expansive gesture indicating all that she was. 'Our grandfather was a sadly bitter man.'

'Who took you in.'

'True. He ran a large pharmaceutical company in Firenze which I later took over. Raimondo was wise to stay in medicine.'

'Do you miss being a doctor?' she asked.

'If my grandfather had not needed me to join the firm I would not have chosen pharmacy.'

Which didn't really answer her question. He didn't say he would have returned to medicine, and she wondered why.

'From my perspective, you're a wonderful doctor. I feel very well cared for.'

He smiled at that. 'I am glad. But it has been too long to feel I could give all that is necessary to a wide range of patients. I would not be giving my best, as I would have if I'd continued in the profession.'

Ah. He'd decided he wouldn't be good enough. He'd lost trust in himself. Humility was fine but he was wasting his talents—especially now, when the number of doctors was falling. 'Don't you think a refresher and study would help? You have done some aid work fairly recently.'

'True. My brother seems to think so. But I have not been a doctor in Firenze since early in my marriage.'

Did she address the elephant in the room or back away? Backing away wasn't her style—unless it was from her own story. But neither was trampling on people's feelings. Very gently she asked, 'How long were you married before you lost your wife and son, Dom?'

He was silent and she thought he wasn't going to answer. She waited, not pushing him. He could answer or not, but her fingers tightened on the cup. She was hoping he would.

Finally he said, 'Eight years.'

Isabel tried some mental arithmetic. 'You must have married at a young age. Twenty or so? Childhood sweethearts?'

'Not at all. Ours was an arranged marriage... Teresa was the daughter of a business partner of my grandfather's, but we had known each other for several years before then. Early in our marriage I worked at the hospital in Firenze and the hours were long. When he first became ill, my grandfather suggested I take a sabbatical from medicine, doing only occasional shifts, and mostly I worked for him.

'Once Tomas came along Teresa was eager for me to do more normal hours and take more part in family life. Of course, after his death I took over the company fully.'

He rolled his neck as if to loosen the tension he'd gathered discussing his past. 'I'm glad I chose fewer hours when it turned out I had so little time to share with them.'

'Of course. Losing your family is something you'll never leave behind. It's not possible to forget but hopefully sharing the memories can bring you some solace.'

His anguish made her heart ache. And she had nothing to offer except stupid platitudes. She wanted to reach out and touch his hand. Offer comfort and support? Because she'd brought this on him, asking him to share his story, wanting to hear it for herself. Trying to understand why he had isolated himself from others for so long.

'I'm sorry to have asked. You don't have to talk about this…if it's too much.'

He shifted in his seat, looked away as if seeing another place and time. 'It has been almost six years. Then last month, after the fire…' He paused. 'It destroyed the factory.'

He had been through the mill. 'We heard that from Rai. I'm so sorry.'

'Don't be. That disaster did me a favour in a way, although it left me feeling…unbalanced. Perhaps I needed to lose my only purpose in life, even if it wasn't a purpose I enjoyed.' He looked at her. Hurt, pained and maybe a little embarrassed. 'Rai's wedding has been a very pleasant diversion from unpleasant circumstances.'

'I'm glad. You've added to the occasion by being here. We've enjoyed meeting you. When do you go back?'

'Christmas Eve.'

She'd been leaning forward, riveted by all he shared, wanting to be closer to him—not wanting to miss a word or a nuance of expression?

Isabel sat back, startled. Her hand lifted unconsciously to her chest as if to protect her heart. Protect herself from pain.

No.

Somehow she'd assumed he'd be here for another week. How had that happened? 'Why not wait till after Christmas? Chloe will be sad. You'll miss Rai's joy with his first Christmas as a dad. That's stupid.' She glared at him, suddenly angry with him. 'Crazy man.' Clapped a hand over her mouth. A step too far. 'I'm sorry.'

He looked a little stunned but strangely amused. 'I have commitments made.' He shrugged. 'It is a good time to travel. I would have left earlier, but Rai insisted I stay until he returned.'

He would do what his brother asked. But he was stubborn too, she realised.

Stubborn? Funny how that endeared him to her and not the opposite. But relief swept through her that he'd been brought out of his pain from the past and wasn't holding her lack of subtlety against her. Time to lighten the mood.

'Did he force you to stay, your brother? What a bully.' She tilted her head at him. 'Wait… I thought you were older than him.'

Dom blinked and then his shoulders eased as his mouth tilted crookedly, acknowledging her joke. '*Sì*. By ten minutes. He should show me respect.'

Discreetly she blew out a sigh of relief. It was good to leave heavy topics behind. Especially those she had instigated.

A knock sounded at the door. 'That will be Faith.' Isabel had no doubt. She'd be dying to find out how much Isabel liked Dom. How Isabel got along with Dom? How Isabel had managed with Dom's domineering presence in her home? She'd bet on all of those.

Dom stood. Took her empty cup. 'If so, I will go to Rai and leave you safely in Faith's hands.'

Isabel heard him place the cups in the kitchen before crossing to the front door. When he let Faith into the house she heard, sotto voce, 'Do try to keep her from walking about.'

Faith's amused reply was anything but soft. 'I'll try but I'm not carrying her anywhere.'

Dom laughed. 'My number is in Isabel's mobile, should my woman-carrying services be required. I will return for my computer before I leave.' She heard the door shut behind him.

Faith appeared at the door to the bedroom. 'He actually laughed.' She turned her head to the door he'd disappeared through. 'Who is that guy? Where's Domenico?'

Isabel snorted. 'He is less dark and gloomy. Chloe has really helped him, I think. She threw her arms around him the first night and he looked so taken aback and then gratified.'

'Chloe, huh?' Patent disbelief in her voice. 'What about you? Have you thrown your arms around him?' Faith pretended surprise. 'Hang on. You have. I saw. Your arms went around his neck when he carried you.'

And she'd known that was coming. 'Very funny,' Isabel said. 'Make yourself tea before you sit down. I've just had one, and I want to hear all about the honeymoon.' She considered that statement and shook her head. 'No. Not all of it.'

Faith blushed and ducked back into the open-plan area and the kitchen, which made Isabel smile. Ah… Young love.

When Faith returned two minutes later she sat where Dom had been sitting and leaned forward. 'So? Has he been carrying you around everywhere?'

'I have crutches, but the ankle still throbs when I hang it down. So yes, when necessary. My stupid ankle won't take any weight and yesterday I was still a little groggy and not so stable on the crutches.'

'You hit your head. Chloe told me it made you sleepy. I can see the bruise.'

Isabel sighed. 'I imagine it will get more colourful before it goes away. They X-rayed my ankle before I came home. It is only a sprain but it's driving me mad.'

'I can imagine.' She leaned even further forward and dropped her voice. 'How's Dom as a nurse?'

And there it was.

Amazing. Fabulous.

'Pretty wonderful.' Isabel kept her voice light, but the truth was there; he'd been brilliant. A hard act to follow. She tried a change of subject. 'At least this all happened after your beautiful wedding and not before.'

'Oh, wow, yes. And wasn't it just gorgeous?' Faith smiled dreamily as she thought back to her special day. She sank back into her chair and blew out a contented breath. 'I'm so happy.'

Isabel felt her chest warm with pleasure. Dearest Faith. 'I'm so glad. You deserve happiness. Both of you. The three of you.'

Faith sat straighter. 'And so.' She pointed one finger. 'Do you.'

And here we are again. Isabel managed to stop a sigh from escaping. Just.

'I *am* happy. Once my ankle is healed I'll go back to travelling. I cannot wait.'

Faith's face fell.

Oops. Not tactful or what she'd meant but it was too late.

'We have cramped your style, haven't we, Chloe and I? I don't know how I would have managed without you.'

No, that was exactly what she didn't mean. 'Good grief, Faith. You would have managed fine. Don't be silly. I wouldn't have missed the last five years for a million Qantas Frequent Flyer points. I've loved sharing Chloe's early years and will be rushing home to my own little house between jaunts.' She held her niece's gaze. 'No more of that nonsense. Please.'

'I'm sorry. Thank you.' Mollified, it seemed it was Faith's turn to change the subject. 'Do you think Dom will go back to Italy in a better frame of mind after being here?'

'I think that's possible. He still has two days with you all when he moves back tonight.'

Faith shook her head. 'But he's not. Moving back with us. Didn't you know? He refused to stay when we came back. Newly married couple he said. He's booked a room at Rose's B&B at the edge of town.'

Isabel grimaced. She could feel her own recoil from the idea of Dom staying away down the street when he needed to be with family. The man was determined to isolate himself.

'That's ridiculous. He only has two nights left and he needs to spend it with you guys.'

'Exactly what I said.' An amused glint in Faith's eye made Isabel lean back warily against the pillows. 'You could convince him to stay with you here, if you didn't mind. You've got Chloe's room free now if he could cope with sleeping in a single bed. Pretend you need him?'

Pretend she needed him? She'd do no such thing.

'I'm not telling fibs for you.' But the man was hopeless at caring for himself. He needed his family, especially now he was finally moving towards recovery from his grief. But it wasn't her place to put him up. Yet an inner voice suggested he was already here. She could ask him. No.

Faith pushed. 'That's if you wouldn't mind him sleeping in the cottage without supervision now Chloe's gone…?'

'Don't be silly.' A chaperone? As if she and Dom needed a watcher. Good grief. She was pretty sure a five-year-old wasn't observant either in that regard.

'Just a thought,' Faith said innocently and sipped her tea.

When Dom walked into his brother's house, Rai winked at him. Dom's brows lifted mockingly. 'A facial tic after only two days' marriage, brother?'

Rai's startled laugh turned into a big grin. '*Sì*. Excellent joke. My brother is back?'

'*Accidenti!*' The most polite swear-word he could think of. First Isabel and now his brother, shocked that he had made a joke.

Rai continued, 'So you carry the lovely Isabel everywhere now?'

'I carry Isabel when she is foolish. Which she does not choose to be too often.'

'Chloe tells us the motorbike whizzed past all of you very fast and smashed on the pole.'

Dom flinched. Felt his stomach clench at the remembered fear. '*Sì*. Too close.'

Rai stepped forward and he knew he had seen his distress. He touched his shoulder. 'It was meant for you to be here then, Dom. Thank you for keeping Chloe and Isabel safe.'

Dom itched to divert the attention from himself and to lose the thoughts of Isabel's near miss. That was too much. 'How was your honeymoon?'

A pause and then his brother allowed the change of topic. 'Short but no less perfect. My wife and I are very happy.' Rai clapped him on the shoulder meaningfully. 'It would be good to see you happy too.'

Dom shrugged. There was no answer to that. Yet. 'I must pack. Your house is an excellent dwelling, but I am still moving out for the next two nights.'

'Ridiculous. Stay here. We have many rooms. Or stay across the road and care for Isabel?'

'I will come often. But I will sleep at the small accommodation I spoke about last week. We have had this discussion.'

Rai tilted his head and a sorrowful expression crossed his face. 'What of Isabel? How will she manage?'

Dom narrowed his eyes at him. 'I'm here if Isabel needs me. I believe she is desirous of her independence.' He looked around as if something was missing. 'And Chloe?' Dom smiled. 'You have been home for an hour and have lost her already?'

'There are three ships close on the horizon and she is with her telescope.'

'Then I too will see the ships on my way to my packing.'

'Running away, brother?' Rai's voice followed him up the stairs.

'*Sì.*'

By the time Faith left for her own house, Isabel was sick of resting on her bed with her leg up. She needed to get to the bathroom after all the tea she'd consumed this morning.

The knock at the door, a firm Dom-sounding knock, signalled the return of her nemesis and she called out to him to enter as she slid her feet out of the bed.

'Are you going somewhere?' His question sounded slightly amused as he appeared at her door.

'To the bathroom. And no, I don't want help.'

His brows went up. 'I've come for my computer. Can I do anything else for you before I leave?'

'No. And I'm feeling cross so you'd best hurry away.'

He leant his big frame on the doorframe. 'Cross? Isabel? Is that possible?'

She huffed out a sigh and laughed unwillingly as she straightened and balanced. 'I've just realised I'm stuck here for days until the blasted ankle gets better. And I can't believe you're going across town to sleep and not across the road to your brother.'

'I have no wish to invade the privacy of newlyweds.'

He watched her, leaning on the door, all nonchalant gorgeous male whom she could ask to stay with her. Easily. As a favour to him. To Rai. It wasn't as if she was a young woman with a reputation to guard. But still, it was an awkward thing to say out loud.

He strode into the room and stood beside her, not touching. Just there if she needed him and, despite the frown she gave him, she was glad of his presence. She concentrated on her hands and feet, avoiding the other thoughts that were distracting her.

'I don't seem to have a walking-with-crutches synapse in my brain. It's still tricky to balance on the wooden pegs.' She shook her head at him as she manoeuvred herself towards the bathroom. 'I need to get used to these,' she said, pausing for a break. 'As for staying across the road. There's a five-year-old child living in the house. I doubt you're going to cramp their style.'

He didn't take his eyes off her and moved beside her to the bathroom. 'And yet I shall leave them.'

'You could stay here.' The words were out. She hadn't intended to say them but there they were, spread between them like unopened letter bombs, and she waited with bated breath for him to answer. Now she was terrified she'd encouraged him to think she was asking him to take their odd relationship to the next level. 'Chloe's bedroom is free.' A throwaway comment that almost sounded mocking, but she was mocking her own rollercoaster emotions not him.

'Such a gracious invitation.'

It hadn't been, as well he knew. That made her smile. He made her smile. 'Yes, well. It's only a single bed.'

'It's very kind of you to offer,' Dom said with a slight brow raise. 'Are you sure you wish for a guest?'

No. And not this one in her house for another two

nights. Alone with her. Tempting her. Sharing space and feelings. Telling herself she was crazy, she turned her head to look at him but swayed with the loss of concentration and he put a hand out. 'Steady.'

The swaying stopped. 'I'm fine.' Now. 'Thank you.' Good that she had her balance back. Falling at his feet wasn't an option.

'I have made a booking for a room.'

She looked up. Met his gaze. Held it. 'You shouldn't go and stay with strangers.' This she meant. 'Stay as long as you like...' she forced a smile '...but don't bully me when you see me limping around.'

She closed the door in his face.

When she came out five minutes later her bed was pulled back to order neatly and her new boarder was standing at the door to Chloe's old room.

She felt calmer—which was strange, given the circumstances—but that state had been achieved by a severe yet silent talking-to in the bathroom mirror. 'Faith has made up Chloe's room with clean sheets. I think she was planning on you staying here.'

He didn't smile but she was pretty sure he had an amused glint in his eye. 'I can work for my board. Perhaps bring you tea when you need. Straighten your pillows.'

'There's no need, but I was thinking that was a given. Spend time with your brother and his family. That's what everyone needs, with you leaving so soon. You'll be having your meals with them and Faith has promised to send over dinner for me for a day or two. I'll sort myself for lunch.'

'And you will sit here in a lonely state?'

'I'm fine on my own and my house is handy for you.'

'Handy is not what I think of staying here, Isabel.'

Then what were you thinking about staying here?
The thought made her skin tingle. She wasn't going to
ask him. Her cheeks warmed but silently she swung her
crutches past him and went into the lounge room to sit
back on the sofa and lift her leg up to stop it swelling.
In truth, it was becoming less painful to hang her foot
down for a short time.

Soon she would be better. He would be gone. Life
would go on.

He sat opposite her in the big white armchair he'd
slept in the first night. Another piece of her furniture he
seemed to have imprinted with his personality. 'I will
be happy to know you would not be alone if you fell on
your own in the night.'

Poor, lonely Isabel. Pity.

That was all. No, she wasn't disappointed. Not at all.

She'd jumped to conclusions, thinking he wanted to
spend time with her.

Isabel let her head fall back and she looked at the tall,
gorgeous man relaxing opposite. She was an idiot to in-
vest so much angst into this. 'I'm surprised you'd want
to stay here when I'm so crabby.'

He laughed. 'Crabby? Like a crab, walking sideways
with your crutches?'

'No.' She had to grin at the thought. 'Crabby, cranky,
cross is what I'm looking for. I think I'm going a little
crazy, stuck between my bed and this sofa for more than
a day. I hadn't realised how much I relied on my daily
walks and getting about on my own two feet. It's not your
fault and I may even be glad of your company.'

'Of course. Perhaps I can help with this.'

*You could be more gentle next time when you fall on
me.* A wicked thought. She imagined his big body low-
ering over hers. The heat. The scent of him. And if that

didn't make her blush, nothing would. She resisted the urge to fan her face.

He went on thoughtfully, 'If your ankle is better tomorrow, would you like to go out? I can borrow Rai's car. There is much to see that I have missed since I arrived. You could guide me and lose your "crabbiness" with a little freedom.' His brows lifted innocently. 'Is that a word?'

'Crabbiness?' She laughed. 'Yes, that is definitely a word.' As if he didn't know. She'd come to realise that these Salvanelli men could drop most of their accent or language idiosyncrasies at will. 'Sounds like something I would enjoy for tomorrow. Thank you.'

'Then I will cancel the accommodation and mention to Rai and Faith that I will stay here.' He inclined his head. 'Thank you, Isabel.'

And she needed to have her head read.

CHAPTER SEVEN

WITHOUT THE COMPANY of Chloe sharing their space, the evening with Dom felt more visceral. Everything thrummed. The air. The ocean outside. Her skin.

No amusing chatter from the child like last night, while normal chores and meals were managed. Now that her shock from the accident had receded and her ankle had finally begun to improve, instead of going to bed to rest, they sat in the lounge companionably, but both aware of the other. She could feel something but it wasn't uncomfortable.

He relaxed back in her new recliner while she rested comfortably, her leg propped along the sofa, and they both pretended they were only chance in-laws and house-mates. His dark skin and strong features looked far too good there, framed by the white leather. She'd suggested a movie, one set in Florence during the Second World War, to share memories of familiar scenery, but they'd paused it while he made another pot of tea.

Words slid out unexpectedly. 'I'm surprised it's so easy with you here, Dom.'

He lifted his brows with that hint of quiet amuse-ment in his eyes. 'I have some social skills and practise them on you.'

Yes, he did. 'Thank you.' She laughed. Like a schoolgirl. This was ridiculous. 'I haven't watched a movie for a long time. I thought this particular one might help us find topics of interest. But finding conversation with you is easy.'

She'd thought it would be awkward but any silence that fell between them felt right. Perfectly timed and not rushed.

Not just companionable. There was intimacy, their glances meeting when a scene from the film connected with them, or a place resonated.

Her cheeks had warmed and her body had thrummed. The last time she'd met his gaze he'd taken a long time to look away. Too much delicious connection and the first inkling of the loss she was afraid she would feel when he flew away. Hence the reason she'd suggested they press pause on the movie and have a cup of tea. Hopefully to calm the pulse of awareness that was steadily building between them like a distant jungle drum. Even her breath felt sensitive in her throat.

While he boiled the kettle and assembled mugs, she steered the conversation back to the reality of his leaving and needing to make a life for himself. To remind both of them. 'What are your plans when you return to Florence?'

'I must decide if I am a pharmacist or doctor.'

She hadn't thought there was much choice. 'Might be hard to be a pharmaceutical magnate without a factory?'

'There are concerns with that, of course. And issues that need resolving rapidly or we will all lose much of what we gained. But my priorities have changed.' He smiled. 'I am not the same man who left Florence, reluctantly, for my brother's wedding.'

Humour about his life in Florence. Excellent. 'Should you decide on medicine, will that be a hard decision?'

He looked at her, his scrutiny intense. 'No. Not now

that I have discovered I wish to live and not just exist, which I fear I had fallen deeply into. I should follow a pursuit that draws me and not just diverts my mind.'

'So?' She cocked her head. 'Medicine?'

'Medicine.' He grimaced. 'But there is work to be done to be as useful as I should be.'

She didn't think it would be too hard for Dom to catch up. Fierce intelligence shone from his dark eyes and, except for the darkness he'd dwelt in for so long, she doubted he'd ever had trouble remembering anything.

'Pharmacy would have kept you abreast of treatments, and you have had your field work to keep you credentialled. I think you're hard on yourself.'

'As my brother has mentioned to me.' His turn to incline his head and spread his hands. 'And what is your passion, Isabel? Raimondo says you work at the hospital.'

No. I was a midwife, but one day I ran from it because it hurt too much to watch others achieving what I could not. Women giving birth deserved better than I could give at that time.

Instead she said, 'I take photographs and write travel stories when I can. Meanwhile, office work has good hours, reasonable pay and I like the people I work with. I'll travel again soon.' It wasn't everything she wanted but it was enough. She was perilously close to lying by omission and she wanted out of that position. 'Lighthouse Bay must feel very different to Florence.'

'*Sì*. And beautiful in a different way.' He was watching her again and the heat under her skin was back. 'Your beaches are most amazing, with the white sand. I like the way the waves make everything fresh.'

'We have beaches with pebbles too. In other places in Australia.' Her mood shifted again. Rollercoaster indeed. She turned to him and smiled. They both seemed to be doing a lot of that. Almost as if they'd had a glass of champagne. 'Though maybe not the same pebbles as you have in Italy.' No, now she was gabbling. 'But Australian culture must feel different.'

'*Sì*, but easy. I have been the one who is different.' He shook his head. 'Since coming here, it is as if I can see another life. One I thought I had lost. One I did not care to have lost.'

Yes. She'd heard that of him. And seen it in him during those first few days, and glimpses yesterday as he'd told her about his marriage. She liked this new man better.

'Why do you think that is so?'

'In Firenze, every time I was reminded of Teresa's death the guilt burned me.'

'Why guilt, Dom?' A big question to ask—maybe she shouldn't have. The last thing she wanted was to plunge him back into the darkness and pain, to see that other man he'd risen from. But she wanted to know, to hear the whole story, so she had to ask.

He looked at the silent television and she wondered if he would ask to begin the film again to avoid an answer. Instead, his gaze shifted to her. 'A small thing. But bitter. The morning of the accident, Teresa and I argued about my work. Teresa believed I was overworking, that I spent too little time with my family. It was a typical couple's row, nothing to threaten our relationship but a venting of feelings and opinions. I was to go with them. Instead, I stayed and worked.'

She said softly, 'I think you're being hard on yourself again.'

His eyes darkened with emotion and he ignored her comment. 'That was the last time we spoke. And I remember Tomas looking between us, a worried child with the quiet but hostile voices of his parents filling the room with emotion.' His mouth tightened. 'I struggled to come to terms with my wife and son's deaths, knowing that the last time I saw them alive they were upset…and I was the cause.' His hand gestured vaguely. 'I would have wished to make everything right.'

'That's understandable. And tragic. I'm sorry. So very sorry.' She reached out and touched his knee, gripping it briefly until their eyes met. Wishing she could take his pain and guilt away but knowing that it was his journey. That it was for him to work through them and forgive himself. 'Do you think Teresa would have expected you to hurt so badly for so long?' Her fingers loosened and she sat back.

'Something we will never know.'

'Of course. And you immersed yourself in the business?'

'My grandfather also suffered from the loss of Tomas, the loss of his dream of two generations of heirs. He died soon after and I became eager to fully lose myself in his world like he had always wished. I slept there most nights, but remember little of what I did.' He shrugged. 'The company thrived so I must have made the correct decisions.'

'No wonder your brother was worried about you.'

'Rai escaped to his aid work. I see now he had his own heartbreak. It's not surprising he didn't share his feelings about Faith with me. I was not interested in the love or heartbreak of others.'

The words hung in the air between them. Thought bubbles. Was that an intentional past tense? She hoped so. Quietly she asked, 'And now he has his family. A family you are part of.'

She thought of Chloe hugging him that first night after her mother and new father had left. Dom's look of stiffness fading to one of surprised pleasure and maybe, even then, cautious hope for the future. Yes, he needed children. Children she couldn't give him. 'I think Chloe had something to do with that.'

'Perhaps. She is a delightful child.' He raised one brow. 'Or it could have been the aunt of Chloe.'

She wished. 'Great-aunt. Great-aunt,' she repeated as if it was a shield she could hold up. 'And that one's too old for you. You're a young man. I was just here when you woke up. When you go back to Florence, I hope you find happiness.'

'You are truly obsessed with our minor age difference. You are saying I could not find happiness here?'

'I'm saying you need a young wife, not someone over forty, to carry on your family name.' Oh, dear, had she just said that? Had she just presumed that this could be more than a passing fancy for him, a brief holiday fling as he started to find himself again?

He didn't rush into speech and her own words hung in the air, embarrassing her with a tinge of neediness she hoped he didn't hear.

'My brother has that,' he said finally. 'I would have a woman who made me want to wake each day to the promise of warmth.'

'Good plan.' She reached for the remote. 'No idea how we became so serious. Let's watch the end of the movie and then I'll call it a night.'

Oh, dear, oh, dear, oh, dear, she thought as the unseen movie flashed before her eyes. She could give him warmth but that was all. That woman he would wake to couldn't be her. But she knew inside she wanted it to be.

Such a virile man, with his future ahead of him. Though she had to wonder if her fear came from the scars caused by the last man who had left her because of her infertility, and not her own common sense.

But there were more reasons. It would be even worse if they tried to find happiness together and it didn't work; the ripples could affect Faith and Rai.

He watched her with a thoughtful expression. 'I will wake you with coffee and tomorrow we will drive in the sunshine.'

CHAPTER EIGHT

SUNSHINE ARRIVED AS PROMISED. Her family across the street had gone for last-minute Christmas supplies, heading south to Coffs Harbour. An added bonus was the annual family photo with Santa Claus. This year Rai would be included for the first time. It was a toss-up over who was more excited, Chloe or her papà.

After they left, Dom reminded Isabel about the outing he'd promised. As if she could have forgotten! There was no way that Rai would be driving away in Faith's all-wheel drive if he hadn't promised his car to Dom. Not a chance.

Isabel wasn't sure she needed to be in the confines of a car with Dom after last night's embarrassment, but she couldn't think of a good enough reason to excuse herself. After all, she had inspired the invitation by bemoaning her boredom with being housebound.

'Let us drive to the lighthouse to start,' he suggested. 'I have not been even close to it and you can tell me the history if you know it.'

She knew the history. Backwards. Had been a guide there many times, preferring lighthouse tours to the local caving tours that Faith guided. 'You may regret asking me.'

Despite her misgivings, once she'd limped to the car

at the gate, so pleased that she didn't need the crutches this morning, and was ensconced in the luxury that was Rai's new pride and joy, she felt fine. In fact, Isabel tried to calm the flutters that tickled with pleasure in her belly just from being with Dom.

His scent, his shoulder next to hers, his concern for her—all enclosed in the capsule of the car—were hard to regret. She reminded herself that soon he would be gone. Why not savour the moment?

'We can drive up to the car park,' Isabel suggested. 'From there, admire the external tower of the lighthouse.' Her ankle was better but not up to the hill climb just yet. 'Maybe tomorrow I can make the top, but it's still easy to enjoy the clean lines of the tower against the sky from the bottom of the hill.'

As they drove past the lower bends of the footpath and the row of bench seats that faced the sea, Isabel noticed a friend of Faith's perched awkwardly on a wooden seat beside the path. Something about her posture seemed odd.

Why was Trina out here alone?

'Can you pull over here for a moment? I want to speak to that woman—she's a friend of Faith's. You would've met her at your brother's wedding... Catrina, otherwise known as Trina.'

'Of course.'

The car pulled in smoothly to the side of the road and Isabel reached for her door as the car reached a stop.

Dom leaned towards her, concern on his face. 'Are you sure you are able to walk that far?'

'I'll limp and it feels secure with the bandage. I need to check on her. Her baby's due any day.' Isabel climbed out, careful to place her foot squarely so as to be stable. She could hear Dom opening his door so she guessed he'd be beside her if she stumbled.

'You okay, Trina?' But at the sight of the young woman's face she could see she wasn't. Catrina's face was pulled tight and tears ran in tiny rivulets. She put down the mobile phone in her hand. 'I just went for a walk… My waters broke. I've rung Finn. He's coming.' She turned horrified eyes to Isabel. 'Something else came with the flood. It feels like cord.'

Isabel's stomach sank. 'Catrina's a midwife,' she said over her shoulder to Dom. There'd be no waiting for Trina's husband. 'Dom's here. Let's get you to the hospital.'

Trina's wide eyes met Isabel's. 'I can't move, Izzy. Everything's happening.' Her face shone pale with shock. 'I need to push.'

'Can you wait a little?' Dom came closer, his voice quiet, the question hopeful.

'No.' There was a tinge of hysteria, so very unlike Trina, Isabel thought, and, oh, so very like the transition of labour.

Trina's hands flapped as if she didn't know what to do. 'It's coming. I'm trying not to push.'

'We'll move you. You don't have to do anything,' Isabel said calmly. 'You can't stay here. If baby comes at least we'll be ready to drive straight to the hospital immediately after. Finn will understand we put you in the car.'

Trina blew out a breath and, with several more panting breaths, she nodded.

Isabel turned to the man beside her and said decisively, 'Pick her up, Dom.' She had no doubt he was strong enough and wouldn't be squeamish at getting wet. The thought made her smile. Their gazes met, his startled but appreciative. 'I'll open the back door and put the picnic rug down on the seat.' She walked carefully back towards the car, glancing often over her shoulder as he gathered the pregnant woman in his capable arms.

The rug was more for Trina's comfort than her concern about Rai's car, she thought as she flipped the rug open and tossed it in. The soft cream leather would be cold. She turned to find Dom behind her with Trina in his arms and by the time he eased the trembling woman into the car Isabel knew they were going to have the baby.

'It's coming,' Trina whispered, and Isabel nodded, amazed the mum-to-be had found calm amidst the inevitable.

A baby born here would be better if the cord was first. Isabel wasn't going to give sympathy that might crack Trina's hold on composure.

'Clever baby. Let's get you out of your underwear.'

Isabel had her full weight on her good leg and leant against the side of the car. Between the two women they managed faster than she'd expected, and Trina rolled to her knees on the wide seat with her bottom in the air, her long skirt pushed half up her back, but she panted with effort.

'My word, it's happening,' Isabel said quietly. 'You are amazing, Trina.' Because, below the crease of Trina's buttocks, a glistening coil of thick cord was hanging down and the descending crescent of the baby's head with a stripe of damp hair was behind it.

'Head on view, keep going.' Isabel's words came from her past life. A life she'd tried to forget and now realised she missed with aching loss.

'I can feel it,' gritted out Trina.

Isabel glanced at Dom's face; he was watching them both with a furrowed brow. Then he said softly, 'So, were you a midwife or a doctor?'

'Midwife.'

He inclined his head as if something had been confirmed. 'Do you wish me to assist?' he asked quietly.

'We've got this. You may need to take the baby after, if it needs help...' The words *if the baby doesn't breathe* were unspoken but they were there all the same.

She, like Catrina, felt calm. Being with a woman at a rapid birth was something you never forgot, despite the passing of years. She knew this. Knew what to do. Believed all would progress because there was no other choice. Every second counted with the cord occluded and both of them now wanted the baby born here. 'Push, Catrina. Let's not wait for contractions. Baby is almost here.'

Isabel knew the mother was in a perfect position for rapid delivery. She and Trina both knew, with the cord jammed between the pelvis and the hard head of the baby, foetal blood supply and any oxygen it carried to the baby would be dangerously reduced.

The window of time for a good outcome was too, too horribly short, with baby's reserves falling dangerously low. A fast vaginal birth was the best option and even faster than an emergency caesarean if the mother was ready to push. That wasn't in doubt.

Leaning over the front seat, Dom slid one of Chloe's beach towels towards Isabel—he must have searched for practical supplies in the boot—and she took it gratefully as she leaned in through the back door. Wet babies were slippery, and the towel would be better than Trina's clothes to dry a damp newborn.

With a huge breath and a long drawn-out groan Trina pushed hard.

And pushed again.

The scalp grew larger as baby edged closer to birth. Trina groaned low and deep as the baby's head finally eased completely into the world and then she gasped and panted.

Isabel soothed, her voice reflecting nothing of the fear for Trina and Finn's baby that curled in her stomach. 'You're doing so well.'

Trina puffed and then slowed her breathing to gather herself. 'Not the birth I planned,' she gasped.

'But still amazing. You're fabulous.' Thank goodness her voice remained calm and steady. 'Keep going, Trina.' Isabel's gaze met Dom's and she nodded to agree it was good. Yet, deep in her mind, Isabel's brain screamed *hurry, hurry, hurry.*

Catrina pushed again. The end started with torturous slowness until, with a flood of fluid and limbs and coils of thick cord, came the baby in a rush—neck, shoulders, arms and body and limbs slid into the world and into Isabel's steady hands.

The roar of a car could be heard coming up the hill but there was no time to look.

'A boy. He's stunned but has tone.' A thick umbilical cord was good, Isabel thought in fragments of thoughts and exultation—the fragile umbilical vein and arteries would be well protected by the protective jelly inside a thick cord—but her gaze anxiously scanned the baby for movement as she began to rub his body all over with the towel. Not flaccid, some tone in his limbs was a good sign, but not breathing.

Catrina craned her neck but she couldn't see where he lay on the seat as Isabel rubbed. The new mum tried to shift sideways but there wasn't enough room. 'Still stunned. Let's give him a few seconds to start breathing himself, and if he doesn't I'll hand him to Dom.'

For Isabel, staring into the baby's dark eyes, so wide and blank, it was a jolt back to the past and another baby, tinier, a pale and precious being, who never breathed. Something else she could one day have told Dom. *No. That would not happen.* She rubbed more firmly. 'Come on, baby.' This was not surprising with the speed of his expulsion into the world, and his body was purple and not the white that she feared.

Finally, the frozen eyes blinked slowly and the small chest fluttered. A tiny mewling gasp broke from blue lips and, beside Isabel, Catrina sucked her breath in once softly.

The baby coughed and gurgled in a gasp. Then another deeper gasp and then a breath. 'He's breathing.' Her eyes stung and she blinked. 'He'll be fine.' She needed to say it out loud, for Catrina's benefit as well as her own. To let the words sink in and the relief and the joy to seep into her skin and mind and heart. The baby was well. 'He's good.'

She looked up to see Dom looking between her and the baby. Back and forward, his eyes shiny with emotion.

Isabel nodded. Blew out a breath and met his gaze for a second, almost overcome by the relief from the horror. She looked to the baby and gently swiped the pinking skin. Trina's baby mewled louder as Isabel wrapped him to stop the sea breeze cooling him.

'We've nothing to cut or tie the cord, so he needs to stay close to Mum.' She pulled her thoughts back to the moment, closing the door on that heartbreaking time years ago. 'But there's plenty of cord, Catrina, to allow you to shift.' Seriously—Isabel jollied herself back into a normal frame of mind—that was the longest cord she'd ever seen. Thank goodness.

Dom handed Isabel another clean towel and she unwrapped the baby and rewrapped in the dry towel, wadding the other for Trina to sit on after they'd disentangled cord and legs and baby so the new mum could twist and ease herself back until she could sit on the seat next to her son. Trina winced as she settled but reached for her baby, which Isabel passed across still wrapped in the new towel. Her face shone, streaked with tears, but her eyes glowed with joy and enormous relief.

Isabel smiled at Dom as their eyes met. Suddenly she was glad she could share this miracle with him.

A car pulled up behind them and Catrina's husband Finn wrenched open the other passenger door.

'Trina!'

CHAPTER NINE

HALF AN HOUR LATER, watching Isabel limp into the house, Dom could still not believe they had experienced a birth together at the side of the road. That moment when she had remained so calm as they'd waited for the baby to breathe... Yet he had seen the emotion in her eyes. A reflection of the past perhaps. He wanted to know why and how and when.

Today he had seen a side to Isabel that he had never envisaged. A capable, professional midwife. Was this not spoken about? Something he would find out today, he hoped. They wouldn't drive anywhere else that day.

'Enough excitement for one morning,' Dom said with a smile. He'd given her two mild analgesic tablets for the discomfort. Of course she'd forgotten her ankle. They both had. But she'd barely seemed bothered by it and hopefully the anti-inflammatories would keep it from swelling again.

He left her at her cottage to shower and change her clothes. He had no doubt Isabel would be ready with a strong cup of tea to share. Dom could do with one. They could sit and talk about their adventure when he returned, but first he needed to restore his brother's car to its former glory so he could concentrate on Isabel.

As he walked he muttered, 'My Isabel, you amaze me.

And much needs discussing because there are emotions beneath all of this that I can almost grasp yet remain hidden. What are your secrets and your pain?' But he would be back soon to find out.

Finn had driven Rai's car with the precious cargo to the hospital, while Dom had followed in Finn's car to retrieve the other. But mother and babe were well. That was all that mattered.

It had been years since he'd witnessed a birth, yet during the drama he'd seen Isabel's direction of thought, the sequence of events and best probable outcome. Also there was the not-to-be-underestimated importance of the mother being attended by someone she trusted. Perhaps there was hope for his medical intuition and abilities after all, he thought ruefully, because though he'd been ready he hadn't felt the need to interfere. And his Isabel? She had managed as if this were an everyday occurrence for her. He knew it was not.

He stopped. Stared unseeingly as he wiped over the inside of the car, which had very little damage, and out to the ocean beyond. Struck by a memory.

Except Isabel had not been calm for that moment when the baby had been slow to breathe. He had seen an expression of horror. Remembered horror. And fear in Isabel's eyes. He mulled over that moment, thought back to the last time he had seen that expression, at one of their earliest exchanges of words, and he wondered now if there were big things she hadn't shared with him. Things he didn't know, that might explain much.

But again, that was something for a later time.

When Dom returned to Isabel's cottage he found her resting on the sofa, her beautiful face calm in repose and smiling. Relief flooded through him that she had gained comfort. He nodded approval. 'This is good. You and your foot have had a busy morning.'

Two steaming cups of tea sat beside the teapot on her side table. She must have heard him coming up the path and poured. The scene set for the two of them pleased his soul.

Her lack of disclosure about her past did not.

'You've been busy too.' She pushed his cup towards him as he sat down in his usual chair.

Dom considered the setting and the company. They were comfortable together, ready to share thoughts and opinions, except they were not in a relationship. The thought startled him and he veered rapidly away from that discomfort.

She said, 'Speaking of which, how is your brother's car?'

That made him smile. 'It appears to have suffered no lasting ill.' Rai would accept he had done the best he could. He gestured to her lower leg. 'And you?'

'Fine. But resting is nice too.'

She looked sad. Or pensive. And he considered the morning and the secrets that she hadn't shared. Her obvious expertise with attending a birth and the calmness and knowledge she'd displayed—of course these were not skills a photographer or a receptionist would have.

'So you were a midwife?' he asked.

The tea sloshed in her cup and he watched her frown at the small spill on the sofa cushion. Her hand steadied, she put the mug down, pulled out one of Chloe's hand-wipes and dabbed the spill and sat back. Lifted her chin at him with that composure he'd come to expect and admire from Isabel.

'The young Isabel was a midwife. Fifteen years ago.

Her fiancé left when she lost her baby at twenty-four weeks. Stillbirth. She never went back to midwifery.'

It was disquieting that she had spoken as if it were all to do with some other person and not herself, but it explained much. But far too briefly.

'This is a sadness, Isabel. Yet you speak as if it wasn't you who suffered this pain.'

'That's not me anymore. I'm a different person. That was Isabel before. And, like you, she hung onto that grief too long. Until it changed all of her future plans.'

'Because your heart was broken? Or because the loss of the child could not be borne?'

Her mouth twisted into the sad semblance of a smile. 'Something like that.'

'You never went back to that man, I hope?'

At that she smiled, a smile that held a grim quality which made him frown. 'Any man, really. Short-term relationships don't require explanations.'

And yet she had given him an account, Dom thought with some hope that there could be more between them.

'What of me? I want you, Isabel. The passionate woman inside that I sense could be my soulmate. This obsession with your age and my need for a wife who will bear babies...does it come from this history? Your previous tragic birth?' He leaned forward. Reached out and took her hand now it was free. Lifted it to his lips and said quietly, 'You are enough for any man.'

She stared, perhaps shocked, perhaps tempted. He hoped for the latter but then she pulled away and her face pinched. 'Apart from my age, which makes conception less likely and more risky, I have a bicornate uterus and it is unlikely I would ever carry a baby to full term. So if you ever changed your mind...' She let the sentence trail off.

The shock hit him.

Not for himself. No. But for this pain that he saw in Isabel. He ached with sorrow for her as her mouth turned down with unaccustomed bitterness. It was not an emotion he associated with his Isabel.

Her gaze slid away. 'Any man would later regret the limitations I bring.' She swung her foot down and stood. 'I'm going to lie down, Dom. You'll have to amuse yourself for the rest of the day.'

He couldn't remember the last time he had been dismissed. And this was not the time for her to leave.

'Isabel?' But she had turned away.

Finally he was seeing inside the real Isabel, not the woman who provided a calm haven for the rest of the world—he could see the pain she suffered, and yet she shut him out.

Dom watched her go. He wanted to call her back more forcefully but the pain on her face was pain he had worn himself, as he'd pushed people away. So instead he thought about her words and the emotions beneath them and her insistence that she did not hold false hope for a child of her own.

That, on top of the drama of the birth today and the fact that she had assumed responsibility for Catrina's baby's safe arrival, would have been draining after many years away from her profession.

He wanted to go to her. Hold her. Offer comfort. But he knew she would push him away.

He was leaving tomorrow. There was no time. It had been hard enough to be here for the wedding, with all that needed to be done in Florence. But a sense of urgency was building between him and Isabel and he couldn't help but think he'd missed the opportunity to break through her barriers if he'd just taken her in his arms.

* * *

Isabel closed the door to her room and sagged back against it. Today, like every day since Dom had arrived, felt like a wild rollercoaster that filled her with hope one minute and the next moment something would happen to sting with the pain of loss.

Even this morning, the initial anticipation of sitting in a car close to Dom for hours had swiftly changed to the fear and later exhilaration of Catrina's baby's safe arrival.

Then the closeness they'd found in simple things like drinking tea and debriefing together had suddenly broken her heart. All had been surrounded by the caring that Dom showed towards her in all of his actions. And now he'd said what she'd secretly hoped and absolutely feared.

I want you, Isabel. You would be enough for any man.

Well, she knew for a fact that wasn't true. Had found that before with another man, whom she'd not been enough for. As for Dom...

She'd seen forty-one summers. He only thirty-four. So young. So virile. She looked at the bed and waiting pillows.

She wanted to hide her head beneath the covers and cry.

But she didn't cry any more.

Had told herself to stop years ago.

When Isabel woke she found her common sense had re-asserted itself. Dom would go home to Italy and her life would return to normal.

Of course it would.

Earlier she'd been overwrought after the danger of the prolapsed cord and then the excitement of Catrina's baby's healthy arrival. Only natural emotions after the first midwifery she'd practised in fifteen years, along with its unexpected drama.

She lay listening but the cottage felt empty. She didn't know how she knew, but the aura of Dom that she seemed to be able to sense in the air felt absent.

Empty.

No—this was good.

She would start being normal from this moment on. She would phone Faith and suggest they have Dom alone, without Isabel, for dinner tonight as he was leaving tomorrow and should spend time with his brother and family.

She would have a quiet evening on her own.

Yes.

She'd like that.

Ten minutes later Isabel put down her phone. Well, that hadn't gone well. Faith was making a family dinner, Isabel must be there, and wouldn't Isabel have months to have quiet evenings? Isabel could tell that Faith was disappointed Dom had been un-swayed about leaving for Italy on Christmas Eve. He'd reiterated that it proved the best time to fly without a family.

Isabel wondered just how many times Dom had scheduled flights or business to avoid Christmas in the years since his family had been killed.

He should be staying for Christmas. Someone should have convinced him to stay. She should have.

She shook her head. These were not sensible thoughts. And what about the one she was having now, of just having him hold her while she pressed her nose into his chest and breathed. To find the haven she needed and was beginning to think Dom could provide. Though she suspected that once he had his arms around her she wouldn't want to let him go. Would want to drag Dom into her bedroom and have her way with him. Like Mrs Robinson. Though he might be just as happy to have his way with her.

He had said she would be enough for any man.

Would she be enough for him?

Would her own dissatisfaction for what she could not give him ruin them both? And, by default, impact on her dear Faith and Rai.

Enough. Time to be sensible. To think of Dom's last night. Sensible thoughts would help her decide how to provide a side dish or a dessert for tonight, so she walked to the kitchen—with barely a limp, thank goodness— and opened the fridge to stare inside. The shelves seemed crowded when she hadn't shopped for days...

Then she understood. Dom. She'd asked him to amuse himself. So he'd replenished her food supply and then some, because he was leaving.

Typical, and kind of him. She wouldn't have to carry grocery bags, something he would have taken into account, she suspected. She studied the shelves. Milk, bread, meat, vegetables, three types of wine, soft and hard cheese. Fruit of all colours. A balanced diet for the supposed invalid. Though she doubted she'd eat the olives, anchovies and artichoke, peperoni and cheeses in oil—unless she held an Italian night with antipasto for Myra and Reg.

No, she'd make that plate for tonight and at least half of those ingredients would be used...and wouldn't be left to remind her of the man who'd supplied them.

She texted Faith, telling her what she would bring, and set about preparing.

* * *

When Dom arrived an hour later she had the splendid plate finished but her dilemma had been it wouldn't fit back in the cold storage.

'Perfect timing, Mr Salvanelli.' Said breezily, as if she hadn't noticed his gorgeously windblown hair across his forehead, the curved steel ridges of his abdominal muscles through his damp shirt and his scent of the sea. Obviously, he'd come straight from the beach, like a merman out of her dreams.

No. She hadn't noticed any of that. Much.

'You look rested.' His eyes said she looked good and she felt her cheeks warm.

'Thank you for the shopping.' Her stomach tightened but she forced herself to say the words. 'I'm sorry for being a drama queen, Dom.'

'You are a queen.' His eyes were kind. 'As for drama, I would talk of this more.'

She shook her head decisively. 'And I would like to have a light, fun conversation with my house guest. Let's leave drama for another day.' Except they didn't have another day after tomorrow. Which was a good thing.

He inclined his head. 'Fun it is, Isabel.' There was a wicked glint in his eye and she might have just got more than she bargained for with her stated house guest.

She looked down at the platter in her hands, fighting her blush. 'Would you take this across to Faith to put in her larger refrigerator, please?' She sealed the last of the plastic wrap over the dish and handed it to him. 'Now I know why your brother bought such a huge appliance.'

He inclined his head, put down his damp towel on a wooden chair and took it from her. Stepping close. The heat from his body warming her more. His mouth kinked up. 'You know, Isabel—' his eyes darkened, teased her, invited her '—I too have a large appliance. Rai and I are twins after all.'

She blinked. Her mouth kinked. He did not just say that. Well, she'd asked for fun. Who'd have thought he had that in him? She snorted. She couldn't help herself.

'Does Isabel snort?' His eyes twinkled and suddenly their camaraderie was back. Angst was stupid and he was leaving.

Oh, Dom. You are a gorgeous man and I will so badly miss you.

'It seems I do.' Her shoulders dropped with the tension she'd held for what seemed liked days and her mouth lifted. A real smile. Throwing caution out of her seaside window she added, 'As this is your last night, when you come back from your errand we should sit on my little veranda and toast our friendship.'

There. That sounded very sensible and grown-up and angst-free.

He gestured to the fridge with a free finger as his hands were taken up with the platter. 'And I have just the thing in there. A glorious Prosecco I discovered in your little shop.' He glanced down. 'I will take this across and return for a shower if you do not mind the delay. Your seawater is a joy, but your beach sand sticks in awkward places.' He raised his brows. 'Unlike our beach pebbles.'

Isabel tried not think where the beach sand had stuck but she was smiling at the door as she opened it for him. 'I can wait.'

Not long later Dom held the cold-beaded bottle of sparkling wine and filled Isabel's flute, the swirl of the liquid mimicking the swirl of emotions he held in check. Another memory to take home with him as her eyes sparkled as much as the wine.

He studied her as the salty breeze stirred her hair to float like a dark halo around her calm face and he wondered how much it would be possible to miss this woman when he was on the other side of the world.

'Come to Italy with me.' The words came from deep within, not for the first time in his thoughts, but still he was surprised he had allowed them voice.

She laughed quietly and raised her brows. 'Just like that? Follow you across the world?'

She thought it was a joke. Better than a rapid, *no thank you*, he supposed, just a little miffed. 'Why not?'

She waved an arm, still smiling at his jest. 'Oh, no good reason. Just my job, my family, my independence. My plans to return to travel journalism.'

'All cold bedfellows.'

Such an old-fashioned word. This time she really smiled. Sipped her wine, tasted it and took another sip. 'This is a very nice drop.' Then she looked at him again beneath raised brows. 'Were we talking bedfellows?'

'It has crossed my mind.' He paused. Nodded sagely. Playing light-hearted, if that was what she wanted. 'Often in the last two days. Hoping. Praying.'

'And I thought you were such a serious young man.'

'*Sì*. I said praying. I'm serious about this.'

Her smile disappeared. 'Then no. I won't follow you to Italy. We barely know each other.' She lifted her glass. Gestured to the view. 'I like you. Very much. But this is a definite no. Drink your wine, Dom, and we'll go across and see your brother and his family for your last night here.'

'All right,' Dom replied in the same even tone she had used. 'We shall do as you wish, Isabel.'

And then he would make it his business—later tonight, when they returned home—to make real memories.

CHAPTER TEN

'UNCLE DOM, UNCLE DOM, we missed you today.' Dom's slight awkwardness with the child was still there but improving every day, Isabel thought. He had no choice because every time she saw him Chloe made a fuss of her uncle.

Isabel stood at the door and watched Dom as a slow smile creased his face. He'd hung back but Chloe allowed none of that. She'd raced straight into his arms and hugged him. Again, his hands came down to cuddle her back like they had the first night, when they'd all shared pizza.

'We had Santa photos today. Mummy and I have them every year, but this year my papà was *in* them!' The importance of that statement was evidenced by Chloe's outflicked hands. 'Do you want to see?'

'Of course.' Dom had no choice but he looked genuinely interested, which was a good sign for a man who—according to Rai—had avoided children and family occasions since his own loss.

Rai leaned against the wall, watching Chloe, flicking amused glances at his brother and Isabel.

Chloe brought the Santa portrait over to her uncle. Isabel watched Dom's face. From where she stood she could see it was a gorgeous photo, but she waited for Chloe to come around and show her so the little girl could drag out and enjoy every moment.

The picture caught tall, handsome Rai in full grin. Faith looked supremely happy with her red hair spilling free around her face. And Chloe looked like the cat that got the cream.

'Even Santa looks good,' Isabel said, teasing.

'What do you think, Dom?' Rai asked. 'Is that a good Christmas photo or not?'

'Excellent, my brother.'

Isabel decided he looked remarkably comfortable as he nodded at Chloe's explanations of where the photos had been taken in the shopping mall. It was wonderful to see Dom so at ease, compared to the broken, stilted man who had arrived from Italy. A return to the world of other families and, she thought with a spasm of loss, another brick in the wall of her certainty that Dom needed a family of his own. Something she couldn't give him.

Chloe spun to her. 'Look, Aunty Izzy. Don't we look happy? And that's Santa in the red suit. He has a white beard, see? And that's his sleigh behind his chair.'

Who knew you would need to explain every element of a family portrait, right down to Santa's attire? Isabel smiled. 'You all look very happy, darling.' She looked up and caught the laughter in Faith's eyes. Rai was watching Dom and he seemed satisfied that his brother was fine with this.

'And there is my papà next to Mummy.'

And Chloe wasn't the only one who was proud. Rai's face beamed from the photo. 'You look dashing,' Dom said with a note of teasing in his voice.

'Of course.' Rai met his brother's eye and laughed. 'I am the most handsome of the two of us.'

'Funny,' Isabel said. 'I heard another version of that recently.'

And that was the tone of the night.

She wasn't sure if it was the two glasses of Prosecco they'd had beforehand, but there was no tension or doldrums in the Captain's house tonight. Dom looked happy and she couldn't understand how his mental shift had occurred so fast. It was as if he'd made a decision and she had no idea what it was.

There were some lovely memories from the last week and when he was gone Chloe would certainly miss him. As would she, Isabel thought with a hollow feeling in her middle. But, apart from having to care for an invalid and then being ready to resuscitate a baby at the side of the road, nothing had changed. She hadn't changed.

Rai said, 'We have your beautiful antipasto to start, Isabel. Thank you.'

'Dom bought all the ingredients today and they were begging to be put together and shared at a big table.'

'Well chosen, Dom,' Rai said. 'I have selected several wines to complement.'

That would explain why there were so many glasses on the table, Isabel thought. She'd be tipsy by the time they finished.

Isabel asked, 'Are we having a degustation?'

'I have a plan,' Rai said. 'With Caprese we will have Lambrusco to complement the tomatoes and basil. Chardonnay with the peppers and Pinot Grigio with the artichoke. Chianti with the cheese.'

'Stop, no more.' Isabel laughed. 'I'll be as silly as a hen.'

Rai said, 'You Australians. Cannot hold your wine.'

'You Italians make it a part of every meal. I have to walk ten kilometres a day to stay trim.'

Dom looked up at that and his dark eyes glinted with promise. Very softly so nobody but Isabel and Chloe heard, he said, 'I like silly.'

He was smiling, Chloe had climbed on his lap, yet he still looked relaxed and happy. Like a dad. Or a doting uncle.

The hollowness inside Isabel warmed and receded when he looked at her like that.

'Can you help me in the kitchen, Izzy?' Faith said and she nodded. A little time away from her handsome lodger would be good for her equilibrium.

Rai went to the table. 'Perhaps some Sangiovese rosé with the prosciutto, do you think?'

Dom took the small glass his brother offered and a tiny plate of the meat.

Rai went on, 'You look good. Happier. In so short a time. This place is crazy and has magic, eh?'

Dom nodded, not sure where his brother was going with this. 'I feel some of that magic. Yes.'

'And how are you after the excitement of the birth today? Did it make you wish to run from medicine or run back to it?'

Dom smiled. 'You are quick to see things. As always. I had forgotten the impact of participating in a birth. The drama. The exultation. And yes, it has directed my thoughts to the possibilities you mentioned before. A small medical practice between us in Lighthouse Bay is perhaps not so far-fetched.'

'It must be what you want. Not what I want, though, if that is the case,' Rai said quietly.

Dom lifted his chin. 'The baby could have died today,

but didn't. Isabel was amazing, but I was there if needed, she knew that and it worked. The occasion drew me to think of things I had forgotten. Opened my eyes and my heart to my love of medicine. To the power of life and death with knowledge.'

'This is good.' Rai sipped his wine appreciatively. Took another sliver of ham. 'And Isabel?'

'She fights what could be between us.'

Rai nodded. 'They are independent women, these Fetherstones. Strong but steady. Worth fighting for. But if I can offer some advice in this matter… Do not rush her.'

Dom didn't say he was finding that hard. That this feeling of urgency warned him she might run from him with her absurd feelings of inadequacy. Which was ridiculous. Isabel was lacking in no way. But if he said so his brother would give further advice that Dom didn't want. So he said nothing.

Rai went on, 'Then you go back tomorrow. Sell what is left of the company and arrange care for the family homes in Florence. When all is arranged satisfactorily, you can return?'

'That is the plan.' Except now he wanted Isabel with him. The idea had flown into his mind and he couldn't get rid of it. 'I feel a healing. A great change in my life.'

'I am very glad.' Rai clasped his shoulder strongly. 'You worried me. All of us. It will be good to see you in the New Year, perhaps as early as February?'

'That is my wish.'

Isabel carried in the huge dish of lasagne with a rich aroma trailing behind her like a cloud. She heard the words and let them sink in. February. Dom was coming back in February. The idea excited her and made her want to sing. But that was probably the wine.

Her mood flattened a little. This changed nothing. The man needed a family that she couldn't provide.

To protect her heart, she might need to plan a trip away for February. But tonight wasn't for future planning; it was for celebrating the present. To celebrate and toast the newlyweds, Dom's obvious lift in spirits and Chloe's delight with the approach of her family Christmas.

The lasagne Faith and Rai had prepared together was a recipe that had been passed down through the Salvanelli family kitchens. Isabel, full with antipasto even before she started on the newlyweds' lasagne, felt the need to walk off her dinner. Plus, thanks to the excellent wines that had accompanied the meal, maybe dance a little if she wanted to really test her ankle.

But she'd been outvoted on that one.

After goodbyes, when Dom and Isabel crossed to her cottage under the streetlamps, the gentle susurration of waves from the bay filled the air. A warm breeze brushed her skin with a tinge of salty promise. With Dom beside her she felt more sensitive to everything around her, and because tonight was his last night the many sensations felt damnably bittersweet.

She glanced wistfully towards the sweeping light from the cliff across the bay and a longing to be a part of that ethereal landscape drifted into her mind. 'Let me show you the lights at night from the lighthouse. It's something you should see before you go home to Italy.'

Dom stopped and his gaze followed the moving beam of light that swept the bay from the tower. 'The path is steep. That is not a good idea for your ankle.'

She screwed up her face. 'I'm almost fully recovered. I'm sure I could climb up the last path to the lighthouse.'

Suddenly she desperately wanted to go. 'Especially with the bandage on.'

His gaze rested on her, a little quizzical at her insistence, but he nodded. 'As you wish, but we will drive to the car park and walk from there. And I will steady you as we walk. I only sipped, while others indulged, tonight. Let me retrieve Rai's keys and a torch.'

While he went for the keys, Isabel slipped inside her cottage for a scarf in case the breeze turned cooler and a better pair of shoes for walking in the dark. But all the while, with an irrepressible smile perhaps fuelled by the dinner wines, she was wondering just how he would steady her. Hold her hand? Take her elbow like a recalcitrant child? She grinned at that. Perhaps rest his arm around her shoulders as he pulled her against him?

Enough. She saw the car lights through the windows and eased the door shut behind her with a click.

Dom pulled up near the gate and her heart skipped a beat. As if it was finally liberating to do something fun with Dom. Another dangerous suggestion, a moonlight walk under the lighthouse, and she couldn't wait.

Before she could reach the car, Dom appeared beside her and held the door open as he always did, protective of her. She slipped past his big body into the dim interior and of course the faint drift of his aftershave welcomed her.

She sighed as she slid back in the seat. She should enjoy it now because it would all be ending soon, this cosseting that had grown special in the last few days. It was not something she was used to, or had thought she'd enjoy, but Dom offering her old-world courtesy and care could never be unpleasant. *Unpleasant* was definitely not the word. She feared the word might be *unforgettable*.

In silence—an easy silence that she would also miss

when he was gone—he drove sedately down their hill and up the lighthouse hill, past where they'd found Catrina earlier today. They shared a glance and a smile as Dom steered past. The conversation at dinner had been animated as the day's events had been discussed and exclaimed over.

Dom pulled into the deserted parking area of the lighthouse, dimly lit by one lamp at their level and one at the base of the path.

'Do many people come here at night?' Dom's assessment of the area was thorough. A man scanning for threats.

She thought it looked romantic. 'Not often. Though New Year's morning is popular to greet the first sunrise.'

He studied her in the darkness. 'I would like to do that one New Year's Day. Share that sunrise with you.'

As would she. Her cheeks warmed but the car was dimly lit. 'Hard, if you live in Italy.'

He didn't answer for a few seconds. 'Indeed.'

He opened his door and climbed out and she pushed her own. But of course he arrived to pull it wide and offer her a hand.

He took her fingers in his, looking down at her, not saying anything, and as she stood to balance herself he tucked her hand under the crook of his elbow, drawing her closer than strictly required so that their bodies touched.

His thigh was hard against her softer hip. She was well supported from any hint of a stumble, but strangely her knees felt weak. Silly woman.

His warmth seeped into her. As did the warmth flushing her chest.

His hand tightened and she lifted her chin to tilt her face up at him. For a moment she thought he was going to kiss her. The world stopped. And started again when he loosened his grip. 'Let us see this light.'

As they passed the cottages that lay below the lighthouse, once used for the keeper and the assistants, the steepest part of the climb had Isabel slowing.

Dom looked down at her. 'Should I carry you?'

'Up this steep hill? I'd have to resuscitate you at the top.'

'Perhaps. It is steep.' He laughed and she savoured the sound. He hadn't laughed when he'd first arrived, and now he didn't laugh often but his mood had indeed lifted.

He deserved to laugh, this beautiful man. A man who was leaving tomorrow. She couldn't deny that he had become more dear to her every day.

Ahead the lighthouse glinted and shone in reflected light from the massive beams that cut the night.

Surprisingly, with some of her weight on his strong forearm, her ankle was holding up well. She wanted to tell him about the history of the building but she didn't have the breath. She'd tell him later, she thought as she puffed up the final incline.

Instead, the light beams told any stories that needed sharing, the almost solid ray flirting out over the bay as it turned slowly in a wheel of light beams that warned ships of danger. And, fancifully, legend had it that the light also gave the town its hope.

Finally they reached the small courtyard in front of the tower and she leaned on the low white wall to the left of the path, ostensibly to look out over the dark bay and moon-tipped waves below, but really to catch her breath.

Silence stretched. Two people alone at the top of a jutting cliff. A thrum of awareness beat between them, drumming like the waves below on the rocks.

She wanted him.

She knew she couldn't have him.

But oh, how she wanted him.

She licked her lips and opened her mouth. 'The light-house is an octagonal tower. Apparently, it was easier to work the concrete that way. Easier than in the round formwork, that is.' Her sentences were short, but it was the pounding of her heart, not shortness of breath now that made them so.

Stay on track, she warned herself. 'It was one of the last to be built like this in New South Wales.'

His gaze travelled up the soaring height above them and he ran one strong hand caressingly over the still-warm white stone of the tower wall. She wanted to be that wall. To feel that smoothing touch against her bare skin.

He said, 'It gives pleasure to the eye.'

Yes, he does. 'I love it.' Not him. No, not him. But she wondered if she was lying to herself. 'And inside,' she said, forcing herself to focus, 'there's a beautiful steel spiral staircase. Outside, at the top, the small grate ve-randa is black wrought iron lace, both floor and rails. The view's spectacular up there.'

'The view is spectacular already.'

They were in an alcove of the path, not much to be seen at all, except each other in the reflected light.

Not her. He wasn't talking about her. Her heart pounded again.

She moved forward, almost dislodging his hold, and he tightened his hand. Though now she wondered if for her safety, when they'd reached the summit and walked on smooth path, or his own desire to stay connected.

Either way, she was grateful for the darkness hid-ing her hot, hot cheeks. 'Come and sit beneath the light. There's a bench that leans against the white wall and you can tilt your head back and watch the light turn.'

They followed the curve of the white tower until she took one step down to the viewing platform and there, against the wall, stood the bench. She eased down onto the seat and he sat close to her and released her so that her hand slid away. Before she could miss his touch he promptly captured her fingers in his and held them again. He squeezed gently. 'This is nice.'

Very nice. Too nice.

But she spoke about the view. 'It's the surreal impact of watching the light beam shooting out over the sea. Each lighthouse has a different sequence of light timed in seconds.' *Be quiet, Isabel*, she thought. 'It's a simple but powerful pleasure to watch the beams.'

'Ah, and let's not forget the simple pleasure of holding hands.' She could hear the amusement in his voice.

'You can let go now.' Isabel raised their linked hands and when he didn't release her she lowered them. 'I can't fall here.'

'This is a concern.' Said slowly.

Cryptic man. She frowned and he must have seen it despite the dark.

She felt his shrug, a brush of cloth against cloth. That was how close they sat. 'I had hoped you would fall for me, Isabel.'

'I could fall.' She lifted her chin. 'But I'm too old for you, Dom. You need a young woman.'

He shook his head. 'It is your excuse that is too old.'

She tugged at the hand he held. He held on. Not tightly but implacably. 'Do you see me as a callow youth, unable to know my own mind? One who does not know my own wants and needs?'

'No. Of course not.' She'd insulted him. She was so confused. 'I'm sorry.' So she prattled on about the lighthouse. 'I love the blocks of white paint and the blue trim in the day, but I think the night, with the light beams, is my favourite.'

'Hmm,' he said. 'I admire the tilt of your mouth and the directness of your eyes. And your hair.' His other hand lifted and stroked the back of her hair in a slow caress that spread gooseflesh along her arms. 'But not your excuses.'

She couldn't do this. 'Stop talking.'

'I think that is a splendid idea,' he said, and his hand cupped her chin and tilted it towards him. His mouth came down and gently brushed her lips. She opened her mouth to protest and he kissed her.

The taste, the feel, the pressure of him was too beguiling, too fascinating, too mesmerising to deny.

Please. And she gave in. Isabel leaned in and pressed her mouth more firmly against his and his answer came, swift and sure. Gently, his tongue swept against her, his hands sliding up her arms until they drifted to her cheeks. Cupping her face, his eyes were on hers as he supped from her mouth. 'So beautiful,' he murmured. 'So stubborn. So desirable.' Her lids fell, and his kiss deepened. She was lost.

Later, sitting on his lap, when sense had returned and she had been thoroughly kissed, Dom said again, 'Come with me to Italy.'

Her heart cracked. 'No.'

He tightened his hold. 'I want you to come.'

She looked into his dark eyes in the dim light. They were like pools of potent need, pools of passion, pools of forbidden promise. 'People don't always get what they want.'

He tilted his strong chin. 'Before Teresa died, I had what I wanted.'

There was no answer to that. And she understood that

would have been his biggest 'want'. He wanted his wife back. He wanted his son back. He wanted his family back. Family. She understood that. Grieved for him. 'I'm sorry for your loss.'

'No.' His voice was quiet but intense. 'You are wishing I still had a wife because you are tempted.' He sat back and he let her fingers slide from his. Bereft didn't begin to cover the loss she felt but she'd asked for this separation. She slid from his lap to sit beside him in the dim reflected light.

Dom turned his head towards the sea, away from her, and the distance grew between them when only moments ago there was no distance, just the melding of breath and two bodies, two mouths fused in mutual desire. 'Perhaps you are right. You think I am not a whole man. You deserve more.'

No. She wanted him. 'You're everything I could possibly want in a man, but I'm the one with issues I can't seem to get over. You have your life and the chance of a new family ahead of you, Dom. With me you wouldn't get that.' She absolutely believed that.

His head lifted and his voice held a sternness she hadn't heard before. 'Why do you get to decide who or what I want? Isn't that up to me? What if I prefer not to have more children—would that be an issue for you?'

Isabel blinked and opened her mouth. And closed it again.

That would change everything.

She stood. She needed to think. Re-examine her beliefs. But not with him, so big and hot and kissable, beside her. 'I'm glad we came. And glad you saw the lights up here. It is my favourite place in the world.'

He rose beside her and studied her face. 'Think on

that, Isabel, when I am gone. I will remember your face, here in the glow from the beams, my Isabel of the light.'

Then he turned, gathered her hand and placed it back on his arm to keep her safe as they began the descent to the car below.

When he switched the torchlight on for the path she shook her head. 'Please. The moon is up. I prefer the dark.'

So did he. Dom knew he'd somehow ruined everything with Isabel. Had he pushed too soon? Kissed too thoroughly—or not enough? Been too harsh on her preconceived notions of what was good for him? But time was passing and tomorrow he would leave. He wanted more than her kisses before he left. Needed to leave his mark upon her so she would wait for his return.

Did she not share the feelings that burned in his belly? When he had kissed her, she had leaned into him and opened her mouth—it had been there, and that sweetness had swept them both from this place to somewhere more heated. The memory made his chest thrum and his hands ache to shape her beneath him again.

She stumbled once in the dark and his hold tightened, his other arm coming up to steady her. Her breath shuddered in and he did not think it was from pain but from his touch. He had to resist the urge to sweep her up and carry her against his chest, but he knew she would protest and pull against him.

Why did he carry such intense feelings for this woman after so short a time? Yet in those few days she had been with him for almost every hour of the day. He'd watched her sleeping. Been witness to her fearless protection of Chloe and the silent endurance of pain because of that. She hadn't been bitter about the accident, though he would ensure the motorcyclists would suffer the full consequence of their dangerous stupidity. Isabel would disagree, he knew, and her fierce independence made him smile.

He realised now that he'd fallen for her the moment he'd first seen her at his brother's house. That first day after the flight and a woman who had refused to allow him to be distant and morose.

An unassuming woman hiding the delight beneath demure clothing and an unshakable calm. She had woken him from a dark dream with her shining strength and kindness, like the heroine in a modern-day fairy tale, one his small niece would enjoy. If only he could find the happy ending.

He'd been the male version of Sleeping Beauty and Isabel the handsome princess who'd come to awaken him. But she had demons too, though she hadn't shared them all, demons like the ones he carried, and he would have to fight for her. Fight for both of them.

When they reached the light at the bottom of the path he said, 'If you won't come to Italy, come with me to the airport?'

He watched her face, saw the hope, saw the loss of it, watched her struggle to keep her face expressionless, but she had no idea how clearly he could read her now. His Isabel did not want a long goodbye because she cared too much?

Finally she said, 'Surely your brother will want to do that?'

'But having you there is what I want.' He cocked a brow at her. 'I did not think you were a coward, Isabel.'

He saw her spine stiffen. 'Nobody has called me one before.'

'Then, if to drive back from the airport will not be detrimental to your ankle, spend this last time with me.'

She looked away from him. 'If that's what you want, I can do that.'

Dom could not sleep. His body ached with longing to be with Isabel in the room so close to where he now lay. At least now she would drive him to the airport, though, to be accurate, he would drive there and she would bring herself home alone.

He wasn't sure if his insistence to have Isabel there for his departure was a last-minute attempt to convince her to come with him, or his pathetic need to see her face for as long as he could before he left.

Even his brother had advised him to give her time.

But things happened. Unexpected tragedies. What if something happened to Isabel while he was sixteen thousand kilometres away?

He did not remember this angst with Teresa. Everything had been immediate. He was there. Until he wasn't.

With Isabel, he felt like picking her up and running off with her, but she would just tell him to put her down. He had liked it when she had been an invalid and he could care for her. What did that say about him?

Isabel would have an opinion on that. The thought made him smile. Certainly she would tell him to stop being foolish.

He turned his pillow and stared out of the window at the night sky. A beam of light from across the bay travelled across his window as if warning him to chart a safe course. If that course led him safely back to Isabel he would be happy.

CHAPTER ELEVEN

ISABEL LAY STARING at the pink ceiling of her room as the first dusting of colour reached to paint the horizon. Before the sun broke through, rosy light dusted the clouds, turning them pink and purple, gradually turning to deeper and darker hues. Like a soft bruise on the horizon—like the bruise on her heart from falling for Dom.

She'd left the blinds open last night so she would see the sunrise this morning, but this empurpled beauty made her eyes sting.

Dom was leaving. And he'd called her out on her reasons for backing away. Turning it back on her, making her re-examine her beliefs.

In two hours they'd drive to the airport and she'd be going with him for an extended goodbye. She shuddered.

Why on earth had she agreed? Because he'd called her a coward? Or because she'd wanted to be there?

Last night in her bed she'd wondered what she'd been frightened of. If she would still be this careful when she was fifty…or sixty. How many young, virile Italian men would ask her to run away with them then?

Would she have been so foolish to take what he was offering, revel in the moment and risk the consequences of being with Dom in what she suspected would be an explosion of unforgettable folly? And what if she did discover a wonder she suspected might change her for ever? Was she supposed to then stay with a man she barely knew, in a strange city across the world?

By then she would know him well. Biblically, anyway.

What could she lose? What could others lose? She wasn't sure about herself. But others? What if, because of her, he never came back to Lighthouse Bay? Could she do that to Rai and his new family?

No. She wasn't unfeeling, but she wasn't a martyr. That would be Dom's decision and she could always absent herself when needed if her presence was a factor, arrange times he could visit. He could come then.

When the knock came on her door, like it had for the last three days, Isabel sat up and pulled the sheet to cover the rose-embroidered bodice of her thin nightdress. She patted the edges down beside her like a sealed wall of resistance. Even she could see the symbolism in that. But, in fact, it was more for her than him. She trusted him.

'Come in.'

Dom had brought her coffee every morning—glorious coffee, hand-made by a gorgeous man coffee—and placed it beside her bed. Then he would sit with her as she drank it. The best way to start her day, she'd come to realise.

Today was the last day that would happen. Even when—*if*—he came back, he would stay with Faith and Rai.

Unless she broke a leg.

She smiled a little mistily at the ridiculousness of that thought. And touched the wood of her bedhead superstitiously.

As he entered she allowed herself to savour the sight of him. Tall and commanding, virile in shorts and an open-necked shirt, ready for his jog on the beach. His muscled thighs and powerful lower legs covered the ground between them fast and she couldn't read his expression as he carried the coffee across.

Ah, Domenico Salvanelli, her big, dark-haired Italian man. Immense, harshly handsome, with his sometimes grim and always sexy mouth. Dark, dark eyes that searched her face with just a hint of suggestion and all over her body her skin prickled.

He smiled at her, but that smile held a bittersweet tilt this morning. When the cup he carried lowered to the small bedside table where he always rested it, he paused and swung to her so their faces were level.

'Good morning, Isabel,' he said as his face drew closer. He leaned forward and kissed her cheek. Then he turned his face, his hand came up to still her and he kissed her mouth. Firmly. She was too startled to protest. He stood back. 'I needed that. I am sad this morning.'

Her thoughts scattered. She clutched at her shattered composure like she clutched at the sheet and huffed out a small gasp of surprise. Said the first thing that came into her head to relieve the hot wave of awareness between them. 'I'm sad too. No more coffee in bed.' As if to reinforce that innocuous topic, she reached for her mug and pretended to sip.

He raked his hair from his eyes and threw himself back in the chair beside the bed as if forcing himself to relax. Apparently, her calming technique wasn't working. The wood of the chair creaked in protest. The man looked sinfully sexy despite his obvious black mood.

Fierce black eyes locked on hers. 'Pah! This is our last morning together in our odd relationship and I should be in your bed—should have been there all night, doing all the things I dream of with you—not holding this mug with a handle in the morning.' He gestured to the cup in her hands and she felt the prickles of her skin instantly glow with heat and languor. Graphic imaginings were easily conjured. She was so there with him. *Good grief.*

She tore her eyes away before he recognised her response. 'Stop.' Said with a semblance of her usual calm. 'I'll spill the contents.' She put the cup back on the bedside table. She'd never look at morning coffee the same again.

Someone needed to be sensible. 'We don't have a relationship, Dom. Odd or otherwise. And we've done very well to avoid doing something irreversibly foolish.' She blew out a breath before she lifted her head. Then she raised her chin. 'You helped me in my time of need and I helped you. That's all there is.'

His eyes were fierce. 'You are mistaken. Which is strange and unusual for such an intelligent woman. Silent sparks fly between us. The air shimmers and my body tightens when I come within touching distance of you. From afar I can sense your mood and emotions. That is more than boring assistance; this is magic you deny. But you have had walls of resistance set up for a long time and I will give you some space to think. It has not been long and I have asked a lot of you. Perhaps it is unreasonable for me to expect you to follow.'

She shook her head at him. Oh, the gorgeous arrogance. 'Perhaps unreasonable?' she echoed, eyes widening in mock surprise.

He brushed that away with one of his oh-so-Italian sweeps of the hand. 'I only hope that by the time I come back to your Lighthouse Bay you will understand.'

Yes, he was coming back. Her heart thudded hard. 'Have you decided when you will return?'

'I have things to arrange if I am to learn to be a doctor in a distant land. And I will need a job if I am to woo a stubborn woman.'

Woo? Oh, my goodness. He was coming back here to work. And to woo her? He held her gaze then stood as if he didn't trust himself to sit by her bedside any longer.

'I go to the beach to run off the need to lift your bed-covers and show you how I feel. When I return we will prepare to leave.'

Her front door closed with a decided snap this morning and she raised her brows. So, Dom had a limit to his patience and she'd pushed it. Not surprising. Not as surprising as how much she wished he'd lifted the blankets. He certainly wasn't oblivious to her.

She sipped her coffee with a swirl of melancholy and frustration and a crazy delight. They had done well to not jump into bed together because the attraction between them was there. Dom was right. It did spark and sizzle. She finished her coffee and sighed, long and loudly. Lifted the cup. Examined it. Looked at her bed. She probably wouldn't look at her covers the same way either.

The good news was her ankle had healed, no doubt due to the fact her housemate had been so diligent with ice and care and protection. Her gorgeous nurse, doctor, housemate, friend and almost lover who was leaving today.

Enough. Today was a new day. A new start. She laid out the clothes for the day. Opened her drawer and saw the thick brown travel wallet caught in a dancing sunbeam from the window. Lit with light. Glowing with promise.

Isabel opened her handbag and slid the wallet inside. Zipped up the pocket. Unwise and disturbing. She should put it back. But she didn't.

She'd discovered things about herself. She wanted

more from life. And she would search until she found what she was looking for.

If a small voice inside screamed in a frenzy that he was there in front of her she ignored it. Placed the first bricks level at the bottom of the wall and began to rebuild her barriers against foolishness again. Soon the shrewish voice would be blocked.

Dom would be back and he would be over his brief infatuation with an older woman. It wasn't as if she'd never see him again.

It would be good to drive home from the airport, to prove her independence had returned. Then she would get on with finding her new hope for life.

Dom glanced from the road to Isabel in the seat beside him. He'd suggested he drive on the way to the airport as it seemed sensible for her to rest her ankle until the journey home. Also, of course, he hated not being in control and she knew that.

She'd agreed calmly. As she did most things, but only because she chose to. Dear Isabel. He was not feeling calm. They had been driving almost an hour and every minute reminded him that soon they would part.

This was what he wanted. To have her by his side. Always. He couldn't like the fact that he was going back to Italy with nothing resolved between them, but he had to believe that time would come. It was unfortunate that he had to consider how long it would take him to sort and ensure everything went smoothly in Florence before he could return.

But he would win Isabel. Next time he wouldn't rush away with unfinished business he'd had to drop for his brother's wedding. He would take the time to woo her and then they would see if she still resisted his vision for their future. It was a vision he would not have believed possible a fortnight ago and now he wanted it with an immediacy that floored him.

CHAPTER TWELVE

DOM TURNED RIGHT at a roundabout Isabel said was not far from the airport and had to stamp on the brakes to avoid hitting the vehicle in front.

A barrier of disaster lay strewn before them.

Instinctively his left arm went out to protect Isabel as their seat belts slammed them back and the car skidded to a stop a few feet from the rear bumper of the car in front. With urgent precision he reversed their vehicle onto the shoulder of the road, well out of the way in case another car came through at speed.

He turned to face her. 'Are you okay?'

'Of course. Thanks to your quick reaction.' She touched his arm in a gesture of thanks as her gaze scanned the damaged vehicles. Then she scooped her phone from her bag. 'This looks bad. And very recent. I'll phone to make sure the emergency services know.'

Of course she was calm and moving forward. 'I'll see what I can do to assist until they arrive.' Dom switched on the hazard lights of Isabel's car and slipped into the smoky daylight, jogging towards one of the vehicles, which was tipped precariously sideways.

A pall of smoke and dust still hung over the vehicles. It had only just happened. Dom felt a chill of fear run down his neck as he realised if they'd been a few minutes earlier he and Isabel could have been in the tangled mess of metal as well. There were at least four cars involved. 'Too close,' he muttered, unable to imagine anything like this happening to Isabel. He doubted he would stay sane.

He ducked back to Isabel with grim determination. Opening his door, he demanded, 'Stay in the car.' Then he ran back to the nearest vehicle.

Isabel looked after him with wide eyes. 'Right,' she said quietly, not planning to obey. What on earth made him think she would stay safely cocooned in her car and not offer help when it was obviously needed?

But first she needed to complete the job at hand. When the emergency calls had been made and she knew help was on the way, Isabel opened her door and slipped out, bringing her small first aid kit from the glove box and a scarf she kept for cooler weather in case someone urgently needed a makeshift bandage.

A low, wailing cry came from the direction Dom had run towards, and in another direction someone swore, low and repetitively. Somewhere to the left a small voice whispered for help.

She headed for the whispers, stepping over broken glass and torn metal. Her breath hissed at the strewn wreckage and sounds of distress.

She thought briefly of the motorbike and pole, but that had been minor compared to this. The tang of spilt petrol added to the danger and she could imagine how those trapped would be terrified of fire. She was feeling skittish herself.

The first vehicle she reached was a small blue sedan, skewed all the way to the edge of the road with the passenger side crushed viciously by a wide-based gum tree it must have bounced off. The left side of the vehicle had climbed the tree a few feet leaving paint and had then fallen, but it was now jammed against the bark. Even from here Isabel could tell if there was someone in the front seat it wouldn't be good.

There was no entry to that side of the car at all.

She moved to the driver's door but, when she tried to open the mangled metal, not surprisingly, it was jammed tight from impact.

From the damage, it looked as though this car had been hit from several angles at once. The windows were tinted and the sunlight awkwardly shining, but she could just make out someone with their head on the steering wheel. The figure wasn't moving. She tried the front windshield, but it was cracked into tiny broken cubes and she couldn't see anything.

She heard a whisper and she tried the rear door, again jammed and skewed out of shape by a blow.

The rear window had smashed inwards as if a branch or projectile from outside the car had speared it. Shards of glass were scattered in a circle around the wreck, jagged edges around the hole where the window had been.

For the moment it was the only way to see in.

A young voice—a child, she thought, no older than seven or eight—whispered in a broken voice, 'Help me... please...'

Isabel sucked in a breath and moved closer to the rear window hole. 'I'm here,' she called, quietly reassuring. 'Help's on the way. Don't move until they say you can.'

'Help Mummy,' the voice whimpered. 'I'm scared, and Mummy and Daddy won't answer. Mummy's bleeding and there's a lot of blood.'

Isabel's heart contracted and she sucked in a breath. 'I'm here. Help's coming.'

But she couldn't get to the child. Isabel's chest ached with cold at the possible heartbreak to come and she looked around but there was so much damage and devastation she couldn't see Dom to ask for help. He would be busy elsewhere. So much for her own advice not to move anything until help arrived.

'Ten seconds and I'll be back.'

'Don't leave me.'

'I won't leave you. Just getting something until the ambulance arrives. They shouldn't be long.' Ten or fifteen minutes at the most, but in that time a body could bleed to death.

She hurried back to her car and pulled out the beach bag. Most locals kept one in their cars at Lighthouse Bay, always ready for a swim.

When she returned she called out, 'I'm back. I'm going to try to reach the rear window to see your face.'

Isabel used a towel from her bag to brush the shards of glass off the car boot before flicking open the clean side of the towel.

Looking down at her fine trousers and shirt, she was glad she'd worn something which would offer some protection from the glass, although she'd have been better in jeans. Nothing to what she might find inside the car. She tossed the cloth over the jagged window so she could push herself up and peer in the back window, placing her first aid kit close to hand so she could grab it quickly.

Setting one foot on the bumper bar and her knee on the boot, she used a piece of the towel to grab the edge of the window frame and shimmied herself up.

Inside, blood splattered the roof, the windows, the seats. Splashed and dripping, pooling into dark circles on the floor like a room in a slaughterhouse. One glance at the front of the car made her look away. She swallowed the instinctive gag in her throat.

To her right, in the back, still strapped in his booster

seat and seat belt, a young dark-haired boy turned wide tear-stained eyes to her. For some crazy reason she thought of Dom. And Dom's lost son. And how tragedy seemed to come in circles.

Isabel breathed long and slow until her head cleared and her breathing settled. 'Hello, there,' she said softly. 'I'm Isabel. Are you hurt?'

He shook his head and he seemed to move freely when he twisted to see her.

Gently, she asked, 'What's your name?'

'Lucas.' The boy blinked as if he couldn't believe she was there. She'd bet it looked odd to see a strange woman peering in through a broken back window. 'Are you going to get me out?'

'I can't do that, Lucas. Not until the paramedics come. But I can stay with you until then.' Something sharp was pressing into her shoulder where she leaned on the sill. And her leg stung where a piece of glass had pierced both towel and trousers.

He thought about that. 'Can you help Mummy?' Then a frightened glance at the passenger side, crushed around the unmoving body of a man. 'Or Daddy?'

Isabel suspected his daddy was beyond help. 'I can't reach your mum.'

'You could if you came in,' the boy pleaded, and Isabel's heart squeezed.

God, he must be so frightened. Blood dripped from his mother's hair at the shoulder and dribbled down the back of her seat.

Isabel didn't know what to do. She needed help. She needed Dom. He was a doctor. She had distant medical training but she didn't have the equipment needed for a trauma like this. 'I'll go and get help,' she said.

'Don't leave me,' the boy whispered and even more softly, 'I'm scared.'

Her heart squeezed even tighter. 'Oh, Lucas. I know you are. You're such a good boy being patient.' Isabel peered to the left of the boy and the vacant rear seat that she could probably squeeze into if she tried.

Would it cause any problems for the emergency services if she did? She could climb out again when someone came. Would it make things worse for the boy? For anyone?

Well, it would for her if she tore something major herself on all the ragged metal, or the car exploded if a fuel leak ignited. She didn't want to think about that.

It would certainly cause problems with Dom. He'd blow a gasket and say he'd told her to stay. Perhaps someone should have stayed with his son. She wished she could have done something for Dom in the tragedy of his loss.

But that was the least of her worries now.

She needed to think about Lucas now.

It would mean a lot to the boy and from there she should be able to see where the mum was bleeding from. She might be able to stop the flow until help arrived. And check the boy. He said he was fine but, for all she knew, he was quietly exsanguinating as well. He certainly looked pale.

The fuel smell seemed stronger and she guessed it was spilling from a ruptured tank. She hoped no one was smoking. The thought made her shudder.

Isabel forced herself to look again at the front of the car. On the passenger side she could see the man would be extremely lucky to be alive and next to him a woman with long blood-soaked hair remained unmoving despite the conversation going on around her. Lucas's mother's face rested against the steering wheel. Though, watching carefully, Isabel thought she could see a slight rise and fall of the shoulders as the woman breathed.

'You have to help us.' The boy was crying now.

She couldn't not. She pushed the first aid kit into the back seat through the window. With a last assessment of how she would land and manage to right herself, Isabel wriggled her shoulders further through the window of the car and pulled her thighs and feet after her until she was squashed face first into the seat next to Lucas. As she wriggled to awkwardly turn to sit on the seat she heard Dom calling her name.

Methodically, Dom had done what he could for the occupants of each car. Applying pressure to wounds with whatever he could find. Ensuring airways were open and breathing not hampered. That people with injuries did not move until they could be assessed properly by the paramedics.

More bystanders had arrived and after he'd told them he was a doctor he'd stationed one sensible person with each car as he'd moved between them, triaging until the ambulances arrived. Only one car left to check.

He spotted the final car, pushed to the side against a tree, distorted and bent and smelling strongly of fuel. He'd missed it, tucked to the side as it was; this was where he should have first come. It looked by far the worst.

As he moved towards it a movement caught his eye and with incredulous horror he watched as Isabel awkwardly propelled herself through the rear window into the mangled car and disappeared.

Madre di Dio. For a moment he couldn't breathe, and then a red mist descended and he bellowed, 'Isabel! No!'

Adrenalin surged and he sprinted. As he did so the

pungent stink of petrol rose strongly and he noted the reek seemed to flood from under the car. Worse and worse. He had to get her out.

What was the woman thinking? *Idiota.*

He pushed away the white-hot anger at Isabel's foolishness in risking everything they had, and might have. Pushed it away to worry about later. For the moment those who were trapped inside the car were more important.

Isabel was inside that car, his mind growled.

For a moment blind anger surged again and he shoved it down ruthlessly. She must have had a good reason. She'd better. He reminded himself she was a nurse and midwife. Even if it had been years ago, she had been trained to save lives.

By the time he reached the wreck he had himself under control. 'Isabel—' it came out remarkably mild in tone, so much so that he surprised himself '—what is happening? What have you got?' He saw the surprise on her face from his lack of stress, giving him a grim satisfaction.

Yes, he hadn't panicked that she was in danger, not that she could see now, anyway. But they would talk later about this putting herself in harm's way. He could exercise self-control in some instances. He shook his head. Mouthed, 'Later.' Then said out loud, 'What do you need?'

Acknowledgement of the 'later' flashed in her eyes as she replied. 'Something to stop the bleeding.' That so calm voice. 'Lucas's mother has a large puncture laceration on her neck and it's pumping blood. It soaked my small pad and bandages. There are tampons in my handbag. A small red zippered purse. Can you bring them?'

Good grief. Her favourite saying was appropriate in this moment. He nodded, slid back off the car and ran to Isabel's vehicle. Rummaged, found, retrieved and returned.

'Here.' He climbed up the car and held the small purse through the broken window. The sounds of approaching emergency vehicles were finally heard in the distance.

He watched her unwrap the tampon, lift the veil of the woman's hair aside and slide the wad into the deep cut, where it soaked up the flow. He'd seen them used before, but for gunshot wounds.

'When the paramedics get here, they need to come here first. She's critical.'

'Of course.'

'And who are you?' Dom asked the young boy in the back seat, barely visible beneath Isabel's leaning body. His breath caught and for a moment the child looked like his own Tomas. Same age. Same dark hair and eyes. He saw the child who needed help and knew why Isabel was here. For the boy.

'Lucas.'

'I am Dom, Lucas. A doctor. Can you hear the sirens?' The boy nodded.

'Soon they will get you out.'

'And my mummy and daddy?'

'Yes. It is too hard for us to reach and help them now, so we will leave them for the experts. Isabel will need to climb out for the paramedic to enter. Perhaps they will try to cut open your door. If they cannot open it easily they may help you go out the same way. Okay?'

'Okay.'

The sirens were closer now and Dom said softly to Isabel, 'You have done what you could. It is best if you leave the way open so they can climb in as fast as possible.'

She studied his face and he tried to mask the sense of urgency that almost overwhelmed him. What he said was true. But he desperately wanted her out of there as well. 'Come, Isabel. Let me help you.'

Behind him, the sirens ceased and he heard the sound of many vehicles arriving. The shout of people.

Isabel turned to the boy. 'I have to climb out now, Lucas. The paramedics will climb in.'

The child nodded despite the tears that slid down his face. Isabel gently hugged him. 'We will wait for them to lift you out and stay with you until your mummy can be with you.'

'And Daddy?' Fear saturated the boy's whisper.

'Daddy will have to go to the hospital.' That wasn't a lie.

Dom's hand reached in and he watched, breath hitched in his chest, as she wriggled on the cramped seat until she was facing the back window awkwardly. Her cold hands touched his and he gripped one wrist and then the other. With a steady grasp and her own upward pressure he eased her out through the window until she was lying face down on the rear of the car. Once she was free he picked her up and pulled her to him.

'You are safe.' He squeezed her. '*Dio*, woman. Are you trying to kill me with worry?'

'I can't believe you told me to stay in the car,' she said shakily but with a determined tilt to her chin.

'What can I say? I am a fool,' he said, still reassuring himself she was safe. To his relief, she clung to him once convulsively and then kissed his cheek. 'Put me down, please, Dom.'

He didn't want to, but needs must. As he did so, men and women in paramedics' jumpsuits pushed past. 'Do you wish to give them a report or shall I?'

'You do it.' She gestured. 'I want to be back here when they get Lucas out.'

He nodded. 'I will tell them what you found.' He pointed at the car. 'Go. Wash your hands and drink the water after your hard work, and then come back for Lucas.'

It took an hour for the emergency workers to extricate Lucas's mother from the car. When she was removed, post replacement fluids for the blood loss, she was conscious and coherent. Lucas's grandmother had arrived and had taken the boy home with her once his mother was free.

He'd been promised to see his parents at the hospital. Incredibly, his father was still alive, though his crush injuries had caused many conferences on the best way to extricate him. Dom and Isabel left as soon as Lucas did.

Time was running short for Dom's flight departure, but they could still make it. If they hurried.

CHAPTER THIRTEEN

By the time they arrived at the airport they both wanted to think about something other than shattered families and accident victims. Or Dom's distress at Isabel's actions.

When he parked in Coffs Harbour Airport's car park, Dom shook his head that he'd found a spot so easily when his flight was almost due. He observed the scattered cars and the multiple choice of open spots and muttered, 'Australia seems so under-populated.'

'Looks busy to me,' she said with a smile. 'But parking is always easier here than what you're used to in the bustle of Italy.'

'Sixty million souls compared to your twenty-five.' And still he'd found Isabel among them.

'Not the only difference between us.'

Yes, they were dissimilar, but he realised that, instead of finding their disparities, difficult he gloried in that. 'Differences are to be celebrated.'

At that she laughed, a little shakily after their morning, and he savoured the sound. He wanted her less bowed down by other's distress before he left. He wanted his last view of her to be a joyful one. So he smiled at her, putting all of the pleasure he felt when he was with her, what she meant to him, in his expression.

Isabel tilted her head at him like a small bird. 'Who are you? Where is the man who arrived two weeks ago? I swear you are almost playful.'

He could be.

Wanted to be.

With her.

She opened her own door. Of course she would not wait for him to open it for her. He flew from his own and arrived to offer his hand, requiring fast movement from his own side, a game she didn't know she was a part of, but it had become a game he cherished.

Once he knew she was secure, he put his hand over his heart. 'That man has been healed by an angel.'

'Glad to hear it.' She eyed him quizzically and opened her handbag. 'Can I have the entry ticket you were issued with, please? I need to pay for the parking at a machine inside the terminal before I leave.'

'So businesslike. You are killing me. Does it not mean anything to you that we will be parted for possibly months?'

Even he was surprised by the honesty. As if the immediacy of departure—and perhaps the danger and anguish just past—had released a freedom he hadn't felt for many, many years. He wanted her to laugh again. To smile up into his face, because he needed to take that with him. A cure for his own melancholy. 'What if I go into a decline from missing you?'

'Then I would think you stark raving sad.'

He frowned. That expression did not sound right.

Isabel had no idea what Dom was playing at, but her brain hadn't shifted yet. That accident had been harrowing.

She'd thought their parting would be all doom and gloom. This was much better, if a little disconcerting.

He opened the boot and removed his small four-wheeled carry-on case, mostly filled with his computer. She had no idea how he'd lived out of that during his stay, though of course Rai had taken care of the wedding suit for his brother. And anything else she supposed, as they were of a size.

They walked together through the automatic doors into the departure terminal, though at regional level the departures and arrivals were very close, under one roof and separated by a glass wall. This was only the first leg, his short flight to Sydney, where he would board a larger plane for the international travel.

There would be several hours' wait in Sydney between flights, as well as that bus transfer between terminals.

She stood back while he checked in, noting the admiring glances sent his way from other women in the terminal and the extremely attentive check-in agent at the desk. Their scrutiny made her frown at herself because there could be no doubt she felt a tad possessive over the annoying Italian.

Did she have any right to such a response?

It was done. Boarding pass in hand, he and his carry-on were closing the distance between them. It was time to say goodbye.

She would not cry...she would not cry...

Dom stopped directly in front of her. Gently, he placed his warm, large hands on her shoulders, pulling her closer into his chest until the button she stared at blurred in front of her eyes. She lifted her palm and laid it flat on his chest and pushed until she could feel his heartbeat beneath. His chest was so, so warm. So hard. So Dom.

His hand slid up and his finger lifted her chin so he could see into her face and what he saw there made him chew those beautiful lips in concern. 'Come with me to

Italy. The hostess tells me there is a seat that will keep you beside me all the way.'

If only she could. In a small voice she said, 'I don't have my passport.' But she blushed and turned her face away as she said it.

He laughed with delight. 'You lie.' He lifted her face. 'You cannot tell a lie; you are hopeless. You did consider the idea of flying with me, didn't you?'

She couldn't deny the truth. 'I just threw the wallet in, a silly idea. Briefly I considered, but I can't do it, Dom. I can't.'

Silently she added, *I can't risk you being disappointed in me.* Like the last man had been so disappointed in her that he'd left. She'd survived that but she doubted she would survive if she failed Dom's belief in her.

His brow creased, his smile fell, and she feared she'd given him false hope with her inability to hide an untruth.

His hands slid down to grasp her upper arms as if he wanted to shake her. But he held her gently. 'Why would you do that, Isabel? Why would you take the action of bringing your passport, making it possible, and not make it happen?'

Her throat closed on unshed tears. She didn't offer an explanation because she didn't have one. And for the moment she couldn't speak.

It had been a last-minute toss from the drawer to her bag. Almost as if she hadn't wanted to talk to herself about it, let alone Dom.

She looked away, ostensibly to see that no one was paying them any attention, but really to try and think of a way to get herself out of this situation. It was starting to slide out of her control.

His hand cupped her cheek, bringing her gaze back.

Holding her with his intense scrutiny. 'Is it because you too can see that what time we have should not be squandered?'

She pulled back. 'You're so dramatic, Dom.'

'One of us has to be dramatic.' This was accompanied by a charmingly European male shrug. 'For you are too calm and composed and sensible, my love.'

Her head shook but her eyes were caught. Captured by his. 'There is nothing wrong with being sensible. And I'm not your love.'

'I fear you are. Have I not said you are enough for any man? I would have you, my love, if only you would have me. For you have slipped past my frozen heart to lodge at the core of me. Do you not care for me a small amount?'

'No.' But it was a useless denial that sounded slightly petulant to her own ears.

He laughed. 'And I know you lie again.'

Her eyes stung but she blinked away the welling tears. She would not cry. 'Stop it. Please. Goodbye, Dom.' She tore her gaze free. She waved her hand at the X-ray machine and uniformed officers. 'Go through Security or you'll miss your flight. I'm leaving.'

He reached out and pulled her closer. Cupped her cheeks with his big hands and claimed her mouth. His lips were soft at first, with a tenderness that created an ache deep inside her. Isabel breathed slowly, savouring the mingling of breath, her lids fluttering shut as she allowed him a brief glimpse of her loss, until that drew the stinging back to her eyes.

Dom pressed more firmly, demanding, a hint of the desperate need she felt herself and those two needs entwined and flared like a cordite fuse of pure heat.

His breath hissed in and hers was lodged somewhere in her chest. Big, warm hands dropped from her face and he stepped away, the loss of contact shattering them both.

'Goodbye, Isabel. God willing, we will meet again.'
Without looking at her, he turned and headed towards
the security point, his footsteps quiet on the polished
floor, distance stretching between them, his body growing smaller as he moved away.

God willing. Her mouth pulled painfully as she tried
to stop the trembling and her heart pounded. That man
kissed like an angel. Angel? 'God willing', he'd said. She
hadn't thought of that and should have after this morning's example of the fragility of life.

Cold doused her like ice from a bucket, flooding her
skin, her throat, her chest until she couldn't breathe.

What if something happened to Dom and she'd thrown
away the chance of finding even the briefest happiness?
All because she'd been too cowardly to risk upsetting
her comfortable life. Too scared to risk the pain of being
discarded. Too afraid to trust.

There was nothing wrong with being sensible. It kept
her safe from pain when she was cast aside.

But there was worse pain than being discarded. Unimaginable pain if she threw away the only chance she
had to be with Dom. She'd thought it was always about
their age difference and her infertility, but what if it was
really more about her fear of taking that leap into the unknown, daring to trust? Was she a coward?

He'd said, *'I did not think you were a coward, Isabel.'*
Too frightened to trust him.
Too afraid to risk her heart.
Too complacent in her independence to do anything
that threatened her peace of mind. Proving to everyone
that she was happy and fulfilled in her guise as the calm
and serene Aunty Izzy.

Isabel opened her mouth to say his name, the word
aimed silently at his distant back like a sliver of incred-

ulous fear. 'Oh, Dom. Be safe. Find happiness.' And finally, painfully, she whispered, 'I love you.'

She loved him.

Now she found this out?

Idiot. She knew he cared for the woman he thought he knew, but he didn't know the real Isabel. He knew the image she projected to the world. He called her calm and collected and sensible when so often, deep inside, she was none of these things.

Yet Isabel could remember a time when she had been more impulsive, but she'd learned to rein those feelings in, until now with Dom. Since she'd met him she seemed to spend half of her time simultaneously terrified and half tempted, wanting to revisit the old impetuous Isabel.

If she was with Dom she wouldn't recognise herself. Would lose herself. It had taken her a long time to find the Isabel she thought she was, but Domenico Salvanelli had turned it all upside down. Which made her feel anything but calm and comfortable. But alive.

What if? Fear scratched her throat with its talons.

He'd be fine. *God willing.* The phrase he'd chosen chilled her to the bone. Of course he would be fine and she forced herself to turn for the exit.

An aircraft roared overhead as it came in to land. Isabel made it to her car despite her tears-obscured vision and when she did open the car door she slumped into the driver's seat, shivering with a tearing sense of loss she hadn't expected.

In the distance the thundering aircraft touched down and applied its brakes. Soon it would take off again and carry Dom away.

Her hand reached out to start the car and she looked ahead to the exit. And slumped back. The old Isabel would never have forgotten that.

The boom gates out of the parking area needed a freaking ticket; she had to go back and do it all again. Despite her wish to drive as far and fast as she could, she wasn't going anywhere.

She had to go back. The damn ticket. The pay machine to the car park was in the arrivals hall and she had to stamp it with her proof of payment before she could exit the car park.

Maybe she wouldn't see him through the glass as he waited to board.

Back across the expanse outside, Isabel entered the other end of the building, a place of luggage carousels and waiting relatives, but instead of walking to the parking machine she searched through the window to Departures and the faces of those staring towards the tarmac where their plane had just landed. People were standing, massing around the checkpoint as if that would get them away more quickly.

She couldn't see him. Which was good. She just needed to stamp her ticket and leave.

But somehow she couldn't make herself move to the machine. Instead, she drifted through the crowd to the wall of floor-to-ceiling windows until she found the strong lines of his back, his broad shoulders and the ever so slightly arrogant tilt to his head. Yes, there he was, none of his handsome face visible, tension in his neck and shoulders she could see from here.

He wasn't looking to the tarmac; he was looking back towards Security and the check-in area. As if searching for something—or someone.

Waiting for her?

What if he did love her?

And the voice in her head. Accusing. What was she so afraid of that she wouldn't risk finding out?

And it came to her, crystal-clear. Like spring water. A dousing of life and purity. She really did love Dom. He deserved to be allowed to love her.

Finally, the only thing that terrified Isabel on the deepest primal level was the idea that she might not see Domenico Salvanelli ever again.

What if something did happen and she wasn't there?

What if she never knew what it was like to lie in his arms?

What if he never knew that she loved him?

The first passengers from the aircraft on the tarmac began to stream into the arrivals hall, greeting relatives, children running, the volume suddenly increased as if someone had turned a dial.

The carousel for luggage beeped and groaned and began to turn with grinding slowness.

All she needed was a little more time to decide.

She could fly to Sydney and talk to him. Heck, she could buy a set of clothes in the airport and even a carry-on bag if she decided to go all the way to Italy. But she couldn't think of that yet. The parking bill would grow until Faith or Rai could retrieve her car, but that was fine. Faith had spare keys, could eat the food in her fridge, lock her doors, hold the fort until her return.

There really was no reason for her not to go.

Isabel laughed, turned and prepared to do the craziest thing she'd ever done in her life. To follow a man seven years her junior and offer herself as a lover.

Isabel spun, walked briskly out of Arrivals, down the footpath to Departures and entered the now almost deserted building. The loud speaker announced that boarding had commenced for the flight to Sydney and through the windows the scrum of passengers shuffled forward to offer their boarding passes and Dom was lost in a sea of milling people.

The agent at the check-in counter shot Isabel a quizzical look that said, *You're very late...or very early for the next flight.*

'Can I buy a ticket on that flight to Sydney, please? Heck, give me one to Rome. Last-minute decision. I don't have any luggage.' She smiled and it felt as if her face might break open with the sudden excitement that glowed inside.

The glow must have shone externally too. 'It looks like a good choice.' The woman glanced at her watch and smiled. 'I think we can manage that, if we're super-fast.'

Isabel already had her driver's licence and credit card.

The agent's shoulders drooped. 'Oh, I'm sorry. I knew we were cutting it fine, but I'm afraid it was too fine. The flight has just closed.'

CHAPTER FOURTEEN

SHE WASN'T COMING. Dom accepted he'd been mistaken to nurture even the tiniest hope that Isabel would throw caution to the winds. Though she had once been so brave, and his body thrummed with the memory of her glorious body against his in that last kiss. But this insistent dream and craziness to want her to fly across the world with him had been too much to ask and he was a fool to think she would change her mind at the last minute.

He'd maintained hope until the last few passengers came through Security into the departure lounge. Now he called himself an idiot as he crossed the tarmac and ascended the steps into the front of the aircraft. He stowed his bag above his seat and settled beside his allocated window in the small plane.

The cabin was barely half full. Only fools and family flew at Christmas. His business class ticket to Rome and then Florence meant the seat next to him was empty and he had room to stretch his legs. He opened his phone and texted his brother that he was on board.

The text came back. 'What of Isabel?'

Had Raimondo known what he was thinking? Had she shared her indecision with Faith? His heart thundered with renewed hope as he stared at his phone. The

announcement asked passengers to switch all electronic
equipment to flight mode.

The hostess stood waiting at the cockpit, a cardboard
instruction sheet in her hand. She smiled at him and
said softly, 'One more passenger and then we'll close
the door.'

Isabel's heart sank to the cold tiled floor under her feet.
Too late. She'd blown it with her indecision. Her inability
to see what was crystal-clear in front of her eyes. 'Isn't
there anything you can do?'

The woman looked suitably apologetic. 'Not for this
flight.' She tapped screens and stared at her computer.
'There's a flight departing Port Macquarie in two hours.
It gets you to Sydney two hours before the Rome departure and it takes roughly an hour and a half to drive to
Port. It'll be close. You still might not make it but at least
you don't have luggage. I can check you in from here.'

'Do it. Book it. Check me in. Take my card. Sydney
to Florence via Rome.' She was mad. Crazy. Crazy in
love. And in no condition to drive fast so she'd have to
drive carefully.

She didn't stay to see Dom's plane take off. She ran
to Arrivals and paid the wonderful parking machine that
had changed her mind. Thank goodness she'd filled her
car up last week and wouldn't run out of petrol with an
extra hundred and fifty kilometres to drive.

On the way back to the highway the link road was
down to one lane and banked back more than she'd expected. She glanced at her watch. She had one hundred
minutes.

Of course! The accident!

She put on her indicator and performed a quick U-turn
and headed a different way to the highway. Longer dis-

tance but moving traffic. Her head began to throb with the strain of the morning and the fact she needed food.

She grabbed her water bottle and drained most of it. Probably dehydrated as well with adrenalin. She kept twenty mils in the bottom. She might have to run later and she'd need a sip.

Glancing at the car clock, she worked out how many minutes she had. Halfway there and seventy minutes until take-off. She shook her head. What was she doing?

Once on the M1, Isabel overtook another slow car and kept her speed legal, something she didn't normally have trouble with but today she was on edge. Thankfully, the new highway was conducive to fast travel but still she watched the minutes tick by.

She had to make it. Such a crazy thing to attempt. She would not think of that; she would drive, drive, drive.

Exactly one hundred minutes after exiting the Coffs Harbour car park, she rolled into Port Macquarie airport with a grunt of relief. Took the ticket from the parking machine and bared her teeth at it in a grimace of a smile. She could leave that in the car for Faith.

Striding across the car park to the terminal, she saw her plane had already landed. Passengers were boarding. That was okay. She had her boarding pass. She'd done it.

With a jubilant fist pump, Isabel strode into the departure lounge and headed for the security check. Through the window she could see the line of passengers snaking towards the plane. Still time. She couldn't believe she'd made it.

She placed her handbag on the conveyer belt and it disappeared through as she imagined Dom's face when she arrived in Sydney. A smile spread across her face and her heart leapt in anticipation of that moment.

Bells rang. Lights flashed. And Isabel's heart stuttered. Now what? Her bag reversed out of the X-ray back into sight and her stomach sank.

The tall grey-haired man said in a bored tone, 'You have scissors, lady.'

Isabel blinked. Resisted the urge to grab her bag and upend it in the middle of the conveyor belt. Instead, she forced a smile and followed after the officer as he carried her bag to the side table, where he pulled on nitrile gloves. With torturous slowness. She glanced through the window at the last boarding passengers.

This had all been in vain. The universe was trying to tell her something—via a pair of darn nail scissors!— and she watched the last passenger for her flight step onto the plane.

'You'll have to leave them.'

Isabel blinked. 'What?' Her thoughts jerked back from the loss of a dream.

'The scissors,' the man said. 'If you want to catch that flight you'll have to leave the scissors.'

In Sydney Airport, Dom accepted he'd lost. She hadn't boarded in Coffs Harbour. He'd been so certain that one final passenger would be Isabel. He'd been convinced she would appear. Instead, it had been a young man with a backpack who'd scurried up the stairs and into the cabin, and they'd closed the doors.

He raked his hand through his hair and swore silently as he looked at his watch. He had two hours to decide if he would toss his business worries, and a small fortune, to the wind and go back to claim Isabel. Or catch the flight to Florence and return to Lighthouse Bay another day.

He rocked gently as he squeezed the bridge of his nose

between his fingers. His phone rang. He almost dropped it in his haste to see if it was Isabel.

Not Isabel. 'Rai. Yes. In Sydney. Thank you. Is Isabel safely home?'

His brother's denial made his brows draw together. 'Faith hasn't heard from her?'

Rai suggested, 'Perhaps she has gone shopping. The shops are better in Coffs Harbour.'

Dom did not think his Isabel would be shopping today. Thoughts skittered and hope flared. 'I am considering my return. Not taking the flight to Rome.'

'What?' Rai's disbelief carried clearly down the line. 'Brother. Do not rue a decision made in haste.'

Dom didn't like that. 'I am still deciding.'

'You have to return to Florence at some point for the factory.' Rai's opinion was clear. 'I appreciate your attendance at my wedding but we both know it is you who will lose a large sum if you delay much longer.'

Dom's chin lifted and he narrowed his eyes at the phone. Glaring at his brother, who had found his happiness and seemed intent on denying him the same. 'And yet today I consider returning to Lighthouse Bay, rather than boarding my flight.'

Rai's dissenting mutter made Dom smile. His words did not. 'You will be coming back to Lighthouse Bay within months. If Isabel is the right woman for you, she will be waiting. Give her time and space; do not rush her. She is a cautious woman, and an independent one. She needs to make her own decisions.'

Except Dom knew his Isabel was many things, and that he'd encouraged her to be more impulsive. To grab the life she wanted and the happiness she deserved. Who knew what that quixotic woman would do while he was gone? She might head off on a round-the-world

adventure without him and he would spend years waiting. Would he risk that?

Isabel arrived in Sydney, was one of the first to stand up
when the seat belt sign went off, but she was well down
the aircraft and had to wait for those in front to alight.

Finally, she stepped out…

And there was a bus. Not a walkway to the terminal that she could run through. *Saints preserve her.* She
climbed on and stood in the bus, holding a hand strap
from the roof with white knuckles and a twisting stomach. Turning her arm to stare at the moving numbers on
her watch. Finally all the passengers from the aircraft
transferred into the bus. With all the speed of the slow-
est tortoise.

Eventually the bus started, moving at a different tortoise's pace, and then stopped, waited for an aircraft to
cross the runway, before it headed again through molas-
ses towards the terminal.

Five minutes later it docked at the terminal. 'Excuse
me,' she said. 'Sorry,' as she bumped a man who scowled
at her. Desperately she slipped between disembarking
passengers and took off briskly in front of the crowd.
Terrified she'd be behind a long line of slow movers up
the escalators to the departure hall floor.

She knew the way. Had travelled from Sydney often
and headed for the inter-terminal bus that would take
her to the international departure gates. Seventy minutes
until Dom's aircraft departed.

Dom's and hers, she corrected herself.

The doors were open, a bus must be near to departing and she quickened her pace. The attendant looked
up, took her boarding pass and glanced at it. 'You'll be
pushing to make this flight.'

Isabel sucked in a breath and felt the rush of tears. Forced them back. Swallowed as she took back the boarding pass. 'I know.' Lifted her head and looked the woman in the eye. 'The man I love is on that flight and he doesn't know I'm here. I must make it.'

The woman nodded. Handed her an Express Lane Pass for immigration and picked up the phone. 'I'll let them know you're coming but I can't promise they'll hold it for you.'

'Thank you,' she called over her shoulder and took the descending escalators fast to the almost full bus below.

Again, she stood swaying, holding onto the hand strap in a bus she'd had no idea she'd be travelling on when she'd woken this morning.

This morning.

So long ago.

So much had happened.

There was still a chance she would make it. No chance for clothes or luggage or food. But food could happen on the plane. Dom would happen on the plane. She would not lose sight of that.

Jogging up the long stairs because she couldn't stand quietly in a line on the escalator, Isabel reached the international departure hall. She headed straight for the departing passengers gate and slipped into the immigration and customs hall. The queues were staggeringly long and she almost sobbed before she remembered her Express Pass in her shaking hand.

She held it up to the border control officer and he allowed her past his gate, but still there were a dozen ahead of her with waving passports and she had less than five minutes until her flight boarded.

At least she no longer had the scissors to hold her up when she made it to the X-ray machines.

Except they waved her across to the random explosives test. She almost laughed with hysteria. The officer studied her strange facial tic with suspicion, and she waved her hand at the flashing lights overhead. 'The departures board is flashing "Boarding" next to my flight number.'

Totally unmoved, the man offered his obviously standard answer. 'This won't take a moment.'

Isabel bit back the caustic reply that it didn't take long to shut an aircraft door either, but he was just doing his job. She held out her arms and he ran the sensor over her sleeves, her back, her front, shoes and inside her handbag.

While they waited for the sensor machine to spit out the verdict she asked, 'Do you know how far away Gate Sixty-One is?'

He nodded to his right. 'Seven minutes that way.'

Good grief didn't begin to cover that.

'Clear. Good luck.' His tone said she had little chance.

Isabel ran. Saw a sign directing her right. Kept running. Saw another sign and kept right. Ran. Puffed. Felt her chest tighten with the effort but kept on trucking.

Who knew she could be so determined?

There it was. Gate Sixty-One. Her footsteps slowed. No passengers. One cleaner emptying a bin. No flight attendants. The door was shut. The sign said *Flight Closed*.

A sob burst from Isabel's mouth. She flopped into the nearest seat, head bowed, and sucked badly-needed air into her lungs. She'd actually never thought she would miss that flight. She'd thought she was meant to be on board. With Dom. Surprising him.

Now she felt like an idiot. A prize fool.

Embarrassed by the whole idea of chasing the one that got away.

She pulled her drink bottle out of her bag, but it was

dry. Not even a drip. She'd had to tip out the last water at the last security check. This sucked big time.

Isabel drew in a long juddering breath and stood. Walked to the nearest bubbler and filled her bottle. After a long swallow she let the tension of the last four hours gurgle down the drain with the stream of water.

She'd tried. What more could she do? She'd fly home. Maybe stay the night in Coffs Harbour.

Except her car was at Port Macquarie, not Coffs Harbour, and she didn't know the town. A dingy hotel would do her in. Best make the almost three-hour drive home.

Heart in her shoes, Isabel walked slowly back through the terminal, not even sure how she went from Departures to Arrivals in this terminal.

Who knew?

She'd never missed a flight before.

She'd never chased a man before.

She really should let Faith know what was going on, which she hadn't earlier because there'd not been a spare minute between all the deciding and rushing and running.

She drew her mobile from her bag and pressed the number for her niece. 'Hey, Faith.'

'Isabel, where are you? How are you?' Before she could answer, Faith went on. 'You sound strange. Dom told Rai you should have arrived home hours ago.'

Did he? Well, she guessed that was the impression she'd given. 'Long story. I'm at Sydney Airport.'

'Sydney?' A pause. 'Oh, my,' Faith said softly. Incredulously. 'You followed him. You're going to Italy, aren't you?'

No one said her niece was slow on the uptake. 'That was the plan, but I missed the flight to Rome. Now I'm just sitting here, wondering what to do next.'

'Um… Izzy. Darling Izzy…' Now Faith sounded strange.

'What?'

'Dom's not on that plane either.' Faith sounded breathless with excitement. 'He's flying back here.'

Isabel stared at the phone for a moment before lifting it back to her ear. 'What flight number?'

'QF2164. Leaves at fifteen-forty.'

Her chest faint with growing excitement, Isabel stood. Started back the way she'd come with renewed purpose. 'Faith, I have to run. I'll call you later.' And she hung up.

Dom glanced out of the window to the woman striding across the tarmac towards his aircraft and his breath caught in his throat. 'Isabel…' he breathed. Her hair flowed behind her, her chin tilted up to the aircraft, long steps decisive.

Disbelievingly, joy-filled, he savoured the side angle he had of her face as she entered and greeted the hostess. Showed her the boarding ticket. Then she stood for a moment at the front of the cabin, scanning passenger faces.

Her search skimmed over his and swung back. Their eyes met, held, locked and Dom's heart soared and his eyes widened. She'd come to fly with him. His brave Isabel had been coming to Italy.

The hostess spoke to her.

Isabel smiled and nodded and she looked back at him to wave her boarding pass. All he could do was stare at her incredulously with sudden joy bubbling up inside him like Vesuvius on its most spectacular day. They would go together. On the next flight.

Dom's hand flew to his seat belt and unclipped it. He rose, and in his haste almost hit his head on the hand luggage compartment. He ducked away.

'Isabel…' His voice came out hoarse, exultant, uncaring of the faces that turned to him as he slid from behind the seat and closed the distance between them.

Took her small, precious hand in his larger one, looked down at her fingers curled in his briefly in disbelief, and then back at her face. She waved the boarding pass under his nose.

His other arm slid around her and he squeezed her to him before he let her go. Indicated with his head towards the door she'd just entered.

'You won't need that pass. We're flying to Italy.'

EPILOGUE

One year later

IT FELT AS if Isabel had been waiting to share Christmas morning in Lighthouse Bay with her husband for ever. In two months it would be their first wedding anniversary—so only a year—yet so much had happened.

Apart from falling more in love every day, sharing a joy in each other's company that permeated the solid relationship between them, they'd travelled through Italy for a month after Dom's business had been concluded, and then home to a beautiful Lighthouse Bay wedding organised by Faith and Rai in their absence.

They'd just had their honeymoon first.

The factory site in Florence and new build had been sold, the Villa Salvanelli had been left with a skeleton staff to maintain it, and they'd shipped Dom's personal belongings to Lighthouse Bay.

Since then, they'd settled into Isabel's little house and her husband had eased into working at the new medical centre with his brother. The town was delighted to have two new doctors open for business.

Dr Reg had retired, both he and Myra happy he was no longer leaving the hospital short-staffed.

Isabel had even done a few shifts at the cottage hospital after a refresher course in midwifery and general nursing that had brought unexpected satisfaction to her heart.

But now everything had changed.

Changed by an unexpected missive from Dom and Rai's family priest in Florence and a whirlwind of twin country organisation her husband had managed with remarkable ease considering the legal red tape.

Two toddlers, two years old. Twins. A boy and a girl. A crazy, tumultuous, terrible two of toddlerhood had flown home with them a month ago on an epic flight with two fractious children, and Isabel and Dom, despite the culture shock, couldn't be happier.

Matteo and Bianca, sudden orphans, distant relations to the Salvanellis, with no closer family able to take them, had come to live in Lighthouse Bay with her and Dom. First, they were fostered and later the adoption would be finalised.

Isabel placed the small Santa sack at the bottom of one bed. Bianca, deeply asleep, the older by half an hour, was a strong and boisterous child who looked after her brother even at that age. The dark-haired little girl bossed Matteo yet was the first to run to him if he cried, her bright eyes observing her surroundings and learning quickly to understand the language of her new mother.

Isabel carefully placed the other sack and decided their new son was near to waking. While the more timid of the two, Matteo, slower to talk and slower to cuddle, shared everything from his sandwich to his toys with his sister and looked to her for guidance in their new world. His eyes followed Dom when he passed, and for the moment Dom had more luck in making the child smile.

But they'd get there.

Early days yet. And she remembered a time when she'd said to Dom that God's plans could not be understood by mortals. She could only be thankful for this grand plan.

Now, with the dawn light painting pink across the clouds out to sea, Isabel looked across to the two miniature beds in the corner of Chloe's old room. These two small children had come into their life and already given them so much joy and love.

The new house plans had been submitted to join the house next door to theirs in a renovation to rival his brother's across the road. Their house would grow more crowded as the children grew and Dom had snapped up the premises when it had gone on the market before Isabel had realised what he was planning. Apparently, he could be as impulsive as his brother.

She heard Dom's footsteps behind her and he rested his hands on her shoulder as he leant down to nuzzle her neck. 'All my love to you at Christmas, my wife.'

She turned in his arms, reaching up to touch the glorious stubble on his chin. Feeling the warmth of his mouth and prickly chin as he turned his face to kiss her palm. Heat sizzled through her in this now accustomed storm of lightning strikes she'd never known existed.

'And to you, my love,' she whispered, not to wake the children. 'And our first Christmas with Bianca and Matteo.'

'We are blessed. Let's sneak back to bed before our children wake.' His laughing whisper was warm in her ear, making her skin tingle and her mouth curve. 'I have something for you for Christmas that requires privacy,' he murmured.

She didn't like his chances and laughed. 'We could try.'

Holding hands, they turned and began to tiptoe out of the room.

* * * * *

COMING SOON!

We really hope you enjoyed reading this book.
If you're looking for more romance, be sure to
head to the shops when new books are
available on

Thursday 20th January

To see which titles are coming soon, please visit

millsandboon.co.uk/nextmonth

MILLS & BOON

THE HEART OF ROMANCE

A ROMANCE FOR EVERY READER

MODERN

Prepare to be swept off your feet by sophisticated, sexy and seductive heroes, in some of the world's most glamourous and romantic locations, where power and passion collide.

HISTORICAL

Escape with historical heroes from time gone by. Whether your passion is for wicked Regency Rakes, muscled Vikings or rugged Highlanders, awak the romance of the past.

MEDICAL

Set your pulse racing with dedicated, delectable doctors in the high-pres sure world of medicine, where emotions run high and passion, comfort an love are the best medicine.

True Love

Celebrate true love with tender stories of heartfelt romance, from the rush of falling in love to the joy a new baby can bring, and a focus on the emotional heart of a relationship.

Desire

Indulge in secrets and scandal, intense drama and plenty of sizzling hot action with powerful and passionate heroes who have it all: wealth, status good looks…everything but the right woman.

HEROES

Experience all the excitement of a gripping thriller, with an intense ro mance at its heart. Resourceful, true-to-life women and strong, fearless m face danger and desire - a killer combination!

To see which titles are coming soon, please visit

millsandboon.co.uk/nextmonth

MILLS & BOON

Coming next month

THE MIDWIFE'S MIRACLE TWINS
Caroline Anderson

The rest of the clinic was busy but routine, with no dramas or crises, and she ended her shift only an hour late.

She went into the locker room to change, found the pregnancy tests strips still in her pocket and put them in her locker, then changed her clothes, dropping the scrubs into the laundry bin. Then she pulled out her bag and a tampon fell out. She bent down and picked it up, then stared at it thoughtfully.

Was her period overdue?

She wasn't sure. Her cycle wasn't an issue, so she never really bothered to make a note, but her periods usually started on a Tuesday, and it was Thursday.

Her heart gave a dull thud and she stared at it for another moment, then put it and the test strips in her bag and shut her locker.

There was no way she could be pregnant—was there? Surely not.

But all the way home her heart was racing, and the first thing she did once she'd closed the front door was run upstairs to the bathroom to do the test.

How could a minute be so long?

She perched on the edge of the bath, staring at the little strip and not quite sure what she wanted to see, one line or two.

One appeared instantly, to show the test was working. Not that anything else was going to happen—

Another line? Really? And a strong, dark line, too, not some vague little shadow.

She got up, her legs like jelly, and walked slowly out of the bathroom, sank down onto the bed and stared blankly at the test strip.

How could she possibly be pregnant? Dan had said it was a tiny tear, and she and Mark had tried for years. How could she be? Unless they'd just been incompatible, but even so…

She slid a hand down over her board-flat tummy. Was there really a baby in there? Dan's baby?

Please, no.

Please, yes!

But…

She'd have to tell him. Not yet, though. It might have been a fluke. She'd do another test in a while.

And then another one, until all the tests were used up.

Four of them couldn't be wrong.

She started to cry, great tearing sobs welling up from deep inside her where the pain she'd hidden for so long had festered like poison, and then the tears died away, leaving only joy.

Continue reading
THE MIDWIFE'S MIRACLE TWINS
Caroline Anderson

Available next month
www.millsandboon.co.uk

MILLS & BOON
True Love
Romance from the Heart

Celebrate true love with tender stories of heartfelt romance, from the rush of falling in love to the joy a new baby can bring, and a focus on the emotional heart of a relationship.

Four True Love stories published every month, find them all at:

millsandboon.co.uk/TrueLove